Prodigious Praise
from the Cast of "Hickey"

EDWARD HERRMANN (*Headmaster*): "Owen Johnson's stories have so much good-natured vitality that it is easy to miss the tough edge of the kids he writes about. Perhaps the most precious thing, though, is that they are really funny. Who can forget Goat Phillips eating Turkey Reiter's necktie—these stories are great stuff!"

ROBERT JOY (*Tapping*): "To act in 'The Prodigious Hickey' is to participate in the classic American conflict between spirited youth and conservative authority—the same conflict that produced the American Revolution. And the mock-epic tone of the stories makes the whole thing tremendous fun. It's *Tom Sawyer* retold as Arthurian legend."

ZACH GALLIGAN (*Hickey*): "The only thing that is more fun than reading about Hickey is playing him. Owen Johnson creates his own encapsulated little world of special friendships in special circumstances, and I loved being a part of it."

ALBERT SCHULTZ (*Doc*): "What I love about the production of 'The Prodigious Hickey' is that the charm, innocence, and spirit of Owen Johnson's stories is kept throughout. The quirkiness of the characters, combined with the comradery they shared, continues to have universal appeal."

JOSH HAMILTON (*Lovely*): " 'The Prodigious Hickey' and *The Lawrenceville Stories* embody the importance of close friendships and the incredible potential of youth. I'd go back to 1905 any day."

STEPHEN BALDWIN (*Gutter Pup*): "When I read *The Lawrenceville Stories* I felt I had been zapped back to a time that seemed simpler, stronger, filled with affection and youthful discovery. I'd like to see more of them come to life on screen."

HANS ENGEL (*Hungry*): "The reason that the stories are so charming is that the characters are not one-dimensional. The people are real, with a genuine warmth to them."

The
Lawrenceville Stories

OWEN JOHNSON

A TOUCHSTONE BOOK
SIMON & SCHUSTER, INC. • NEW YORK

FIRST TOUCHSTONE EDITION, 1987
PUBLISHED BY SIMON & SCHUSTER, INC.
SIMON & SCHUSTER BUILDING
ROCKEFELLER CENTER
1230 AVENUE OF THE AMERICAS
NEW YORK, NEW YORK 10020

THIS IS A REVISED EDITION OF A WORK ORIGINALLY PUBLISHED IN 1967
BY SIMON & SCHUSTER, INC.

TOUCHSTONE AND COLOPHON ARE REGISTERED TRADEMARKS
OF SIMON & SCHUSTER, INC.

MANUFACTURED IN THE UNITED STATES OF AMERICA

1 3 5 7 9 10 8 6 4 2 PBK.

LIBRARY OF CONGRESS CATALOGING-IN-PUBLICATION DATA

JOHNSON, OWEN MCMAHON, 1878–1952.
THE LAWRENCEVILLE STORIES.

REPRINT. ORIGINALLY PUBLISHED: NEW YORK:
SIMON AND SCHUSTER, 1967.
I. TITLE.
PS3519.O284L39   1987   813'.52   86-31314
ISBN 0-671-64248-0 PBK.

CONTENTS

FOREWORD

Peter Schwed

Have you ever met Hungry Smeed? Doc Macnooder? The Triumphant Egghead? The Gutter Pup? The Coffee-Colored Angel? The Waladoo Bird? The Uncooked Beefsteak? Dennis de Brian de Boru Finnegan? As a matter of fact, have you ever met *any* of the fabulous characters who people Owen Johnson's classic prep school stories?

If not, you're in for a treat when you read the two famous books that are brought together in this volume: *The Prodigious Hickey* and *The Tennessee Shad*. The first-ever edition in paperback and the very first after decades of being available only in hard cover, is now being published in conjunction with the Public Broadcasting Service's "American Playhouse" presentation of *The Prodigious Hickey*. Should you see that show and enjoy these stories as much as have the millions of readers in the past who reveled in them in magazine and hardcover book form (when they first came out, Booth Tarkington said that they "had given me more pleasure than anything I had ever read") you'll also want to read *The Varmint*, Owen Johnson's full-length novel about Dink Stover's years at the school before he went on to Yale.

Meanwhile, sit back and come to the table with Hungry Smeed as he goes all out after "The Great Pancake Record." Join a midnight Welsh rabbit party where the host has all the fixings except one vital ingredient, beer—when the Tennessee Shad, backed by Doc Macnooder's medical opinion, persuades the group that witch hazel can be used instead. And read of the several inspired schemes of the firm of the Shad and Doc Macnooder that finally educated the millionaire kid, The Uncooked Beefsteak, and broiled him to a crisp.

"American Playhouse" can show only so much. These pages will let you in on even more of the fun.

———

An alumnus and former trustee of The Lawrenceville School, Peter Schwed was responsible for re-publishing and reviving interest in *The Lawrenceville Stories* in the late 1960s.

The Prodigious Hickey

THE AWAKENING OF HICKEY

" 'HE FORGED a thunderbolt and hurled it at what? At the proudest blood in Europe, the Spaniard, and sent him home conquered; at the most warlike blood in Europe, the French . . .' "

Shrimp Davis, on the platform, piped forth the familiar periods of Phillips's oration on Toussaint L'Ouverture, while the Third Form in declamation, disposed to sleep, stirred fitfully on one another's shoulders, resenting the adolescent squeak that rendered perfect rest impossible. Pa Dater followed from the last bench, marking the position of the heels, the adjustment of the gesture to the phrase, and the rise and fall of the voice with patient enthusiasm, undismayed by the memory of the thousand Toussaints who had passed, or the certainty of the thousands who were to come.

" 'I would call him Napoleon, but Napoleon made his way to empire over broken oaths and through a sea of *blood*,' " shrieked the diminutive orator with a sudden crescendo as a spitball, artfully thrown, sang by his nose.

At this sudden shrill notice of approaching manhood, Hickey, in the front row, roused himself with a jerk, put both fists in his eyes and glanced with indignant reproach at the embattled disturber of his privileges. Rest now being impossible, he decided to revenge himself by putting forth a series of faces as a sort of running illustration to the swelling cadences. Shrimp Davis struggled manfully to keep his eyes from the antics of his tormentor. He accosted the ceiling, he looked sadly on the floor. He gazed east and west profoundly, through the open windows, seeking forgetfulness in the distant vistas. All to no purpose. Turn where he might, the mocking face of Hickey danced after him. At the height of his eloquence Shrimp choked, clutched at his mouth, exploded into laughter and tumbled ingloriously to his seat amid the delighted shrieks of the class.

Pa Dater, surprised and puzzled, rose with solemnity and examined the benches for the cause of the outbreak. Then taking up a position on the platform from which he could command each face, he scanned the roll thoughtfully and announced, "William Orville Hicks."

Utterly unprepared and off his guard, Hickey drew up slowly to his feet. Then a flash of inspiration came to him.

"Please, Mr. Dater," he said with simulated regret, "I chose the same piece."

Delighted, he settled down, confident that the fortunate coincidence would at least postpone his appearance.

"Indeed," said Mr. Dater with a merciless smile, "isn't that extraordinary! Well, Hicks, try and lend it a new charm."

Hickey hesitated with a calculating glance at the already snickering class. Then, forced to carry through the bravado, he climbed over the legs of his seatmates and up to the platform, made Mr. Dater a deep bow, and gave the class a quick bob of his head, accompanied by a confidential wink from that eye which happened to be out of the master's scrutiny. He glanced down, shook the wrinkles from his trousers, buttoned his coat, shot his cuffs and assumed the recognized Websterian attitude. Twice he cleared his throat while the class waited expectantly for the eloquence that did not surge. Next he frowned, took one step forward and two back, sank his hands in his trousers and searched for the missing sentences on the molding that ran around the edge of the ceiling.

"Well, Hicks, what's wrong?" said the master with difficult seriousness. "Haven't learned it?"

"Oh, yes, sir," said Hickey with dignity.

"What's the matter then?"

"Please, sir," said Hickey, with innocent frankness, "I'm afraid I'm a little embarrassed."

The class guffawed loud and long. The idea of Hickey succumbing to such an emotion was irresistible. Shrimp Davis sobbed hysterically and gratefully.

Hickey alone remained solemn, grieved and misunderstood.

"Well, Hicks," continued the master with the ghost of a smile, "embarrassment is something that you should try to overcome."

At this Turkey Reiter led Shrimp Davis out in agony.

"Very well," said Hickey with an injured look, "I'll try, sir. I'll do my best. But I don't think the conditions are favorable."

Mr. Dater commanded silence. Hickey bowed again and raised his head, cloaked in seriousness. A titter acclaimed him. He stopped and looked appealingly at the master.

"Go on, Hicks, go on," said Mr. Dater. "Do your best. At least, let us hear the words."

Another inspiration came to Hickey. "I don't think that this is quite regular, sir," he said aggressively. "I have always taken an interest in my work, and I don't see why I should be made to sacrifice a good mark."

Mr. Dater bit his lips and quieted the storm with two upraised fingers.

"Nevertheless, Hicks," he said, "I think we shall allow you to continue."

"What!" exclaimed Hickey as though loath to credit his ears. Then adding calm to dignity, he said, "Very well, sir—not prepared!"

With the limp of a martyr, he turned his back on Mr. Dater and returned to his seat, where he sat in injured dignity, disdaining to notice the grimaces of his companions.

Class over, the master summoned Hicks and bent his brows, boring him with a look of inquisitorial accusation.

"Hicks," he said, spacing his words, "I have felt, for the last two weeks, a certain lack of discipline here. Just a word to the wise, Hicks, just a word to *the wise!*"

Hickey was pained. Where was the evidence to warrant such a flat accusation? He had been arraigned on suspicion, that was all, absolutely on mere haphazard suspicion. And this was justice?

Moreover, Hickey's sensitive nature was shocked. He had always looked upon Pa Dater as an antagonist for whose sense of fair play he would have answered as for his own. And now to be accused thus with innuendo and veiled menace—then he could have faith in no master, not one in the whole faculty! And this grieved Hickey mightily as he went moodily along the halls.

Now, the code of a schoolboy's ethics is a marvelously fashioned thing—and by that each master stands or falls. To be accused of an offense of which he is innocent means nothing, for it simply demonstrates the lower caliber of the master's intelligence. But to be suspected and accused on mere suspicion of something which he has just committed—that is unpardonable, and in absolute violation of the laws of warfare, which decree that the struggle shall be one of wits, without recourse to the methods of the inquisition.

Hickey, disillusioned and shocked, went glumly down the brownstone steps of Memorial and slowly about the green circle, resisting the shouted invitations to tarry under the nourishing apple trees.

He felt in him an imperative need to strike back, to instantly break some rule of the tyranny that encompassed him. With this heroic intention he walked nonchalantly up the main street to the Jigger Shop, which no underformer may enter until after four. As he approached the forbidden haunt, suddenly the figure of Mr. Lorenzo Blackstone Tapping, the young assistant housemaster at the Dickinson, more popularly known as "Tabby," rolled up on a bicycle.

"Humph, Hicks!" Mr. Tapping said at once, with a suspicious glance at the Jigger Shop directly opposite. "How do you happen to be here out of hours?"

"Please, sir," said Hickey glibly, "I've got a nail that's sticking into my foot. I was just going to Bill Orum's to get it fixed."

"Humph!" Mr. Tapping gave him a searching look, hesitated, and mounting his wheel continued, unconvinced.

"He looked back," said Hickey wrathfully, peering through the misty windows of the cobbler's shop. Then smarting at the injury, he added, "He didn't believe me—the sneak!"

It was a second reminder of the tyranny he lived under. He

waited a moment, found the coast clear and flashed across to the Jigger Shop. Half drugstore, half confectioner's, the Jigger Shop was the property of Doctor Furnell, whose chief interest in life consisted in a devotion to the theory of the millennium, to the lengthy expounding of which an impoverished boy would sometimes listen in the vain hope of establishing a larger credit. On everyday occasions the shop was under the charge of "Al," a creature without heart or pity, who knew the exact financial status of each of the four hundred odd boys, even to the amount and date of his allowance. Al made no errors, his sympathies were deaf to the call, and he never (like the doctor) committed the mistake of returning too much change.

Al welcomed him with a grunt, carefully closing the little glass doors that protected the tray of éclairs and fruit cake, and leaning back, drawled, "What's the matter, Hickey? You look kind of discouraged."

"Give me a coffee jigger, with chocolate syrup and a dash of whipped cream—stick a meringue in it," said Hickey. Then as Al remained passively expectant, he drew out a coin, saying, "Oh, I've got the money!"

He ate gloomily and in silence, refusing to be drawn into conversation. Something was wrong in the scheme of things. Twice in the same hour he had been regarded with suspicion and an accusing glance—his simplest explanation discountenanced! Up to this time, he had been like a hundred other growing boys, loving mischief for mischief's sake, entering into a lark with no more definite purpose than the zest of an adventure. Of course he regarded a master as the Natural Enemy, but he had viewed him with the tolerance of an agile monkey for a wolf who does not climb. Now slowly it began to dawn upon him that there was an ethical side.

He vanished suddenly behind the counter as Mr. Tapping, returning, made directly for the Jigger Shop. Hickey, at the end of the long counter, crouching amid stationery, heard him moving suspiciously toward his hiding place. Quickly he flicked a pencil down behind the counter and vanished through the back entrance as Tapping, falling into the trap, sprang in the direction of the noise.

The adventure served two purposes: it gave Hickey the measure of the enemy, and it revealed to him where first to strike.

II

The President of the Dickinson, by virtue of the necessary authority to suppress all insubordination, was Turkey Reiter, broad of shoulder, speckled and battling of face, but the spirit of the Dickinson was Hickey. Hickey it was, lank of figure and keen of feature, bustling of gait and drawling of speech, with face as innocent as a choir boy's, who planned the revolts against the masters, organized the midnight feasts and the painting of water towers. His genius lived in the nicknames of the Egghead, Beauty Sawtelle, Morning Glory, Red Dog, Wash Simmons and the Coffee Cooler, which he had bestowed on his comrades with unfailing felicity.

Great was Hickey, and Macnooder was his prophet. Doc Macnooder roomed just across the hall. He was a sort of genius of all trades. He played quarter on the eleven and ran the half-mile close to the two-minute mark. He was the mainstay of Banjo, Mandolin and Glee Clubs. He played the organ in chapel and had composed the famous Hamill House March in memory of his requested departure from that abode. He organized the school dramatic club. He was secretary and treasurer of his class and of every organization to which he belonged. He received a commission from a dozen firms to sell to his likenesses, stationery, athletic goods, choice sets of books, fin de siècle neckties, fancy waistcoats, fountain pens and safety razors, all of which articles, if report is to be credited, he sold with ease and eloquence at ten per cent above the retail price. His room was a combination of a sorcerer's den and junk shop. At one corner a row of shelves held a villainous array of ill-smelling black, green and blue bottles, with which he was prepared to instantly cure anything from lockjaw to snake bite.

The full measure of Macnooder's activities was never known. Turkey Reiter had even surprised him drawing up a will for Bill Orum, the cobbler, to whom he had just sold a cure for rheumatism.

It was to Macnooder that Hickey opened his heart and his need of vengeance. It cannot be said that the ethical side of the struggle appealed to Macnooder, who had small predilection for philosophy and none at all for the moral sciences, but the love of mischief was strong. The encounter with Tapping in the morning had suggested

8

a victim near at hand and conveniently inexperienced.

Mr. Tapping, in advance of young Mr. Baldwin (of whom it shall be related), had arrived at Lawrenceville the previous year with latter-day theories on the education of boys. As luck would have it, Mr. Rogers, the housemaster, would be absent that evening at a little dinner of old classmates in Princeton, leaving the entire conduct of the Dickinson in the hands of his assistant. In passing, it must be noted that between the two masters there was little sympathy. Mr. Rogers had lived too long in the lair of the boy to be at all impressed with the new ideas on education that Mr. Tapping and later Mr. Baldwin advocated in the blissful state of their ignorance.

At three o'clock, Tapping departed to convey to a class of impatient boys, decked out in athletic costumes with baseballs stuffed in their pockets and tennis rackets waiting at their sides, the interesting shades of distinction in that exciting study, Greek prose composition. Then Hickey gleefully, while Macnooder guarded the stairs, entered the study, and with a screwdriver loosened the screw which held the inner doorknob, to the extent that it could later be easily removed with the fingers.

At half past seven o'clock, when study hour had begun, Hickey entered the sanctum ostensibly for advice on a perplexing problem in advanced algebra.

Mr. Tapping did not like Hickey. He regarded him with suspicion, with an instinctive recognition of an enemy. Also he was engaged in the difficult expression of a certain letter which, at that time, presented more difficulties than the binomial theorem. So he inquired with short cordiality, concealing the written page under a blotter:

"Well, Hicks, what is it?"

"Please, Mr. Tapping," said Hickey, who had perceived the move with malignant delight, "I wish you'd look at this problem— it won't work out." He added (shades of a thousand boys!), "I think there must be some mistake in the book."

Now, the chief miseries of a young assistant master center about the study hours—when theory demands that he should be ready to advise and instruct the discouraged boyish mind on any subject figuring in the curriculum, whatever be his preference or his prejudice. Mr. Tapping, who romped over the Greek and Latin page, had an hereditary weakness in the mathematics, a failing that the boys had discovered and instantly turned to their profit. He took the book, glanced at the problem and began to jot down a line of figures. Hickey, meanwhile, with his back to the door, brazenly extracted the loosened screw.

Finally, Mr. Tapping, becoming hopelessly entangled, raised his head and said with a disdainful smile, "Hicks, I think you had better put a little work on this—just a little work!"

"Mr. Tapping, I don't understand it," said Hickey, adding to himself, "Old Tabby is up a tree!"

"Nonsense—perfectly easy, perfectly simple," said Tapping, returning the book with a gesture of dismissal, "requires a little application, Hicks, just a little application—that's all."

Hickey, putting on his most injured look, bowed to injustice and departed at the moment that Turkey Reiter entered, seeking assistance in French. Upon his tracks, without an interval, succeeded Macnooder with a German composition, Hungry Smeed to discuss history, the Egghead on a question of spelling, and Beauty Sawtelle in thirst for information about the Middle Ages. Finally, Mr. Tapping's patience, according to Macnooder's prophetic calculation, burst on a question of biblical interpretation, and announcing wrathfully that he could no longer be disturbed, he ushered out the last tormentor and shut the door with violence.

Presently Hickey stole up on tiptoe and fastening a noose over the knob, gave a signal. The string, pulled by a dozen equally responsible hands, carried away the knob, which fell with a tiny crash and spun in crazy circles on the floor. The fall of the inner useless knob was heard on the inside of the door and the exclamation that burst from the startled master. The tyrant was caged—the house was at their pleasure!

Mr. Tapping committed the initial mistake of knocking twice imperiously on the door and commanding, "Open at once."

Two knocks answered him. Then he struck three violent blows and three violent echoes returned, while a bunch of wriggling, chuckling boys clustered at every crack of the door, listening with strained ears for the muffled roars that came from within.

While one group began a game of leapfrog, another, under the guidance of Hickey, descended into the housemaster's quarters and proceeded to attend to the rearrangement of the various rooms.

Working beaverlike with whispered cautions, they rapidly exchanged the furniture of the parlor with the dining room, grouping each transformed room exactly as the original had been.

Then they placed the six-foot water-cooler directly in front of the entrance with a tin pan balanced, to give the alarm, and shaking with silent expectant laughter extinguished all lights, undressed and returned to the corridors, white, shadowy forms, to wait developments. Meanwhile, the caged assistant master continued to pound upon the door with a fury that betokened a state of approaching hysteria.

At half past ten, suddenly the tin pan crashed horribly on the floor. A second later every boy was sleeping loudly in his bed. Astonished at such a reception, Mr. Rogers groped into the darkness and fell against the water-cooler, which in his excitement he embraced and carried over with him to the floor. Recovering himself, he lighted the gas and perceived the transformed parlor and dining room. Then he started for the assistant housemaster's rooms, with long, angry bounds, saying incoherent, expressive things to himself.

The ordeal that young Mr. Tapping faced from his superior, one hour later when the door had been opened, was distinctly unpleasant, and was not made the more agreeable from the fact that every rebuke resounded through the house and carried joy and comfort to the listening boys.

The housemaster would hear no explanation; in fact, explanations were about the last thing he wanted. He desired to express his disgust, his indignation and his rage, and he did so magnificently.

"May I say one word, sir?" said Mr. Tapping in a lull.

"Quite unnecessary, Mr. Tapping," cut in the still angry master. "I don't wish any explanations. Such a thing as this has never happened in the history of this institution. That's all I wish to know. You forget that you are not left in charge of a young ladies' seminary."

"Very well, sir," said the mortified Mr. Tapping. "May I ask what you intend to do about this act of insubordination?"

"That is what I intend to ask *you*, sir," replied his superior. "Good night."

The next day after luncheon, Mr. Tapping summoned the house to his study and addressed them as follows:

"Young gentlemen of the Dickinson House, I don't think you have any doubt as to why I have called you here. A very serious breach of discipline has taken place—one that cannot be overlooked. The sooner we meet the situation in the right spirit, gravely, with seriousness, the sooner will we meet each other in that spirit of harmony and friendly understanding that should exist between pupil and master. I am willing to make some allowance for the spirit of mischief, but none for an exhibition of untruthfulness. I warn you that I know, that I *know* who were the ringleaders in last night's outrage."

Here he stopped and glanced in succession at each individual boy. Then suddenly turning, he said, "Hicks, were you concerned in this?"

"Mr. Tapping," said Hickey, with the air of a martyr, "I refuse to answer."

"On what ground?"

"On the ground that I will not furnish any clue whatsoever."

"I shall deal with your case later."

"Very well, sir."

"Macnooder," continued Mr. Tapping, "what do you know about this?"

"I refuse to answer, sir."

At each demand, the same refusal.

Tapping, repulsed in his first attempt, hesitated and reflected. Above all things he did not wish to perpetuate last night's humiliation, and to continue the combat meant an accusation *en bloc* against the Dickinson House before the headmaster.

"Hicks, Macnooder and Reiter, wait here," he said suddenly; "the rest may go."

He walked up and down before the three a moment, and then said, "Reiter, you may go; you, too, Macnooder."

Hickey, thus deprived of all support, remained defiant.

"May I ask," he said indignantly, "why I am picked out?"

"Hicks," said Mr. Tapping sternly, without replying to the question, "I know pretty well who was the ringleader in this, and other things that have been going on in the past. I warn you, my boy, I shall keep my eye on you from this time forth. That's all I want to say to you. Look out for yourself!"

Hickey could hardly restrain the tears. He went out with deadly wrath boiling in his heart. The idea of signaling him out from the whole house in that way! So then every hand was against him; he had no security; he was marked for suspicion, his downfall determined upon!

For one brief moment his spirit, the spirit of indomitable, battling boyhood, failed him, and he felt the gray impossibility of contending against tyrants. But only a moment, and then with a return of the old fighting spirit he suddenly conceived the idea of single-handedly defying the whole organized, hereditary and entrenched tyranny that sought to crush him, of matching his wits against the hydra despotism, perhaps going down gloriously like Spartacus, for the cause, but leaving behind a name that should roll down the generations of future boys.

THE GREAT PANCAKE RECORD

LITTLE SMEED stood apart, in the obscure shelter of the station, waiting to take his place on the stage which would carry him to the great new boarding school. He was frail and undersized, with a long, pointed nose and vacant eyes that stupidly assisted the wide mouth to make up a famished face. The scarred bag in his hand hung from one clasp, the premature trousers were at half-mast, while pink polka dots blazed from the cuffs of his nervous sleeves.

By the wheels of the stage Fire Crackers Glendenning and Jock Hasbrouck, veterans of the Kennedy House, sporting the varsity initials on their sweaters and caps, were busily engaged in cross-examining the new boys who clambered timidly to their places on top. Presently, Fire Crackers, perceiving Smeed, hailed him.

"Hello, over there—what's your name?"

"Smeed, sir."

"Smeed what?"

"Johnnie Smeed."

The questioner looked him over with disfavor and said aggressively:

"You're not for the Kennedy?"

"No, sir."

"What house?"

"The Dickinson, sir."

"The Dickinson, eh? That's a good one," said Fire Crackers, with a laugh, and, turning to his companion, he added, "Say, Jock, won't Hickey and the old Turkey be wild when they get this one?"

Little Smeed, uncomprehending of the judgment that had been passed, stowed his bag inside and clambered up to a place on the top. Jimmy, at the reins, gave a warning shout. The horses, stirred by the whip, churned obediently through the sideways of Trenton.

Lounging on the stage were half a dozen newcomers, six well-assorted types, from the well-groomed stripling of the city to the aggressive, big-limbed animal from the West, all profoundly under the sway of the two old boys who sat on the box with Jimmy and rattled on with quiet superiority. The coach left the outskirts of the city and rolled into the white highway that leads to Lawrenceville. The known world departed for Smeed. He gazed fearfully ahead, waiting the first glimpse of the new continent.

Suddenly Fire Crackers turned and, scanning the embarrassed group, singled out the strong Westerner with an approving glance.

"You're for the Kennedy?"

The boy, stirring uneasily, blurted out, "Yes, sir."

"What's your name?"

"Tom Walsh."

"How old are you?"

"Eighteen."

"What do you weigh?"

"One hundred and seventy."

"Stripped?"

"What? Oh, no, sir—regular way."

"You've played a good deal of football?"

"Yes, sir."

Hasbrouck took up the questioning with a critical appreciation.
"What position?"

"Guard and tackle."

"You know Bill Stevens?"

"Yes, sir."

"He spoke about you; said you played on the Military Academy. You'll try for the varsity?"

"I guess so."

Hasbrouck turned to Fire Crackers in solemn conclave.

"He ought to stand up against Turkey if he knows anything about the game. If we get a good end we ought to give that Dickinson crowd the fight of their lives."

"There's a fellow came from Montclair they say is pretty good," Fire Crackers said, with solicitous gravity. "The line'll be all right if we can get some good halves. That's where the Dickinson has it on us."

Smeed listened in awe to the two statesmen studying out the chances of the Kennedy eleven for the house championship, realizing suddenly that there were new and sacred purposes about his new life of which he had no conception. Then, absorbed by the fantasy of the trip and the strange unfolding world into which he was jogging, he forgot the lords of the Kennedy, forgot his fellows in ignorance, forgot that he didn't play football and was only a stripling, forgot everything but the fascination of the moment when the great school would rise out of the distance and fix itself indelibly in his memory.

"There's the water tower," said Jimmy, extending the whip; "you'll see the school from the top of the hill."

Little Smeed craned forward with a sudden thumping of his heart. In the distance, a mile away, a cluster of brick and tile sprang out of the green, like a herd of red deer surprised in the forest. Groups of boys began to show on the roadside. Strange greetings were flung back and forth.

"Hello-oo, Fire Crackers!"

"How-de-do, Saphead!"

"Oh, there, Jock Hasbrouck!"

"Oh, you Morning Glory!"

"Oh, you Kennedys, we're going to lick you!"

"Yes you are, Dickinson!"

The coach passed down the shaded vault of the village street, turned into the campus, passed the ivy-clad house of the headmaster and rolled around a circle of well-trimmed lawn, past the long, low Upper House where the Fourth Form gazed at them in senior superiority; past the great brown masses of Memorial Hall and the pointed chapel, around to where the houses were ranged in red, extended bodies. Little Smeed felt an abject sinking of the heart at this sudden exposure to the thousand eyes fastened upon him from the wide esplanade of the Upper, from the steps of Memorial, from house, windows and stoops, from the shade of apple trees and the glistening road.

All at once the stage stopped and Jimmy cried, "Dickinson!"

At one end of the red-brick building, overrun with cool vines, a group of boys were lolling in flannels and light jerseys. A chorus went up.

"Hello, Fire Crackers!"

"Hello, Jock!"

"Hello, you Hickey boy!"

"Hello, Turkey; see what we've brought you!"

Smeed dropped to the ground amid a sudden hush.

"Fare," said Jimmy aggressively.

Smeed dug into his pocket and tendered the necessary coin. The coach squeaked away, while from the top Fire Crackers' exulting voice returned in insolent exultation:

"Hard luck, Dickinson! Hard luck, you, old Hickey!"

Little Smeed, his hat askew, his collar rolled up, his bag at his feet, stood in the road, alone in the world, miserable and thoroughly frightened. One path led to the silent, hostile group on the steps, another went in safety to the master's entrance. He picked up his bag hastily.

"Hello, you—over there!"

Smeed understood it was a command. He turned submissively and approached with embarrassed steps. Face to face with these superior beings, tanned and muscular, stretched in Olympian attitudes, he realized all at once the hopelessness of his ever daring to associate with such demigods. Still he stood, shifting from foot to foot, eyeing the steps, waiting for the solemn ordeal of examination and classification to be over.

"Well, Hungry—what's your name?"

Smeed comprehended that the future was decided, and that to the grave he would go down as "Hungry" Smeed. With a sigh of relief he answered, "Smeed—John Smeed."

"Sir!"

"Sir."

"How old?"

"Fifteen."

"Sir!!"

"Sir."

"What do you weigh?"

"One hundred and six—sir!"

A grim silence succeeded this depressing information. Then someone in the back, as a mere matter of form, asked, "Never played football?"

"No, sir."

"Baseball?"

"No, sir."

"Anything on the track?"

"No, sir."

"Sing?"

"No, sir," said Smeed, humbly.

"Do anything at all?"

Little Smeed glanced at the eaves where the swallows were swaying and then down at the soft couch of green at his feet and answered faintly, "No, sir—I'm afraid not."

Another silence came, then someone said, in a voice of deepest conviction: "A dead loss!"

Smeed went sadly into the house.

At the door he lingered long enough to hear the chorus burst out:

"A fine football team we'll have!"

"It's a put-up job!"

"They don't want us to win the championship again—that's it!"

"I say, we ought to kick."

Then, after a little, the same deep voice:

"A dead loss!"

With each succeeding week Hungry Smeed comprehended more fully the enormity of his offense in doing nothing and weighing one hundred and six pounds. He saw the new boys arrive, pass through the fire of christening, give respectable weights and go forth to the gridiron to be whipped into shape by Turkey and the Butcher, who played on the school eleven. Smeed humbly and thankfully went down each afternoon to the practice, carrying the sweaters and shin-guards, like the grateful little beast of burden that he was. He watched his juniors, Spider and Red Dog, rolling in the mud or flung gloriously under an avalanche of bodies; but then, they weighed over one hundred and thirty, while he was still at one hundred and six—a dead loss! The fever of house loyalty invaded him; he even came to look with resentment on the Faculty and to repeat secretly to himself that they never would have unloaded him on the Dickinson if they hadn't been willing to stoop to any methods to prevent the House again securing the championship.

The fact that the Dickinson, in an extraordinary manner, finally won by the closest of margins, consoled Smeed but a little while. There were no more sweaters to carry, or pails of barley water to fetch, or guard to be mounted on the old rail fence, to make certain that the spies from the Davis and Kennedy did not surprise the secret plays which Hickey and Slugger Jones had craftily evolved.

With the long winter months he felt more keenly his obscurity and the hopelessness of ever leaving a mark on the great desert of school life that would bring honor to the Dickinson. He resented even the lack of the mild hazing the other boys received—he was too insignificant to be so honored. He was only a "dead loss," good for nothing but to squeeze through his recitations, to sleep enormously, and to eat like a glutton with a hunger that could never be satisfied, little suspecting the future that lay in this famine of his stomach.

For it was written in the inscrutable fates that Hungry Smeed should leave a name that would go down imperishably to decades of schoolboys, when Dibbles' touchdown against Princeton and Kafer's home run should be only tinkling sounds. So it happened, and the agent of this divine destiny was Hickey.

It so happened that examinations being still in the threatening distance, Hickey's fertile brain was unoccupied with methods of facilitating his scholarly progress by homely inventions that allowed formulas and dates to be concealed in the palm and disappear obligingly up the sleeve on the approach of the Natural Enemy. Moreover, Hickey and Hickey's friends were in straitened circumstances, with all credit gone at the Jigger Shop, and the appetite for jiggers in an acute stage of deprivation.

In this keenly sensitive, famished state of his imagination, Hickey suddenly became aware of a fact fraught with possibilities. Hungry Smeed had an appetite distinguished and remarkable even in that company of aching voids.

No sooner had this pregnant idea become his property than Hickey confided his hopes to Doc Macnooder, his chum and partner in plans that were dark and mysterious. Macnooder saw in a flash the glorious and lucrative possibilities. A very short series of tests sufficed to convince the twain that in little Smeed they had a phenomenon who needed only to be properly developed to pass into history.

Accordingly, on a certain muddy morning in March, Hickey and Doc Macnooder, with Smeed in tow, stole into the Jigger Shop at an hour in defiance of regulations and fraught with delightful risks of detection.

Al, the watchdog of the Jigger, was tilted back, near a farther window, the parted tow hair falling doglike over his eyes, absorbed in the reading of Spenser's *Faerie Queene,* an abnormal taste which made him absolutely incomprehensible to the boyish mind. At the sound of the stolen entrance, Al put down the volume and started mechanically to rise. Then, recognizing his visitors, he returned to his chair, saying wearily, "Nothing doing, Hickey."

"Guess again," said Hickey, cheerily. "We're not asking you to hang us up this time, Al."

"You haven't got any money," said Al, the recorder of allowances; "not unless you stole it."

"Al, we don't come to take your hard-earned money, but to do you good," put in Macnooder impudently. "We're bringing you a little sporting proposition."

"Have you come to pay up that account of yours?" said Al. "If not, run along, you Macnooder. Don't waste my time with your wildcat schemes."

"Al, this is a sporting proposition," took up Hickey.

"Has *he* any money?" said Al, who suddenly remembered that Smeed was not yet under suspicion.

"See here, Al," said Macnooder, "we'll back Smeed to eat the jiggers against you—for the crowd!"

"Where's your money?"

"Here," said Hickey; "this goes up if we lose." He produced a gold watch of Smeed's, and was about to tender it when he withdrew it with a sudden caution. "On the condition, if we win I get it back and you won't hold it up against my account."

"All right. Let's see it."

The watch was given to Al, who looked it over, grunted in approval, and then looked at little Smeed.

"Now, Al," said Macnooder softly, "give us a gambling chance. He's only a runt."

Al considered and Al was wise. The proposition came often and he had never lost. A jigger is unlike any other ice cream. It is dipped from the creamy tin by a cone-shaped scoop called a jigger, which gives it an unusual and peculiar flavor. Since those days the original jigger has been contaminated and made ridiculous by offensive alliances with upstart syrups, meringues and macaroons with absurd titles, but then the boy went to the simple jigger as the sturdy Roman went to the cold waters of the Tiber. A double jigger fills a large soda glass when ten cents has been laid on the counter, and two such glasses quench all desire in the normal appetite.

"If he can eat twelve double jiggers," Al said slowly, "I'll set them up and the jiggers for youse. Otherwise, I'll hold the watch."

At this there was a protest from the backers of the champion, with the result that the limit was reduced to ten.

"Is it a go?" Al said, turning to Smeed, who had waited modestly in the background.

"Sure," he answered, with calm certainty.

"You've got nerve, you have," said Al, with a scornful smile, scooping up the first jiggers and shoving the glass to him. "Ten doubles is the record in these parts, young fellow!"

Then little Smeed, methodically, and without apparent pain, ate the ten doubles.

Conover's was not in the catalogue that anxious parents study, but then catalogues are like epitaphs in a cemetery. Next to the Jigger Shop, Conover's was quite the most important institution in the school. In a little white Colonial cottage, Conover, veteran of the late war, and Mrs. Conover, still in active service, supplied pancakes and maple syrup on a cash basis, two dollars credit to second-year boys in good repute. Conover's, too, had its traditions. Twenty-six pancakes, large and thick, in one continuous sitting, was the record, five years old, standing to the credit of Guzzler Wilkins, which succeeding classes had attacked in vain. Wily Conover, to stimulate such profitable tests, had solemnly pledged himself to the delivery of free pancakes to all comers during that day on which any boy, at one continuous sitting, unaided, should succeed in swallowing the awful number of thirty-two. Conover was not considered a prodigal.

This deed of heroic accomplishment and public benefaction was the true goal of Hickey's planning. The test of the Jigger Shop was but a preliminary trying out. With medical caution, Doc Macnooder refused to permit Smeed to go beyond the ten doubles, holding very wisely that the jigger record could wait for a further day. The amazed Al was sworn to secrecy.

It was Wednesday, and the following Saturday was decided upon for the supreme test at Conover's. Smeed at once was subjected to a graduated system of starvation. Thursday he was hungry, but Friday he was so ravenous that a watch was instituted on all his movements.

The next morning the Dickinson House, let into the secret, accompanied Smeed to Conover's. If there was even a possibility of free pancakes, the House intended to be satisfied before the deluge broke.

Great was the astonishment at Conover's at the arrival of the procession.

"Mr. Conover," said Hickey, in the quality of manager, "we're going after that pancake record."

"Mr. Wilkins' record?" said Conover, seeking vainly the champion in the crowd.

"No—after that record of *yours*," answered Hickey. "Thirty-two pancakes—we're here to get free pancakes today—that's what we're here for."

"So, boys, so," said Conover, smiling pleasantly; "and you want to begin now?"

"Right off the bat."

"Well, where is he?"

Little Smeed, famished to the point of tears, was thrust forward. Conover, who was expecting something on the lines of a buffalo, smiled confidently.

"So, boys, so," he said, leading the way with alacrity. "I guess we're ready, too."

"Thirty-two pancakes, Conover—and we get 'em free!"

"That's right," answered Conover, secure in his knowledge of boyish capacity. "If that little boy there can eat thirty-two, I'll make them all day free to the school. That's what I said, and what I say goes—and that's what I say now."

Hickey and Doc Macnooder whispered the last instructions in Smeed's ear.

"Cut out the syrup."

"Loosen your belt."

"Eat slowly."

In a low room, with the white rafters impending over his head, beside a basement window flanked with geraniums, little Smeed sat down to battle for the honor of the Dickinson and the record of the school. Directly under his eyes, carved on the wooden table, a name challenged him, standing out of the numerous initials— Guzzzler Wilkins.

"I'll keep count," said Hickey. "Macnooder and Turkey, watch the pancakes."

"Regulation size, Conover," cried that cautious Red Dog, "no doubling now. All fair and aboveboard."

"All right, Hickey, all right," said Conover, leering wickedly from the door. "If that little grasshopper can do it, you get the cakes."

"Now, Hungry," said Turkey, clapping Smeed on the shoulder. "Here is where you get your chance. Remember, kid, old sport, it's for the Dickinson."

Smeed heard in ecstasy; it was just the way Turkey talked to the eleven on the eve of a match. He nodded his head with a grim little shake and smiled nervously at the thirty-odd Dickinsonians who formed around him a pit of expectant and hungry boyhood from the floor to the ceiling.

"All ready!" sang out Turkey, from the doorway.

"Six pancakes!"

"Six it is," replied Hickey, chalking up a monster 6 on the slate that swung from the rafters. The pancakes placed before the ravenous Smeed vanished like snowflakes on a July lawn.

A cheer went up, mingled with cries of caution.

"Not so fast."

"Take your time."

"Don't let them be too hot."

"Not too hot, Hickey!"

Macnooder was instructed to watch carefully over the temperature as well as the dimensions.

"Ready again," came the cry.

"Ready—how many?"

"Six more."

"Six it is," said Hickey, adding a second figure to the score. "Six and six are twelve."

The second batch went the way of the first.

"Why, that boy is starving," said Conover, opening his eyes.

"Sure he is," said Hickey. "He's eating 'way back in last week— he hasn't had a thing for ten days."

"Six more," cried Macnooder.

"Six it is," answered Hickey. "Six and twelve is eighteen."

"Eat them one at a time, Hungry."

"No, let him alone."

"He knows best."

"Not too fast, Hungry, not too fast."

"Eighteen for Hungry, eighteen. Hurrah!"

"Thirty-two is a long ways to go," said Conover, gazing apprehensively at the little David who had come so impudently into his domain. "Fourteen pancakes is an awful lot."

"Shut up, Conover."

"No trying to influence him there."

"Don't listen to him, Hungry."

"He's only trying to get you nervous."

"Fourteen more, Hungry—fourteen more."

"Ready again," sang out Macnooder.

"Ready here."

"Three pancakes."

"Three it is," responded Hickey. "Eighteen and three is twenty-one."

But a storm of protest arose.

"Here, that's not fair!"

"I say, Hickey, don't let them do that."

"I say, Hickey, it's twice as hard that way."

"Oh, go on."

"Sure it is."

"Of course it is."

"Don't you know that you can't drink a glass of beer if you take it with a teaspoon?"

"That's right, Red Dog's right! Six at a time."

"Six at a time!"

A hurried consultation was now held and the reasoning approved. Macnooder was charged with the responsibility of seeing to the number as well as the temperature and dimensions.

Meanwhile Smeed had eaten the pancakes.

"Coming again!"

"All ready here."

"Six pancakes!"

"Six," said Hickey. "Twenty-one and six is twenty-seven."

"That'll beat Guzzler Wilkins."

"So it will."

"Five more makes thirty-two."

"Easy, Hungry, easy."

"Hungry's done it; he's done it."

"Twenty-seven and the record!"

"Hurrah!"

At this point Smeed looked about anxiously.

"It's pretty dry," he said, speaking for the first time.

Instantly there was a panic. Smeed was reaching his limit—a groan went up.

"Oh, Hungry."

"Only five more."

"Give him some water."

"Water, you loon; do you want to end him?"

"Why?"

"Water'll swell up the pancakes, crazy."

"No water, no water."

Hickey approached his man with anxiety.

"What is it, Hungry? Anything wrong?" he said tenderly.

"No, only it's a little dry," said Smeed, unmoved. "I'm all right, but I'd like just a drop of syrup now."

The syrup was discussed, approved and voted.

"You're sure you're all right?" said Hickey.

"Oh, yes."

Conover, in the last ditch, said carefully, "I don't want no fits around here."

A cry of protest greeted him.

"Well, son, the boy can't stand much more. That's just like the Guzzler. He was taken short and we had to work over him for an hour."

"Conover, shut up!"

"Conover, you're beaten."

"Conover, that's an old game."

"Get out."

"Shut up."

"Fair play."

"Fair play! Fair play!"

A new interruption came from the kitchen. Macnooder claimed that Mrs. Conover was doubling the size of the cakes. The dish was brought. There was no doubt about it. The cakes were swollen. Pandemonium broke loose. Conover capitulated, the cakes were rejected.

"Don't be fazed by that," said Hickey, warningly to Smeed.

"I'm not," said Smeed.

"All ready," came Macnooder's cry.

"Ready here."

"Six pancakes!"

"Regulation size?"

"Regulation."

"Six it is," said Hickey, at the slate. "Six and twenty-seven is thirty-three."

"Wait a moment," sang out the Butcher. "He has only to eat thirty-two."

"That's so—take one off."

"Give him five, Hickey—five only."

"If Hungry says he can eat six," said Hickey, firmly, glancing at his protégé, "he can. We're out for big things. Can you do it, Hungry?"

And Smeed, fired with the heroism of the moment, answered in disdainful simplicity, "Sure!"

A cheer that brought two Davis House boys running in greeted the disappearance of the thirty-third. Then everything was forgotten in the amazement of the deed.

"Please, I'd like to go on," said Smeed.

"Oh, Hungry, can you do it?"

"Really?"

"You're goin' on?"

"Holy cats!"

"How'll you take them?" said Hickey, anxiously.

"I'll try another six," said Smeed, thoughtfully, "and then we'll see."

Conover, vanquished and convinced, no longer sought to intimidate him with horrid suggestions.

"Mr. Smeed," he said, giving him his hand in admiration, "you go ahead; you make a great record."

"Six more," cried Macnooder.

"Six it is," said Hickey, in an awed voice; "six and thirty-three makes thirty-nine!"

Mrs. Conover and Macnooder, no longer antagonists, came in from the kitchen to watch the great spectacle. Little Smeed alone, calm and unconscious, with the light of a great ambition on his forehead, ate steadily, without vacillation.

"Gee, what a stride!"

"By Jiminy, where does he put it?" said Conover, staring helplessly.

"Holy cats!"

"Thirty-nine—thirty-nine pancakes—gee!!!"

"Hungry," said Hickey, entreatingly, "do you think you could eat another—make it an even forty?"

"Three more," said Smeed, pounding the table with a new authority. This time no voice rose in remonstrance. The clouds had rolled away. They were in the presence of a master.

"Pancakes coming."

"Bring them in!"

"Three more."

"Three it is," said Hickey, faintly. "Thirty-nine and three makes forty-two—forty-two. Gee!"

In profound silence the three pancakes passed regularly from the plate down the throat of little Smeed. Forty-two pancakes!

"Three more," said Smeed.

Doc Macnooder rushed in hysterically.

"Hungry, go the limit—the limit! If anything happens I'll bleed you."

"Shut up, Doc!"

"Get out, you wild man."

Macnooder was sent ignominiously back into the kitchen, with the curses of the Dickinson, and Smeed assured of their unfaltering protection.

"Three more," came the cry from the chastened Macnooder.

"Three it is," said Hickey. "Forty-two and three makes—forty-five."

"Holy cats!"

Still little Smeed, without appreciable abatement of hunger, continued to eat. A sense of impending calamity and alarm began to spread. Forty-five pancakes, and still eating! It might turn into a tragedy.

"Say, bub—say, now," said Hickey, gazing anxiously down into the pointed face, "you've done enough—don't get rash."

"I'll stop when it's time," said Smeed. "Bring 'em on now, one at a time."

"Forty-six, forty-seven, forty-eight, forty-nine!"

Suddenly, at the moment when they expected him to go on forever, little Smeed stopped, gazed at his plate, then at the fiftieth pancake, and said:

"That's all."

Forty-nine pancakes! Then, and only then, did they return to a realization of what had happened. They cheered Smeed, they sang his praises, they cheered again, and then, pounding the table, they cried, in a mighty chorus, "We want pancakes!"

"Bring us pancakes!"

"Pancakes, pancakes, we want pancakes!"

Twenty minutes later, Red Dog and the Egghead, fed to bursting, rolled out of Conover's, spreading the uproarious news.

"Free pancakes! Free pancakes!"

The nearest houses, the Davis and the Rouse, heard and came with a rush.

Red Dog and the Egghead staggered down into the village and over to the circle of houses, throwing out their arms like returning bacchanalians.

"Free pancakes!"

"Hungry Smeed's broken the record!"

"Pancakes at Conover's—free pancakes!"

The word jumped from house to house, the campus was emptied in a trice. The road became choked with the hungry stream that struggled, fought, laughed and shouted as it stormed to Conover's.

"Free pancakes! Free pancakes!"

"Hurrah for Smeed!"

"Hurrah for Hungry Smeed!!"

THE RUN THAT TURNED THE GAME

In THIS same fall of Hungry Smeed's arrival, when the Dickinson, the Cleve, the Woodhull, the Griswold, the Hamill, the Kennedy, and the Davis, were each separately convinced that the faculty was seeking to prevent its winning the football championship by filling the house with boys under weight and under size, there arrived at the Kennedy the now-celebrated "Piggy" Moore. He did not come on the top of the stage as new boys should, but drove up in a carriage, in the company of an aunt, who departed with misgivings after kissing him in the full sight of the campus.

For she had raised Piggy on the bottle of gentle manners and rocked him in the cradle of innocent and edifying ambitions until the manly age of sixteen. His hands were soft and manicured, he entered a room with grace and left it with distinction. His body was swathed in plumpness. His face was chubby and well nourished, with fat, indolent eyes and wide nostrils. He was five feet eight and weighed a hundred and fifty.

Without embarrassment or anxiety he went to his room, removed his coat, folded it neatly on a chair, turned up his sleeves and proceeded to spread on his bureau a toilet set of chaste silver. He was neatly arranging eight pairs of shoes, carefully treed, when his name was shouted from the hall.

"Oh, Moore! Hello there!"

He emerged hurriedly to find Captain Hasbrouck in football togs, eying him critically and without enthusiasm.

"Football practice, Moore!"

"It will take me an hour or so, I'm afraid," said Moore, smiling politely. "That is, to put my things in order and get thoroughly unpacked."

"Sir!"

Piggy was surprised. The voice was harsh, rude and ominous, and the figure of Hasbrouck quite obscured the doorway.

"Yes, sir!" he said hastily. "I'll be right down, sir."

"Have you got any football togs?" said Hasbrouck, looking at the toilet set.

"No, sir."

"A sweater?"

"No, sir."

"Well, we only want a little light practice. Get your things tonight in the village. On the jump now!"

Moore hastily trooped down with the others and followed across the long green stretches in the tingly September air, a little apprehensive of what the term "light practice" might mean. The veterans in scarred suits and rent jerseys marched gloriously in front, gamboling and romping with the ball, shouting out salutations to parties who swarmed over the campus from other houses on the way to the playgrounds. The newcomers in hastily patched-up costumes, incongruous and absurd, clustered together, talking in broken, forced monosyllables. Suddenly the advance halted and a shout went up.

"Here come the Dickinsons! Gee, look at the material they've got!"

Piggy, uncomprehending, beheld a group of thirty-odd boys swinging toward them, shouting and laughing as they came. From the advancing crowd came a challenging yell.

"We're going to wipe the earth up with you, Kennedy."

31

"Goodbye, Kennedy. Goodbye!"

From the Kennedys the challenge was flung back:

"We've got you where we want you."

"You'll be easy, Dickinson."

"We'll attend to the championship this year."

The two crowds halted while the leaders inspected their antagonists, sizing up the new material. Moore, in a tailor-cut suit of English tweed, a stiff collar and a derby hat, felt for the first time a little out of the picture when Hickey of the enemy paused in front of him and derisively asked, "Where did that come from?"

"Oh, that's been specially raised for us."

"He has? In a hothouse, yes! What'll *he* play?"

"He'll play all over the field. *He's* a regular demon!"

"Huh!"

"We'll twist your tail, Dickinson."

"We'll skin you, Kennedy."

"Yes, you will!"

"Yes, we will!"

The groups departed, each vowing that it was disheartening the way the faculty had favored the other.

On the playground Jock Hasbrouck and Fire Crackers Glendenning held a consultation while the old boys frolicked with the ball and the new arrivals huddled in an embarrassed group.

The new material was excellent, beyond expectation, but no joy appeared on the face of the captain.

"How in the deuce are we ever going to beat the Dickinsons with such a bunch as that?" he said, with a shake of his head. "What do we need anyhow?"

"Both ends, a tackle and the halves," said Fire Crackers gloomily.

"Well, we've got to do our best, that's all," said the captain, with a glance that made every newcomer miserable. "Let's see how we can line up. Fatty Harris, get in at center there. Keg, you'll have to go in at right guard. Buffalo, you stay at left."

The old boys, brawny and hard, formed into a center trio.

"If you take left tackle we'd better put Walsh in at right to face Turkey," said Fire Crackers. "Legs Brockett there plays end, he says."

Walsh and Brockett, eyes to the ground, took their places in the line at a nod from Jock.

"Duke Wilson, full; Fire Crackers, quarter. What then?" he said slowly to his counsel. "Suppose we give Pebbles Stone a chance at half this year?"

"What do you weigh, Pebbles?" asked Fire Crackers.

"One hundred and forty-five," brazenly answered the lithe but rather frail person addressed.

"Honest?"

"Honest to God, Jock."

"Stripped?"

"No—o-o. With ten pounds in me pockets."

"Well, get in there, you old liar; you've got the sand all right."

Pebbles, with a delighted whoop, sprang into line. Then Fire Crackers and Jock stopped before a trim, cleanly built boy with a suit that looked worthy.

"You're Francis, ain't you?"

"Yes, sir."

"Played half?"

"Yes, sir."

"What do you weigh?"

"One hundred and fifty, stripped, sir."

"Take right half."

Francis, quickly, but with an air of ease, took his place. Only one position remained vacant, left end. Hasbrouck glanced over the squad of slight, overgrown boys, and his eye by a process of elimination, rested on Moore, standing stiff and immaculate.

"Moore, get in to right end."

"Me?" said Moore in horror.

"Sir!"

"Sir."

"Quick!"

"But I—I've never played, sir!"

"Get into line!"

Piggy went sullenly, indignant and cherishing resistance. Hasbrouck gave a professionally pessimistic glance at the whole and said, "Well, fellows, we'll only take a little light practice today. Try a few starts."

The candidates in threes and fours crouched on a designated line, dug their toes in the sod, and raced forward at the clap of a hand for a good fifteen yards.

"Take your place, Moore," said Jock finally. "Dig down and get off with a jump."

Piggy, embarrassed by the stiffness of his collar and the difficulty of retaining his derby without loss of dignity, made a lumbering attempt.

"Try again. You're not racing a baby buggy! Get back on your marks," said Hasbrouck, and moving to a position directly behind him, he thundered, "Now, one—two—*three!*"

A stinging hand descended upon the crouching Piggy, who leaped forward in indignant amazement.

"That helped," said Jock, with an approving nod. "Once more."

Piggy, red to the ears, a second time was forced to humble himself and receive the indignity of such propulsion.

"Here, Piggy, catch!"

Moore had just time to spin around, when a football vigorously thrown, smote him full in the stomach.

"Oh, butterfingers!"

"Clumsy!"

"Get your arms into it!"

"Now!"

Warned by a chorus of instructions Moore strove a dozen times to retain the tantalizing spinning oval, which constantly slipped his grasp with a smart reminder as it bounded away.

"My boy, your education has been neglected," said Jock in disgust. "At least try and learn how to fall on the ball. Watch."

Rolling the pigskin in front of him, he dove for it, pounding on it as a beagle on a rabbit.

"Now, Piggy, let her go!"

Moore, who loved his tailor suit with the pride and affection which a father bestows only on the firstborn, desperately essayed to secure the pigskin with the minimum of danger possible.

A shriek of derision burst forth.

"No, my dear Miss Moore, I did not ask you to lie down and pillow your head upon it," said Jock in disgust. "That is *not* what is called falling on the ball. Go at it like a demon; chew it up, mangle it! Here, Morning Glory," he added, turning to a scrubby little urchin who was gamboling about, "take this young lady and show her how it's done."

To Piggy's culminating mortification, the diminutive Morning

Glory, with a contemptuous sneer, began to instruct him in the new art, with a rattling fire of insults which drew shrieks of laughter from the squad.

"Now then, old ice-wagon—get your nose in it."

"Don't spare the daisies, dearest."

"Jump, you Indian, jump!"

"Ah, watch me—like this."

The urchin hurled himself viciously on the ball, plowing up the soft turf, and bounding gloriously to his feet, with scornful, mud-stained face, cried, "Ah, what're you afraid of! Now then, old houseboat!"

Piggy's collar clung limply to his neck, half the buttons of his coat had gone, streaks of yellow and green decorated the suit a custom tailor had fashioned for fifty dollars cash, but still he was forced to go tumbling after the ball, down and up, up and down, head over heels, at the staccato shriek of the Morning Glory, like the one dog in the show who circles about the stage, tumbling somersaults.

"That's enough for today," came at last Jock's welcome command. "We must begin easily. Tomorrow we'll get into it. Practice over! Moore, jog around the circle six times and cut out pastry at supper."

During the dinner a great light dawned over Moore as he sat silently investigating his new masters with sidelong, calculated glances. He went to his room and with one sweep eliminated the solid silver toilet set, removed the trees from his boots, packed away the pink embroidered bedroom slippers so neatly arranged under the bed and pruned solicitously among the gorgeous cravats. Then he went to the village and, under skillful prompting, bought a pair of corduroy trousers, a cap, a red-and-black jersey, the softest pair of football trousers in stock, a jersey padded at the elbows and shoulders, a sweater, a pair of heavy shoes, a nose protector, and a pair of shin-guards. Encased in every possible protection he reported next day for the dreadful ordeal of tackling and being tackled.

"So you've all got your togs," said Fire Crackers, surveying the squad of freshmen on the field. "Let's see how you made out."

With Keg Smith and Jock, he passed them over in inspection, punching and poking the new suits with brief interjections, until Moore was reached. Before that swollen figure the three halted in mock amazement.

"Who's this?" said Keg, with a blank face.

"It's Moore, sir," said Piggy innocently.

"What's happened to you?" continued Fire Crackers with great seriousness.

Moore, perceiving he had blundered again, grew red with mortification, while Fire Crackers stripped the sweater from him and examined the jersey.

"Say, just see what Bill sold him!" he exclaimed. "Isn't it a shame how he'll impose on the green ones? Look at that bedticking! And those pads! Gee, I'll fix that!"

Before Moore could protest, Fire Crackers had ripped off the protections and flung them away.

"Now you'll feel easier,'" he said with a friendly smile. "Bill Appleby is an infernal old swindler, selling you shin-guards and a nose protecter! Huh! Throw 'em away."

'Thank you, sir," said Moore gratefully, "I'll make him take them back."

"That's right," said his inquisitor with a queer nod, "you're pretty green at this, aren't you?"

"I have never done much, sir."

"Well, let me give you a pointer; when you tackle, you want to grit your teeth and slam down hard, then you don't feel it at all."

"Thank you, sir."

"And when you're tackled," continued Fire Crackers with perfect seriousness, "just let yourself go limp; then you can't break any bones—see?"

"Yes, sir."

"You like the game, don't you?"

"Oh, very much."

Fire Crackers' advice did him scant good. On the whole it was probably the most painful afternoon he had ever known in his life. He had no instinct for tackling, that was certain. His arms slipped, his hands could not fasten to anything and he accomplished nothing more than to go sprawling, face downward.

"Funny you don't get on to that," said Jock, shaking his head.

"I tell you what you do. Run down the line and take a few tackles; then you'll see how it's done."

Moore stood balancing, looking down to where Jock's one hundred and sixty-five pounds were gathering for a model tackle. Every natural instinct in him bade him turn tail and run.

"Come on now!" cried Jock, spitting on his hands. "Hard as you can."

Piggy went as a horse goes to a road crusher, faltering and finally stopping dead. The next moment, Jock, cleaving the air in a perfect dive, caught him about the knees and threw him crashing to the ground. Piggy rose with difficulty.

"Do you get it now?" said Jock solicitously.

"I think I do," said Moore faintly.

"Well now, try one on me," said Jock, brightening. "Put your shoulder into it and squeeze it. Remember now."

Piggy remembered only the sensation of being tackled, and with the thought of that greater evil, improved astonishingly.

"That's the way to learn," said Jock approvingly. "Now, notice how I pull your legs from under you, and try to get that."

That evening after supper, Moore valiantly determined to take the bull by the horns. Seizing a favorable opportunity, he accosted his captain with the resolution of despair, and told him point blank that he would not be eligible for the team.

"Why not?" said Jock aggressively.

"I don't know anything about the game, sir," said Moore defiantly, "and I don't like it."

"Is that the only reason?"

"I don't want to play, sir—that ought to be enough."

"We're not *asking* you what you want to do."

"But, sir, I don't like it," said Moore, beginning to shrink under the cold, boring gaze of Hasbrouck.

"That has nothing to do with it, either."

"Nothing—"

"Certainly not. We don't want you; in fact, we're crying because we've got to take you. You're a flubdub and a quitter. But there's no one else, and so, Piggy, mark you—we're going to make a demon out of you, a regular demon. Mark my words!"

All of which was accomplished easily and naturally within a short two weeks by the discipline and tradition which has put courage into the hearts of generations of natural cowards.

The crisis came in the first game of the series, when, for the first time, Piggy beheld the terrifying spectacle of an end run started in his direction. At the sight of the solid front of bone and muscle ready to sweep him off his feet and send him tumbling head over heels, he shut his eyes and funked deliberately and ingloriously.

The next moment Jock had him by the small of the neck; Jock's hand jerked him to his feet and Jock's voice cried, "You cowardly little pup! You do that again and I'll tear the hide off you!"

Piggy, chilled to the bone, went to his position. The opposing team, with a shout of exultation, sent the same play crashing in his direction. Piggy, desperate with fear, tore through the advancing mass, found the runner and hurled him to the ground. Jock smiled contentedly. Moore was a coward, he knew, but from that time forth, no passing menace before him could compare with the abiding terror that waited behind.

Had Moore been possessed of even moderate courage the task would have been difficult, for then it would have resolved itself into a mere question of natural ability. But being an arrant and utter coward, his very cowardice drove him into feats of desperate recklessness. For always, in lull or storm, in the confusion of the melee or the open scramble down the field to cover a punt, Moore felt the ominous presence of Hasbrouck just at his shoulder and heard the sharp and threatening cry, "Get that man, you, Piggy!"

So blindly and rebelliously he served the tyrant, and unwilling and revolting learned to despise fear, little suspecting how many reckless spirits of other teams had been formed under the same rude discipline.

The earlier contests developed the strength of the two long-time rivals, the Kennedy and the Dickinson, between whom at last lay the question of supremacy. The last week approached with excitement at fierce heat. Every day a fresh rumor was served up; Hickey, the wily Dickinson quarter, had a weak ankle; Turkey, the captain, was behind in his studies; a Princeton varsity man was over, coaching the enemy; the signals were discovered and a dozen trick plays were being held in reserve, each good for a touchdown.

Each night on the Kennedy steps, the council of war convened and plans were discussed in utter gravity for temporarily crippling and eliminating from the contest Turkey, Slugger Jones, Hickey and the Butcher. For, of course, it was conceded that Jock, Tom Walsh and Fire Crackers would probably be maimed for life by the brutal and unscrupulous enemy.

Piggy, whose critical sense of humor had been under early disadvantages, took this as exact truth and beheld the horrible day arrive with an absolute conviction that it would be his last. He did not sleep during the night; he could eat nothing during the day; his fingers trembled and snarled up the lacings as he forced himself into his football clothes. Then he stood a long moment, viewing his white face in the mirror—the last look, perhaps—and went weakly to join the squad below. He heard nothing of the magnificent address of Jock to his followers. One idea only was in his head: to sell his life as dearly as possible.

While the captains conferred and tossed for position, the two teams, face to face at last, paced up and down, eying each other with contempt, breathing forth furious threats.

The Egghead assured Fatty Harris that the first scrimmage would be his last. Fatty Harris returned the compliment and suggested that the Egghead leave a memorandum for the hearse. The Coffee Cooler looked Buffalo Brown over and sneered; Keg Smith did as much to the Butcher and laughed. The diminutive Spider at right end, approached his dear friend Legs Brockett, his opponent, and muttered through his teeth, "I'm going to slug you!"

While these friendly salutations were taking place, Flea Obie and Wash Simmons, the Dickinson halves, approached Piggy, who, sick at heart, was stamping his feet and churning his arms to convey to Red Dog, opposite, the impression that he was thirsting for his blood.

Wash gave Piggy one withering glance and said loudly to the Red Dog, "This fellow's a quitter. He's got yellow in his eyes. Smash him good and hard, Red Dog. Don't waste any time about it, either."

"He's got a chicken liver," said Red Dog, who looked a reed beside the sturdy Piggy. "He shuts his eyes when he tackles! I'll fix him. Huh!"

"Ah, go on now, go on, go on," said Piggy, with a desperate attempt at lightheartedness.

Flea Obie, lovely no longer in mud-stained jacket and pirate band around his forehead, strode up to Piggy and added, "Old Sport, let me give you a word of advice. When we strike your end, the best thing you can do is to lie down *quick and soft. Savez?*"

Luckily for Piggy, whose imagination was panic-driven by this perfectly innocuous braggadocio, the torrent of conversation was checked by a cry of exultation.

The Kennedy had won the toss and chose the kickoff. Bat Finney, umpire from the Fourth Form, called the two teams together and said solemnly, "Now I want it understood by you fellows this is going to be a gentleman's game. No roughing it, no slugging, nothing bru-tal. Take your sides."

Immediately the air resounded with war cries:

"Get in there, Dickinson."

"Chew 'em up, Kennedy."

"Hit 'em hard, Buffalo."

"Sock 'em, Turkey."

"Knock 'em out, boys!"

Piggy, at left end with his eye on the ball, waited hopelessly for Jock to send the oval spinning into Dickinson territory. He was shivering, in a dead funk. The whistle blew, the run was on. Piggy went perfunctorily, helplessly, down the field to where the dreaded Hickey, ball under arm, was dodging toward him. Suddenly the vigorous form of Wash Simmons hove into view, headed directly for him. He wavered and the next moment was knocked off his feet, while Hickey, the way thus cleared for him, went bounding back for a run of forty yards.

Meanwhile Piggy was in the hands of Jock, who administered to him before the eyes of every spectator, a humiliating and well-placed kick.

"You funked, I saw you funk, you miserable shivery little coward!" he cried, shaking his fist in his face. "You jump in there now and cripple a few of those fellows or I'll massacre you!"

He added a few words which shall remain sacred between them and shoved him into place. The old fear awoke triumphant in Piggy. He rushed in like a demon, whirling over the field, upsetting play after play, making tackles that brought Flea Obie and Wash Simmons to their feet rubbing their sides. Nothing could stop him, for at last he was panic-stricken, utterly and horribly afraid.

The two teams, evenly matched, fought each other to a stand-still. The first half closed without any perceptible advantage. The second half continued the deadlock, the precious minutes slipping away. Such a struggle had never been known in a House contest. Several eyes were closed, several bandages had appeared. The frenzy of battle had taken possession of the descendants of Goth and Viking. Challenges to future encounters were flung recklessly and recklessly accepted. After each melee little clusters of battling boyhood were disentangled with difficulty, while Bat Finney, the umpire, joyfully proclaimed, "No roughing it, fellows—remember, this is a *gentleman's* game."

The dusk began to cloud the field and the players, one of those tragic, melancholy mists that come only at the close of a desperate second half. Two minutes only to play and the ball in the Kennedy's possession, exactly at midfield, without a score.

"6-5-8-15-2-3!" shrieked Fire Crackers, grimy and unrecognizable.

The team, converging swiftly for a revolving mass play on tackle, strove wearily to make headway against the reeling Dickinsons, who, too fagged to upset the play, could only hold, surging and twisting. Piggy, scrambling and pushing, head down in the melee, whirled and spun with the revolving mass. Then his feet tripped and he went underneath, shielding his head from the vortex of legs that swirled above him. Suddenly, lying free, a scant five yards in front of him, he perceived to his horror the precious ball! With a lurch, he freed himself from the mass, scrambled to his feet, picked up the ball and set out, break-a-neck, for the faraway goal. Five yards behind was Hickey, the fleet quarter, bounding after him.

In a twinkling the whole scene had changed into the extraordinary spectacle of a stern chase, two figures well in front, striving for the mastery of the fates, and behind the futile, scrambling, exulting or desperate mass of players, sweeping helplessly on the tracks of destiny.

Forty yards to the interminable goal! Piggy remembered with dread the stories of Hickey's fleetness. He glanced back. His pursuer had not gained an inch. On the contrary, his freckled face was distorted, his arms were churning, his teeth were horribly displayed, biting at the stinging air, with the agony of the effort to increase his speed. So he was beating out Hickey, the famous Hickey! Then the touchdown was a fact! Above the uproar he heard a strident shriek:

"Piggy, oh, you damned Piggy!"

The terror of that familiar voice gave a new impetus to his chubby legs. Someone else must be gaining on him. Thirty yards still to go!

He ran and ran, hugging the ball in his arms, his head thrown back, gasping for breath. Twenty yards—fifteen yards! Suddenly swift, glorious visions rose before him, scenes of jubilation and exultation, of cheering comrades, celebrations that would wipe out the long record of humiliation. Hickey was closer now, but Piggy did not dare to turn his head; five yards more and the game would be over and the kingdom of the Kennedy in his grasp. He sped over the last white chalk line and dropped triumphant behind the goal posts. The next moment, Hickey, wily Hickey, screaming with laughter, flung himself on him.

Piggy gazed about wildly with a sudden horrible suspicion. He had run over his own goal line and scored a safety for the Dickinson.

Then Hasbrouck arrived.

THE FUTURE PRESIDENT

"Snorky" Green, at the fourth desk of the middle aisle, gazed dreamily at the forgotten pages of the divine Virgil. The wide windows let in the warm breath of June meadows and the tiny sounds of contented insects roaming in unhuman liberty. Outside were soft banks to loll upon, from which to watch the baseball candidates gamboling over the neat diamond, tennis courts calling to be played upon, and the friendly jigger ready to soothe the parched highway to the aching void. And for an hour the tugging souls of forty-two imprisoned little pagans would have to construe, and parse, and decline, secretly cursing the fossils who rediscovered those unnecessary Latin documents.

Eight rows of desks, nine deep, were swept by the Argus eye of the master from his raised pulpit. Around the room, immense vacant blackboards shut them in—dark, hopeless walls over which no convict might clamber, on which a thousand boys had blundered and guessed and writ in water.

Lucius Cassius Hopkins, the Roman, man of heroic and consular mold, flunker of boys and deviser of systems against which even the ingenuity of a Hickey hurled itself in vain, sat on the rostrum, pitilessly mowing down the unresisting ranks.

Snorky's tousled hair was more rumpled than ever, a smudge was on one cheek where his grimy, ball-stained hand had unknowingly left its mark. He was dirty, bored, and unprepared. The dickey at his throat, formed by the junction of a collar and two joined cuffs, saved the proprieties and allowed the body to keep cool. But the spirit of dreams was upon Snorky, and the hard, rectangular room began to recede.

He heard indistinctly the low, mocking rumble of the Roman as his scythe passed down the rows.

"Anything from the Simpson twins today? No, no? Anything from the Davis House combination? Too bad! Too bad! Nothing from the illuminating Hicks? Yes? No? Too bad! Too bad!"

Snorky did not hear him; his eyes were on the firm torsos of Flash Condit and Charley De Soto before him—Condit, wonder of the football field, hero of the touchdown against the Princeton varsity, and De Soto the phenomenal shortstop, both Olympian spirits doomed to endure the barbed shafts of Lucius Cassius Hopkins.

He, too—Snorky—would go down in the annals of school history. He remembered the beginning of an outcurve he had developed that morning in the lot back of the Woodhull—a genuine outcurve, Ginger Pop Rooker to the contrary notwithstanding. With a little practice he would master the perplexing incurve and the drop. And the Woodhull needed a pitcher badly. McCarty had no courage; the Dickinson would batter him all over the field in the afternoon's game, and then goodbye to the championship. In his mind he began the game, trotting hopelessly out into left field. He saw Hickey, first up for the Dickinson, get a base on balls—four wide ones in succession. Slugger Jones, four balls—heavens, to be beaten like that! Turkey Reiter, third man up, hit a two-bagger; two runs. Doc Macnooder knocked the first ball pitched for a clean single; a two-bagger for the Egghead! Again four balls for Butcher Stevens! The Red Dog, of all people in the world, to hit safely! And still they allowed the slaughter to go on! The Dickinson House was shrieking with joy, dancing war dances back of third, and singing derisive songs of triumph. Flea Obie went to first on another base on balls, filling the bases. And five runs over the plate! Hickey and Turkey on the line began to dance a cakewalk. From the uproarious Dickinsonians rose the humiliating wail:

We're on to his curves, we're on to his curves;
Long-legged McCarty has lost his nerves.

McCarty *had* lost his nerves. Five runs, the bases full, and Wash
Simmons, the Dickinson pitcher, to the bat. The infield, badly
rattled, played in to catch the runner at home in approved professional style. Snorky stole in closer and closer until he was almost
back of shortstop. Simmons, he knew, couldn't send it out of the
diamond. But Wash knocked what looked to be a clean single, clear
over the heads of the near infield. That was what he had been
waiting for; on the full run he made a desperate dive, caught the
ball one-handed, close to the ground, turned a somersault, scrambled to second base, and shot the ball to first before the runner
could even check himself!

Nothing like it had ever been seen in Lawrenceville. Even the
Dickinsons generously applauded him as he came up happy and
flushed.

"Snorky, that's the greatest play I ever saw pulled off. I wish I
had made it myself."

He looked up. The speaker was the dashing De Soto. That from
Charley, the greatest ballplayer who ever came to Lawrenceville!
Snorky's throat swelled with emotion. At last they knew his worth.

One run for the Woodhull. Again the Dickinsons to the bat, and
again the rout; one single, a base on balls, two bases on balls—oh,
if he only would get his chance! One ball, two balls, three balls.
Suddenly McCarty stopped and clutched his arm with an exclamation of pain. The team gathered about him. Snorky sniffed in
disdain; he knew that trick, pretending it was all on account of
his arm! What a quitter McCarty was, after all! Still, what was to
be done? The team gathered in grave discussion. No one else had
ever pitched.

"Give me a chance," he said suddenly to Rock Bemis, the captain.

"You!" said Rock, with a laugh. "You, Snorky!"

"Look at me! I can do it," he answered, and met the other's glare
with steady look as heroes do. Something of the fire in that look
convinced Bemis.

"Why not?" he said. "The game's gone, anyhow. Go into the
box, Snorky, and put them over if you can."

The teams lined up. With clenched teeth and a cold streak down his spine he strode into the box. An insulting yelp went up from the enemy.

Three balls, no strikes, and the bases full! Turkey at the plate stepped back scornfully to wait for the fourth ball.

"Strike one!"

Turkey advanced to the utmost limit of the batter's box, turned his back deliberately on Snorky, and called out, "You hit me, and I'll break your neck!"

"Strike two!"

Turkey turned in surprise, looked at him, and deliberated.

"He can't put it over," yelled the gallery. "Yi, yi, yi!"

Then Turkey seated himself Indian fashion, his back still to Snorky, and gazed up into the face of Tug Moffat, the catcher. A furious wrangle ensued, the Woodhull claiming that his position was illegal, the Dickinson insisting that nothing in the rules prohibited it. Stonewall Jackson, the umpire, a weak-minded fellow from the Rouse House, allowed the play.

"Strike three!"

Turkey, crestfallen and muttering, arose and dusted himself amid the jeers of the onlookers. Doc Macnooder smote high and low, and then forgot to smite—three strikes and out. The Egghead, despite the entreaties of the Dickinson to bring in his housemates, could only foul out. The Woodhulls went wild with delight. He heard Tug, the catcher, whispering excitedly to De Soto.

"Charley, just watch him! He's got everything—everything!"

Then the Woodhull tied the score on two bases on balls, and his own two-bagger.

When he walked lightly into the box for the third inning, Stonewall Jackson had been replaced by De Soto with the imperious remark: "Here, get out! I want to watch this."

He gave the great Charley a modest nod.

"When did you ever pitch?" said De Soto, critically.

"Oh, now and then," he answered.

"Well, Snorky, let yourself out."

"Tug can't hold me," he said impudently. "That's the trouble, Charley."

"Try him."

Tug signaled for an in-shoot. He wound himself up and let fly. Butcher Stevens flung himself from the plate, Moffat threw up his mitt in sudden fear. The ball caromed off and went frolicking past the backstop.

"Strike one!"

Tug, puzzled and apprehensive, came up for a consultation.

"Gee, Snorky, give me warning! What do you think I am—a Statue of Liberty?"

"Charley wants me to let myself out. I'll slow down on the third strike," he said loftily. "Let the others go if you want."

Tug, like a Roman gladiator, with undying resolve, squatted back of the plate and signaled for an outcurve. No use; no mitt of his could ever stop the frightful velocity of that shoot.

"Stri-ike two!"

"Now ease up a bit," cautioned De Soto.

He sent a floating outdrop that seemed headed for Butcher Stevens' head, and finally settled gently over the plate at the waistline.

"Striker out!"

Moffat no longer tried to hold him, admitting himself outclassed by the blinding speed of ins and outs, jump balls, and cross fire that Snorky hurled unerringly across the plate. The Red Dog and Flea Obie, plainly unnerved, died like babes in their tracks. Five strike-outs in two innings!

Then De Soto spoke.

"Here, Snorky, you get out of this!"

A cry of protest came from the Woodhull.

"Yell all you like," said De Soto; "Snorky is going with me where he belongs."

And, to the amazement of the two houses, he drew his arm under Snorky's and marched him right over to the varsity diamond.

How the school buzzed and chattered about the phenomenal rise of the new pitcher! He saw himself pitching wonderful curves to burly Cap Kiefer, the veteran backstop, built like a mastodon, who had all he could do to hold those frightful balls. He saw the crowds of boys, six deep, who stood reverentially between times to watch the amazing curves. He heard pleasurably the chorus of "Ahs!" and "Ohs!" and "Gees!" which followed each delivery. Then suddenly he was in the box on the great, clean diamond, with the eyes of hundreds of boys fastened prayerfully on him, and the orange-and-black stripes of a Princeton varsity man facing him at the plate. To beat the Princeton varsity—what a goal!

He saw each striped champion come up gracefully and retire

crestfallen to the bench, even as the Dickinson batters had done. Inning after inning passed without a score; not a Princeton man reached first. Then in the seventh an accident happened. The first Princeton man up deliberately stepped into the ball, and the umpire allowed him to take his base. It was outrageous, but worse was to follow. On the attempt to steal second, Cap lined a beautiful ball to the base, but no one covered it—a mistake in signals! And the runner kept on to third! Snorky settled down and struck out the next two batters. The Lawrenceville bleachers rose *en masse* and shrieked his praises. Then suddenly Kiefer, to catch the runner off third, snapped the ball to Waladoo a trifle, just a trifle, wild; but the damage was done. 1 to 0 in favor of Princeton. Even the great Princeton captain, Barrett, said to him, "Hard luck, Green! Blamed hard luck!"

But Snorky wasn't beaten yet. The eighth and ninth innings passed without another Princeton man reaching first. Nine innings without a hit—wonderful!—and yet to be beaten by a fluke. One out for Lawrenceville; two out. The third man up, Cap Kiefer himself, reached first on an error. "Green to the bat," sang out the scorer.

Snorky looked around, picked up his bat and calmly strode to the plate. He had no fear; he knew what was going to happen. One ball, one strike, two strikes. He let the drop pass. What he wanted was a swift in-shoot. Two balls—too high. Three balls—wide of the plate. He was not to be tempted by any such. Two strikes and three balls; now he must get what he wanted. He cast one glance at the bleachers, alive with the frantic red-and-black flags; he heard his comrades calling, beseeching, imploring. Then his eye settled on the far green stretch between right and center field and the brown masses of Memorial where no ball before had ever reached. A home run would drive in Kiefer and win the game! The chance had come. The Princeton pitcher slowly began to wind up for the delivery. Snorky settled into the box, caught his bat with the grip of desperation, gathered together all his sinews, and—

"Green!" called the sharp, jeering voice of Lucius Cassius Hopkins.

Snorky sprang to his feet in fright, clutching at his book. The great home run died in the air.

"Translate."

Snorky gazed helplessly at the page, seeking the place. He heard the muffled voice of Hickey behind him:

"The advance, the advance, you chump!"

But to find the place under the hawk eyes of the Roman was an impossibility. He stared at the page in a well-simulated attempt, shook his head, and sat down.

"A very creditable attempt, Green," said the master, now with a gentle voice. "De Soto?—Nothing from De Soto? Dear, dear! We'll have to try Macnooder then. What? Studied the wrong lesson? How sad! Mistakes will happen. Don't want to try that, either? No feeling of confidence today; no feeling of confidence." He began to call them by rows. "Dark, Davis, Denton, Dibble—nothing in the D's. Farr, Francis, Frey, Frick—nothing from the F's; nothing from the D. F's. Very strange! very strange! Little spring fever—yes? Too bad! too bad! Lesson too long? Yes? Too long to get any of it? Dear, dear! Everyone studied the review, I see. Excellent moral idea, conscientious; wouldn't go on until you have mastered yesterday's lesson. Well, well, so we'll have a beautiful recitation in the review."

How absurd it was to be flunking under the Roman! Next year he would show them. He would rise early in the morning and study hours before breakfast; he would master everything, absorb everything—declensions and conjugations, Greek, Roman, and medieval civilization; he would frolic in equations and toy with logarithms; his translation would be the wonder of the faculty. He would crush Red Dog and Crazy Opdyke; he would be valedictorian of his class. They would speak of him as a phenomenon, as a prodigy, like Pascal—was it Pascal? What a tribute the headmaster would pay him at commencement! There on the stage before all the people, the fathers and mothers and sisters, before the Red Dog, and Ginger Pop Rooker, and Hickey, and all the rest, sitting open-mouthed while he, Snorky Green, the crack pitcher and valedictorian of his class, a scholar such as Lawrenceville had never known—

"Green, Gay, and Hammond, go to the board. Take your books."

Snorky went hastily and clumsily, waiting as a gambler waits for his chance.

"Gay, decline *hic, haec, hoc;* Green, write out the gerundive forms of all the verbs in the first paragraph top of page 163."

Snorky gazed helplessly at the chronicles of Aeneas, and then blankly at the inexorable blackboard, where so many gerundives had not been inscribed.

He drew his name in lagging letters exactly midway, at the top, with a symmetrical space above.

R. B. GREEN

Then he searched anxiously for the gerundives that lurked some-where in the first paragraph, top of page 163. Then returning to the board he rubbed out the name with little reluctant dabs and wrote

ROGER B. GREEN

Abandoning the chase for gerundives, he stood off a few feet and surveyed his labors on the blackboard, frowned, erased it and wrote dashingly

ROGER BALLINGTON GREEN

Satisfied, he drew a strong line under it, added two short crosses and a dot or two, and returned to his seat.

Once more in the abode of dreams he was transported to college, president of his class, the idol of his mates, the marvel of the faculty. He hesitated on the borderline of a great football victory, where, single-handed, bruised, and suffering, he would win the game for his college—and then found higher levels. War had been declared swiftly and treacherously by the German Empire. The whole country was rising to the President's call to arms. A great meeting of the university was held, and he spoke with a sudden revelation of a power for oratory he had never before suspected.

That very afternoon a company was formed under his leadership. Twenty-four hours later they marched to the station, and, amid a whirlwind of cheers and godspeeds, embarked for the front. During the night, while others slept, he pored over books of tactics; he studied the campaigns of Caesar, Napoleon, Grant, and Moltke. In the first disastrous year of the war, when the American army was beaten back at every point and an invading force of Germans was penetrating from the coast in three sections, he rose to the command of his regiment, with the reputation of being the finest disciplinarian in the army. Their corps was always at the front, checking the resistless advance of the enemy, saving their comrades time after time at frightful loss. Then came that dreadful day when it seemed as though the Army of the South was doomed to be surrounded and crushed by the sudden tightening of the enemy's net before the Army of the Center could effect a junction. In the gloomy council he spoke out. One way of escape there was, but it meant the sacrifice of five thousand men. Clearly and quickly he traced his plan, while general, brigadier-general, and general-in-chief stared in amazement at the new genius that flashed before their minds.

"That is the plan," he said calmly, with the authority of a master mind. "It means the safety of a hundred thousand, and if a junction can be made with the Army of the Center, the Germans can be stopped and driven back at so-and-so. But this means the death of five thousand men. There is only one man who has the right to die so—the man who proposes it. Give me five regiments, and I will hold the enemy for thirty-six hours."

He threw his regiments boldly into the enemy's line of march, and by a sudden rush carried the spur that dominated the valley. The German army, surprised and threatened in its most vulnerable spot, forced to abandon the pursuit, turned to crush the handful of heroes.

All day long the desperate battalions flung themselves in vain against the little band. All day long he walked with drawn sword up and down the thinning ranks, stiffening their courage. Red Dog and Ginger Pop called to him, imploring him not to expose himself —Red Dog and Ginger Pop whose idol he now was; yes, and Hickey's and Condit's, too. But carelessly, defiantly, he stood in full view, his clothes pierced, his head bared. Then came the night—the long, fatiguing night, without an instant's cessation. The carnage was frightful. Half of the force gone, and twelve hours more to hold out! That was his promise. And the sickening dawn, with the shrouded clouds and the expectant vultures, came stealing out of the east. Until night came again they must cling to the spur-top and manage to live in that hurricane of lead. He went down the line, calling each man by name, rousing them like a prophet inspired. The fury of sacrifice seized them. They fought on, parched and bleeding, while the sun rose above them and slowly fell. A thousand lives; half that, and half that again. Five o'clock, and still two hours to go. He looked about him. Only a few hundred remained to meet the next charge. Red Dog and Ginger Pop were cold in death, Hickey was dying. Of all his school friends, only Flash Condit remained, staggering at his side. And then the great masses of the enemy swept over them like an avalanche, and he fell, unconscious but happy, with the vision of martyrdom shining above him.

Red Dog, on his way back to his seat, knocked against him, saying angrily, "Oh, you clumsy!"

Red Dog, of all the world! Red Dog, whom he had just cheered into a hero's death. Snorky, thus brought to earth, decided to resuscitate himself and read the papers, with their big page-broad scareheads of the fight on the spur. This accomplished, he decided to end the war. The President, driven by public clamor, put him in command of the Army of the South. In three weeks, by a series of rapid Napoleonic marches, he flung the enemy into morasses and wilderness, cut their line of communication and starved them into surrender; then flinging his army north, he effected a junction with the Army of the Center, sending a laconic message to the President: "I am here. Give me command, and I will feed the sea with the remnants of Germany's glory."

Official Washington, intriguing and jealous, cried out for a court martial; but the voice of the people, echoing from coast to coast, gave him his wish. In one month he swept the middle coast bare of resistance, fought three enormous battles, and annihilated the armies of the invaders, ending the war. What a triumph was his! That wonderful entry into Washington, with the frenzied roars of multitudes that greeted him, as he rode simply and modestly, but greatly, down the Avenue at the head of his old regiment, in their worn and ragged uniforms, with the flag shot to shreds proudly carried by the resuscitated Hickey and Flash Condit, seeing in the crowd the tear-stained faces of the Roman and the headmaster and all his old comrades, amid the waving handkerchiefs of frantic thousands.

At this point Snorky's emotion overmastered him. A lump was in his throat. He controlled himself with difficulty and dignity. He went over the quiet, stately years until a grateful nation carried him in triumph into the Presidential chair, nominated by acclamation and without opposition! He saw the wonderful years of his ascendancy, the wrongs righted, peace and concord returning to all classes, the development of science, the uniting into one system of all the warring branches of education, the amalgamation of Canada and Mexico into the United States, the development of an immense merchant fleet, the consolidation of all laws into one national code, the establishment of free concerts and theaters for the people. Then suddenly there fell a terrible blow, the hand of a maniac struck him down as he passed through the multitudes who loved him. He was carried unconscious to the nearest house. The greatest physicians flocked to him, striving in vain to fight off the inevitable end. He saw the street filled with tanbark and the faces of the grief-stricken multitude, with Hickey and Red Dog and Ginger Pop sobbing on the steps and refusing to leave all that fateful night, while bulletins of the final struggle were constantly sent to every part of the globe. And then he died. He heard the muffled peal of bells, and the sobs that went up from every home in the land; he saw the houses being decked with crepe, and the people, with aching hearts, trooping into the churches: for he, the President, the beloved, the great military genius, the wisest of human rulers, was dead—dead.

Suddenly a titter, a horrible, mocking laugh, broke through the stately dignity of the national grief. Snorky, with tears trembling in his eyes, suddenly brought back to reality, looked up to see Lucius Cassius Hopkins standing over him with mocking smile. From their desks Red Dog and Hickey were making faces at him, roaring at his discomfiture.

"So Green is dreaming again! Dear, dear! Dreaming again!" said the deliberate voice. "Dreaming of chocolate eclairs and the Jigger Shop, eh, Green?"

FURTHER PERSECUTION OF HICKEY

EVER SINCE the disillusioning encounter with Tabby, Hickey, like the obscure Bonaparte before the trenches of Toulon, walked moodily alone, absorbed in his own resolves, evolving his immense scheme of a colossal rebellion. Macnooder alone received the full confidence of the war *à outrance* with the faculty which he gradually evolved.

Macnooder was the man of peace, the Mazarin and the Machiavelli of the Dickinson. He risked nothing in action, but to his cunning mind with its legal sense of dangers to be met and avoided, were brought all the problems of conspiracies against the discipline of the school. Macnooder pronounced the scheme of a revolt heroic, all the more so that he saw an opportunity of essaying his strategy on large lines.

"We must begin on a small scale, Hickey," he said wisely, "and keep working up to something really big."

"I thought we might organize a secret society," said Hickey, ruminating, "something Masonic, all sworn to silence and secrecy and all that sort of thing."

"No," said Doc, "just as few as possible and no real confidants, Hickey; we'll take assistants as we need them."

"What would you begin with?"

"We must strike a blow at Tabby," said Macnooder. "We must show him that we don't propose to stand for any of his underhanded methods."

"He needs a lesson," Hickey asserted savagely.

"How about the skeleton?"

"Humph!" said Hickey, considering. "Perhaps, but that's rather old."

"Not up the flagpole—something new."

"What is it, Doc?"

Hickey looked at Macnooder with expectant admiration.

"I noticed something yesterday in Memorial, during chapel, that gave me an idea," said Macnooder profoundly. "There is a great big ventilator in the ceiling; now there must be some way of getting to that and letting a rope down." Macnooder stopped and looked at Hickey. Hickey returned a look full of admiration, then by a mutual movement they clasped hands in ecstatic, sudden delight.

That night they reconnoitered with the aid of a dark lantern, borrowed from Legs Brownell of the Griswold, and the passkeys, of which Hickey was the hereditary possessor.

They found to their delight that there was in fact a small opening through which one boy could wriggle with difficulty.

The attempt was fixed for the following night, and as a third boy was indispensable, it was decided that etiquette demanded that the owner of the lantern should have the first call.

At two o'clock that night Hickey and Macnooder stole down the creaking stairs, and out Sawtelle's window (the highway to the outer world). The night was misty, with a pleasant, ghostly chill that heightened measurably the delight of the adventure. In the shadow of the Griswold a third shivering form cautiously developed into the possessor of the dark lantern.

After a whispered consultation, they proceeded to Foundation

House, where they secured the necessary rope from the clothes line, it being deemed eminently fitting to secure the cooperation of the best society.

Memorial Hall entered, they soon found themselves, by the aid of the smelly lantern, in front of the closet that held the skeleton which twice a week served as demonstration to the class in anatomy, and twice a year was dragged forth to decorate the flagpole or some such exalted and inaccessible station. In a short time the door yielded to the prying of the hatchet Macnooder had thoughtfully brought along, and the white, chalky outlines of the melancholy skeleton appeared.

The three stood gazing, awed. It was black and still, and the hour of the night when dogs howl and bats go hunting.

"Who's going to take him?" said Legs in a whisper.

"Take it yourself," said Macnooder, unhooking the wriggling form. "Hickey's got to crawl through the air hole, and I've got to work the lantern. You're not superstitious, are you?"

"Sure I'm not," retorted Legs, who received the skeleton in his arms with a shiver that raised the gooseflesh from his crown to his heels.

"Come on," said Hickey in a whisper, "softly now."

"What's that?" exclaimed Legs, drawing in his breath.

"That's nothing," said Macnooder loftily; "all buildings creak at night."

"I swear I heard a step. There, again. Listen."

"Legs is right," said Hickey in a whisper. "It's outside."

"Rats! It's nothing but Jimmy," said Macnooder with enforced calm. "Keep quiet until he passes on."

They stood breathless until the sounds of the watchman on his nightly rounds died away. Then they started on tiptoe up the first flight for the chapel, Macnooder leading with the lantern, Legs next with the skeleton gingerly carried in his arms, Hickey bringing up the rear with the coil of rope.

"Here we are," said Macnooder at length. "Legs, you wait here —see, that's where we're going to hoist him." He flashed the bull's-eye upward to the perforated circle directly above the rostrum, and added, "I'll get Hickey started and then I'll be right back."

"Are you going to take the lantern?" said Legs, whose courage began to fail him.

"Sure," said Hickey, indignantly. "Legs, you're getting scared."

"No, I'm not," protested Legs faintly, "but I don't like to be left all alone with this thing in my arms!"

"Say, do you want my job," said Hickey, scornfully, "crawling down thirty feet of air hole with bugs and spiders and mice? Do you? 'Cause if you do just say so."

"No-o-o," said Legs with a sigh. "No, I'll stay here."

"You don't believe in ghosts and that sort of thing, do you?" said Macnooder solicitously.

" 'Course, I don't!"

"All right then, 'cause if you do we won't leave you."

"You chaps go on," said Legs bravely, "only be quick about it."

"All right?"

"All right."

Hickey and Macnooder stole away; then suddenly Hickey, returning, whispered, "Say, Legs!"

"What?"

"If you catch your coat don't think it's the dead man's hand grabbing you, will you?"

"Darn you, Hickey," said Legs, "if you don't shut up I'll quit."

"Sh-h—goodbye, old man."

"Hurry up!"

In the crawling, howling darkness Legs waited, holding the skeleton at arm's length, trembling like a leaf, listening tensely for a sound, vowing that if he ever got safely back into his bed he would never break another law of the school. At the moment when his courage was wavering, he heard the muffled, slipping tread of Macnooder returning. He drew a long comfortable breath, threw one leg nonchalantly over the back of a nearby seat and clasped the skeleton in an affectionate embrace.

"Hist—Legs."

The lantern flashed upon him. Legs yawned a bored, tranquil yawn.

"Is that you, Doc?"

"Were you scared?"

"Of what!"

"Say, you've got nerve for a youngster," said Macnooder admiringly. "Honestly, how did it feel hugging old Bonesy, all alone there in the dark?"

"You know, I rather liked it," said Legs with a drawl. "I tried to imagine what it would be like to see a ghost. Only, I could hardly keep awake. Good Lord! What's that?"

The coil of rope descending had brushed against his face and the start which he gave completely destroyed the effect of his narrative. Macnooder, seizing the rope, made it fast to the skeleton. Then, producing a large pasteboard from under his sweater, he attached it to a foot so that it would display to the morrow's audience the inscription, TABBY.

He gave two quick tugs, and the skeleton slowly ascended, twisting and turning in unnatural white gyrations, throwing grotesque shadows against the ceiling.

"Now, let's get up to see Hickey come out," said Macnooder with a chuckle. "He's a sight."

Ten minutes later, as they waited expectantly, listening at the opening of the narrow passage, a sneeze resounded.

"What's that?" exclaimed Legs, whose nerves were tense.

"That's Hickey," said Macnooder with a chuckle. "He'll be along in a minute. He's scattering red pepper after him so no one can crawl in to get the skeleton down. Gee, he must have swallowed half of it!"

A succession of sneezes resounded, and then with a scramble an unrecognizable form shot out of the opening, covered with cobwebs and the accumulated dust of years.

"For heaven's sake, Hickey, stop sneezing!" cried Macnooder in tremor. "You'll get us pinched."

"I—I—can't help it," returned Hickey between sneezes. "Great idea of yours—red pepper!"

"Just think of the fellow that goes in after you," said Macnooder, "and stop sneezing."

"It's in my eyes, down my throat, everywhere!" said Hickey helplessly.

They got him out of the building and down by the pond where he plunged his head gratefully into the cooling waters. Then they slapped the dust from him and rubbed the cobwebs out of his hair, until he begged for mercy.

"Never mind, Hickey," said Macnooder helpfully. "Just think of Tabby when he comes in tomorrow."

Fortified by this delicious thought, Hickey submitted to being cleaned. Then Macnooder examined him carefully, saying, "There mustn't be the slightest clue; if there is a button missing you'll have to go back for it." Suddenly he stopped. "Hickey, there's one gone— off the left sleeve."

"I lost that scrapping with the Egghead last week," explained Hickey, "and both of the left suspender ones are gone, too."

"Honest?"

"I swear it."

"There's been many a murder tracked down," said Macnooder impressively, "on just a little button."

"Gee, Doc." said Legs in chilled admiration. "Say, what a bully criminal you would make!"

And on this spontaneous expression of young ambition, the three separated.

The next morning, when the school filed in to Memorial for chapel, they beheld with rapture the uncanny figure suspended directly over the rostrum. In an instant the name was whispered over the benches—"Tabby." It was then a feat of the Dickinson House. Every Dickinsonian was questioned excitedly and professed the blankest ignorance, but with such an insistent air that twenty were instantly credited with the deed. Then, with a common impulse, the school turned to watch the entrance of the faculty. Each master on entering started, repressed an involuntary smile, looked to see the name attached, frowned, gazed fiercely at the nearest boys and took his seat.

Suddenly a thrill of excitement ran over the school and like a huge sigh the exclamation welled up, "Tabby!"

Mr. Lorenzo Blackstone Tapping had entered. His eyes met the skeleton and he colored. A smile would have saved him, but the young Greek and Latin expert understood nothing of the humanizing sciences. He tried to look unconcerned and failed; he tried to look dignified and appeared sheepish; he tried to appear calm and became red with anger. It was a moment that carried joy into the heart of Hickey, joy and the forgetfulness of red pepper, cobwebs and dust.

Then the headmaster arrived and a frightened calm fell over the awed assemblage. Did he see the skeleton? There was not the slightest evidence of recognition. He walked to his seat without a break and began the services without once lifting his eyes. The school was vexed, mystified and apprehensive. But at the close of the services the headmaster spoke, seeking the culprits among the four hundred, and under that terrifying glance each innocent boy looked guilty.

Such an outrage had never before occurred in the history of the institution, he assured them. Not only had a gross desecration been done to the sacredness of the spot, but wanton and cowardly insult had been perpetrated on one of the masters (Tapping thought the specific allusion might have been omitted). It was as cowardly as the miserable wretch who writes an anonymous letter, as cowardly as the drunken bully who shoots from the dark. He repelled the thought that this was a manifestation of the spirit of the school; it was rather the isolated act of misguided unfortunates who should never have entered the institution, who would leave it the day of their detection. And he promised the school that they would be detected, that he would neither rest nor spare an effort to ferret out this cancer and remove it.

Hickey drank in the terrific onslaught with delight. He had struck the enemy, he had made it wince and cry out. The first battle was his. He rose with the school and shuffled up the aisle. Suddenly at the exit, he beheld Mr. Tapping waiting. Their glances met in a long, hostile clash. There was no mistaking the master's meaning; it was a direct accusation that sought in Hickey's face to surprise a telltale look.

A great lump rose in Hickey's throat; all the joy of a moment ago passed, a profound melancholy enveloped him; he felt alone, horribly alone, fighting against the impossible.

"Why," he said, bitterly, "why should he always pick on me—the sneak!"

During the next few days a few minor skirmishes ensued which showed only too clearly to Hickey the implacable persecution he must expect from Tabby. The first day it was the question of breakfast.

At seven o'clock every morning the rising bell fills the air with its clamor from the belfry of the old gymnasium, but no one rises. There is half an hour until the gong sounds for breakfast, a long delicious half hour—the best half hour of the day or night to prolong under the covers. After twenty minutes a few effeminate members rise to prink, five minutes later there is a general tumbling out of the bed and a wild scamper into garments arranged in ingenious time-saving combinations.

At exactly the half hour, with the first sounds of the breakfast gong, Hickey would start from his warm bed, piunge his head into the already filled basin, wash with circumspection in eight seconds (drying included), thrust his legs into an arrangement of trousers, socks and unmentionables, pull a jersey over his head, stick his feet into the waiting pair of slippers, part and brush his hair, snap a dickey about his neck, and run down the stairs struggling into his coat, tying his tie and attending to the buttons, the whole process varying between twenty-one and one-eighth seconds and twenty-two and three-quarters.

But on the morning after the exposing of the skeleton Hickey had trouble with the dickey. The school regulations tyrannically demanded that each boy should appear at breakfast and chapel properly dressed, i.e., in collar and shirt. But as the appearance is accepted for the fact, the dickey comes to the rescue and permits not only dispatch in dressing, but, by suppressing a luxury from the wash list, to attend to the necessities of the stomach. The dickey is formed by the junction of two flat cuffs, held together by a stud, to which is attached a collar, and later a tie. When the coat is added even the most practiced eye may be deceived by the enclosed exhibition of linen.

On the aforesaid morning, as Hickey hastily donned his dickey, the stud snapped and he was forced to waste precious seconds in not only procuring another stud but in arranging the component parts. He tore down the stairs to find the door shut in his face—Tabby's orders, of course!

The next night the same malignant enemy surprised him at ten o'clock returning on tiptoe from the Egghead's room—marks and penal service on Saturday afternoon. Hickey soon perceived that he was to be subjected to a constant surveillance, that the slightest absence from his room after dark would expose him to detection and punishment. Macnooder counseled seeming submission and a certain interval of patient caution. Hickey indignantly repelled the advice; the more the danger the greater the glory.

On Friday morning a strange calm pervaded the school, a lethargy universal and sweet. Seven o'clock, half-past seven, a quarter of eight, and not a stir. Then suddenly in every house, exclamations of amazement burst from the rooms, watches were scanned incredulously and excited boys called from house to house. Gradually the wonder dawned, welcomed by cries of rejoicing—the clapper had been stolen!

In the Dickinson, Hickey and Macnooder were the first in the halls, the loudest in their questions, the most dumfounded at the occurrence. Breakfast, forty minutes late, was eaten in a buzz of excitement, interrupted by the arrival of a messenger from the headmaster with peremptory orders to convene at once in Memorial.

The Doctor was in no pleasant mood. The theft of the clapper, coming so soon upon the incident of the skeleton, had roused his fighting blood. His discourse was terse, to the point, and uncompromising. There could no longer be any doubt that individuals were in rebellion against the peace and discipline of the school. He would accept the defiance. If it was to be war, war it should be. It was for the majority to say how long they, the law-abiding, the studious, the decent, would suffer from the reckless outrages of a few without standards or seriousness of purpose. The clapper would not be replaced. All marks for tardiness and absence from recitations would be doubled, and the moment any total reached twenty, that boy would be immediately suspended from the institution. The clapper would not be replaced until the school itself replaced it!

Hickey drank in the sweet discourse, reveling in the buzz of conjecture that rose about him, concentrating all his powers on appearing innocent and unconcerned before the fusillade of admiring, alluring glances that spontaneously sought him out.

The school went to the recitation rooms joyfully, discussing how best to draw from the ultimatum all the amusement possible. By the afternoon every boy was armed with an alarm clock which he carried into each recitation, placing it in the aisle at his feet after a solicitous comparison of the time with his neighbors. Five minutes before the close of the hour the bombardment would begin, and as each clock exploded, the owner would grab it up frantically and depart for the next recitation in a gallop. Bright, happy days, when even the monotony of the classroom disappeared under the expectation of a sudden alarm!

With a perfect simulation of seriousness, expeditions known as clapper parties were organized to search for the missing clapper.

Orchards, gardens, streams—nothing was spared in the search. Complaints began to pour in from neighboring farmers with threats of defending their property with shotguns. The school gardener arrived in a panic to implore protection for his lawns. Then the alarm clocks became strangely unreliable. At every moment the sound of the alarm, singly, or in bunches, was heard in the halls of Memorial. Several of the older members of the faculty, who were addicted to insomnia and nervous indigestion, sent in their ultimatum. Thus forced to a decision, the headmaster compromised. He had the clapper replaced and assessed the school for the costs.

During those glorious, turbulent days, Hickey perceived with melancholy that Tabby still persisted in suspecting him. It was disheartening but there was no blinking the fact. Tabby suspected him!

At the table Tabby's eyes restlessly returned again and again in his direction. Tabby's ears were strained to catch the slightest word he might utter; in fact, everything in Tabby's bearing indicated a malignant determination to see in him the author of every escapade. This fresh injustice roused Hickey's ire to such an extent that, despite the cautious Macnooder, he determined upon a further deed of bravado.

One morning, Mr. Lorenzo Blackstone Tapping, exactly as Hickey planned, perceived a curious watch charm on Hickey's watch chain, which he soon made out to be a miniature silver clapper. Immediately suspicious, he noticed that every boy in the room was in a state of excitement. On examining them, he discovered that every waitscoat was adorned with the same suspect emblem. During the day, a chance remark overheard revealed to him the fact that Hickey was selling the souvenirs at a dollar apiece. Assuredly here was an important clue. That afternoon all his doubts were answered. He was seated at his study window when his attention was attracted by a group directly beneath. Against the wall Hickey was standing, with a large box under his arm, selling souvenirs as fast as he could make change to the breathless crowd which augmented at every moment.

Meanwhile, Hickey, fully aware of his enemy's proximity, took special pains that the conversation should carry. About him the excited crowd pressed in a frantic endeavor to purchase before the store was exhausted.

To all inquiries Hickey maintained a dark secrecy.

"I'm saying nothing, fellows, nothing at all," he said with a canny smile. "It isn't wise sometimes to do much talking. The impression has somehow got around that these little 'suveneers' are made out of the original clapper. I'm not responsible for that impression, gents, and I make no remarks thereupon. These little 'suveneers' I hold in my hand are silver-plated—*silver-plated,* gents, and when a thing is silver-plated there must be something inside. And I further remark that these 'suveneers' will sell for one dollar apiece only until five o'clock, that after that time they will sell at one dollar and a half, and I further remark that there are only forty-five left!" Then, rattling the box, he continued with simulated innocence, "Nothing but a 'suveneer,' gents, nothing guaranteed. We sell nothing under false pretenses!"

At half past four he had sold the last of a lot of two hundred and fifty amid scenes of excitement worthy of Wall Street.

At five o'clock, Hickey received a summons to Foundation House. There, to his delight, he found the headmaster in the company of Mr. Tapping.

Hickey entered with the candor of a cherub, plainly quite at loss as to the object of the summons.

"Hicks," said the headmaster in his solemnest tones, "you are under very grave suspicion."

"Me, sir?" said Hickey in ungrammatical astonishment.

"Hicks, it has come to my knowledge that you are selling as souvenirs bits of the clapper that was stolen from the gymnasium."

"May I ask, sir," said Hickey with indignation, "who has accused me?"

At this Mr. Tapping spoke up severely.

"I have informed the Doctor of facts which have come into my possession."

"Sir," said Hickey, addressing the headmaster, "Mr. Tapping has *honored* me with his enmity for a long while. He has not even hesitated to *threaten* me. I am not surprised that he should accuse me, only I insist that he state what evidence he has for bringing this accusation."

"Doctor, allow me," said Mr. Tapping, somewhat ill at ease. Then turning to Hickey he said, with the air of a cross-examiner: "Hicks, are you or are you not selling souvenirs at one dollar apiece, in the shape of small silver clappers?"

"Certainly."

"Made out of the original clapper?"

"Certainly *not!*"

"What!" exclaimed the amazed Tapping.

"Certainly not."

"Do you mean to say that two hundred and fifty boys would have bought those souvenirs at a dollar apiece for any other reason than that they contained a bit of the stolen clapper?"

Hickey smiled proudly.

"They may have been under that impression."

"Because you told them!"

"No, sir," said Hickey with righteous anger. "You have no right, sir, to say such a thing. On the contrary, I refused to answer one way or the other. You listened this afternoon from your window and you heard exactly my answer. If you will do me the *justice,* sir, to tell the Doctor what I did say, I shall be very much obliged to you."

"Enough, Hicks," said the headmaster with a frown. "Answer me directly. Are these watch charms made up out of the original clapper?"

"No, sir."

The Doctor, in his turn, looked amazed.

"Come, Hicks, that is not possible," he said. "I warn you I shall trace them without any difficulty."

Then Hickey smiled, a long delicious smile of culminating triumph. Slowly he drew forth from his pocket an envelope, from which he produced a legal document.

"If you will kindly read this, sir," he said, tending it with deepest respect.

The Doctor took it, glanced curiously at Hickey, and then began to read. Presently his face relaxed, and despite a struggle a smile appeared. Then he handed the document to Mr. Tapping, who read as follows:

I, John J. Goodsell, representing the firm of White, Brown and Bangs, jewelers, of Trenton, New Jersey, take oath that I have this day engaged to manufacture for William Orville Hicks of The Lawrenceville School 250 small clappers, design submitted, of iron plated with silver, and that the iron which forms the

foundation comes from scrap iron entirely furnished by us.
Sworn to in the presence of notary.

JOHN J. GOODSELL.

Attached to the document was a bill as follows:

William Orville Hicks, Dr.,
To White, Brown and Bangs.
250 silver gilt clappers, at 11c apiece................. $27.50
Received payment.

MAKING FRIENDS

"That was just before I licked Whitey Brown," said Lazelle, alias Gazelle, alias the Rocky Mountain Goat and the Gutter Pup. "Cracky, that was a fight!"

"How many rounds?" asked Lovely Mead, disrobing for the night.

"Eleven and a half. Knocked him to the count in the middle of the twelfth with a left jab to the bellows," said the Gutter Pup professionally. "He weighed ten pounds more than me. Ever do any fighting?"

"Sure," said the new arrival instantly.

"How many times?"

"Oh, I can't remember."

"You don't look it."

"Why not?"

"Your complexion's too lovely; and you're only a shaver, you know."

"I'm fifteen, almost sixteen," said Lovely, bridling up and surveying his new roommate with a calculating glance. "How old are you?"

"I've been three years at Lawrenceville, freshman," said the Gutter Pup severely. "That's the difference. What's your longest fight?"

"Twenty-one rounds," said Lovely, promptly.

"Oh," said the Gutter Pup in profound disappointment. "He licked you?"

"No."

"You licked him?"

"No."

"What then?"

"They stopped us."

"Huh!"

"We had to let it go over to the next day."

"And then?"

"Then I put him out in the thirteenth."

"Yes, you did!"

"Yes, I did."

The two fiery-haired champions stood measuring each other with their glances. Lovely Mead ran his eye over the wiry arms and chest opposite him and wondered. The Gutter Pup in veteran disdain was about to remark that Lovely was a cheerful liar when the tolling of the gym bell broke in on a dangerous situation. The Gutter Pup dove into bed and, reaching for a slipper, hurled it across the room, striking the candle fair and square and plunging the room into darkness.

"I learned that trick," he said, "the year I put the Welsh Rabbit to sleep in six." He stopped and ruminated over Lovely's story of his two-day fight, and then spoke scornfully from the dark: "I never fought anybody over eleven rounds. I never *had* to."

Lovely heard and possessed his soul in patience. He was on his second day at the school, his spirit not a whit subdued, though considerably awed, by the sacred dignities of the old boys. He liked the

Gutter Pup, with one reservation, and that was an instinctive antagonism for which there was no logical explanation. But at the first fistic reminiscence of the Gutter Pup he had sought in his soul anxiously and asked himself, "Can I lick him?" Each time the question repeated itself he felt an overwhelming impulse to throw down the gage and settle the awful doubt then and there. It was pure instinct, nothing more. The Gutter Pup was really a good sort and had adopted him in quite a decent way without taking an undue advantage. In fact, Lovely was certain that in his roommate he had met the congenial soul, the chum, the best friend among all friends for whom he had waited and yearned. His heart went out to the joyous, friendly Gazelle, but his fingers contracted convulsively. Theirs was to be an enduring friendship, a sacred, Three Musketeer sort of friendship—after one small detail was settled.

The next morning Lovely Mead bounded up with the rising bell and started nervously to dress. There was a lazy commotion in the opposite bed, and then, after a few languid movements of the covers, the Gutter Pup's reddish head appeared in surprise.

"Why, Lovely, what are you doing?"

"Dressing. Didn't you hear the bell?"

"Jiminy crickets, what a waste, what an awful waste of time," said the Gutter Pup, luxuriously, stretching his arms and yawning. "Say, Lovely, I like you. You're a good sort and that was a rattlin' plucky tackle you made yesterday. Say, we're going to get on famously together, only, Lovely, you *are* green, you know."

"I suppose I am."

"You are. Of course, you can't help it, you know. Everyone starts that way. Lordy, Lovely, you remind me of the first time I hit this old place, three weeks after I fought Mucker Dennis of the Seventy-second Street gang."

Lovely Mead's gorge swelled up with indignation. To hide his emotion, he plunged his head into the basin and emerged dripping.

"I say, Lovely, I must give you some pointers," said the Gutter Pup affably. "Everything depends, you know, on the start. You want to stand in with the masters, you know. Study hard the first week and get your lessons down fine, and work up their weak points, and you'll slide through the term with ease and pleasure."

"What are these weak points?" inquired Lovely from the depths of a clean shirt.

"Oh, I mean the side they're most approachable. Now the Roman, you know, when he makes a joke you always want to laugh as though you were going to die."

"Does he make many jokes?" asked Lovely.

"Cracky, yes. Then there's one very important one he makes around Thanksgiving that everyone watches for. I'll put you on, but you must be very careful."

"What? The same joke every year?" said Lovely.

"Regular. It's about Volturcius in Caesar—the 'c' is soft, you know, but you have to pronounce it—Vol-turk-ious."

"Why so?"

"So the Roman can say, 'No-o, no-o, not even the near approach of Thanksgiving will justify such a pronunciation.' See? That's the cue to laugh until the tears wet the page. It's most important."

"What about the Doctor?"

"Easy, dead easy; just ask questions, side-path questions that'll lead him away from the lesson and give him a chance to discourse. Say—another thing, Lovely, don't go and buy anything in the village; let me do that for you."

"Thanks."

"I'm on to their games, you know; I'm wise. Oh, say, another pointer—about the Jigger Shop. You want to build up your credit with Al, you know."

"How d'you mean?"

"The best way is to get trusted right off while you've got the chink and then pay up promptly at the end of a week, and repeat the operation a couple of times. Then Al thinks you're conscientious about debts and that sort of thing, and when the hard-up months come he'll let you go the limit."

"I say, Lazelle," said Lovely, admiringly, "you've got it down pretty fine, haven't you? It's real white of you to look after me this way."

"You're all right," said the Gutter Pup, still lolling in bed. "All you want is to lay low for a month or so and no one'll bother you. Besides, I'll see to that."

"Thank you."

"You see, Lovely, I've taken a fancy to you: a real, live, fat, young fancy. You remind me of Bozy Walker that was fired for introducing geese into the Muffin Head's bedroom; dear old Bozy, he stood up to me for seven rounds."

Lovely Mead dropped the hairbrush in his agitation and drew a long breath. How much longer could his weak human nature hold out? Downstairs the gong began to call them to breakfast. With the first sound the Gutter Pup was in the middle of the floor, out of his pajamas and into his clothes before the gong had ceased to ring. He plunged his head into the basin already filled with water, dried himself, parted the moist hair with one sweeping stroke of his comb, snapped a dickey about his neck and struggled into his coat while Lovely was still staring with amazement.

"That's the way it's done," said the Gutter Pup, triumphantly. "There's only one fellow in the school can beat me out, and that's that old Hickey, over in the Dickinson; but I'll beat him yet. Are you ready? Come on!"

The trouble was that the Gutter Pup was absolutely unaware of the disturbance in Lovely's mind, or that his reminiscences provoked such thoughts of combat. He took Lovely to the village and fitted him out, hectoring the tradesmen and smashing prices with debonair impudence that Lovely sneakingly envied. Certainly the Gutter Pup was unusually cordial and did not in the least make him feel the indignities of his position of newcomer, as he had a right to do.

After supper they worked on the arrangement of their room. The Gutter Pup grew ecstatic as Lovely produced his treasures from the bottom of the trunk.

"My aunt's cat's kittens!" he ejaculated as Lovely produced a set of pennants in gaudy arrangement. "Will we have the boss room, though! Lovely, you are a treasure! This will make the Waladoo Bird turn pale and weep for sorrow. Supposin' we ruminate."

They ranged their accumulated possessions on the floor, and sat back to consider.

"Well," said the Gutter Pup, "let's begin by putting the cushions on the window seat and the rugs on the floor. Now the question is —what's to have the place of honor?"

"What have you got?" asked Lovely, considering.

"I've got a signed photograph of John L. Sullivan," said the Gutter Pup, proudly producing it. "It used to be cleaner, but Butsey White blew up with a root beer bottle and spattered it."

"Is it his own signature?" inquired Lovely, gazing in awe.

"Sure. Dear old John L. He *was* a fighter. Now, what have *you* got?"

"I've got a picture of an actress."

"Honest?"

"Sure."

"Who is it?"

"Maude Adams."

"You don't say so!"

"Fact."

"It isn't signed, Lovely—it can't be?"

"It is."

"Cracky! That *is* a prize. Maude Adams! Think of it! What will the Waladoo Bird say?"

The Gutter Pup gazed reverently at the priceless photograph and said in a breath, "Maude Adams and John L.; think of it, Lovely!" He paused and added in a burst of gratitude, "Say, you can call me Gazelle or Razzle-dazzle now, if you want; afterward we'll see about Gutter Pup."

Lovely was too overcome by this advance to voice his feelings, but his heart went out to his new friend, all irritation forgotten. After long discussion it was decided that the two photographs, being of unique and equal value, should be hung side by side on the background of an American flag. The pennants were strung as a border around the walls, but were speedily hidden under an imposing procession of lightweight and middleweight champions, sporting prints, posters and lithographic reproductions of comic opera favorites, boxing gloves, fencing masks, lacrosse sticks, Japanese swords, bird nests, stolen signs, photographs of athletic teams, cotillion favors and emblems of the school and the Woodhull. They stopped and gazed in awe and admiration, and falling gleefully into each other's arms, executed a dance about the room. Then Lovely Mead, in an unthinking moment, standing before the photograph of the mighty John L., exclaimed, "Say, Gazelle, isn't he a wonder, though! How long have you had it?"

"I got it," said the Gutter Pup, putting his head on one side and reflecting, "right after I fought Whitey Brown—just before my mill with Doggie Shephard—a year and a half ago, I should say."

All the joy of the home-building left Lovely. He sat down on the bed and pulled at his shoestrings so viciously that they broke off in his hand.

"What's the matter?" said the Gutter Pup in surprise.

"Nothing."

"You look sort of put out."

"Oh, no."

"Whitey was a tough one," resumed the Gutter Pup, lolling on the window seat, "but Doggie was no great shakes. Too fat and overgrown. He did look big, but he had no footwork and his wind was bad—very bad."

Lovely Mead listened with averted eyes.

If he had only been an old boy he would have thrown down the gauntlet then and there; but he was a freshman and must check the tugging within. Besides, there must be some excuse. He could not openly, out of clear sky, provoke an old boy who had taken him under his protection and had done everything to make him feel at home. Such an act would be fresh, and would bring down on him the condemnation of the whole school.

"Why the deuce should I care, after all?" he asked himself gloomily that night. "What difference does it make how many fellows he's licked. I suppose it's because I'm a coward. That's it; it's because I'm afraid that he would lick me that it rankles so. Am I a coward, after all, I wonder?"

This internal questioning became an obsession. It clouded his days and took the edges from the keen joy of romping over the football field and earning the good word of Tough McCarty for his neat diving tackles. Could the Gutter Pup lick him, after all? He wondered, he debated, he doubted. He began to brood over it until he became perfectly unapproachable, and the Gutter Pup, without a suspicion of the real cause, began to assure Hasbrouck that Lovely was being overtrained.

Meanwhile, matters were approaching a crisis with Lovely. Each morning he calculated the strength of the Gutter Pup's chest and arms, and wondered what was the staying power of his legs. Sometimes he admitted to himself that he wouldn't last three rounds. At others he figured out a whole plan of campaign that must wear down the Gutter Pup and send him to a crashing defeat. Waking, he went through imaginary rounds, received without wincing tremendous, imaginary blows, and sent in sledge-hammer replies that inevitably landed the champion prone on his back. At night his dreams were a long conglomeration of tussling and battle in the most unexpected places. He fought the Gutter Pup at the top of

73

the water tower and saw him vanish over the edge as the result of a smashing blow on the point of the jaw; he fought him on the football field and in the classroom, while the Roman held the watch and the headmaster insisted on refereeing.

The worst of it was, he knew he was going to pieces and moping in a way to render himself a nuisance to all his associates; and yet he couldn't help it. Try as he would to skip the mention of any subject that could be tagged to a date, every now and then an opening would come, and the Gutter Pup would begin: "Let me see; that must have been just after I fought—"

At last, one night, unable to bear the strain longer, Lovely went to his room resolved to end it. He bided his opportunity, gazing with unseeing eyes at the pages of the divine Virgil. Finally he raised his head and said, abruptly, "Say, Lazelle, what do you think of our chances for the football championship?"

"Fair, only fair," said the Gutter, glad for any excuse to stop studying. "The Davis and the Dickinson look better to me."

"How long has it been since we won?" said Lovely, scarcely breathing.

"Let me see," said the Gutter Pup, unsuspecting. "We won the fall I fought Legs Brownell behind the Davis house."

"Lazelle," said Lovely, rising desperately, "I can lick you!"

"What?"

"I can lick you!"

"Hello," said the Gutter Pup, considering him in amazement, "what does this mean?"

"It means I can lick you," repeated Lovely doggedly, advancing and clenching his fists.

"You want a fight?"

"I do."

"Why, bully for you!"

The Gutter Pup considered, joyfully, with a glance at the clock. "It's too late now to pull it off. We'll let it go until tomorrow night. Besides, you'll be in better condition then, and you can watch your food, which is important. I'll notify Hickey. You don't mind fighting by lamplight?"

"Huh!"

"Of course, we'll fight under the auspices of the Sporting Club, with a ring and sponges and that sort of thing," said the Gutter Pup cheerfully. "You'll like it. It's a secret organization and it's a great honor to belong. Hickey, at the Dickinson, got it up. He's president, and referees. I'm the official timekeeper, but that don't matter. They'll arrange for seconds and all that sort of thing, and Doc Macnooder is always there for medical assistance. You're sure the light won't bother you?"

"No."

"It's a queer effect, though. First time I fought Snapper Bell—"

"Lazelle," said Lovely, choking with rage, "I can lick you, right now—here—and I don't believe you ever licked anyone in your life!"

"Look here, freshman," said the Gutter Pup, at once on his dignity; "I've stood enough of your impertinence. You'll do just as I say, and you'll act like a gentleman and a sport and not like a member of the Seventy-second Street gang. We'll fight like sportsmen, tomorrow, at midnight, under the auspices of the Sporting Club, in the baseball cage, and until then I'll dispense with your conversation! Do you hear me?"

Lovely Mead felt the justice of the reproof. Yes, he *had* acted like a member of the Seventy-second Street gang! He glanced up at the photograph (slightly spotted) of John L. and he thought of Ivanhoe and the Three Musketeers, and Sir Nigel of the White Company, and presently he said, tentatively, "I say—"

No answer.

"Lazelle—"

Still no answer.

"Say, I want to—to apologize. You're right about the Seventy-second Street gang. I'm sorry."

"All right," said the Gutter Pup, not quite appeased. "I'm glad you apologized."

"But we fight to-morrow—to the end—to the limit!"

"You're on!"

They spoke no more that night, undressing in silence, each covertly swelling his muscles and glancing with stolen looks at his opponent's knotted torso. By morning the Gutter Pup's serenity had returned.

"Well, how're you feeling? How did you sleep?" he asked, poking his nose over the coverlets.

"Like a log," returned Lovely, lying gloriously.

"Good. Better take a nap in the afternoon, though, if you're not used to midnight scrapping."

"Thanks."

"Mind the food—no hot biscuits and that sort of thing. A dish of popovers almost put me to the bad the first time I met Bull Dunham. Fact, and he didn't know enough to counter."

Lovely dressed and hurriedly left the room.

At two o'clock, to his amazement, Charley De Soto, the great quarterback, in person, waited on him in company with the gigantic Turkey Reiter, tackle on the eleven, and informed him that they had been appointed his seconds and anxiously inquired after his welfare.

"I—oh, I'm doing pretty well, thank you, sir," said Lovely, overcome with embarrassment and pride.

"Say, Charley," said Turkey, after an approving examination, "I kind of hanker to the looks of this here bantam. He's got the proper color hair and the protruding jaw. Danged if I don't believe he'll give the Gutter Pup the fight of his life."

"Can you lick him?" said De Soto, looking Lovely tensely in the eyes.

"I'll do it or die," said Lovely, with a lump in his throat.

"Good, but mind this, youngster: no funking. I don't stand second to any quitter. If I'm behind you, you've *got* to win."

Lovely thought at that moment that death on the rack would be a delight if it only could win a nod of approbation from Charley De Soto.

"How's your muscles?" asked Turkey. He ran his fingers over him, slapped his chest and punched his hips, saying, "Hard as a rock, Charley."

"How's your wind?" said De Soto.

"Pretty well, thank you, sir," said Lovely, quite overcome by the august presence.

"Now keep your mind off things. Don't let the Gutter Pup bluff you. Slip over to the Upper, right after lights, and I'll take charge of the rest. By the way, Turk, who's in the corner with the Gutter Pup?"

"Billy Condit and the Triumphant Egghead."

"Good. We'll just saunter over and lay a little bet. So long, youngster. No jiggers or eclairs. See you later."

"So long, old Sporting Life," added Turkey, with a friendly tap on the shoulder. "Mind now, keep cheerful."

Lovely's mood was not exactly cheerful. In fact he felt as if the bottom had fallen out of things. He tried his best to follow Charley De Soto's advice and not think of the coming encounter, but, do what he would, his mind slipped ahead to the crowded baseball cage, the small, ill-lighted ring, and the Gutter Pup.

"After all, will he lick me?" he said, almost aloud. His heart sank, or rather it was a depression in the pit of his stomach.

"Supposing he does?" he went on, pressing his knuckles against his teeth. What a humiliation after his boast! There would be only one thing to do—leave school at once, and never, never return!

He had wandered down to the football field where the candidates for the school eleven were passing and falling on the ball under the shouted directions of the veterans. The bulky figure of Turkey Reiter, gigantic with its padded shoulders and voluminous sweater, hove into view, and the tackle's rumbling voice cried out:

"Hi there, old Sockarooster, this won't do! Keep a-laughin'; keep cheerful; tumble down here and shag for me."

Lovely Mead went gratefully to fetch the balls that Turkey booted, far down the field, to the waiting halfbacks.

"Feeling a bit serious, eh?" said Turkey.

"Well—"

"Sure you are. That's nothing. Don't let the Gutter Pup see it, though. He's got to believe we are holding you in, chaining you up, keepin' you under the bars, 'cause you're barking to get at him. Savvy? Chuck in a bluff, old sport, and—keep cheerful. Better now?"

"Yes, thank you," said Lovely, who was in nowise suffering from an excess of hilarity.

He did not see the Gutter Pup until supper, and then had to undergo again his solicitous inquiries. By a horrible effort he succeeded in telling a funny story at the table, and laughed until his own voice alarmed him. Then he relapsed into silence, smiling furiously at every remark, and chewing endlessly on food that had no flavor for him.

"Lovely," said the Gutter Pup upstairs, shaking his head, "you don't look fit; you're getting nervous."

"Sure," said Lovely, remembering Turkey's injunction. "I'm a high-strung, *vicious* temperament!"

"Your eye acts sort of loose," said the Gutter Pup, unconvinced.

"You're new to fighting before a big assemblage. It's no wonder. I don't want any *accidental* advantages. Say the word and we'll put it over."

"No," said Lovely, quite upset by his friendly offer. "I only hope, Lazelle, I can hold myself in. I've got an awful temper; I'm afraid I'll kill a man some day."

"No, Lovely," said Gutter Pup, shaking his head. "You don't deceive me. You are ill—ill, I tell you, and you might as well own up."

The truth was, Lovely was ill and rapidly getting worse under the insouciance of the veteran of the ring.

"Why, my aunt's cat's pants, Lovely," said the Gutter Pup seriously. "That's nothing to be ashamed of. Didn't I get it the same way the first time I went up against Bloody Davis of the Murray Hill gang, on a bet I'd stick out three rounds?"

Lovely Mead drew a sigh of relief. The red blood seemed to rush back into his veins once more, and his lungs to resume their appointed functions.

"September's a good month for these little things," he said hopefully.

"October's better, more snap in the air," said the Gutter Pup. "September's muggy. I remember when I was matched against Slugger Kelly; it was so hot I lost ten pounds, and the fight only went five rounds at that."

The old provocation had roused up the old antagonism in Lovely. He hardly dared trust himself longer in the room, so he bolted and slipped down to the Waladoo's room and out into the campus.

"Gee," he said to himself, with a sigh of relief, "if I could only get at him *now!*"

At taps he went cautiously to the Upper, by the back way, and gained the room of Charley De Soto, where he was told to turn in on the window seat and take it easy.

Presently Turkey Reiter and Macnooder arrived to discuss the probabilities. Then Bojo Lowry, who could play anything, sat down at the piano and performed the most wonderful variations and medleys, until Lovely forgot any future engagement in the delight of gazing from his cushioned recess on real Fourth Formers, enjoying the perquisites and liberties of the Upper House.

Suddenly Macnooder glanced at his watch and announced that it was almost midnight. Lovely sprang up feverishly.

"Here, young Sporting Life," cried Turkey, "no champing on the bit! Just a dash of calm and tranquility."

"Easy, easy there," said De Soto, with a professional glance.

"Ready here," said Macnooder, picking up a brown satchel. "I'll bleed him if he faints."

They separated, and, on tiptoe, by various routes, departed from the Upper, making wide circles in the darkness before seeking the baseball cage, Lovely Mead supported on either side by Charley De Soto and Turkey.

They gave the countersign at the door, and were admitted noiselessly into the utter blackness of the baseball cage. Lovely waited in awe, unable to distinguish anything, clutching at Turkey's arm.

"Is the Gutter Pup here yet?" said De Soto's voice, in a whisper.

Another voice, equally guarded, replied: "Just in."

From time to time the door opened on the starry night and vague forms flitted in. Then other voices spoke:

"What time is it?"

"Midnight, Hickey."

"Lock the door; no admittance now. Egghead, show up with the light. Strike up, Morning Glory!"

A bull's-eye flashed out from one corner, and then two lanterns filled the gloom with their trembling flicker.

Out of the mist suddenly sprang forty-odd members of the Sporting Club, grouped about a vacant square in the middle of the cage which had been roped off. De Soto and Turkey pushed forward to their appointed stations, where chairs had been placed for the principals. Lovely seated himself and glanced across the ropes. The Gutter Pup was already in his corner, stripped to the waist, and being gently massaged by the Triumphant Egghead and Billy Condit, captain of the eleven.

In the middle of the ring, Hickey, in his quality of president and referee, was giving his directions in low, quick syllables. The assembled sporting gentlemen pressed forward for the advantage of position; the two front ranks assuming sitting or crouching positions, over which the back rows craned. Lovely gazed in awe at the select assembly. The élite of the school was there. He saw Glendenning, Rock Bemis and Tough McCarty of his own house, scattered among such celebrities as Crazy Opdyke, the Mugwump Politician, Goat Phillips who ate the necktie, and the Duke of Bilgewater, Wash Simmons, Cap Kiefer, Stonewall Jackson, Tug Moffat, Slugger Jones, Ginger-Pop Rooker, Cheyenne Baxter, Red Dog, Hungry Smeed, and Beauty Sawtelle, all silently estimating the strength of the freshman who had to go up against the veteran Gutter Pup.

Referee Hickey paid a quick visit to the contending camps, and was assured that each antagonist was restrained from flying at his opponent's throat only by the combined efforts of his seconds.

"Gentlemen of the Sporting Club," said Hickey, scraping one foot and shooting his collar, as referees do, "before proceeding with the evening's entertainment, the management begs to remind you that the labors incident to the opening of the school have been un-usually heavy—unusually so; and, as we particularly desire that nothing shall be done to disturb the slumbers of our overworked faculty, we will ask you to applaud only in the English fashion, by whispering to your neighbor, 'Oh, very well struck, indeed,' when you are moved to excitement. We gently remind you that anyone breaking forth into cheers will be first slugged and then expelled.

"Gentlemen of the Sporting Club, I have the honor to present to you the evening's contestants. On the right, our well-known sport-ing authority, Mr. Gutter Pup Lazelle, known professionally as the Crouching Kangaroo. On the left, Mr. Lovely Mead, the dark horse from Erie, Pennsylvania, who has been specially fed on raw beef in preparation for the encounter. Both boys are members of the Woodhull branch of this club. The rounds will be of three minutes each—one minute intermission. Mr. Welsh Rabbit Simpson will act as timekeeper, and will return the stop watch *immediately* on con-clusion of the exercises. Both contestants have signified their desire to abide strictly to the rules laid down by the late Marquis of Queensberry, bless him! No fouls will be tolerated, and only one blow may be struck in the breakaway.

"In the corner for the Gutter Pup, Mr. William Condit, the tiddledy-winks champion, and the only Triumphant Egghead in captivity.

"In the corner for Lovely, Mr. Turkey Reiter, the Dickinson Mud Lark, and Mr. Charles De Soto, the famous crochet expert. Doctor Macnooder, the Trenton veterinary, is in attendance, but will *not* be allowed to practice. The referee of the evening will be that upright and popular sportsman, the Honorable Hickey Hicks. Let the contestants step into the ring."

Lovely was shoved to his feet and propelled forward by a resounding slap on his shoulders from Turkey Reiter. He had sat in a daze, awed by the strange, imposing countenances of the school celebrities, duly submitting to the invigorating massage of his seconds, hearing nothing of the directions showered on him. Now he was actually in the ring, feeling the hard earth under his feet, looking into the eyes of the Gutter Pup, who came up cheerfully extending his hand. Surprised, Lovely took it, and grinned a sheepish grin.

"Ready—go!" came the command.

Instantly the Gutter Pup sprang back, assuming that low, protective attitude which had earned from Hickey the epithet of the Crouching Kangaroo. Lovely, very much embarrassed, extended his left arm, holding his right in readiness while he moved mechanically forward on the point of his toes. The Gutter Pup, smiling at him, churned his arms and shifted slightly to one side. Strangely enough, Lovely felt all his resentment vanish. He no longer had the slightest desire to hurl himself on his antagonist. Indeed, it would at that moment have seemed quite a natural act to extend his hand to the joyful Gutter Pup and close the incident with a laugh. But there he was, irrevocably destined to fight before the assembled Sporting Club, under penalty of everlasting disgrace. He made a tentative jab and sprang lightly back from the Gutter Pup's reply. Then he moved forward and backward, feinting with his left and right, wishing all the time that the Gutter Pup would rush in and strike him, that he might attack with anger instead of this weakening mental attitude to which he was at present a prisoner. Twice the Gutter Pup's blows grazed his head, and once landed lightly on his chest, without his being at all moved from his calm. The call of "Time" surprised him. He went to his seconds frowning.

"What's wrong, young'n?" said De Soto. "You're not in the game."

"No," said Lovely, shaking his head. "I—I've got to get mad first."

"All right, that'll come. Keep cool and play to tire him out," said De Soto, satisfied. "Make him do the prancing around; don't you waste any energy."

"Time!" whispered the Welsh Rabbit.

Again he was in the ring, experiencing once more that same incomprehensible feeling of sympathy for the Gutter Pup. The more he danced about, shaking his head and feinting with quick, nervous jabs, the more Lovely's heart warmed up to him. Wasn't he a jolly, genial chap, though? Desperately Lovely strove to remember some fault, a word or a look that had once offended him. In vain; nothing came. He liked the chap better than he had ever liked anyone before. He struck out as one strikes at his dearest friend, and a low groan of disgust rose from the Sporting Club.

"Ah, put some steam in it!"

"Do you think you're pickin' cherries?"

"That's it—be polite!"

"Sister, don't hurt little brother!"

The Welsh Rabbit spoke:

"Time!"

Not a real blow had yet been struck. Lovely went to his corner perplexed.

"That's the boy," said De Soto, with a satisfied shake of his head. "That's the game! Don't mind what you hear. Play the long game. The Crouching Kangaroo style is all very pretty, but it doesn't save the wind."

"Never mind the ballet steps, Sport," added Turkey, vigorously applying the towel. "Hold in, but when you do start, rip the in'ards out of things."

"They think I'm doing it on purpose," said Lovely to himself.

"Time!" called the Welsh Rabbit.

The Gutter Pup, changing his tactics, as though he had sufficiently reconnoitered, began to attack with rapid, pestiferous blows that annoyed Lovely as a swarm of gnats annoys a dog. He shook his head angrily and sought an opportunity to strike, but the fusillade continued, light but disconcerting. When he struck, the Gutter Pup slipped away or ducked and returned smiling and professional to attack. Lovely began to be irritated by the Gutter Pup's complacency. He wasn't serious enough—his levity was insulting. Also, he was furious because the Gutter Pup would not strike him a blow that hurt. His jaw set and he started to rush.

"Time!" said the Welsh Rabbit.

Lovely went to his corner unconvinced.

"Are the rounds three minutes?" he asked.

"Sure," said Turkey. "Don't worry; they'll get longer."

Lovely looked across at the opposite camp. The adherents of the Gutter Pup were patting him on the back, exulting over his work.

"What's he done?" said Lovely, angrily, to himself. "That sort of work wouldn't hurt a fly."

"Time!" said the Welsh Rabbit.

Lovely walked slowly to meet the Gutter Pup, bursting with irritation. He waited, and as the Gutter Pup attacked he plunged forward, taking a blow in the face, and drove his fist joyfully into the chest before him. The Gutter Pup went back like a tenpin, staggered, and kept his footing. When he came up there was no longer a smile in his eyes.

They threw boxing to the winds. It was give and take, fast and furious, back and forth against the ropes, and rolling over and over on the ground.

"Time!" announced the Welsh Rabbit, and Hickey had to pry them apart.

Lovely thought the intermission would never end. He sat stolidly, paying no heed to his seconds' prayers to go slow, to rest up this next round, to make the Gutter Pup work. He would fight his fight his own way, without assistance.

"Time!" said the Welsh Rabbit.

Lovely started from his corner for the thing that came to meet him without yielding, exchanging blows without attempt at blocking, rushing into clinches, locking against the heaving chest, looking into the strange, wild eyes, pausing for neither breath nor rest.

Once he was rushed across the ring, fighting back like a tiger, and jammed over the ropes into the ranks of the spectators. Then he caught the Gutter Pup off his balance, and drove him the same way, his arms working like pistons. The rounds continued and ended with nothing to choose between them.

Lovely felt neither the blows received nor the rough rubbing-down of his seconds. He heard nothing but the sharp cries of "Time!" and sometimes he didn't hear that; but a rough hand would seize him (was it Hickey's?) and tear him away from the body against him.

He went down several times, wondering what had caused it, remembered standing moments triumphantly, while the fallen Gutter Pup raised himself from the ground.

Then he lost track of the rounds; and the rows of sweaters and funny white faces about the ring seemed to swell and multiply into crowds that stretched far back and up. The lights seemed to be going out—getting terribly dim and unsteady.

Once in his corner he thought he heard someone say: "Fifteenth round"—fifteen, and he could remember only six. In fact, he had forgotten whom he was fighting or what it was about, only that someone on whose knee he was resting was shrieking in his ear, "He's all out, Lovely. You've got him. Just one good soak—just one *lovely* one!"

That was a joke, he supposed—a poor joke—but he would see to that "one soak" the next round.

"Time!" cried the Welsh Rabbit.

For the sixteenth time the seconds raised their champions, steadied them, and sent them forth. One good blow would send either toppling over to the final count. So they craned forward in wild excitement, exhorting them in hoarse whispers.

The two contestants gyrated up and stood blankly regarding each other. About them rose a murmur of voices:

"Sail in!"

"Soak him, Lovely!"

"Clean him up, Gutter Pup!"

"One to the jaw!"

"Now's your time!"

With a simultaneous movement each raised his right and shot it lumberingly forward, past the hazy, confronting head, fruitlessly into the air. Renewed whispers, dangerously loud, arose:

"Now's your chance, Gutter Pup!"

"Draw off and smash him!"

"He's all yours, Lovely!"

"Oh, Lovely, hit him! Hit him!"

"Just once!"

They neither heard nor cared. Their arms locked lovingly about their shoulders, and they began to settle. New cries:

"Break away!"

"Don't let him pull you down!"

"Keep your feet, Lovely!"

"They're both going!"

With a gradual, deliberate motion, Lovely and the Gutter Pup sat down, still affectionately embraced; then, wavering a moment, careened over and lay blissfully unconscious. Amazement and perplexity burst forth.

"Why, they're done for!"

"They're out—they're both out!"

"Sure enough."

"What happens?"

"Who wins?"

"Well, did you ever—"

Suddenly Hickey, standing forward, began to count:

"One, two, three—"

"What's he doing that for?"

"Aren't they both down?"

"Four, five, six, seven—"

"But Lovely went first!"

"No, the Gutter Pup."

"Eight, nine, *TEN!*" cried Hickey. "I declare both men down and out. The Sporting Club will register one knockout to the credit of the Gutter Pup and one to Lovely Mead. All bets off. The Welsh Rabbit will proceed to return that watch!!"

At seven o'clock the next morning Lovely, from his delicious bed, gazed across at the swollen head of the Gutter Pup. At the same instant the Gutter Pup, opening his eyes, perceived the altered map of Lovely's features.

"Lovely," he said brokenly, "you're the finest ever. You're a man after my own heart!"

"Razzle-dazzle," replied Lovely, choking, "you're the finest sport and gentleman in the land. I love you better than a brother."

"Lovely, that was the greatest fight that has ever been fought," said the Gutter Pup. "You are *the* daisy scrapper!"

"Razzle-dazzle—"

"Call me Gutter Pup."

"Gutter Pup, you've got the nerve market cornered."

"Lovely, I haven't felt so happy since the day I stood up five rounds—"

Suddenly the Gutter Pup stopped and added apologetically: "Say, Lovely, honest, does my au-to-biography annoy you?"

And Lovely replied happily:

"No, Gutter Pup, honest—not now."

THE HERO OF AN HOUR

GEORGE BARKER SMITH was one of the four hundred-odd boys whose names figure in the school catalogue at the commencement of each year. He had passed from the shell into the first form, from the first form into the second, where he had remained an extra year, during the elongating, dormant period of his growth, and another year, during the dormant, elongating one. Then in the seventh year of his career he finally achieved the fourth form and entered the Upper House.

During this generous stay he had done nothing to distinguish himself from his neighbor. He had never accomplished anything heroic, attempted anything daring, or done anything ridiculous. After seven years his record was so blank that even the fertile imaginations of Hickey and Macnooder could find nothing on which to hang a nickname. Besides, it is doubtful if they ever stopped to think of George Barker Smith. He filled in, he was the average—a part of the great background of school life, which made up the second teams in athletic contests and substituted occasionally on the banjo and mandolin clubs, after borrowing a dress suit across the hall.

He ran in debt at the Jigger Shop, like everyone else, or he might have been called Miser. He flunked in Greek and mathematics sufficiently to escape the epithet of Poler. He had occasionally been read out at roll call for absence from bath, thus invalidating the right to Soapsuds or Wash.

Sometimes, when his neighbors dropped in on him in quest of stamps or a collar or a jersey, they called him affectionately Smithy, old Sockarooster. But he was not deceived, and loaned from his wardrobe with a full comprehension of the value of endearing terms. Smithy! After seven years he was just Smithy—his whole story was there.

And in the secret places of his heart, which no boy reveals, George Barker Smith grieved. Covertly he felt his obscureness and rebelled. After seven years' afflictions he would pass from Lawrenceville and be forgotten. And all for the lack of a nickname! If Nature had only formed him so that he might have aspired to the appellation of the Triumphant Egghead. The Triumphant Egghead—that was a name to be proud of! Who could ever forget that? There was fame secure and imperishable; neither years nor distance could dim the memory!

No, Nature had not been considerate of him. His nose was just a nose, not a Beekstein; his ears were ordinary ears, not Flop Ears; his teeth were regular and all present. No one would ever call him Walrus or Tuskarora Smith, which sounds so well. He was not tall enough to be called Ladders or Beanpole; he was not small enough for Runt, Tiny, Wee-wee, or The Man. He was just average size, average weight, which barred a whole category, such as Skinny, Puff-Ball, Shanks, Slab-Sides, Jumbo, Flea, Bigboy and Razors.

To pass into the world and be forgotten! To fade from the memory of his classmates or to linger indistinctly as one of the Smiths between Charles D. and George R.! And all for the lack of a nickname! George Barker Smith, brooding thereon, envied the Gutter Pup, who likewise rejoiced in the appellation of Razzle-dazzle and the Rocky Mountains Gazelle; he envied the Waladoo Bird, the Coffee Cooler, the Morning Glory; he envied Two-Inches Brown, whose indiscreet remark that he needed but that to make the varsity nine had at least enrolled his name on the list of celebrities; but most of all he envied the Triumphant Egghead. With that glorious title as model, he sought in himself for something which might reclaim him—and found nothing. From Barker Smith might be made Doggie or Bow-wow Smith, but even that lacked naturalness and application. No, there was no turning his destiny; Smithy it was decreed and Smithy it would remain.

It was not fame Smith sought. His spirit was not of the sort that drags angels down. Naturally there had been periods in his youth when he had dreamed of reaching the Homeric proportions of Turkey Reiter or Slugger Jones; of scurrying over the gridiron, darting through a maze of frantic tacklers like Flash Condit, who had scored against the Princeton varsity in that glorious eight-to-four game; of knocking out dramatic home runs like Cap Kiefer, that bring joy out of sorrow and end in towering bonfires. These are glories which all may dream of but few attain.

Neither did he ask for the gifts of a Hungry Smeed, for to possess the ability to eat forty-nine pancakes at a sitting was a talent that is not lightly bestowed. No, he did not ask for fame; all he asked was to be remembered; for some incident or accident to come which would mark him with a glorious, fantastic nickname that would live with the Triumphant Egghead and the Duke of Bilgewater. And Fate, which sometimes listens to prayers, was kind and brought him not only a nickname but fame—real enduring fame. For in the most extraordinary way it came to pass that George Barker Smith unwittingly accomplished a feat which no boy had ever dared before and which it is extremely unlikely will ever be duplicated in the future. And this is the manner in which greatness was thrust upon him.

In the last days of the month of September the school returned from the fatiguing period of vacation to seek recuperation and needed sleep in the classrooms. George Barker Smith found himself at last a full-fledged fourth former, one of the lords of the school, member of a free governing body, with license to burn the midnight lamp unchallenged, to stray into the village at all hours, to visit the Jigger Shop during school and remain tranquilly seated when a master bore down from the horizon, instead of joining the palpitating under-formers that just at his back crouched, glasses in hand, behind the counter. No longer did he have to stand in file once a week before the Bursar to claim a beggarly half-dollar allowance. Instead, once a month he strolled in at his pleasure and nonchalantly tendered checks for fifty dollars, with which allowance his parents, for one blissful year only, fondly expected him to purchase all the clothes necessary—per agreement.

He could hire a buggy at ruinous rates and disappear in search of distant cider-mills or visit friends in Princeton, who had gone before. Finally, his room was his castle, where no imperious tapping of a lurking undermaster would come to disturb a little party at the national game, for chips only, of course.

George Barker Smith's room was on the third floor back and had attached to it certain communal rights. Even as the possession of the ground-floor rooms in the under-form houses entailed the obligation to assist at all hours of the night the passage to the outer world, and to assure the safe return therefrom, so room 67 was the recognized highway to the roof of the Upper, when the thermometer had mounted above seventy-eight degrees Fahrenheit.

Those who sought the cooling heights sought security and (be it confessed, now that an inconsiderate faculty's sanction has made smoking no longer a pleasure but a choice) the companionship of the Demon Cigarette or the "Coffin Nail," as it was more affectionately known. The guardianship of this highway, if it entailed responsibilities, also brought with it certain perquisites and tariffs in the shape of an invitation without expense.

Now, George Barker Smith did not like the odor of tobacco in the least, and he particularly disliked the effects produced by the cheap cigarette which the price rendered popular. But once a fourth former there were so few rules to break that this opportunity had to be embraced as an imperative duty, and so he resigned himself, pretending (like how many others!) to inhale and enjoy it.

The last weeks of September were unusually hot and distressing. The stiff collar disappeared. Two-piece suits became the fashion for full dress and fatigue uniform consisted of considerably less. The day was passed in long, grumbling siestas under the shade of apple trees or in a complete surrender to the cooling contact of peach and strawberry jiggers. Even games lost their attraction, and the only sign of life was the pleasant spectacle of the heavy squad on the football team, puffing protestingly about the circle under the cruel necessity of reducing weight.

After dark, bands were organized which stole away, through Negro villages, arousing frantic dogs, to the banks of the not-too-fragrant canal, where they spent a long, blissful hour frolicking in the moonlit water or raising their voices in close harmony on the bank. Other spirits, not so adventurous, contented themselves with lining up behind the Upper in white, shivering line, where the hose brought comfort as it played over grateful backs.

Naturally, at night, smoking up the flue, even with the whispered conversations with the boy below and the boy across, lost all charm. The roof became a veritable rookery. Mattresses were carried up and hot, suffocating boys lolled through the raging night swapping yarns and gazing at the inscrutable stars.

On a certain evening, hot among the hottest, George Barker Smith, in that costume which obtained before the publication of the first fashions, was sitting at his desk in a conscientious endeavor to translate one paragraph of Cicero, which he held in his right hand, for every chapter of *The Count of Monte Cristo,* which he held in his left.

At his door suddenly appeared the Triumphant Egghead and Goat Phillips, whose title at this time had been conveyed solely for the butting manner of his attack. Each had likewise reached that stage of dishabille where there is little more to shed.

"Hello, old Sockbutts," said Egghead, genially.

"Hello yourself," returned Smith, noncommittally.

"We're going up on the roof," continued the Egghead. "Anyone up yet?"

"Not yet."

"It's as hot as blazes," said the Goat. "Better come along."

"I ought to finish this Cicero," said Smith, wondering if he could leave his hero in a sack, ready to be plunged into the dizzy waters below.

"Oh, come on," said the Egghead; "I'll give you that when we come down. Have you any matches? I've got the coffin nails."

A slight shower had ended a few minutes before without bringing relief from the heat.

"Are you coming?" said the Egghead, already out of the window. "Don't be a grind, Smithy."

"Sure, I'm with you," replied Smith, thus forced to repel the insinuation.

The Goat had gone first, then the Egghead, with Smith bringing up the rear.

"Look out, fellows," whispered the pilot, lost in the darkness ahead. "It's slippery as the deuce!"

The way led up a gutter to the peak of one slope, down that, up another and over to a cranny which formed about the back chimneys. The still moist tiles were, in fact, slippery and treacherous, and their movements were made with calculation and solicitude.

Smith, arriving the last at the top of the first peak, waited until the Egghead had descended and climbed in safety to the next ridge, glanced down the twenty feet of slippery slate, and, tempted, called out, "Look out, fellows, I'm going to slide!"

The Goat and the Egghead, in unison, cried to him to desist, for the second ridge which ended the slope of the first had a downward inclination toward the edge of the roof that made it exceedingly dangerous.

Just how it happened has never been satisfactorily settled: whether Smith actually intended to slide or whether he lost his grip and started unwillingly. However it may be, Egghead and the Goat, astride the second ridge, were suddenly horrified to see Smith's naked body shoot down the slope, strike the moist incline at the bottom, and, bounding down that, with increased velocity disappear over the roof. They heard one thud and then another in the gravel path, three stories below.

The two clung to each other with a dreadful sinking feeling.

"He's dead," said the Goat, solemnly. "Poor old Smith is dead."

"Squashed like a bug," said the Egghead. "We won't even recognize his remains."

"Egghead, it's all our fault—all our fault."

"Shut up, Goat, and don't blubber!"

"I'm not."

"You are—for Heaven's sake, brace up! We've got to get down to him!"

They started fearfully over the treacherous return, reaching Smith's room thoroughly unnerved. Then they began to run down the stairs, calling out:

"Smithy's dead!"

"Smithy's fallen off the roof!"

On their trail came a motley assortment of excited boys, rushing out of every room. Without a single hope they tore around to the back of the Upper, and there, sitting bolt upright in the position in which he had fallen, they found George Barker Smith. They stopped, astounded.

"Smith, is that you!" Egghead said, in a hoarse, incredulous whisper, and the answer returned faintly:

"It's me, Egghead."

"Are you dying?"

"I don't know."

"Are your bones all broken?"

"I don't know—I'm full of gravel!"

The boys gazed astounded up at the dark outline three stories above them. Halfway, the slanting roof of the porch had broken the fall and saved him from certain death. They gazed in silence, and then the chorus arose:

"Holy cats!"

"Great snakes!"

"Marvelous!"

"Can you beat that!"

"Mamma!"

"Simply marvelous!"

Smith, still in a comatose condition, caught the sounds of astonishment, and suddenly comprehended, first, that he had done something without parallel in school history, and, second, that he was alive.

"You fellows, get me upstairs," he said, gruffly, "and send for Doctor Charlie. I want to get this gravel out of me."

Macnooder and Turkey reverently carried him to his room, while Shy Thomas, who was clothed in a dressing gown, went streaming across the campus for the doctor.

A quick examination revealed the amazing fact that not a bone had been fractured.

"You've got a few bruises, and that's all, by George!" said the doctor, looking at him in open-eyed wonder.

"It's the gravel that bothers me," said Smith, twisting on his side.

"You did sit down rather hard," remarked the doctor, with a twitch of his lips. In half an hour he had removed thirty-seven pieces of gravel, large and small, and departed, after ordering rest and a few days' sojourn in bed.

Hardly had the doctor departed when Hickey arrived, full of importance and enthusiasm. For a moment he stood at the foot of the bed surveying the bruised hero with the affectionate and fatherly joy of a Barnum suddenly discovering a new freak.

"My boy," he said, happily, "you're a wonder. You're great. You're it. There's been nothing like it ever happened. Smithy, my boy, you're a genius. You're the wonder of the age!"

"I suppose everyone's excited?" said Smith, faintly realizing that Fate had touched him in her flight and made him famous.

"Excited? Why, they're howling with curiosity," responded Hickey, who, having cautiously turned the key in the door, returned and continued with importance: "Say, but I suppose you don't realize what we can make of this, do you?"

"What do you mean?" said Smith.

"First, where are those thirty-seven pieces of gravel?"

"I threw them away."

"My boy, my boy!" said Hickey, sitting down and burying his head in his arms. "Pearls before swine."

"But they're over there in the basket."

Hickey, with a cry of joy, flung himself on them, counted them and thrust them into his pocket.

"Smith," he said, condescendingly, "you've got certain qualities, I'll admit, but what you need is a manager!"

"Why, what are you thinking of?" said Smith, who began to have a suspicion of Hickey's plan.

"I suppose you would expose your honorable scars," said Hickey, disdainfully, "to anyone who asks to see them?"

"Why not?"

"Just out of friendliness?"

"Yes."

"Smith, you *are* a nincompoop! Why, my boy, there's money in it—big money! Never thought of that, eh?"

"How so?"

"Exhibitions—paid exhibitions, my boy! We'll organize the greatest sideshow ever known."

Smith blushed at the thought.

"Won't it be rather undignified?" he said doubtfully.

"Dignity, rats!" said Hickey. "Talk to me of dignity when you hear the gold rattling in your pocket, when you lodge in a marble palace and drive fast horses up Fifth Avenue. My boy, you don't know what you're worth. I'll have Macnooder paper the campus tomorrow. I'll get up scareheads that'll bring every mother's son of them scampering here to see you."

"What do I get out of it?" said Smith cautiously.

"Half!"

"You low-down robber!"

"Who had the idea? Would you ever have made a cent if it hadn't been for me? Do you suppose any attraction ever makes as much as his manager? My boy, I'm generous! I oughtn't to do it! Come now—is it a go?"

"Well—yes!"

"Wait—till you see the posters," said Hickey, squeezing his hand joyfully, "and mind, no private exhibitions. Promise?"

"I promise."

"Under oath?"

"So help me."

"Ta, ta."

Left at last alone, George Barker Smith could hardly seize the full measure of his future. Hickey was right, it was the biggest thing that had ever happened. In one short hour everything had changed. Now he was of the elect—a part of history, a tale to be told over whenever one old graduate would meet another. Even Hungry Smeed's great pancake record would have to be placed second to this. Other more distinguished appetites might come who would achieve fifty pancakes, but no boy would ever go the path he had gone. He was famous at last. At Prom and Commencement he would be pointed out to visitors in the company of Hickey, Flash Condit, Cap Kiefer and Turkey Reiter. Only yesterday he was plain George Barker Smith, tomorrow he might be . . .

What would the morrow bring? Who would name him? Would it be Hickey, Macnooder or Turkey or the Egghead, or would some unsuspected classmate find the happy expression? He hoped that it would be something picturesque, but a little more dignified than the Triumphant Egghead. He tried to imagine what the nickname would be. Of course, there were certain obvious appellations that immediately suggested themselves, such as Roofie, Jumper, or, better still, Plunger Smith. There was also Tattoo and Rubber and Sliding, but somehow none of these seemed to measure up to the achievement, and in this delightful perplexity Smith fell asleep.

OLD IRONSIDES
THE GREATEST SIDESHOW ON EARTH ON EXHIBITION
AT ROOM 67 UPPER
MANAGEMENT—Hicks & Macnooder.

Come one, Come all! Come and View the HUMAN METEOR, THE YOUNG RUBBER PLANT, THE FAMOUS PLUNGING ROCKET, THE WORLD-RENOWNED SMITH, THE BOY GRAVEL YARD!

Come and see the honorable scars! No private exhibition. This afternoon only! Old Ironsides is under contract not to bathe in the canal this fall. This is your one and only opportunity to see the results of Old Ironsides' encounter with the gravel path!

Come and see the 37 original guaranteed and authentic bits of gravel which dented but could not penetrate!

ADMISSION, 5 CENTS   FRESHMEN, 10 CENTS
$500 REWARD $500

To anyone who will duplicate this mad, death-defying feat. MR. MACNOODER, on behalf of Old Ironsides, will offer the above reward. Doctor's or Undertaker's bills to be shared in case of failure.

ROOM 67   ROOM 67
Exhibition begins at 2 o'clock.

The above posters, prominently displayed, produced a furore. By two o'clock fully one hundred boys were in line before room 67. At two o'clock Hickey addressed the crowd.

"Gentlemen, unfortunately a slight delay has become necessary —only a slight delay. Mr. Ironsides Smith's sense of natural delicacy is at present struggling with Mr. Ironsides Smith's desire not to disappoint his many friends and admirers. Just a slight delay, gentlemen—just a slight delay."

A cry of protest went up and Hickey disappeared. At the end of five minutes he returned radiant, announcing:

"Gentlemen, I am very glad to announce to you that Old Ironsides will not disappoint his many admirers. Only we wish it to be understood that this is a strictly scientific exhibition with an educational purpose in view. No levity will be tolerated. The exhibition is about to begin. Have your nickels in hand, gentlemen; ten cents for freshmen, with the privilege of shaking hands with Old Ironsides himself! Absolutely unique, absolutely unique!"

When the last spectator had filed out, Hickey, Macnooder and Smith divided fifteen dollars and twenty cents as pure profit, of which sum the gravel stones had brought no less than a third.

When on the fourth day Smith was able painfully to descend the stairs and circulate in the world again he felt the full delight of his newly acquired fame. At the Jigger Shop, Al graciously waved aside his tendered money, saying:

"I guess it's up to me, Ironsides, to stand treat. Such things don't happen every day. Go ahead—do your worst."

Bill Appleby and "Mista" Laloo, the rival livery men, Bill Orum, the cobbler, Barnum of the village store, even Doc Cubberly, the bell-ringer, with his little dog, stopped to watch him pass. When he crossed the campus youngsters gamboled up to his side with solicitous inquiries and the inevitable, "Say, weren't you awfully scared?"

Even in the classroom the Roman, after flunking him, would say, "That will do now, Smith. You may sit down—gently."

So he was now "Old Ironsides." He liked the name and was proud of it. It had a certain grim, uncompromising sternness about it that lent it dignity. It sounded well and it had patriotic associations.

For a whole week he knew the intoxications of popularity, of being the celebrity of the hour, of the thrill that runs up and down the back when a dozen glances are following, and the music of a murmured name, admiringly pronounced. Then abruptly another hero was exalted and he fell.

One evening after supper, while the fourth form lounged on the esplanade of the Upper, Turkey Reiter and Slugger Jones amused themselves with teasing Goat Phillips, who, being privileged by his diminutive size, responded by butting his tormentors in vigorous fashion.

"My, what an awful, rambunctious, great big Goat," said Reiter, defending himself. "Do goats eat neckties?"

"I'll eat yours," responded the youngster recklessly.

"Ten double jiggers to one you can't do it," said Slugger Jones, lazily.

"Give me the tie," responded Phillips.

More to continue the joke than for any other reason, Turkey detached the green and yellow cross tie, which was his joy, and tendered it. What was his amazement to see Goat Phillips calmly set to work to devour it, and to devour it to the very last shred in the most classic goat fashion.

When he had swallowed the last mouthful he stood stock-still and gazed at his shrieking audience. Then he began to have doubts; then he began to have premonitions. Then he ended by having settled on rather the most unsettling convictions. The consideration of the act came after the accomplishment, but it came with terrifying force. What would happen now?

"Turkey," he said, grown very solmen, "you don't think I'm going to be poisoned, do you?"

Turkey became serious at once. Everyone became serious.

"What do you fellows think?" said Turkey, addressing the crowd.

No one had any opinions to volunteer. There were no precedents to go by.

"He might get ptomaine poisoning," finally suggested Shy Thomas.

"What's that?" said Goat, horrified. Shy was forced to confess that he did not know. Hungry Smeed thought it was when you cut your toe on an oyster shell.

"See here, Goat," said Turkey, decisively, "we can't fool with this any more. You come with me."

The now thoroughly demoralized and penitent Goat went meekly between Turkey and Slugger toward Foundation House. But on the way, encountering the Roman, they decided to consult him instead.

"Please, sir," said Phillips, with difficult calm, "I'd like to ask you something."

The master stopped and, prepared for any eventuality, said, "Well, Phillips, nothing serious, I hope?"

"Please, sir, I'm afraid it is," said Phillips, all in a breath. "I've just eaten a necktie, sir."

"A what?"

"A necktie, sir, and I want to know if you think I'm in any danger, sir."

The Roman stood stock-still for a long moment, with dropped jaw; then, recovering himself, he said, "A necktie, Phillips?"

"Yes, sir."

"A whole necktie?"

"Yes, sir."

"Well, Phillips, if you can eat a necktie I guess you can digest it!"

The next morning, when Ironsides Smith unsuspectingly strolled out into the campus, no soul did him honor, not a glance turned as he turned, not a first-form youngster, primed with curiosity and admiration, came rushing to his side. Instead, a knot of boys at the far end of the esplanade was clustered in excited contemplation about Goat Phillips, the boy who had heroically eaten a necktie rather than suffer a dare.

Then Ironsides understood—he was the hero of yesterday. A new celebrity had risen for the delectation of the fickle populace. The King was dead—long live the King!

He went to the classroom disillusioned and sat through the hour stolidly tasting the bitterness of Napoleonic isolation. So this was the favor of crowds. In a night to be dethroned and forgotten!

As he descended Memorial steps, Goat Phillips passed, radiant, saluted by capricornian acclamations.

Smith regarded him darkly.

"As though anyone couldn't eat a necktie," he said in righteous disgust.

Unacclaimed he went through the crowd toward the Upper—he who had risked life and limb to amuse them for a week!

From a tower window in the Upper the Triumphant Egghead, lolling on the cushioned window seat, called down lazily, "Oh, you —Ironsides!"

That was the answer. Let popularity run after a dozen unworthy lights. Other boys would come who would eat neckties, no one ever would go the way he had gone. He had nothing to do with transitory emotions. He must be superior to the voice of the hour. He, Ironsides, belonged to history. That, nothing could take from him!

THE PROTEST AGAINST SINKERS

THE FEELING of revolt sprang up at chapel during the headmaster's weekly talk. Ordinarily the school awaited these moments with expectation, received them with tolerance and drew from them all the humor that could be extracted.

These little heart-to-heart talks brought joy to many an overweighted brain and obliterated momentarily the slow, dragging months of slush and hail. They also added, from time to time, picturesque expressions to the school vocabulary—and for that much was forgiven them. No one who heard it will ever forget the slashing that descended from the rostrum on the demon tobacco, in its embodied vice, the cigarette, nor the chill that ran over each of the four hundred cigarette smokers as the headmaster, with his boring glance straight on him, concluded:

"Yes, I know what you boys will say; I know what your plea will be when you are caught. You will come to me and you'll say with tears in your eyes, with tears, 'Doctor, think of my mother—my poor mother—it will kill my mother!'

"I tell you, *now* is the time to think of your mother; *now* is the time to spare her gray hairs. Every cigarette you boys smoke is a *nail in the coffin of your mother.*"

It was terrific. The school was unanimous in its verdict that the old man had outdone himself. Boys, whom a whiff of tobacco rendered instantly ill, smoked up the ventilators that night with shivers of delight, and from that day to this a cigarette has never been called anything but a coffin nail.

Only the week before, in announcing the suspension of Corkscrew Higgins (since with the ministry), for, among other offenses, mistaking the initials on the hat of Bucky Oliver as his own, the headmaster in his determination to abolish forever such deadly practices, had given forth the following:

"Young gentlemen, it is my painful duty, my very painful duty, to announce to you the suspension of the boy Higgins. The boy Higgins was a sloth, the boy Higgins was the prince of sloths! The boy Higgins was a gambler, the boy Higgins was the prince of gamblers! The boy Higgins was a liar, the boy Higgins was the prince of liars! The boy Higgins was a thief, the boy Higgins was the prince of thieves! Therefore, the boy Higgins will no longer be a member of this community!"

The school pardoned the exaggeration in its admiration for the rhetoric, which was rated up to the oration against Catiline. But on the first Monday of that lean month of February the school rose in revolt. In a tirade against the alarming decline in the percentage of scholastic marks the headmaster, flinging all caution to the winds, had terminated with these incendiary words:

"I know what the trouble is, and I'll tell you. The trouble with you boys is *inordinate and immoderate eating*. The trouble with you boys is—*You Eat Too Much!*"

Such a groan as went up! To comprehend the monstrosity of the accusation it is not sufficient to have been a boy; one must have retained the memory of the sharp pains and gnawing appetites of those growing days! Four hundred-odd famished forms, just from breakfast, suddenly galvanized by that unmerited blow, roared forth a unanimous indignant:

"WHAT!"

"Eat too much!"—they could hardly believe their ears. Had the headmaster of the school, with years of personal experience, actually, in his sober mind, proclaimed that they ate too much! The words had been said; the accusation had to stand. And such a time to proclaim it—in the month of sliced bananas and canned vegetables! The protest that rumbled and growled in the under-form houses exploded in the Dickinson.

It so happened that for days there had been a dull grumbling about the monotony of the daily meals and the regularity and frequency of the appearance of certain abhorrent dishes known as "scrag-birds and sinkers." "Scrag-bird" was a generic term, allowing a wide latitude for conjecture, but "sinker" was an opprobrious epithet dedicated to a particularly hard, doughy substance that under more favorable auspices sometimes, without fear of contradiction, achieves the name of "dumpling."

The sinker was, undoubtedly, the deadliest enemy of the growing boy—the most persistent, the most malignant. It knew no laws and it defied all restraint. It languished in the spring, but thrived and multiplied amazingly in the canned, winter term. It was as likely to bob up in a swimming dish of boiled chicken as it was certain to accompany a mutton stew. It associated at times with veal and attached itself to corned beef; it concealed itself in a beefsteak pie and clung to a leg of lamb. What the red rag is to the bull, the pudgy white of the sinker was to the boys, who, in a sort of desperate hope of exterminating the species, never allowed one to return intact to the kitchen. Twice a week was the allotted appearance of the sinker; at a third visit grumbling would break out; at a fourth arose threats of leaving for Andover or Exeter, of writing home, of boycotting the luncheon.

Now, it so happened that during the preceding week the sinker had inflicted itself not four, but actually six, times on that community of aching voids. The brutal accusation of the headmaster was the spark to the powder. The revolt assumed head and form during the day, and a call for a meeting of protest was unanimously made for that very night.

The boys met with the spirit of the Boston Tea Party, resolved to defend their liberties and assert their independence. The inevitable Doc Macnooder was to address the meeting. He spoke naturally, fluently, with great sounding phrases, on any occasion, on any topic, for his own pure delight, and he always continued to speak until violently suppressed.

"Fellows," he began, without apologies to history, "we are met to decide once and for all whether we are a free governing body, to ask ourselves what is all this worth? For weeks we have endured, supinely on our backs, the tyranny of Mrs. Van Asterbilt, the matron of this House. We have, I say, supinely permitted each insult to pass unchallenged. But the hour has struck, the worm has turned, the moment has come and, without the slightest hesitation, I ask you . . . I ask you . . . what do I ask you?" He paused, and appealed for enlightenment.

The meeting found him guilty of levity and threatened him with the ban of silence.

Macnooder looked grieved and continued: "I ask you to strike as your fathers struck. I ask you to string the bow, to whet the knife, to sharpen the tomahawk, to loose the dogs of war—"

Amid a storm of whoops and catcalls, Macnooder was pulled back into his seat. He rose and explained that his peroration was completed and demanded the inalienable right to express his opinions.

The demand was rejected by a vote of eighty-two to one (Macnooder voting).

Butcher Stevens rose with difficulty and, clutching the shoulder of Red Dog in front of him, addressed the gathering as follows:

"Fellows, I am no silver-tongued orator and all I want to say is just a few words. I think we want to treat this thing seriously." (Cries of "Hear! hear!" "Right.") "I think, fellows, this is a very serious matter, and I think we ought to take some action. This food matter is getting pretty bad. I don't think, fellows, that we ought to stand for sinkers the way they're coming at us, without some action. I don't know just what action we ought to take, but I think we ought really to take some action."

The Butcher subsided into his seat amid immense applause. Lovely Mead arose and jangling the keys in his trousers pocket, addressed the ceiling in rapid, jerky periods:

"Fellows, I think we ought to begin by taking a vote—a vote. I think—I think the sentiment of this meeting is about made up— made up. I think my predecessor has very clearly expressed the—the —has voiced the sentiments of this meeting—very clearly. I think a vote would clear the air, therefore I move we take a vote."

He sighed contentedly and returned into the throng. Doc Macnooder sarcastically demanded what they were to vote upon. Lovely Mead, in great confusion, rose and stammered:

"I meant to say, Mr. Chairman, that I move we take a vote, take a vote to—to take some action."

"Action about what?" said the merciless Macnooder.

Lovely Mead remained speechless. Hungry Smeed interposed glibly:

"Mister Chairman, I move that it is the sense of this meeting that we should take some action looking toward the remedying of the present condition of our daily meals."

The motion was passed and the chairman announced that he was ready to hear suggestions as to the nature of the act, as contemplated. A painful silence succeeded.

Macnooder rose and asked permission to offer a suggestion. The demand was repulsed. Wash Simmons moved that at the next appearance of the abhorrent sinkers, they should rise and leave the room *en masse*. It was decided that the plan entailed too many sacrifices, and it was rejected.

Crazy Opdyke from the Woodhull developed the following scheme, full of novelty and imagination:

"I say, fellows, I've got an idea, you know. What we want is an object lesson, you know, something striking. Now, fellows, this is what I propose: We're eighty-five of us in these dining rooms; now, at two sinkers each, that makes one hundred and seventy sinkers every time; at six times that makes one thousand sinkers a week. What we want to do is to carry off the sinkers from table, save them up, and at the end of the week make a circle of them around the campus as an object lesson!"

Macnooder, again, was refused permission to speak in support of this measure, which had an instant appeal to the imagination of the audience. In the end, however, the judgment of the more serious prevailed, and the motion was lost by a close vote. After more discussion the meeting finally decided to appoint an embassy of three, who should instantly proceed to the headmaster's, and firmly lay before him the Woodhull's and the Dickinson's demand for unconditional and immediate suppression of that indigestible and totally ornamental article known as the sinker. Hickey, Wash Simmons and Crazy Opdyke, by virtue of their expressed defiance, were chosen to carry the ultimatum. Someone proposed that Macnooder should go as a fourth, and the motion passed without opposition. Macnooder rose and declined the honor but asked leave to state his reasons. Whereupon the meeting adjourned.

The Messrs. Crazy Opdyke, Hickey, and Wash Simmons held a conference and decided to shave and assume creased trousers in order to render the aspect of their mission properly impressive. After a short delay they united on the steps, where they received the exhortations of their comrades—to speak out boldly, to mince no words, and to insist on their demands.

The distance to Foundation House, where the headmaster resided, was short—thirty seconds in the darkness; and almost before they knew it the three were at the door. There, under the muffled lamp, they stopped, with spontaneous accord, and looked at one another.

"I say," said Hickey, "hadn't we better agree on what we'll say to the old man? We want to be firm, you know."

"That's a good idea," Opdyke assented, and Wash added, "We'll take a turn down the road."

"Now, what's your idea?" said Simmons to Hickey, when they had put a safe distance between them and the residence of the Doctor.

"We'd better keep away from discussion," replied Hickey. "The Doctor'll beat us out there, and I don't think we'd better be too radical either, because we want to be firm."

"What do you call radical?" said Opdyke, with a little defiance.

"Well, now, we don't want to be too aggressive; we don't want to go in with a chip on our shoulder."

"Hickey, you're beginning to hedge!"

Hickey indignantly denied the accusation, and a little quarrel arose between them, terminated by Wash, who broke in.

"Shut up, Crazy—Hickey is dead right. We want to go in friendly-like, just as though we knew the Doctor would side with us at once—sort of take him into our confidence."

"That's it," said Hickey; "we want to be good-natured at first, lay the matter before him calmly, then afterward we can be firm."

"Rats!" said Crazy. "Are we going to tell him, or not, that we represent the Dickinson and the Woodhull and that they have voted the extinction of sinkers?"

"Sure we are!" exclaimed Wash. "You don't think we are afraid, do you?"

"Well, then, let's tell him," said Crazy. "Come on, if you're going to."

They returned resolutely and again entered the dominion of the dreary lamp.

"Say, fellows," Wash suddenly interjected, "are we going to say anything about scrag-birds?"

"Sure," said Crazy.

"The deuce we are!" said Hickey.

"Why not?" said Crazy, militantly.

"Because we don't want to make fools of ourselves."

The three withdrew again and threshed out the point. It was decided to concentrate on the sinker. Crazy gave in because he said he was cold.

"Well, now, it's all settled," said Hickey. "We make a direct demand for knocking out the sinker, and we stand firm on that. Nothing else. Come on."

"Come on."

A third time they came to the terrible door.

"I say," said Wash, suddenly, "we forgot. Who's to do the talking?"

"Crazy, of course," said Hickey, looking hard at Simmons, "since that clapper episode, I'm not dropping in for the dessert!"

"Sure, Crazy, you're just the one," Simmons agreed.

"Hold up," said Crazy, whose fury suddenly cooled. "Let's talk that over."

Again they retired for deliberation.

"Now, see here, fellows," said Crazy, "let's be reasonable. We want this thing to go through, don't we?"

"Who's hedging now?" said Hickey, with a laugh.

"No one," retorted Crazy. "I'll talk up if you say. I'm not afraid, only I don't stand one, two, three with the Doctor and you know it. I've flunked every recitation in Bible this month. What we want is the strongest pull—and Wash is the one. Why, the old man would feed out of Wash's hand."

Wash indignantly repelled the insinuation. Finally it was agreed that Crazy should state the facts, that Hickey should say, "Doctor, we feel strongly, very strongly, about this," and that Wash should then make the direct demand for the suspension for one month of the sinker, and its future regulation to two appearances a week.

"And now, no more backing and filling," said Hickey.

"I'll lay the facts before him, all right," added Crazy, clenching his fists.

"We'll stick together, and we stand firm," said Wash. "Now for it!"

They had reached a point about thirty feet from the threshold when suddenly the door was flung violently open and a luckless boy bolted out, under the lamp, so that the three could distinguish the vehement gestures. The Doctor appeared in a passion of rage, calling after the retreating offender:

"Don't you dare, young man, to come to me again with such a complaint. You get your work up to where it ought to be, or down you go, and there isn't a power in this country that can prevent it."

The door slammed violently and silence returned.

"He's not in a very receptive mood," said Wash, after a long pause.

"Not precisely," said Hickey, thoughtfully.

"I'm catching cold," said Crazy.

"Suppose we put it over?" continued Wash. "What do you say, Hickey?"

"I shall not oppose the will of the majority."

"And you, Crazy?"

"I think so, too."

They returned to the Dickinson, where they were surrounded and assailed with questions: How had the Doctor taken it? What had he said?

"We took no talk from him," said Crazy, with a determined shake of his head, and then Wash added brusquely, "Just keep your eyes on the sinkers."

"You took long enough," put in the suspicious Macnooder.

"We were firm," replied Hickey, bristling at the recollection, "very firm!"

BEAUTY'S SISTER

His hair it is a faded white,
  His eye a watery blue;
He has no buttons on his coat,
  No shoe-strings in his shoe.

"BEAUTY" SAWTELLE, or Chesterton V. Sawtelle, as it was pronounced when each Monday the master of the form read the biweekly absences from bath, sat adjusting his skate on the edge of the pond with a look of ponderous responsibility on the freckled face, crowned by a sheaf of tow hair, like the wisp of a Japanese doll. Presently he drew from his pocket a dance card, glanced over it for the twentieth time, and replaced it with a sigh.

"Cracky!" he said, in despair. "Sixteen regulars and eight extras; sixteen and eight, twenty-four. Gee!"

Beauty's heart was heavy and his hope faint, for the sinister fin-

ger of the Prom had cast its shadow over the lighthearted democ-
racy of boyhood. Into this free republic, where no thoughts of the
outside society should penetrate, the demoralizing swish of coming
petticoats had suddenly intruded its ominous significance of a
world without, where such tyrannies as money and birth stand
ready to divide the unsuspecting hosts.

Now Beauty's woes were manifold: he was only a second former,
and the Prom was the property of the lords of the school, the ma-
jestic fourth formers, who lived in the Upper House and governed
themselves according to the catalogue and a benevolent tempering
of the exact theory of independence.

A few rash under-formers with pretty sisters were admitted on
sufferance, and robbed of their partners if the chance arose. Beauty,
scrubby boy of fourteen, with a like aversion to girls and stiff col-
lars in his ugly little body, had been horrified to learn that his sister, at the invitation of Rogers, the housemaster, was coming to the
Prom. On his shoulders devolved the herculean task of filling a
card from the upper class, only a handful of whom he knew, at a
moment when the cards had been circulated for weeks. So he stood
dejectedly, calculating how to fill the twenty-four spaces that were
so blank and interminable. Twenty-four dances to fill, and the
Prom only two weeks off!

In the middle of the pond boys were darting and swaying in a
furious game of hockey. Beauty lingered, biding his opportunity,
searching the crowd for a familiar face, until presently Wash Simmons, emerging from the melee, darted to his side, grinding his
skates and coming to a halt for breath, with a swift: "Hello, Venus!
How's the Dickinson these days?"

Beauty, murmuring an inaudible reply, stood turning and twisting, desperately seeking to frame a demand.

"What's the secret sorrow, Beauty?" continued Wash, with a
glance of surprise.

"I say, Wash," said Beauty, plunging, "I say, have you got any
dances left?"

"I? Oh, Lord, no!" said the pitcher of the school nine, with a
quick glance. "Gone long ago."

He drew the strap tight, dug his hands into his gloves again, and
with a nod flashed back into the crowd. Beauty, gulping down
something that rose in his throat, started aimlessly to skirt the edge

of the pond. He had understood the look that Wash had given him in that swift moment.

In this abstracted mood, he suddenly came against something angular and small that accompanied him to the ice with a resounding whack.

"Clumsy beast!" said a sharp voice.

From his embarrassed position, Beauty recognized the Red Dog.

"Excuse me, Red Dog," he said hastily; "I didn't see you."

"Why, it's Beauty," said the Red Dog, rubbing himself. "Blast you, all the same."

"I say, Red Dog," said Beauty, "have you any dances left?"

"All gone, Beauty," answered Red Dog, stooping suddenly to recover his skate.

"Nothing left?"

"Nope—filled the last extra today," said Red Dog, with the shining face of prevarication. Then he added, "Why, Venus, are *you* going to the Prom?"

"No," said Sawtelle; "it's my sister."

"Oh, I'm sorry. I'd like to oblige you, but you see how it is," said Red Dog, lamely.

"I see."

"Ta, ta, Beauty! So long!"

Sawtelle shut his lips, struck a valiant blow at an imaginary puck, and began to whistle.

> 'Tis a jolly life we lead
> Care and sorrow we defy—

After piping forth this inspiring chorus with vigorous notes, the will gave way. He began another:

> To Lawrenceville my father sent me,
> Where for college I should prepare;
> And so I settled down,
> In this queer, forsaken town,
> About five miles away from anywhere.

The bellows gave out. Overcome by the mournfulness of the last verse, he dropped wearily on the bank, continuing doggedly:

> About five miles from anywhere, my boys,
> Where old Lawrenceville evermore shall stand;

For has she not stood,
Since the time of the flood—

Whether the accuracy of the last statement or the forced rhyme displeased him, he broke off, heaved a sigh, and said viciously, "They lied, both of 'em."

"Well, how's the boy?" said a familiar voice.

Beauty came out of the vale of bitterness to perceive at his side the great form of Turkey Reiter, preparing to adjust his skates.

"Oh, Turkey," said Beauty, clutching at the straw, "I've been looking everywhere—"

"What's the matter?"

"Turkey, I'm in an awful hole."

"Out with it."

"I say, Turkey," said Sawtelle, stumbling and blushing, "I say, you know, my sister's coming to the Prom, and I thought if you'd like—that is, I wanted to know if—if you wouldn't take her dance card and get it filled for me." Then he added abjectly, "I'm awfully sorry."

Turkey looked thoughtful. This was a commission he did not relish. Beauty looked particularly unattractive that afternoon, in a red tobogganing toque that swore at his faded white hair, and the orange freckles that stared out from every point of vantage.

"Why, Beauty," he began hesitatingly, "the way it is, you see, my card's already filled, and I'm afraid, honestly, that's about the case with all the others."

"She's an awfully nice girl," said Sawtelle, looking down in a desperate endeavor to control his voice.

"Nice girl," thought Turkey, "ahem! Yes, must be a good-looker, too, something on Venus's particular line of beauty."

He glanced at his companion and mentally pictured a lanky girl with sandy hair, a little upstart nose, and a mass of orange freckles. But between Turkey and Sawtelle relations had been peculiar. There had been many moments in the last year at the Dickinson when the ordinary luxuries of life would have been difficult had it not been for the superior financial standing of Chesterton V. Sawtelle. The account had been a long one, and there was a slight haziness in Turkey's mind as to the exact status of the balance. Also, Turkey was genuinely grateful, with that sense of gratitude which is described as a lively looking forward to favors to come.

"Oh, well, young 'un," he said with rough good humor, "give us the card. I'll do what I can. But, mind you, I can't take any myself. My card's full, and it wouldn't do for me to cut dances."

Jumping up, he started to escape the effusive thanks of the over-joyed Sawtelle, but suddenly wheeled and came skating back.

"Hello, Beauty!" he called out. "I say, what's your sister's name?"

"Sally—that is, Sarah," came the timid answer.

"Heavens!" said Turkey to himself as he flashed over the ice. "That settles it. Sally—Sally! A nice pickle I'm in! Wonder if she sports spectacles and old-fashioned frocks. A nice pickle—I'll be the laughingstock of the whole school. Guess I won't have much trouble recognizing Beauty's sister. Whew! That comes from having a kind heart!"

With these and similar pleasant reflections he threaded his way among the crowd of skaters until at length he perceived Hickey skimming over the ice, stealing the puck from a bunch of scrambling players, until his progress checked, and the puck vanishing into a distant melee, he came to a stop for breath. Turkey, profiting by the occasion, descended on his victim.

"Whoa there, Hickey!"

"Whoa it is!"

"How's your dance card?"

"A dazzling galaxy of beauty, a symposium of grace, a feast of—"

"Got anything left? I have a wonder for you if you have."

"Sure, twelfth regular and sixth extra—but the duchess will be awfully cut up."

"Twelfth and sixth," said Turkey, with a nod; "that's a go."

"Who's the heart-smasher?" asked Hickey, with an eye on the approaching puck.

"A wonder, Hickey; a screamer. There'll be nothing to it. Ta, ta! Much obliged."

"What's her name?"

"Sawtelle—some distant relative of the Beauty's, I believe. I'm filling out her card. Obliged for the dance. Ta, ta!"

"Hold up!" said Hickey, quickly. "Hold up! Jiminy! I almost forgot—why, I do believe I went and promised those two to Has-brouck. Isn't that a shame! Sorry. To think of my forgetting that! Try to give you some other. Confound it! I have no luck." With the most mournful look in the world he waved his hand and sped ostentatiously toward the bunch of players.

"Hickey's on to me," thought Turkey as he watched him disengage himself from the crowd and skate off with Sawtelle; "no hope in that quarter."

Finally, after an hour's persistent work, during which he pleaded and argued, commanded and threatened, he succeeded in filling exactly six of the necessary twenty-four dances. Indeed, he would have had no difficulty in completing the card if he could have passed over that fatal name. But each time, just as he was congratulating himself on another conquest, his victim would ask, "By the way, what name shall I put down?"

"Oh—er—Miss Sawtelle," he would answer nonchalantly; "a distant relative of the Beauty—though nothing like him—ha! ha!"

Then each would suddenly remember that the dances in question were already half-promised—a sort of an understanding; but of course he would have to look it up—but of course, if he found they were free, why, then of course, he wanted, above all things in the world, to dance with Miss Sawtelle.

"Well, anyhow," said Turkey to himself, recapitulating, "I've got six, provided they don't all back out. Let me see. I can make the Kid take three—that's nine—and Snookers will have to take three—that's twelve—and, hang it! Butcher and Egghead have got to take two each—that would make sixteen. The other eight I can fill up with some harmless freaks: some will snap at anything."

That night at the supper table Turkey had to face the music.

"You're a nice one, you are," said Hickey, starting in immediately, "you arch-deceiver. You are a fine friend; I have my opinion of you. 'Handsome girl,' 'a wonder,' 'fine talker,' 'a screamer'—that's the sort of game you try on your friends, is it? Who is she? Oh—ah, yes, a *distant* relative of the Beauty."

"What's up now?" said the Kid, editor of the *Lawrence,* and partner of Turkey's secrets, joys, and debts.

"Hasn't he tried to deceive you yet?" continued Hickey, with an accusing look at Turkey. "No? That's a wonder! What do you think of a fellow who tries to pass off on his friends such a girl as the Beauty's sister?"

"No!" said Butcher Stevens.

"What!" exclaimed Macnooder, laying down his knife with a thud.

"Beauty's sister," said the Egghead, gaping with astonishment.

"Well, why not?" said Turkey, defiantly.

"Listen to that!" continued Hickey. "The brazenness of it!"

The four graduates of the Dickinson, after a moment of stupefied examination of Hickey and Reiter, suddenly burst into roars of laughter that produced a craning of necks and a storm of inquiries from the adjoining tables.

When the hilarity had been somewhat checked, Hickey returned to the persecution of the blushing Turkey.

"Bet you three to one she's a mass of freckles," he said. "Bet you even she wears glasses; bet you one to three she's cross-eyed; bet you four to one she won't open her mouth."

"Hang you, Hickey!" said Turkey, flushing, "I won't have her talked about so."

"Did you take any dances?" said the Kid to Hickey.

"Me?" exclaimed the latter, in great dudgeon. "Me! Well, I guess not! I wouldn't touch any of that tribe with a ten-foot pole."

"Look here, you fellows have got to shut up," said Turkey, forced at last into a virtuous attitude by the exigency of the situation. "I promised the Beauty I'd fill his sister's card for him, and I'm going to do it. The girl can't help her looks. You talk like a lot of cads. What you fellows ought to do is to join in and give her a treat. The girl is probably from the backwoods, and this ought to be made the time of her life."

"Turkey," said the malicious Hickey, "how many dances have you eagerly appropriated?"

Turkey stopped point-blank, greeted by derisive jeers.

"Oho!"

"That's it, is it?"

"Fake!"

"Humbug!"

"Not at all," said Turkey, indignantly. "What do you think I am?"

"Pass over your list and let's see the company you're going to introduce her to," said Hickey, stretching out his hand for the dance card. "Ah, I must congratulate you, my boy; your selection is magnificent; the young lady will be charmed." He flipped the card disdainfully to the Egghead, saying, "A bunch of freaks!"

"Hang it all," said the Egghead, "that's too hard on any girl. A fine opinion she'll have of Lawrenceville fellows! We can't stand for that."

"Look here," said the Kid, suddenly. "Turkey is at fault, and has got to be punished. Here's what we'll do, though: let's each take a dance on condition that Turkey takes her out to supper."

"Oh, I say!" protested Turkey, who had other plans.

The others acclaimed the plan gleefully, rejoicing in his discomfiture, until Turkey, driven to a corner, was forced to capitulate.

That evening on the esplanade he called Snookers to him, and resting his hand affectionately on the little fellow's shoulder, said, "Old man, do you want to do me a favor?"

"Sure."

"I'm filling up a girl's card for the Prom, and I want you to help me out."

"Certainly; give me a couple, if the girl's the real thing."

"Much obliged. I'll put your name down."

"Second and fifth. Say, who is she?"

"Oh, some relative of Sawtelle's—you remember you used to go with him a good deal in the Dickinson. It's his sister."

"Whew!" said Snookers, with a long-drawn whistle. "Say, give me three more, will you?"

"Hardly," answered Turkey, with a laugh; "but I'll spare you another."

"I didn't think it quite fair to the girl," he explained later, "to give her too big a dose of Snookers. Queer, though, how eager the little brute was!"

The last week dragged interminably in multiplied preparations for the great event. In the evenings the war of strings resounded across the campus from the gym, where the Banjo and Mandolin clubs strove desperately to perfect themselves for the concert. The Dramatic Club, in sudden fear, crowded the day with rehearsals, while from the window of Room 65, Upper, the voice of Biddy Hampton, soloist of the Glee Club, was heard chanting "The Pride of the House is Papa's Baby," behind doors stout enough to resist the assaults of his neighbors.

Oil stoves and flatirons immediately came into demand, cushions were rolled back from window seats, and trousers that were limp and discouraged grew smooth and well-creased under the pressure of the hot iron. Turkey and Doc Macnooder, who from their long experience in the Dickinson had become expert tailors, advertised on the bulletin board:

REITER AND MACNOODER
BON TON TAILORS

Trousers neatly pressed, at fifteen cents per pair; all payments strictly cash—*in advance.*

Each night the dining room of the Upper was cleared, and the extraordinary spectacle was seen of boys of all sizes in sweaters and jerseys, clasping each other desperately around the waist, spinning and bumping their way about the reeling room to the chorus of:

"Get off my feet!"

"Reverse, you lubber!"

"Now, *one,* two, three—"

"A fine lady you are!"

"Do you expect me to carry you around the room?"

"Darn you, fatty!"

"Hold tight!"

"Let 'er rip now!"

From the end of the room the cynics and misogynists, roosting on the piled-up tables and chairs, croaked forth their contempt:

"Oh, you fussers!"

"You lady-killers!"

"Dance, my darling, dance!"

"Squeeze her tight, Bill!"

"That's the way!"

"Look at Skinny!"

"Keep a-hoppin', Skinny!"

"Look at him spin!"

"For heaven's sake, someone stop Skinny!"

Of evenings certain of the boys would wander in pairs to the edge of the woods and confide to each other the secret attachments and dark, forlorn hopes that were wasting them away. Turkey and the Kid, who were going as stags, opened their hearts to each other and spoke of the girl, the one distant girl, whose image not all the fair faces that would come could for a moment dim.

"Kid," said Turkey, in solemn conclusion, speaking from the experience of eighteen years, "I am going to make that little girl—my wife."

"Turkey, old man, God bless you!" answered the confidant, with nice regard for old precedents. Then he added, a little choked, "Turkey, I, too—I—"

"I understand, Kid," said Turkey, gravely clapping his shoulder; "I've known it all along."

"Dear old boy!"

They walked in silence.

"What's her name?" asked Turkey, slowly.

"Lucille. And hers?"

"Marie Louise."

Another silence.

"Kid, is it all right?"

The romanticist considered a moment, and then shook his head.

"No, Turk."

"Dear old boy, you'll win out."

"I must. And you, Turk, does she care?"

A heavy sigh was the answer. They walked back arm in arm, each fully believing in the other's sorrow, and almost convinced of his own. At the esplanade of the Upper they stopped and listened to the thumping of the piano and the systematic beat from the dancers.

"I wish it were all over," said Turkey, gloomily. "This can mean nothing to me."

"Nor to me," said the Kid, staring at the melancholy moon.

On the fateful day the school arose, so to speak, as one boy, shaved, and put on a clean collar. Every boot was blacked, every pair of trousers creased to a cutting edge. The array of neckties that suddenly appeared in gigantic puffs or fluttering wings was like the turn of autumn in a single night.

Chapel and the first two recitations over, the esplanade of the Upper was crowded with fourth formers, circulating critically in the dandified throng, chattering excitedly of the coming event. Perish the memory of the fashion there displayed! It seemed magnificent then: let that be the epitaph.

The bell called, and the group slowly departed to the last recitation. From each house a stream of boys came pouring out and made their lagging way around the campus toward Memorial. Slower and slower rang the bell, and faster came the unwilling slaves—those in front with dignity; those behind with dispatch, and so on down the line to the last scattered stragglers who came racing over the lawns. The last peal sounded, the last laggard tore up Memorial steps, and vanished within. A moment later the gong in the hall clanged, and the next recitation was on. The circle, a moment before alive with figures, was quiet and deserted. A group of seven or eight lounging on the esplanade were chatting indolently, tossing a ball back and forth with the occupant of a third-story window.

At this moment Turkey emerged from the doorway in shining russets, a Gladstone collar, a tie of robin's-egg-blue, and a suit of red and green plaids, such as the innocent curiosity of a boy on his first allowance goes to with the thirst of possession.

"Hurrah for Turkey!" cried the Kid. "He looks like a regular fashion plate."

In an instant he was surrounded, punched, examined, and complimented.

"Well, fellows, it's time to give ourselves them finishing touches," said the Egghead, with a glance of envy. "Turkey is trying to steal a march on us. The girls are coming."

"Hello!" cried the Kid, suddenly. "Who's this?"

All turned. From behind Foundation House came a carriage. It drove on briskly until nearly opposite the group on the steps, when the driver reined in, and someone within looked out dubiously.

"Turkey, you're in luck," said the Gutter Pup. "You're the only one with the rouge on. Go down gracefully and see what the lady wants."

So down went Turkey to his duty. They watched him approach the carriage and speak to someone inside. Then he closed the door and spoke to the driver, evidently pointing out his destination, for the cab continued around the circle.

Then Turkey made a jump for the esplanade, and, deaf to all inquiries, seized upon his roommate and dragged him aside.

"Great guns! Kid," he exclaimed, "I've seen her—Beauty's sister! She isn't like Beauty at all. She's a stunner, a dream! Look here! Get that dance card. Get it, if you have to lie and steal. He's in recitation now. You've got to catch him when he comes out. For heaven's sake, don't let anyone get ahead of you! Tell him two girls have backed out, and I want five more dances. Tell him I'm to take her to the debate tonight, and the Dramatic Club tomorrow. Kid, get that card!"

Releasing his astounded roommate, he went tearing across the campus to meet the carriage.

"What's happened to our staid and dignified president?" cried the Gutter Pup in wonder. "Is he crazy?"

"Oh, say, fellows," exclaimed the Kid, overcome by the humor of the situation, "who do you think that was?"

The carriage had now stopped before the Dickinson, and Turkey, arrived in time, was helping out a tall, slender figure in black. A light flashed over the group.

"Beauty's sister."

"No!"

"Yes."

"Impossible!"

"Beauty's sister it is," cried the Kid; "and the joke is, she's a stunner, a dream!"

"A dream!" piped up the inevitable Snookers. "Well, I guess! She's an all-round A-No. 1. Gee! I just got a glimpse of her at a theater, and I tell you, boys, she's a paralyzer."

But his remark ended on the air, for all, with a common impulse, had disappeared. Snookers, struck with the same thought, hastened to his room.

Ten minutes later they reappeared. Hickey, in a suit of pronounced checks, his trousers carefully turned up *à l'Anglais*, glanced approvingly at the array of manly fashion.

"And now, fellows," he said, pointing to the Chapel, which Turkey was entering with Miss Sawtelle, "that traitor shall be punished. We'll guard every entrance to Memorial, capture our friend, 'Chesterton V. Sawtelle (absent from bath),' relieve him of that little dance card, and then, Romans, to the victors belong the spoils!"

The Kid, having delayed over the choice between a red-and-yellow necktie or one of simple purple, did not appear until Hickey had stationed his forces. Taking in the situation at a glance, he chuckled to himself and picking up a couple of books, started for the entrance.

"Lucky it's Hungry and the Egghead," he said to himself as he passed them and entered the Lower Hall. "Hickey would have guessed the game."

He called Sawtelle from the second form, and, slipping his arm through his, drew him down the corridor.

"Sawtelle," he said, "I want your sister's dance card. There's some mistake, and Turkey wants to fix it up. Thanks; that's all. Oh, no, it isn't, either. Turkey said he'd be over after supper to take your sister to the debate, and that he had seats for the Dramatic Club tomorrow. Don't forget all that. So long! See you later."

In high feather at the success of this stratagem, he skipped downstairs, and avoiding Hickey, went to meet Turkey in the Chapel, where he was duly presented.

When Sawtelle emerged at length from the study room, he was amazed at the spontaneity of his reception. He was no longer "Beauty" or "Apollo" or "Venus."

"Sawtelle, old man," they said to him, "I want to see you a moment."

"Chesterton, where have you been?"

"Old man, have you got anything to do?"

Each strove to draw him away from the others, and failing in this, accompanied him to the Jigger Shop, where he was plied with substantial flattery, until having disposed of jiggers, soda, and éclairs, he cast one lingering glance at the tempting counters, and said with a twinkle in his ugly little eyes:

"And now, fellows, I guess my sister must be over at the house. Come around this afternoon, why don't you, and meet her?"—an invitation which was received with enthusiasm and much evident surprise.

When the Prom opened that evening, Beauty's sister made her entrée flanked by the smitten Turkey and the languishing Hasbrouck, while the stricken Kid brought up the rear, consoled by the responsibility of her fan. Five stags who had been lingering miserably in the shadow searching for something daring and imaginative to lay at her feet, crowded forward only to be stricken dumb at the splendor of her toilette.

Beauty's sister, fresh from a Continental season, was quite overwhelmed by the subtle adoration of the famous Wash Simmons and of Egghead, that pattern of elegance and *savoir-faire*—overwhelmed, but not at all confused. Gradually under her deft manipulation the power of speech returned to the stricken. Then the rout began. The young ladies from city and country finishing schools, still struggling with their teens, were quite eclipsed by the gorgeous Parisian toilette and the science of movement displayed by the sister of Chesterton V. Sawtelle. The ordinary ethics of fair play were thrown to the winds. Before the eyes of everyone, Turkey held up the worthless dance card, and tore it into shreds. Only the brave should deserve the fair. Little Smeed, Poler Fox, and Snorky Green struggled in vain for recognition, and retired crestfallen and defrauded, to watch the scramble for each succeeding dance, which had to be portioned among three and often four clamorers.

In fact, it became epidemic. They fell in love by blocks of five, even as they had sought the privileges of the measles. Each implored a memento to fix imperishably on his wall. The roses she wore consoled a dozen. The Gutter Pup obtained her fan; the Kid her handkerchief, a wonderful scented transparency. Glendenning and Hasbrouck brazenly divided the gloves while Turkey, trembling at his own blurting audacity, was blown to the stars by permission to express in a letter certain delicate thoughts which stifle in the vulgar scramble of the ballroom.

When the last dance had been fought for, divided, and redivided, and the lights peremptorily suppressed, the stags *en masse* accompanied Beauty's sister to the Dickinson, where each separately pressed her hand and strove to give to his "Good night" an accent which would be understood by her alone.

On that next morning that somehow always arises, Turkey and the Kid, envied by all, drove her to the station, listening mutely to her gay chatter, each plunged in melancholy, secretly wondering how she managed to conceal her feelings so well.

They escorted her to the car, and loaded her with magazines and candies and flowers, and each succeeded in whispering in her ear a rapid, daring sentence, which she received from each with just the proper encouragement. Then, imaginary Lucilles and Marie Louises forgot, they drove back, heavy of heart, and uncomprehending, viewing the landscape without joy or hope, suffering stoically as men of eighteen should. Not a word was spoken until from the last hill they caught the first glimmer of the school. Then Turkey hoarsely, flicking the air with the lash of the whip, said:

"Kid—"

"What?"

"That *was* a woman."

"A woman of the world, Turkey."

They left the carriage at the stable, and strolled up to the Jigger Shop, joining the group, all intent on the coming baseball season; and gradually the agony eased a bit. Presently a familiar little figure, freckled and towheaded, sidled into the shop, and stood with fists jammed in empty pockets, sniffing the air for succor.

"Oh, you Beauty! Oh, you astonishing Venus!" cried the inevitable persecutor. Then from the crowd Macnooder began to intone the familiar lines:

> His hair, it is a faded white,
>   His eye a watery blue;
> He has no buttons on his coat,
>   No shoe-strings in his shoe.

"Doc," said the Beauty, blushing sheepishly, "set me up to a jigger, will you? Go on, now!"

Then Macnooder, roaring, shouted back: "Not this year; next year—SISTER!"

THE GREAT BIG MAN

THE NOON bell was about to ring, the one glorious spring note of that inexorable Gym bell that ruled the school with its iron tongue. For at noon, on the first liberating stroke, the long winter term died and the Easter vacation became a fact.

Inside Memorial Hall the impatient classes stirred nervously, counting off the minutes, sitting gingerly on the seat edges for fear of wrinkling the carefully pressed suits, or shifting solicitously the sharpened trousers in peril of a bagging at the knees. Heavens! How interminable the hour was, sitting there in a planked shirt and a fashion-high collar—and what a recitation! Would Easter ever begin, that long-coveted vacation when the growing boy, according to theory, goes home to rest from the fatiguing draining of his brain, but in reality returns exhausted by dinners, dances, and theaters, with perhaps a little touch of the measles to exchange with his neighbors. Even the masters droned through the perfunctory exercises, flunking the boys by twos and threes, by groups, by long rows, but without malice or emotion.

Outside, in the roadway, by the steps, waited a long, incongruous line of vehicles, scraped together from every stable in the countryside, forty-odd. A few buggies for nabobs in the Upper House, two-seated rigs (holding eight), country buckboards, excursion wagons to be filled according to capacity at twenty-five cents the trip, hacks from Trenton, and the regulation stage coach—all piled high with bags and suitcases, waiting for the bell that would start them on the scramble for the Trenton station, five miles away. At the horses' heads the lazy drivers lolled, drawing languid puffs from their cigarettes, unconcerned.

Suddenly the bell rang out, and the supine teamsters, galvanizing into life, jumped to their seats. The next moment, down the steps, pell-mell, scrambling and scuffling, swarming over the carriages, with joyful clamor, the school arrived. In an instant the first buggies were off, with whips frantically plied, disputing at a gallop the race to Trenton.

Then the air was filled with shouts.

"Where's Butsey?"

"Oh, you, Red Dog!"

"Where's my bag?"

"Jump in!"

"Oh, we'll never get there!"

"Drive on!"

"Don't wait!"

"Where's Jack?"

"Hurry up, you loafer!"

"Hurry up, you butterfingers!"

"Get in!"

"Pile in!"

"Haul him in!"

"We're off!"

"Hurrah!"

Wagon after wagon, crammed with joyful boyhood, disappeared in a cloud of dust, while back returned a confused uproar of broken cheers, snatches of songs, with whoops and shrieks for more speed dominating the whole. The last load rollicked away to join the mad race, where far ahead a dozen buggies, with foam-flecked horses, vied with one another, their youthful jockeys waving their hats, hurling defiance back and forth, or shrieking with delight as each antagonist was caught and left behind.

The sounds of striving died away, the campus grew still once more. The few who had elected to wait until after luncheon scattered hurriedly about the circle and disappeared in the houses, to fling last armfuls into the already bursting trunks.

On top of Memorial steps the Great Big Man remained, solitary and marooned, gazing over the fields, down the road to Trenton, where still the rising dust clouds showed the struggle toward vacation. He stood like a monument, gazing fixedly, struggling with all the might of his twelve years to conquer the awful feeling of homesickness that came to him. Homesickness—the very word was an anomaly: what home had he to go to? An orphan without ever having known his father, scarcely remembering his mother in the hazy reflections of years, little Joshua Tibbetts had arrived at the school at the beginning of the winter term, to enter the shell,* and gradually pass through the forms in six or seven years.

The boys of the Dickinson, after a glance at his funny little body and his plaintive, doglike face, had baptized him the "Great Big Man" (Big Man for short), and had elected him the child of the house.

He had never known what homesickness was before. He had had a premonition of it, perhaps, from time to time during the last week, wondering a little in the classroom as each day Snorky Green, beside him, calculated the days until Easter, then the hours, then the minutes. He had watched him with an amused, uncomprehending interest. Why was he so anxious to be off? After all, he, the Big Man, found it a pleasant place, after the wearisome life from hotel to hotel. He liked the boys; they were kind to him, and looked after his moral and spiritual welfare with bluff but affectionate solicitude. It is true, one was always hungry, and only ten-and-a-half hours' sleep was a refinement of cruelty unworthy of a great institution. But it was pleasant running over to the Jigger Shop and doing errands for giants like Reiter and Butcher Stevens, with the privileges of the commission. He liked to be tumbled in the grass by the great tackle of the football eleven, or thrown gently from arm to

* The "shell" is the lowest class.

arm like a medicine ball, quits for the privileges of pummeling his big friends *ad libitum* and without fear of reprisals. And then what a privilege to be allowed to run out on the field and fetch the nose-guard or useless bandage, thrown down haphazard, with the confidence that he, the Big Man, was there to fetch and guard! Then he was permitted to share their studies, to read slowly from handy, literal translations, his head cushioned on the Egghead's knee, while the lounging group swore genially at Pius Æneas or sympathized with Catiline. He shagged elusive balls and paraded the bats at shoulder-arms. He opened the mail, and sorted it, fetching the bag from Farnum's. He was even allowed to stand treat to the mighty men of the house whenever the change in his pocket became too heavy for comfort.

In return he was taught to box, to wind tennis rackets, to blacken shoes, to crease trousers, and sew on the buttons of the House. Nothing was lacking to his complete happiness.

Then lately he had begun to realize that there was something else in the school life, outside it, but very much a part of it—vacation.

At first the idea of quitting such a fascinating life was quite incomprehensible to him. What gorging dinner party could compare with the thrill of feasting at midnight on crackers and cheese, deviled ham, boned chicken, mince pie and root beer by the light of a solitary candle, with the cracks of the doors and windows smothered with rugs and blankets, listening at every mouthful for the tread of the master that sometimes (oh, acme of delight!) actually passed unsuspectingly by the door?

Still, there was a joy in leaving all this. He began to notice it distinctly when the trunks were hauled from the cellar and the packing began. The packing—what a lark that had been! He had folded so many coats and trousers, carefully, in their creases, under Macnooder's generous instructions, and, perched on the edge of the banisters like a queer little marmoset, he had watched Wash Simmons throw great armfuls of assorted clothing into the trays and churn them into place with a baseball bat, while the Triumphant Egghead carefully built up his structure with nicety and tenderness. Only he, the Big Man, sworn to secrecy, knew what Hickey had surreptitiously inserted in the bottom of Egghead's trunk, and also what, from the depths of Wash's muddled clothing, would greet the fond mother or sister who did the unpacking; and every time he thought of it he laughed one of those laughs that pain. Then gleefully he had watched Macnooder stretching a strap until it burst with consequences dire, to the complete satisfaction of Hickey, Turkey, Wash, and the Egghead, who, embracing fondly on the top of another trunk, were assisting Butcher Stevens to close an impossible gap.

Yet into all this amusement a little strain of melancholy had stolen. Here was a sensation of which he was not part, an emotion he did not know. Still, his imagination did not seize it; he could not think of the halls quiet, with no familiar figures lolling out of the windows, or a campus unbrokenly green.

Now from his lonely aerie on Memorial steps, looking down the road to vacation, the Great Big Man suddenly understood—understood and felt. It was he who had gone away, not they. The school he loved was not with him, but roaring down to Trenton. No one had thought to invite him for a visit; but then, why should anyone?

"I'm only a runt, after all," he said angrily to himself. He stuck his fists deep in his pockets, and went down the steps like a soldier and across the campus chanting valorously the football slogan:

> Bill kicked,
> Dunham kicked.
> They both kicked together,
> But Bill kicked mighty hard.
> Flash ran,
> Charlie ran,
> Then Pennington lost her grip;
> She also lost the championship—
> Siss, boom, ah!

After all, he could sleep late; that was something. Then in four days the baseball squad would return, and there would be long afternoon practices to watch, lolling on the turf, with an occasional foul to retrieve. He would read *The Count of Monte Cristo,* and follow *The Three Musketeers* through a thousand far-off adventures, and *Lorna Doone*—there was always the great John Ridd, bigger even than Turkey or the Waladoo Bird.

He arrived resolutely at the Dickinson, and started up the deserted stairs for his room. There was only one thing he feared; he did not want Mrs. Rogers, wife of the housemaster, to "mother" him. Anything but that! He was glad that after luncheon he would have to take his meals at the Lodge. That would avert embarrassing situations, for whatever his friends might think, he, the Great Big Man, was a runt in stature only.

To express fully the excessive gaiety he enjoyed, he tramped to his room, bawling out:

'Tis a jolly life we lead,
Care and sorrow we defy.

All at once a gruff voice spoke:

"My, what a lot of noise for a Great Big Man!"

The Big Man stopped thunderstruck. The voice came from Butcher Stevens' room. Cautiously he tiptoed down the hall and paused, with his funny little nose and eyes peering around the door jamb. Sure enough, there was Butcher, and there were the Butcher's trunks and bags. What could it mean?

"I say," he began, according to etiquette, "is that you, Butcher?"

"Very much so, Big Man."

"What are you doing here?"

"The faculty, Big Man, desire my presence," said the Butcher, sarcastically. "They would like my expert advice on a few problems that are perplexing them."

"Ah," said the Great Big Man, slowly. Then he understood. The Butcher had been caught two nights before returning by Sawtelle's window at a very late hour. He did not know exactly the facts because he had been told not to be too inquisitive, and he was accustomed to obeying instructions. Supposing the faculty should expel him! To the Big Man such a sentence meant the end of all things, something too horrible to contemplate. So he said, "Oh, Butcher, is it serious?"

"Rather, youngster; rather, I should say."

"What *will* the baseball team do?" said the Big Man, overwhelmed.

"That's what's worrying me," replied the crack first baseman, gloomily. He rose and went to the window, where he stood beating a tattoo.

"You don't suppose Crazy Opdyke could cover the bag, do you?" said the Big Man.

"Lord, no!"

"How about Stubby?"

"Too short."

"They might do something with the Waladoo."

"Not for first; he can't stop anything below his knees."

"Then I don't see how we're going to beat Andover, Butcher."

"It does look bad."

"Do you think the faculty will—will—"

"Fire me? Pretty certain, youngster."

"Oh, Butcher!"

"Trouble is, they've got the goods on me—dead to rights."

"But does the Doctor know how it'll break up the nine?"

Butcher laughed loudly.

"He doesn't *ap*-preciate that, youngster."

"No," said the Big Man, reflectively. "They never do, do they?"

The luncheon bell rang, and they hurried down. The Big Man was overwhelmed by the discovery. If Butcher didn't cover first, how could they ever beat Andover and the Princeton freshmen? Even Hill School and Pennington might trounce them. He fell into a brown melancholy until suddenly he caught the sympathetic glance of Mrs. Rogers on him, and for fear that she would think it was due to his own weakness, he began to chat volubly.

He had always been a little in awe of the Butcher. Not that the Butcher had not been friendly; but he was so blunt and rough and unbending that he rather repelled intimacy. He watched him covertly, admiring the bravado with which he pretended unconcern. It must be awful to be threatened with expulsion and actually to be expelled, to have your whole life ruined, once and forever—the Big Man's heart was stirred. He said to himself that he had not been sympathetic enough, and he resolved to repair the error. So, luncheon over, he said with an appearance of carelessness, "I say, old man, come on over to the Jigger Shop. I'll set 'em up. I'm pretty flush, you know."

The Butcher looked down at the funny face and saw the kindly motive under the exaggerated bluffness. Being touched by it, he said gruffly, "Well, come on, then, you old billionaire!"

The Big Man felt a great movement of sympathy in him for his big comrade. He would have liked to slip his little fist in the great brown hand and say something appropriate, only he could think of nothing appropriate. Then he remembered that among men there should be no letting down, no sentimentality. So he lounged along, squinting up at the Butcher and trying to copy his rolling gait.

At the Jigger Shop, Al lifted his eyebrows in well-informed disapproval, saying curtly, "What are you doing here, you Butcher, you?"

"Building up my constitution," said Stevens, with a frown. "I'm staying because I like it, of course. Lawrenceville is just lovely at Easter: spring birds and violets, and that sort of thing."

"You're a nice one," said Al, a baseball enthusiast. "Why couldn't you behave until after the Andover game?"

"Of course; but you needn't rub it in," replied the Butcher, staring at the floor. "Give me a double strawberry, and heave it over."

Al, seeing him not insensible, relented. He added another dab to the double jigger already delivered, and said, shoving over the glass, "It's pretty hard luck on the team, Butcher. There's no one hereabouts can hold down the bag like you. Heard anything definite?"

"No."

"What do you think?"

"I'd hate to say."

"Is anyone doing anything?"

"Cap Kiefer is to see the Doctor tonight."

"I say, Butcher," said the Big Man, in sudden fear, "you won't go up to Andover and play against us, will you?"

"Against the school! Well, rather not!" said the Butcher, indignantly. Then he added, "No; if they fire me, I know what I'll do."

The Big Man wondered if he contemplated suicide; that must be the natural thing to do when one is expelled. He felt that he must keep near Butcher, close all the day. So he made bold to wander about with him, watching him with solicitude.

They stopped at Lalo's for a hot dog, and lingered at Bill Appleby's, where the Butcher mournfully tried the new mitts and swung the bats with critical consideration. Then feeling hungry, they trudged up to Conover's for pancakes and syrup. Everywhere was the same feeling of dismay; what would become of the baseball nine?

Then it suddenly dawned upon the Big Man that no one seemed to be sorry on the Butcher's account. He stopped with a pancake poised on his fork, looked about to make sure no one could hear him, and blurted out, "I say, Butcher, it's not only on account of first base, you know; I'm darn sorry for *you*, honest!"

"Why, you profane little cuss," said the Butcher, frowning, "who told you to swear?"

"Don't make fun of me, Butcher," said the Great Big Man, feeling very little; "I meant it."

"Conover," said the Butcher, loudly, "more pancakes, and brown 'em!'"

He, too, had been struck by the fact that in the general mourning there had been scant attention paid to his personal fortunes. He had prided himself on the fact that he was not susceptible to "feelings," that he neither gave nor asked for sympathy. He was older than his associates, but years had never reconciled him to Latin or Greek or, for that matter, to mathematics in simple or aggravated form. He had been the bully of his village out in northern Iowa, and when a stranger came, he trounced him first, and cemented the friendship afterward. He liked hard knocks, give and take. He liked the school because there was the long football season in the autumn, with the joy of battling, with every sinew of the body alert and the humming of cheers indistinctly heard, as he rammed through the yielding line. Then the spring meant long hours of romping over the smooth diamond, cutting down impossible hits, guarding first base like a bulldog, pulling down the high ones, smothering the wild throws that came ripping along the ground, threatening to jump up against his eyes, throws that other fellows dodged. He was in the company of equals, of good fighters, like Charley De Soto, Hickey, Flash Condit, and Turkey, fellows it was a joy to fight beside. Also, it was good to feel that four hundred-odd wearers of the red and black put their trust in him, and that trust became very sacred to him. He played hard—very hard, but cleanly, because combat was the joy of his life to him. He broke other rules, not as a lark, but out of the same fierce desire for battle, to seek out danger wherever he could find it. He had been caught fair and square, and he knew that for that particular offense there was only one punishment. Yet he hoped against hope, suddenly realizing what it would cost him to give up the great school where, however, he had never sought friendships or anything beyond the admiration of his mates.

The sympathy of the Big Man startled him, then made him

uncomfortable. He had no intention of crying out, and he did not like or understand the new emotion that rose in him as he wondered when his sentence would come.

"Well, youngster," he said, gruffly, "had enough? Have another round?"

"I've had enough," said the Big Man, heaving a sigh. "Let me treat, Butcher."

"Not today, youngster."

"Butcher, I—I'd like to. I'm awfully flush."

"Not today."

"Let's match for it."

"What!" said the Butcher, fiercely. "Don't let me hear any more of that talk. You've got to grow up first."

The Big Man, thus rebuked, acquiesced meekly. The two strolled back to the campus in silence.

"Suppose we have a catch," said the Big Man, tentatively.

"All right," said the Butcher, smiling.

Entrenched behind a gigantic mitt, the Big Man strove valorously to hold the difficult balls. After a long period of this mitigated pleasure they sat down to rest. Then Cap Kiefer's stocky figure appeared around the Dickinson, and the Butcher went off for a long, solemn consultation.

The Big Man, thus relieved of responsibility, felt terribly alone. He went to his room and took down volume two of *The Count of Monte Cristo,* and stretched out on the window seat. Somehow the stupendous adventures failed to enthrall him. It was still throughout the house. He caught himself listening for the patter of Hickey's shoes above, dancing a breakdown, or the rumble of Egghead's laugh down the hall, or a voice calling, "Who can lend me a pair of suspenders?"

And the window was empty. It seemed so strange to look up from the printed page and find no one in the Woodhull opposite, shaving painfully at the window, or lolling like himself over a novel, all the time keeping an eye on the life below. He could not jeer at Two Inches Brown and Crazy Opdyke practicing curves, nor assure them that the Dickinson nine would just fatten on those easy ones. No one halloed from house to house, no voice below drawled out, "Oh, you Great Big Man! Stick your head out of the window!"

There was no one to call across for the time o' day, or for just a nickel to buy stamps, or for the loan of a baseball glove, or a sweater, or a collar button, scissors, button-hook, or fifty and one articles that are never bought but borrowed.

The Great Big Man let *The Count of Monte Cristo* tumble unheeded on the floor, seized a tennis ball, and went across the campus to the esplanade of the Upper House, where for half an hour he bounced the ball against the rim of the ledge, a privilege that only a fourth former may enjoy. Tiring of this, he wandered down to the pond where he skimmed innumerable flat stones until he had exhausted the attractions of this limited amusement.

"I—I'm getting homesick," he admitted finally. "I wish I had a dog—something living—around."

At suppertime he saw the Butcher again, and forgot his own loneliness in the concern he felt for his big friend. He remembered that the Butcher had said that if he were expelled he knew what he would do. What had he meant by that? Something terrible. He glanced up at the Butcher and, being very apprehensive, made bold to ask, "Butcher, I say, what does Cap think?"

"He hasn't seen the Doctor yet," said the Butcher. "He'll see him tonight. I guess I'll go over myself, just to leave a calling card accordin' to *et*-iquette!"

The Big Man kept his own counsel but when the Butcher, after dinner, disappeared through the awful portal of Foundation House, he sat down in the dark under a distant tree to watch. In a short five minutes the Butcher reappeared, stood a moment undecided on the steps, stooped, picked up a handful of gravel, flung it into the air with a laugh, and started along the circle.

"Butcher!"

"Hello, who's that!"

"It's me, Butcher," said the Big Man, slipping his hand into the other's; "I—I wanted to know."

"You aren't going to get sentimental, are you, youngster?" said Stevens, disapprovingly.

"Please, Butcher," said the Great Big Man, pleadingly, "don't be cross with me! Is there any hope?"

"The Doctor won't see me, young one," said the Butcher, "but the *at*-mosphere was not encouraging."

"I'm sorry."

"Honest?"

"Honest."

"You *damn* little runt!"

They went hand in hand over to the chapel, where they chose the back steps and settled down with the great walls at their back and plenty of gravel at their feet to fling aimlessly into the dusky night.

"Butcher?"

"Well, Big Man!"

"What will you do if—if they fire you?"

"Oh, lots of things. I'll go hunting for gold somewhere, or strike out for South America or Africa."

"Oh!" The Big Man was immensely relieved; but he added incredulously, "Then you'll give up football and baseball?"

"Looks that way."

"You won't mind?"

"Yes," said the Butcher, suddenly, "I will mind. I'll hate to leave the old school. I'd like to have one chance more."

"Why don't you tell the Doctor that?"

"Never! I don't cry out when I'm caught, youngster. I take my punishment."

"Yes," said the Big Man, reflecting. "That's right, I suppose; but, then, there's the team to think of, you know."

They sat for a long time in silence, broken suddenly by the Butcher's voice, not so gruff as usual.

"Say, Big Man—feeling sort of homesick?"

No answer.

"Just a bit?"

Still no answer. The Butcher looked down, and saw the Big Man struggling desperately to hold in the sobs.

"Here, none of that, youngster!" he exclaimed in alarm. "Brace up, old man!"

"I—I'm all right," said the Great Big Man with difficulty. "It's nothing."

The Butcher patted him on the shoulder, and then drew his arm around the little body. The Big Man put his head down and blubbered, just as though he had been a little fellow, while his companion sat perplexed, wondering what to do or say in the strange situation.

"So he's a little homesick, is he?" he said lamely.

"No-o-o," said the Great Big Man, "not just that; it's—it's all the fellows I miss."

The Butcher was silent. He, too, began to understand that feeling; only he, in his battling pride, fiercely resisted the weakness.

"You've got an uncle somewhere, haven't you, youngster?" he said gently. "Doesn't he look after you in vacation time?"

"I don't miss *him*," replied the Big Man, shaking his head. Then he pulled himself together and said apologetically, "It's just being left behind that makes me such a damned cry-baby."

"Youngster," said the Butcher, sternly, "your language is *atrocious*. Such words do not sound well in the mouth of a suckling of your size."

"I didn't mean to," said the Big Man, blushing.

"You must leave something to grow up for, young man," said the Butcher, profoundly. "Now tell me about that uncle of yours. I don't fancy his silhouette."

The Great Big Man, thus encouraged, poured out his lonely, starved little heart, while the Butcher listened sympathetically, feeling a certain comfort in sitting with his arm around a little fellow being. Not that he was sensible of giving much comfort; his comments, he felt, were certainly inadequate; nor did he measure in any way up to the situation.

"Now it's better, eh, Big Man?" he said at last when the little fellow had stopped. "Does you sort of good to talk things out."

"Oh, yes; thank you, Butcher."

"All right, then, youngster."

"All right. I say, you—you don't ever feel that way, do you—homesick, I mean?"

"Not much."

"You've got a home, haven't you?"

"Quite too much, young one. If they fire me, I'll keep away from there. Strike out for myself."

"Of course, then, it's different."

"Young one," said the Butcher, suddenly, "that's not quite honest. If I have to clear out of here, it will cut me up *con*-siderable."

"Honest?"

"A fact. I didn't know it before; but it will cut me up to strike out and leave all this behind. I want another chance; and do you know why?"

"Why?"

"I'd like to make friends. Oh, I haven't got any real friends, youngster; you needn't shake your head. It's my fault. I know it. You're the first mortal soul who cared what became of me. All the rest are thinking of the team."

"Now, Butcher—"

"Lord, don't think I'm crying out!" said the Butcher, in instant alarm. "It's all been up to me. Truth is, I've been too darned proud. But I'd like to get another whack at it."

"Perhaps you will, Butcher."

"No, no, there's no reason why I should." The Butcher sat solemnly a moment, flinging pebbles down into the dark tennis courts. Suddenly he said, "Look here, Big Man, I'm going to give you some good advice."

"All right, Butcher."

"And I want you to tuck it away in your thinker—*savez?* You're a nice kid now, a good sort, but you've got a lot of chances for being spoiled. Don't get fresh. Don't get a swelled head just because a lot of the older fellows let you play around. There's nothing so hateful in the sight of God or man as a fresh kid."

"You don't think—" began the Big Man in dismay.

"No; you're all right now. You're quiet, and don't tag around, and you're a good sort, darned if you aren't, and that's why I don't want to see you spoiled. Now a straight question: Do you smoke?"

"Why, that is—well, Butcher, I did try once a puff on Snookers' cigarette."

"You ought to be spanked!" said the Butcher, angrily. "And when I get hold of Snookers, I'll tan him. The idea of his letting you! Don't you monkey around tobacco yet a while. First of all, it's fresh, and second, you've got to *grow*. You want to make a team, don't you, while you're here?"

"O-o-oh!" said the Great Big Man with a long sigh.

"Then just stick to growing. 'Cause you've got work cut out for you there. Now I'm not preachin'; I'm saying that you want to fill out and grow up and do something. Harkee."

"All right."

"Cut out Snookers and that gang. Pick out the fellows that count, as you go along, and just remember this, if you forget the rest: if you want to put ducks in Tabby's bed or nail down his desk, do it because *you* want to do it, not because some other fellow wants you to do it. D'ye hear?"

"Yes, Butcher."

"Remember that, youngster; if I'd stuck to it, I'd kept out of a peck of trouble." He reflected a moment and added, "Then I'd study a little. It's not a bad thing, I guess, in the long run, and it gets the masters on your side. And now jump up and we'll trot home."

The following night the Big Man, again under his tree, waited for the result of the conference that was going on inside Foundation House between the Doctor and the Butcher and Cap Kiefer. It was long, very long. The minutes went slowly, and it was very dark there, with hardly a light showing in the circle of houses that ordinarily seemed like a procession of lighted ferryboats. After an interminable hour, the Butcher and Cap came out. He needed no word to tell what their attitudes showed only too plainly: the Butcher was expelled!

The Big Man waited until the two had passed into the night, and then, with a sudden resolve, went bravely to the doorbell and rang. Before he quite appreciated the audacity of his act, he found himself in the sanctum facing a much-perplexed headmaster.

"Doctor, I—I—" The Big Man stopped, overwhelmed by the awful majesty of the Doctor, on whose face still sat the grimness of the past conference.

"Well, Joshua, what's the matter?" said the headmaster, relaxing a bit before one of his favorites.

"Please, sir, I'm a little—a little embarrassed, I'm afraid," said the Great Big Man, desperately.

"Am I so terrible as all that?" said the Doctor, smiling.

"Yes, sir—you are," the Big Man replied frankly. Then he said, plunging in, "Doctor, is the Butcher—is Stevens—are you going to—expel him?"

"That is my painful duty, Joshua," said the Doctor, frowning.

"Oh, Doctor," said the Big Man all in a breath, "you don't know —you're making a mistake."

"I am? Why, Joshua?"

"Because—you don't know. Because the Butcher won't tell you, he's too proud, sir; because he doesn't want to cry out, sir."

"What do you mean exactly?" said the Doctor in surprise. "Does Stevens know you're here?"

"Oh, Heavens, no, sir!" said the Big Man in horror. "And you must never tell him, sir; that would be too terrible."

"Joshua," said the Doctor, impressively, "I am expelling Stevens because he is just the influence I don't want boys of your age to come under."

"Oh, yes, sir," said the Big Man, "I know you think that, sir; but really, Doctor, that's where you are wrong; really you are, sir."

The Doctor saw there was something under the surface, and he encouraged the little fellow to talk. The Big Man, forgetting all fear in the seriousness of the situation, told the listening headmaster all the Butcher's conversation with him on the chapel steps the night before—told it simply and eloquently, with an ardor that bespoke absolute faith. Then suddenly he stopped.

"That's all, sir," he said, frightened.

The Doctor rose and walked back and forth, troubled and perplexed. There was no doubting the sincerity of the recital; it was a side of Stevens he had not guessed. Finally he turned and rested his hand on the Big Man's shoulders.

"Thank you," he said; "it does put another light on the question. I'll think it over."

When, ten days later, the school came trickling home along the road from vacation, they saw, against all hope, the Butcher holding down first base, frolicking over the diamond in the old familiar way, and a great shout of joy and relief went up. But how it had happened no one ever knew, least of all Cap and the Butcher, who had gone from Foundation House that night in settled despair.

To add to Butcher's mystification, the Doctor, in announcing his reprieve, had added, "I've decided to make a change, Stevens. I'm going to put Tibbetts in to room with you. I place him in your charge. I'm going to try a little responsibility on you."

THE POLITICAL EDUCATION
OF MR. BALDWIN

IF HICKEY had not been woefully weak in mathematics the famous Fed and anti-Fed riots would probably never have happened. But as revolutions turn on minor axes, Hickey, who could follow a football like a hound, could not for the life of him trace X, the unknown factor, through the hedges of the simplest equation.

It was, therefore, with feelings of the acutest interest that he waited, in the upper corridor of Memorial Hall, on the opening morning of the spring term, for the appearance of Mr. Baldwin, the new recruit to the mathematics department. The Hall was choked with old boys chattering over the doings of the Easter vacation, calling back and forth, punching one another affectionately, or critically examining the returning stragglers.

"His name is Ernest Garrison Baldwin," said the Gutter Pup. "Just graduated, full of honors and that sort of thing."

"He ought to be easy," said Crazy Opdyke, hopefully.

"These mathematical sharks are always fancy markers," interposed Macnooder.

"If I'm stuck in the first row," said the Egghead gloomily, "it's all up—I never could do anything with figures."

"If we want short lessons," said Hickey, waking out of his reverie, "we've all got to flunk in the beginning."

At this Machiavellian analysis there was a chorus of assent.

"Sure."

"Hickey's the boy!"

"Red Dog and Poler Fox have got to be kept down."

"We're not packhorses."

"Say, is he green?"

"Sure—never taught before."

"Cheese it—he's coming."

The group stood aside, intent on the arrival of the new adversary. They saw a stiff young man, already bald, with a set, affable manner and a pervading smile of cordiality, who entered the classroom with a confident step, after a nodded, "Ah, boys—good morning."

The class filed in, eyeing the natural enemy closely for the first indications of value to aid them in the approaching conflicts.

"He's awfully serious," said the Egghead to his neighbor.

"He'll try to drive us," replied Macnooder, with instinctive resentment.

Hickey said nothing, absorbed in contemplation of a momentous question—how would the new master hear recitations? To solve a master's system is to be prepared in advance, and with the exception of the Roman's there was not a system which he had not solved. Popular masters, like Pa Dater, called you up every third day, which is eminently just and conducive to a high standard of scholarship. The Muffin Head, in stealthy craftiness, had a way of calling you up twice in succession after you had flunked and were expecting a brief period of immunity; but this system once solved gave ample opportunity to redeem yourself. The Doctor, wiser than the rest, wrote each name on a card, shuffled the pack and called for a recitation according to chance—but even the Doctor left the pack on his desk, nor counted the cards as all careful players should. Other masters, like Tapping and Baranson, trusted to their intuitions, seizing upon the boy whose countenance betrayed a lurking apprehension. Hickey took kindly to this method and had thrived amazingly, by sudden flagrant inattentions or noticeable gazing out of the windows, which invariably procured him a staccato summons to recite just as the recitation neared the limited portion he had studied.

So Hickey sat, examining Mr. Baldwin, and speculating into which classification he would fall.

"Now, boys," said Mr. Baldwin, with an expanding smile, "we're beginning the new term. I hope you'll like me—I know I shall like you. I'm quite a boy myself—quite a boy, you know. Now I'm going ahead on a new principle. I'm going to assume that you all take an interest in your work [the class sat up]. I'm going to assume that you look upon life with seriousness and purpose. I'm going to assume that you realize the sacrifices your parents are making to afford you an education. I'm not here as a taskmaster. I'm here to help you, as your friend, as your companion—as an older brother—that's it, as an older brother. I hope our interest in one another will not be limited to this classroom."

Hickey and the Egghead, who had prominently installed themselves in the front seats, led the applause with serious, responsive faces. Mr. Baldwin acknowledged it, noticing pleasantly the leaders of the demonstration.

Then he rapped for order and began to call the roll, seating the boys alphabetically. He ran rapidly through the F's, the G's and H's and, pausing, inquired, "Are there any J's in the class?"

At this excruciatingly witty remark, which every master annually blunders upon, the waiting class roared in unison, while Hinsdale was forced to slap Hickey mercilessly on the back to save him from violent hysterics.

Mr. Baldwin, who suddenly perceived he had made a pun, hastily assumed a roguish expression and allowed a considerable moment for laughter to die away. The session ended in a gale of cordiality.

Hickey and the Egghead paid a visit that afternoon to the Griswold, to make the new arrival feel quite at home.

"Ah, boys," said Mr. Baldwin, with a wringing handshake, "this is very friendly of you, very friendly."

"Mr. Baldwin," said Hickey seriously, "we were very much interested in what you said to us this morning."

"Indeed," said Baldwin, gratified. "Well, that pleases me very much. And I am glad to see that you take me at my word, and I hope you will drop in often. There are lots of things I want to talk over with you."

"Yes, sir," said the Egghead. "It's very kind of you."

"Not at all," said Baldwin, with a wave of his hand. "My theory is that a master should be your companion, and I have one or two ideas about education I am anxious to have my boys interested in. Now, for instance, take politics; what do you know about politics?"

"Why, nothing," said Hickey in acquiescent surprise.

"And yet that is the most vital thing you will have to face as men. Here's a great national election approaching, and yet, I am certain not one in four hundred of you has any clear conception of the political system."

"That's so, Egghead," said Hickey, nodding impressively at his companion. "It *is* so."

"I have a scheme I'm going to talk over with you," continued Baldwin, "and I want your advice. Sit down; make yourselves comfortable."

Later in the afternoon Mr. Baranson, Baldwin's superior in the Griswold, dropped in with a friendly inquiry. Young Mr. Baldwin was gazing out of the window in indulgent amusement. Mr. Baranson, following his gaze, beheld, in the far campus, Hickey and Egghead rolling over each other like two trick bears.

"Well, Baldwin, how goes it?" said Baranson genially.

"Splendidly. The boys are more than friendly. We shall get on famously."

" 'Danaos timeo et dona ferentes,' " said Baranson shrewdly.

"Oh—" Baldwin objected.

"Yes, yes—I'm an old fogy—old style," said Baranson, cutting in, "but it's based on good scientific researches, Baldwin. I just dropped in for a hint or two, which you won't pay attention to—never mind. When you've lived with the young human animal as long as I have, you won't have any illusions. He doesn't want to be enlightened. He hasn't the slightest desire to be educated. He isn't educated. He never will be. His memory simply *detains* for a short while, a larger and larger number of facts—Latin, Greek, history, mathematics, it's all the same—facts, nothing but facts. He remembers when he is compelled to, but he is supremely bored by the performance. All he wants is to grow, to play and to get into sufficient mischief. My dear fellow, treat him as a splendid young savage, who breaks a rule for the joy of matching his wits against yours, and don't take him seriously, as you are in danger of doing. Don't let him take you seriously or he will lead you to a cropper."

Ernest Garrison Baldwin did not deign to reply—the voice of the older generation, of course! He was of the new, he would replace old prejudices with new methods. There were a great many things in the world he intended to change—among others this whole antagonistic spirit of education. So he remained silent, and looked very dignified.

Baranson studied him, saw the workings of his mind, and smiled.

"Never were at boarding school, were you?" he asked.

"No," said Baldwin, drily.

Baranson gave a glance at the study, remarked the advanced note in the shelves, and went to the door.

"After all," he said, with his hand on the knob, "the first year, Baldwin, we learn more than we teach."

"Gee! I think it's an awful bore," said the Gutter Pup.

"I don't see it either," said the Egghead.

"Who started it?" asked Turkey Reiter.

"Hickey and Elder Brother Baldwin," said the Egghead. "Hickey's improving his stand."

"Hickey, boy," said Butcher Stevens, professionally, "you're consorting with awful low company."

"Hickey, you are getting to be a greasy grind," said the Gutter Pup.

"I am, am I," said Hickey indignantly. "I'd like to know if I'm not a patriot. I'd like to know if I'm not responsible for the atmosphere of brotherly love and the dove of peace that floats around Baldwin's classroom. I'd like to know if I'm not responsible for his calling us up alphabetically, regular order, every other day, no suspicion, perfect trust—mutual confidence. Am I right?"

"You are right, Hickey, you are right," said Turkey apologetically. "The binomial theorem is a delight and a joy, when, as you say, the master has mutual trust in the scholar. But where in blazes, Hickey, did you get this political shindy into your thinker?"

"It's Elder Brother's theory of education," said Hickey carefully, "*one* of his theories. Elder Brother is very much distressed at the ignorance, the political ignorance, of the modern boy. Brother is right."

"Come off," said the Egghead, glancing at him suspiciously, but Hickey maintained a serious face.

"What's up?" said Macnooder, sauntering over to the crowd on the lawn.

"Hickey's fixed up a plan with Brotherly Love to have a political campaign," said the Gutter Pup, "and is trying to rouse our enthusiasm."

"A campaign here in the school, in the Lawrenceville School, John C. Green Foundation!" said Macnooder incredulously.

"The same!"

"No! I won't believe it. It's a dream—it's a beautiful, satisfying dream," said Macnooder, shaking his head. "A political campaign in school; Hickey, my bounding boy, I see your cunning hand!"

"Now Doc's gone nutty," said the unimaginative Egghead. "What the deuce do you see in it?"

"Hickey, you old rambunctious, foxy, prodigious Hickey, I knew something was brewing," said Doc, not deigning to notice the Egghead. "You have been quiet, most quiet of late. Hickey, how did you do it?"

"Sympathy, Doc," said Hickey blandly. "I've been most sympathetic with Elder Brother, sympathetic and most encouraging. Sympathy is a beautiful thing, Doc, beautiful and rare."

"Hickey, don't torture me with curiosity," said Doc. "Where are we at?"

"At the present moment, Brother is asking the Doctor for permission to launch the campaign, and the sympathetic, popular and serious Hickey Hicks is proceeding to select a preliminary conference committee."

"And what then?" said Turkey, with sudden interest.

"What then?" said Hickey. "Bonfires, parades, stump speeches, proclamations, et cetera, et ceteray."

"Oh, Hickey," said the now enthusiastic Gutter Pup, "do you think the Doctor ever will permit it?"

"What's the use of getting excited?" said the Egghead contemptuously. "You don't fancy for a moment, do you, there's a chance of fooling the Doctor?"

"Sure, Egghead's right," said Butcher Stevens; "you won't get the Doctor to bite. Baldwin is green, but the Doctor is quite ripe, thank you!"

Even Macnooder looked dubiously at Hickey, who assumed an air of superhuman wisdom and answered, "I have two chances, Baldwin and the De-coy Ducks!"

"The what?"

"Decoy Ducks—the committee that will confer tomorrow afternoon with the Doctor."

Turkey emitted a long, admiring whistle.

"I have given the matter thought—serious thought, as Baldwin would say," said Hickey. "The following collection of Archangels and young High Markers will be rounded up for the Doctor's inspection tomorrow."

"As Decoy Ducks?"

"As Decoy Ducks, you intelligent Turkey. High Markers: Red Dog, Poler Fox, Biddy Hampton and Ginger Pop Rooker, Wash Simmons—the Doctor would feed out of Wash's hand—Crazy Opdyke—he reads Greek like Jules Verne. Everything must be done to make this a strictly ed-u-cational affair. Now to demonstrate that it has the sanction of the religious element of this community the following notorious and flagrant Archangels will qualify: Halo Brown, Pink Rabbit, Parson Eddy, and Saphead and the Coffee Cooler—the Doctor is real affectionate with the Coffee Cooler."

"What a beoo-ti-ful bunch!" said the Gutter Pup rapturously.

"It is," said Hickey, proudly; "the Doctor would let any one of them correct his own examination papers and raise the mark afterward on the ground of overconscientiousness."

"Well, where's the fun?" said the Egghead obstinately. "If Crazy Opdyke and that bunch is to run the campaign, where do we come in?"

"There will be a small preliminary representation of professional politicians," said Hickey, smiling, "very small at present, limited to the handsome and popular Hickey Hicks, who will represent the large body of professional politicians who will be detained at home by hard work and serious application, but—"

"But what?" said Macnooder.

"But who will find time to ac-tively assist this quiet, orderly campaign of education, *after* their presence will not be misunderstood!"

At half-past one the next day, the Doctor, sympathetically inclined by the enthusiastic, if inexperienced, Mr. Baldwin, received the Decoy Ducks in his study at Foundation House.

The Doctor, while interested, had not been convinced, and had expressed a desire to know into whose guidance the nurturing of such a tender plant had been entrusted. As the impresssive gathering defiled before him, his instinctive caution vanished, his glance warmed with satisfaction, and assuming the genial and conversational attitude he reserved for his favorites, he began:

"Well, boys, this appears to be a responsible gathering, an unusually responsible one. It is gratifying to see you approaching such subjects with serious purpose and earnestness. It is gratifying that the leaders of this school" (here his glance rested fondly on Wash Simmons, Crazy Opdyke and the Coffee Cooler, prominently placed) "that the earnest, purposeful boys show this interest in the political welfare of the nation. Mr. Baldwin's plan seems to me to be a most excellent one. I am in hearty accord with its motive. We cannot begin too soon to interest the youth, the intelligent, serious youth of our country in honest government and clean political methods." (Hickey, in noble effacement by the window seat, here gazed dreamily over the campus to the red circle of houses.) "Much can be accomplished from the earnest and purposeful pursuit of this instructive experiment. The experiment should be educational in the largest sense; the more I study it the more worthy it appears. I should not be surprised if your experiment should attract the consideration of the educational world. Mr. Baldwin, it gives me pleasure to express to you my thanks and my gratification for the authorship of so worthy an undertaking. I will leave you to a discussion of the necessary details."

"Well, boys," said Baldwin briskly, "let me briefly outline the plan agreed upon. The election shall be for a school council, before which legislation affecting the interests of the school shall come. Each of the four forms shall elect two representatives, each of the ten houses shall elect one representative, making a deliberative body of eighteen. In view of the fact that the approaching national election might inject unnecessary bitterness if the election should be on national issues, we have decided, on the very excellent suggestion of Hicks, who has indeed given many valuable suggestions" (Hickey looked preternaturally solemn), "to have the election on a matter of school policy, and have settled upon the athletic finances as an issue of sufficient interest and yet one that can be calmly and orderly discussed. At present, the management of the athletic finances is in the hands of selected officers from the fourth form. The issue, then, is whether this method shall be continued or whether a member of the faculty shall administer the finances. I should suggest Federalists and Anti-Federalists as names for the parties you will form. One week will be given to campaigning and the election will take place according to the Australian ballot system. Now, boys, I wish you success. You will acquire a taste for public combat and a facility in the necessary art of politics that will nurture in you a desire to enter public life, to take your part in the fight for honest politics, clean methods, independent thinking, and will make you foes of intimidation, bribery, cheating and that demagoguery that is the despair of our present system. At present you may be indifferent, a little bored, perhaps, at this experiment, but you will like it—I am sure you will like it. I prophesy it will interest you once you get started."

Hickey lingered after the meeting to explain that the duties incident to the organizing of such an important undertaking had unfortunately deprived him of the time necessary to prepare his advanced algebra.

"Well, that is a little matter we'll overlook, Hicks," said the enthusiast genially. "I congratulate you on your selection, an admirable committee, one that inspires confidence. Keep me in touch with developments and call on me for advice at any time."

"Yes, indeed, sir."

"Good luck."

"Thank you, sir."

A half hour later Hickey announced the addition of the following professional politicians: Tough McCarty, Doc Macnooder, the Triumphant Egghead, Slugger Jones, Turkey Reiter, Cheyenne Baxter, Jock Hasbrouck, Butcher Stevens, Rock Bemis, and Bat Greer.

The reinforced committee then met, divided equitably, and having tossed for sides, announced their organization, as follows:

FEDERALIST PARTY
Chairman: THE HON. TOUGH McCARTY
Vice-Chairman: THE HON. GINGER POP ROOKER
ANTI-FEDERALIST PARTY
Chairman: HON. CHEYENNE BAXTER
Vice-Chairman: HON. HICKEY HICKS

The school was at first apathetic, then mildly interested. The scheme was examined with suspicion as perhaps being a veiled attempt of the faculty to increase the already outrageous taxes on the mind. It looked prosy enough at first glance—perhaps an attempt to revive the interest in debating and so to be fiercely resisted.

For an hour the great campaign for political education hung fire and then suddenly it began to catch on. A few leading imaginations had seen the latent possibilities. In another hour apathy had disappeared and every house was discussing the momentous question whether to go Fed or Anti-Fed.

The executive committee of the Federalist party met immediately, on a call from the Honorable Cheyenne Baxter, in the Triumphant Egghead's rooms for organization and conference.

"We've got the short end of it, all right, all right," said Butcher Stevens gloomily. "The idea of our standing up for the faculty."

"That's right, Cheyenne," said Turkey, shaking his head. "We'll be left high and dry."

"We won't carry any house outside the Dickinson and the Woodhull," said Slugger Jones.

"I'd like to make a suggestion," said Crazy Opdyke.

"We've got to plan two campaigns," said Cheyenne, "one for the election from the forms and one for the control of the houses. Let's take up the forms—the fourth form will go solidly against us."

"Sure," said Doc Macnooder, "because if we win they lose control of the finances."

"I have a suggestion," said Crazy Opdyke for the second time.

"Now," said Cheyenne, "we've got to make this a matter of the school against the fourth form, and it oughtn't to be so hard, either. Now, how're we going to do it? First, what have we got?"

"The Dickinson and the Woodhull," said Hickey.

"Yes, we can be sure of those, but that's all. Now, those Feds, with Jock Hasbrouck and Tough McCarty, will swing the Kennedy and the Griswold."

"The Davis House will be against us," said Macnooder, with conviction. "They're just aching to get back at the Dickinson."

"That's so," said Turkey. "They're still sore because we won the football championship."

"The Davis will pull the Rouse House with it," said Hickey gloomily. "They're forty in the Davis and only twelve in the Rouse.

The Davis would mangle them if they ever dared go our way."

"We've got to counteract that by getting the Green," said Cheyenne. "They're only ten there, but it makes a vote. The fight'll be in the Hamill and the Cleve."

"The Cleve is sore on us," said Turkey of the Dickinson, "because we swiped the ice cream last year for their commencement dinner."

"I've got an idea," said Crazy Opdyke, trying to be heard.

"Shut up, Crazy," said Doc. "You've served your purpose; you're a Decoy Duck and nothing else."

"Harmony!" said Cheyenne warningly. "The way to get the Green is to give Butsey White, down there, the nomination from the second form, if he'll swing the house."

"And put up Bronc Andrews in the Hamill," added Macnooder.

"Where do I come in?" said Crazy Opdyke, who had aspirations.

"You subordinate yourself to the success of your party," said Cheyenne.

"The devil I do," said Opdyke. "If you think I'm a backwater delegate, you've got another think coming. I may be a Decoy Duck, but either I'm made chairman of a Finance Committee or I lead a bolt right out of this convention."

"A Finance Committee?" said Butcher Stevens, mystified.

"Sure," said Cheyenne Baxter. "That's most important."

"I'll take that myself, then," said Macnooder aggressively. "I'd like to know what claim Crazy's got to a position of trust and responsibility."

"Claim or no claim," said Opdyke, pulling his hat over his eyes and tilting back, "either I handle the funds of this here campaign or the Anti-Federalist party begins to split."

"Shall a half-plucked rooster from the Cleve House hold up this convention?" said Wash Simmons militantly. "If we're going to be blackjacked by every squid that comes down the road, *I'm* going to get out."

"I have spoken," said Crazy.

"So have I."

"Gentlemen, gentlemen," protested the Honorable Cheyenne Baxter, "we must have harmony."

"Rats!" said Opdyke. "I demand a vote."

"I insist upon it," said Wash.

The vote was taken and Macnooder was declared chairman of the Finance Committee. Crazy Opdyke arose and made them a profound bow.

"Gentlemen, I have the honor of bidding you farewell," he said, loftily. "The voice of freedom has been stifled. This great party is in the hands of commercial interests and private privilege. This is nothing but a Dickinson House sinecure. I retire, I withdraw, I shake the dust from my feet. I depart, but I shall not sleep, I shall not rest, I shall neither forget nor forgive. Remember, gentlemen of the Anti-Federalist party, this hour, and when in the stillness of the night you hear the swish of the poisoned arrow, the swirl of the tomahawk, the thud of the secret stone, pause and say to yourself, 'Crazy Opdyke done it!' "

"It is unfortunate," said Cheyenne, when Crazy had departed, "most unfortunate, but that's politics."

"Crazy has no influence," said Wash, contemptuously.

"He has our secrets," said Cheyenne gloomily.

"Let's get to work," said Macnooder. "You can bet Tough Mc-Carty's on the job; his father's an alderman."

At six o'clock the campaign was off with a rush. At seven the headmaster, all unsuspecting, stepped out from Foundation House, cast one fond glance at the familiar school, reposing peacefully in the twilight, and departed to carry the message of increased liberty in primary education to a waiting conference at Boston. Shortly after, a delegation of the school faculty, who had just learned of the prospective campaign, hurried over in amazed, indignant and incredulous protest. They missed the headmaster by ten minutes— but ten minutes make history.

"Jiminy crickets!"

"Suffering Moses!"

"Call Hickey!"

"Tell Hickey!"

"Hickey, stick your head out of the window!"

Hickey, slumbering peacefully, in that choicest period between the rising bell and breakfast, leaped to the middle of the floor at the uproar that suddenly resounded through the Dickinson.

He thrust his head out of the window and beheld from the upper stories of the Griswold an immense white sheet sagging in the breeze, displaying in crude red-flannel letters the following device:

NO APRON STRINGS FOR US
THE FEDERAL PARTY
WILL FIGHT TO THE END
FACULTY USURPATION

Hardly had his blinking eyes become accustomed to the sight when a fresh uproar broke out on the other side of the Dickinson.

"Hully Gee!"

"Look at the Kennedy!"

"Great cats and little kittens!"

"Snakes alive!"

"Look at the Kennedy, will you!"

"Hickey, oh you, Hickey!"

At the sound of Macnooder's voice in distress, Hickey realized the situation was serious and rushed across the hall. He found Macnooder with stern and belligerent gaze fixed out of the window. From the Kennedy House another banner insolently displayed this amazing proclamation:

DOWN WITH THE GOO-GOOS
LAWRENCEVILLE SHALL NOT BE
A KINDERGARTEN.
RALLY TO THE FEDERALISTS AND
DOWN THE DICKINSON GOO-GOOS

Hickey looked at Macnooder. Macnooder looked at Hickey.

"Goo-Goo," said Hickey, grieved.

"Goo-Goo," repeated Doc sadly. "Goo-Goo and Apron strings. Hickey, my boy, we have got to be up and doing."

"Doc," said Hickey, "that's Tough McCarty's work. We never ought to have let him get away from us."

"Hickey, we must nail the lie," said Doc solemnly.

"The Executive Committee of the Anti-Fed party will meet in my rooms," said Hickey determinedly, "directly after first recitation. We have been caught napping by a gang of ballot stuffers, but we will come back—Doc, we *will* come back!"

The Executive Committee met with stern and angry resolve, like battling football players between the halves of a desperate game.

"Fellows," said Hickey, "while we have slept the enemy has been busy. We are mutts, and the original pie-faced mutt is yours truly."

"No, Hickey, if there's going to be a competition for mutts," said Cheyenne Baxter, "I'm the blue ribbon."

"Before we bestow any more bouquets," said Macnooder sarcastically, "let's examine the situation. Let's see the worst. The Feds have the jump on us. They've raised the cry of 'Apron strings' on us, and it's going to be a mighty hard one to meet."

"We'll never answer it," said the gloomy Egghead; "we're beaten now. It's a rotten issue and a rotten game."

At this moment the Gutter Pup rushed in like a white fuzzy dog, his eyes bulging with importance as he delivered the bombshell, that Crazy Opdyke had organized a Mugwump party and carried the Cleve House for it.

"No."

"A Mugwump party!"

"What the deuce is he up to?"

"Order," said Hickey, stilling the tumult with a shoe vigorously applied to a wash-basin. "This meeting is not a bunch of undertakers. We are here to save the party."

"Hickey's right," said Turkey; "let's get down to business."

"First," said Hickey, "let's have reports. What has Treasurer Macnooder to report?"

The Mark Hanna of the campaign rose, tightened his belt, adjusted his glasses, and announced amid cheers that the Finance Committee had to report sixty-two dollars and forty cents in promissory notes, twelve dollars and thirty-eight cents in cash, three tennis rackets, two jerseys, one dozen caps, a bull's-eye lantern (loaned) and a Flobert rifle.

"We can always have a banquet, even if we're beaten," said the Triumphant Egghead. The gloom began to dissipate.

"What has the Honorable Gutter Pup to report?" said Cheyenne Baxter.

The Rocky Mountain Gazelle proudly announced the establishment of a thorough system of espionage, through the corrupting of Mr. Klondike Jackson, the cooperative gentleman who waited on the table at the Kennedy, and Mr. Alcibiades Bonaparte, who shook up the beds at the Griswold. He likewise reported that young Muskrat Foster, who was not overpopular at the Davis House, had perceived the great truths of Anti-Federalism. He then presented a bill of two dollars and forty-five cents for the corrupting of the

Messrs. Jackson and Bonaparte, with an addition of fifty cents for the further contaminating of young Muskrat Foster.

"The Honorable Wash Simmons will report," said Cheyenne Baxter.

"Fellows," said Wash, "I ain't no silver-tongued orator, and all I've got to say is that Butsey White, down at the Green House, is most sensible to the honor of representing this great and glorious party of moral ideas, as congressman from the second form, but—"

"But what?" said Slugger Jones.

"But he kind of fears that the other members of the Green House aren't quite up on Anti-Federalism, and he reckons it will take quite a little literature to educate them."

"Literature?" said Cheyenne, mystified.

"About eight volumes," said Wash. "Eight green-backed pieces of *literature!*"

"The robber!"

"Why, that's corruption."

"Gentlemen," said Cheyenne, rapping for order, "the question is, does he get the literature? Ayes or noes."

"I protest," interrupted Hickey. "Remember, gents, this is a campaign for clean politics. We will not buy votes, no! We will only encourage local enterprises. The Green is trying to fit themselves out for the baseball season. I suggest contributing toward a catcher's mitt and a mask, and letting it go at that."

On the announcement of a unanimous vote, the Honorable Wash Simmons departed to encourage local enterprises.

"And now, fellows," said Hickey, "we come to the serious proposition—the real business of the meeting. We have got to treat with Crazy Opdyke."

"Never!"

"Macnooder must sacrifice himself," said Hickey. "Am I right, Cheyenne?"

"You are," said Cheyenne. "The campaign has reached a serious stage. The Upper, the Kennedy, the Griswold, the Davis, are already Fed; the Rouse will go next. Even if we get the Green, we're lost if the Cleve goes against us, and Crazy is just holding out to make terms."

"We have misjudged Crazy," said Hickey. "His record was against him, but we have misjudged him. He's been the only live one in the bunch. Now we've got to meet his terms."

The door opened and Crazy Opdyke sauntered in.

"Hello, fellows," he drawled. "How's the campaign going? Are you satisfied with your progress?" He stretched languidly into an armchair. "Am I still welcome in the home of great moral ideas?"

"Crazy, our feelings for you are both of sorrow and of affection," said Cheyenne, conciliatingly. "You certainly are a boss politician. What's this new wrinkle of yours over in the Cleve?"

"I've been amusing myself," said Crazy with a drawl, "organizing the Mugwumps, the intelligent and independent vote, the balance of power, you know, the party that doesn't heel to any boss, but votes according to its, to its—"

"To its what, Crazy?" said Hickey, gently.

"To its conscience," replied Crazy firmly. "To its conscience, when its conscience is intelligently approached."

"Oh, you're for sale, are you?" said Turkey aggressively.

"No, Turkey, no-o-o! And yet we've organized the Blocks of Five Marching Club; rather significant, eh?"

"Well, what's your game; what have you come for?"

"Oh, just to be friendly," said Crazy, rising languidly.

"Stop," said Hickey. "Sit down. Let's have a few words."

Crazy slouched back, sank into the armchair and assumed a listening position.

"Crazy," said Hickey, "we've made a mistake. We didn't know you. You are the surprise of the campaign. We apologize. We are merely amateurs; you are the only original, professional politician."

"This is very gratifying," said Crazy, without a blush.

"Crazy, from this moment," said Hickey, firmly, "you are the treasurer of the Campaign Committee, and we're listening for any words of wisdom you have ready to uncork."

"No, Hickey, no," said Crazy, rising amid general dismay, "I no longer hanker to be a treasurer. It was just a passing fancy. Independence is better and more profitable; I appreciate your kind offer, I do appreciate it, Hickey, but I'm a Mugwump; I couldn't wear a dog collar, I couldn't!"

"Sit down again, Crazy," said Hickey, persuasively; "sit down. It's a pleasure to talk with you. You're right; your independent and intelligent nature would be thrown away in a matter of books and figures. We've been looking round for a fearless, upright, popular and eloquent figure to stand for the Cleve, and, Crazy, we're just aching to have you step up into the frame."

"Hickey, you mistake me, you mistake me and my motives," said Crazy, sadly. "My soul does not hanker for personal glorification or the flattery of the multitude. I'm a child of nature, Hickey, and my ambitions are few and simple."

"It's right to have ambitions, Crazy," said Hickey, soothingly, "and they don't need to be few or simple. We regret that we cannot honor your eminent qualities as we wish to, but we still have hopes, Crazy, that we may have the benefit of your guiding hand."

"Guiding hand?" said Crazy, looking at the ceiling.

"Exactly," said Hickey, magnanimously; "in fact, I realize how unworthy I am to fill the great position of trust and responsibility of vice-chairman of this committee, and I long to see it in the hands—"

"I thought you said guiding hand," said Crazy, interrupting.

The assembled committee looked in amazement at Crazy. Then the storm broke out.

"Why, you insolent, impudent pup!"

"Do you think we'll make you chairman?"

"Kick him out!"

"Roughhouse!"

"Order!" cried Cheyenne. "Crazy, out with it. You want to be chairman, don't you?"

"Have I made any demands?" said Crazy, coolly.

"Come now—yes or no!"

"Are you handing it to me?"

A fresh storm of indignation was interrupted by the sudden tumultuous reappearance of Wash Simmons, shouting, "Fellows, Butsey White and the Green have sold out to the Mugwumps!"

Crazy Opdyke sat down again.

A long silence succeeded. Then Cheyenne Baxter, mutely interrogating every glance, rose and said, "Crazy, you win. The chairmanship is yours. Will you take it on a silver platter or with a bouquet of roses?"

That evening, when Hickey went to report to Ernest Garrison Baldwin, he found that civic reformer in a somewhat perturbed condition.

"I'm afraid, Hicks," he said dubiously, "that the campaign is getting a wrong emphasis. It seems to me that those Federalist banners are not only in questionable taste, but show a frivolous and trifling attitude toward this great opportunity."

"It's just the humor of the campaign, sir," said Hickey reassuringly; "I wouldn't take them seriously."

"Another thing, Hicks; I'm rather surprised that the management of the campaign does not seem to be in the hands of the very representative committee you originally selected."

"Yes, sir," said Hickey; "we realize that; but we're making a change in our party at least which will please you. Opdyke is going to take control."

"Indeed! That is reassuring; that is a guarantee on your side, at least, of a dignified, honorable canvass."

"Oh, yes, sir," said Hickey.

He left gravely and scampered across the campus. Suddenly from the Woodhull Toots Cortell's trumpet squeaked out. At the same moment the first Anti-Fed banner was flung out, thus conceived:

TURN THE ROBBERS OUT
NO MORE GRAFTING
NO MORE GOUGING THE UNDER-FORMERS
FACULTY SUPERVISION MEANS
SAVING TO THE POCKET
OUT WITH THE BLACKMAILERS

The astute and professional hand of the Honorable Crazy Opdyke was felt at once. The Anti-Fed party, while still advocating faculty control of the athletic finances for purposes of efficiency and economy, now shifted the ground by a series of brilliant strokes.

The third day of the campaign had hardly opened when the four fusion houses displayed prominently the following proclamation:

ECONOMY AND JIGGERS
FACULTY MANAGEMENT OF THE FINANCES
MEANS RIGID ECONOMY
PROTECTION OF THE WEAK
FROM THE TYRANNY OF THE TAX GATHERER
EQUITABLE PRO-RATA
LEVYING OF CONTRIBUTIONS
ECONOMY MEANS MORE JIGGERS
MORE JIGGERS MEANS
MORE HAPPINESS FOR THE GREATER NUMBER
VOTE FOR THE FATTER POCKETBOOK

Hardly had this argument to the universal appetite been posted before the Feds retorted by posting a proclamation:

FACULTY PLOT
EVIDENCE IS PILING UP THAT THE PRESENT POLITICAL CAMPAIGN IS A HUGE FACULTY CONSPIRACY TO DEPRIVE THE SCHOOL OF ITS LIBERTIES BY UNDERGROUND DARK-LANTERN METHODS, WHERE IT DOES NOT DARE TO ATTEMPT IT OPENLY
THE APRON STRINGS ARE IN POSSESSION OF A GIGANTIC CORRUPTION FUND   WHO IS PUTTING UP?

When this attack became public the Anti-Feds were in deep deliberation, planning a descent on the Hamill House. The news of the outrageous charge was borne to the conference by Hungry Smeed, with tears in his eyes.

"Crazy," said Doc, "we must meet the charge, now, at once."

There was a chorus of assent.

"We will," said Crazy, diving into his pocket and producing a wad of paper. "This is what I've had up my sleeve from the beginning. This is the greatest state paper ever conceived."

"Let's have it," said Hickey, and Crazy proudly read:

THE FULL PROGRAM

The Campaign of Slander and Vilification Instituted by Tough McCarty and His Myrmidons Will Not Deceive the Intelligent and Independent Voter. Anti-Federalist Candidates Only Are the Defendants of the Liberties of the School.

Anti-Fed Candidates Stand Solemnly Pledged to Work For Increased Privileges.

ACCESS TO THE JIGGER SHOP AT ALL TIMES
REMOVING THE LIMIT ON WEEKLY ALLOWANCES
ABOLITION OF THE HATEFUL COMPULSORY
BATH SYSTEM
BETTER FOOD   MORE FOOD
REGULATION OF SINKERS AND SCRAG-BIRDS
ESTABLISHMENT OF TWO SLEIGHING HOLIDAYS
CUSHIONED SEATS FOR CHAPEL

When this momentous declaration of principles was read there was an appalled silence, while Crazy, in the center of the admiring circle, grew perceptibly.

Then a shriek burst out and Crazy was smothered in the arms of the regenerated Anti-Feds.

"Crazy will be President of the United States," said Turkey admiringly.

"Wonderful!"

"The bathroom plank will win us fifty votes."

"And what about the jigger vote?"

At this moment an egg passed rapidly through the open window and spread itself on the wall, while across the campus the figure of Mucker Reilly of the Kennedy was seen zigzagging for safety, with his thumb vulgarly applied to his nose.

The Executive Committee gazed at the wall, watching the yellow desecration gradually trickling into a map of South America.

"This means the end of argument," said Cheyenne sadly. "The campaign from now on will be bitter."

"If the appeal to force is going to be made," said Crazy, applying a towel, "we shall endeavor—Doc, shut the window—we shall endeavor to meet it."

"We have now a chance," said Egghead, brightening, "to prove that we are not Goo-Goos."

"Egghead, you are both intelligent and comforting," said Hickey. "The first thing is to corner the egg market."

"The Finance Committee," said Crazy wrathfully, "is empowered to buy, beg or borrow every egg, every squashy apple, every mushy tomato that can be detected and run down. From now on we shall wage a vigorous campaign."

The publication of the Anti-Fed program roused the party cohorts to cheers and song. The panicky Feds strove desperately to turn the tide with the following warning:

HA! HA!
IT WON'T DO!
WE KNOW THE HAND!

Don't Be Deceived. Hickey is the Sheep in Wolf's Clothing. Stung to the Quick by Our Detection of the Criminal Alliance Between the Anti-Feds and the Faculty, Hickey, the King of the Goo-Goos,

is Trying to Bleat Like a Wolf. It Won't Do! They Cannot Dodge
the Issue. Stand Firm. Lawrenceville Must Not Be Made Into a
Kindergarten.

But this could not stem the rising wave. The Hamill House
turned its back on Federalism and threw in its lot with the foes
of compulsory bath. Just before supper the Anti-Feds were roused
to frenzy by the astounding news that the little Rouse House,
isolated though it was from the rest of the school and under the
very wing of the Davis, had declared Anti-Fed, for the love of combat that burned in its heroic band led by the redoubtable Charley
De Soto and Scrapper Morrissey.

With the declaration of the different houses the first stage of the
campaign ended. By supper every house was on a military footing
and the dove of peace was hastening toward the horizon.

That night Mr. Baldwin waited in vain for the report of Hickey,
waited and wondered. For the first time Baldwin, the enthusiast,
began to be a little apprehensive of the forces he had unchained.

A little later Mr. Baranson chose to pay him a visit.

"Well, Baldwin, what news?" he said drily. "Thoroughly satisfied
with your new course in political education?"

"Why, the boys seem to take to it with enthusiasm," said Baldwin rather dubiously. "I think they're thoroughly interested."

"Interested? Yes—quite so. By the way, Baldwin," Baranson
stopped a moment and scanned his young subordinate with pitying
knowledge, "I'm going to retire for the night. If I had a cyclone
cellar I'd move to it. I put you in charge of the house. If any attempt is made to set it on fire or dynamite it, go out and argue
gently with the boys, and above all, impress upon them that they are
the hope of the country and must set a standard. Reason with them,
Baldwin, and above all, appeal to their better natures. Good
night."

Baldwin did not answer. He stood meditatively gazing out the
window. From the Dickinson and the Kennedy magic lanterns
were flashing campaign slogans on white sheets suspended at opposite houses. The uproar of catcalls and hoots that accompanied the
exhibitions left small reason to hope that they were couched in that
clear, reasoning style which would uplift future American politics.

As he looked, from the Upper House the indignant and now

thoroughly aroused fourth form started to parade with torchlights and transparencies. Presently the winding procession, clothed in superimposed night shirts, arrived with hideous clamor. Dangling from a pole were two grotesque figures stuffed with straw and decked with aprons; overhead was the inscription, "Kings of the Goo-Goos," and one was labeled Hickey and one was labeled Brother. Opposite his window they halted and chanted in soft unison:

> Hush, hush, tread softly,
> Hush, hush, make no noise,
> Baldwin is the King of the Goo-Goos,
> Let him sleep,
> Let him sleep.
> SHOUTED: LET HIM SLEEP!!!

Then the transparencies succeeded one another, bobbing over the rolling current of indignant seniors.

> BACK TO THE KINDERGARTEN!
> WE WANT NO BROTHERLY LOVE!
> GOODBYE, BALDWIN! GOODBYE!

Baldwin drew down the shade and stepped from the window. He heard a familiar step in the corridor, and quickly locked the door. Baranson knocked; then he knocked again; after which he moved away, chuckling.

When the fourth-form procession arrived on its tour around the circle the Dickinsonians were prepared to welcome it. Crazy Opdyke, head of the literary bureau, stood by the lantern directing the proclamations to be flashed on the sheet that hung from the opposite house.

Hickey and Macnooder posted the orators at strategic windows, supplying them with compressed arguments in the form of eggs and soft apples.

"All ready?" said Opdyke as Hickey returned, chuckling.

"Ready and willing," said Hickey.

"Here they come," said the Big Man.

"Is the Kennedy and the Woodhull with them?" asked Hickey.

"Sure, they're trailing on behind," said Turkey.

A yell of defiance burst from the head of the procession as it reached the headquarters of the enemy.

"Start the literature," said Crazy.

Egghead, at the lantern, slipped in the first slides, flashing them on the opposite sheet.

IT'S ALL OVER, BOYS
FEDERALISM IS IN THE SOUP
FEDERALISTS
THE UPPER HOUSE MYRMIDONS
THE DAVIS JAYHAWKERS
THE WOODHULL SORE HEADS
THE KENNEDY MUCKERS
ANTI-FEDERALISTS
THE ROUSE INVINCIBLES
THE CLEVE INDEPENDENTS
THE GRISWOLD INTELLECTUALS
THE GREEN MUGWUMPS
THE DICKINSON SCHOLARS
THE HAMILL MISSIONARIES
GOODBYE, FEDS! GOODBYE!

"Now for a few personal references," said Crazy, smiling happily at the howls that greeted his first effort. "Egghead, shove them right along."

Another series was put forth:

WHY, WOODHULL, DID WE STEAL
YOUR ICE CREAM?
IS TOUGH McCARTY'S GANG OF
BALLOT STUFFERS WITH YOU?
WE ARE NOT FOURTH-FORM PUPPY DOGS
HELLO, TOUGH, HOW DOES IT FEEL TO
BE A PUPPY DOG?

"What are they shouting now?" said Hickey, peering over at the turbulent chaos below.

"They are re-questing us to come out!" said the Egghead.

The night was filled with the shrieks of the helpless Feds.

"Come out!"

"We dare you to come out!"

"Come out, you Dickinson Goo-Goos."

"Why, they're really getting excited," said Hickey. "They're hopping right up and down."

"We will give them a declaration of principles," said Crazy. "Egghead, give them the principles; Hickey, notify the orators to prepare the compressed arguments. The word is 'BIFF.'"

Hickey went tumbling upstairs; the Egghead delivered the new series.

WHY, FEDS, DON'T GET PEEVISH
THIS IS AN ORDERLY CAMPAIGN
A QUIET, ORDERLY CAMPAIGN
REMEMBER, WE MUST UPLIFT THE
NATION

Outside, the chorus of hoots and catcalls gave way to a steady rhythmic chant:

GOO-GOOS, GOO-GOOS, GOO-GOOS!

"How unjust!" said Crazy, sadly. "We must clear ourselves; we must nail the lie—in a quiet, orderly way! Let her go, Egghead; Cheyenne, give Hickey the cue."

On the sheet suddenly flashed out:

WE ARE GOO-GOOS, ARE WE? BIFF!

At the same moment, from a dozen windows descended a terrific broadside of middle-aged eggs, assorted vegetables and squashy fruit.

The Federalist forces, utterly off their guard, dripping with egg and tomato, vanished like a heap of leaves before a whirlwind, while from the Anti-Federalist houses exultant shrieks of victory burst forth.

"If we are to be called Goo-Goos," said Crazy, proudly, "we have, at least, made Goo-Goo a term of honor."

"Tomorrow should be a very critical day in the campaign," said Macnooder, pensively.

"I suggest that on account of the uncertain state of the weather," said Hickey, wisely, "that all window blinds should be closed and locked."

"I think," said Cheyenne, "that we had better march to chapel in close formation."

"Are there any more arguments left?" said Crazy.

"Quite a number."

"They must be delivered tonight," said Crazy, firmly. "No egg shall be allowed to spoil—in this house."

At eleven o'clock that night, as the headmaster sat in his room in distant Boston, giving the last touches to the address which he had prepared for the following day on the "Experiment of Self-Government and Increased Individual Responsibility in Primary Education," the following telegram was handed to him:

> Come back instantly. School in state of anarchy. Rioting and pillaging unchecked. Another day may be too late. Baldwin's course in political education.
>
> BARANSON

When the Doctor, after a night's precipitous travel, drove onto the campus he had left picturesque and peaceful but a few days before, he could hardly believe his eyes. The circle of houses was stained and spotted with the marks of hundreds of eggs and the softer vegetables. From almost every upper window a banner (often ripped to shreds) or a mutilated proclamation was displayed. Proclamations blossomed on every tree, couched in vitriolic language. Two large groups of embattled boys, bearing strange banners, were converging across the campus with haggard, hysterical faces, fists clenched and muscles strung in nervous tension, waiting the shock of the approaching clash.

The Doctor sprang from the buggy and advanced toward chapel with determined, angry strides. At the sight of the familiar figure a swift change went over the two armies, on the point of flying at each other's throats. The most bloodthirsty suddenly quailed, the most martial scowls gave place to looks of innocence. In the twinkling of an eye every banner had disappeared, and the two armies, breaking formation, went meekly and fearfully into chapel.

The Doctor from his rostrum looked down upon the school. Under his fierce examination every glance fell to the hymn-book.

"Young gentlemen of the Lawrenceville School, I will say just one word," began the headmaster. "This political campaign will

STOP, NOW, *AT ONCE!*" He paused at the spectacle of row on row of blooming eyes and gory features, and, despite himself, his lips twitched.

In an instant the first ranks began to titter, then a roar of laughter went up from the pent-up, hysterical boys. They laughed until they sobbed, for the first time aware of the ridiculousness of the situation. Then as the Doctor, wisely refraining from further discourse, dismissed them, they swayed out on the campus where the Davis fell into the arms of the Dickinson, and Fed and Anti-Fed rolled with laughter on the ground.

When Hickey, that afternoon, brazenly sought out Mr. Baldwin, a certain staccato note in the greeting caused a dozen careful phrases to die on his tongue.

"Don't hesitate, Hicks," said Baldwin, smiling coldly.

"I came, sir," said Hicks, looking down, "I came—that is, I—Mr. Baldwin, sir, I'm sorry it turned out such a failure."

"Of course, Hicks," said Baldwin, softly, "of course. It must be a great disappointment—to you. But it is not a failure, Hicks. On the contrary, it has been a great success—this campaign of education. I have learned greatly. By the way, Hicks, kindly announce to the class that I shall change my method of hearing recitations. I have a new system—based on the latest discoveries in the laws of probability. Announce also an examination for tomorrow."

"Tomorrow?" said Hickey, astounded.

"On the review—in the interest of education—my education. Don't look down, Hicks—I cherish no resentment against you—none at all."

"Against me?" said Hickey, aggrieved.

"My feelings are of gratitude and affection only. You have been the teacher and I the scholar—but—" He paused and surveyed the persecuted Hicks with the smile of the anaconda for the canary, "but, Hicks, my boy, whatever else may be the *indifference* of the masters toward your education, when you leave Lawrenceville you will not be weak in—mathematics."

THE MARTYRDOM OF WILLIAM HICKS

HICKEY HAD now reached the height of his fame. Intoxicated by success, he forgot all prudence, or rather his revolt became an appetite that demanded constant feeding. He no longer concealed his past exploits; he even went so far as to announce the escapades he planned.

"You are running your head into the noose, Hickey, my boy," said Macnooder, sadly; "every master in the school has got his eye on you."

"I know it," said Hickey proudly, "but they've got to catch me."

"Your position is different," objected Macnooder, "now you are suspected. And do you want me to tell you the truth? Your trick about the clappers was too clever. If you could imagine that, you were at the bottom of other things. That's what the Doctor will say to himself when he thinks it over."

"The Doctor plays square," retorted Hickey; "he won't do anything on suspicion. Let him try and catch me, let them all try. If they get me fair and square, I'll take my punishment. I say, Doc, just you wait. I've got something up my sleeve that'll make them all sit up."

"Good Lord!" said the Egghead, who was of the party. "You don't mean you're going on?"

"Egghead," said Hickey, impressively, "I've made up my mind that I just can't live without doing one thing more!"

"Heavens, Hickey! What now?"

"I've got a craving, Egghead, to sleep in Tabby's bed."

"No!"

"Fact."

"What do you mean?"

"Just that. I intend to sleep, not just pop in and out, to *sleep* two hours in Tabby's nice white little bed."

"Gee whiz, Hickey! When?"

"Some night that's coming pretty soon."

"When Tabby's away——"

"No, sir, when Tabby's here—after Tabby himself has been in it. After that I'm going to get back at Big Brother."

"You're crazy!"

"I'm backing my feelings."

"You'll bet on it?"

"As much as you want."

The scornful Egghead, thus provoked, offered ten to one against him. Hickey accepted at once.

During the day the news spread and the bets came flying in. As to his plans, Hickey preserved a cloaked mystery, promising only that the feat should take place within the fortnight.

Each night toward midnight, he slipped out of Sawtelle's window (Sawtelle being sworn to deadly secrecy). He remained out an hour, sometimes two, and came back sleepy and chuckling. About this time the report began to spread that burglars were in the vicinity.

The Gutter Pup, who roomed on the first floor of the Woodhull, took a solemn oath that having been waked up by a strange scratching noise at his window, he had seen four masked figures with bull's-eye lanterns scurrying away. The next report came from

Davis with added picturesqueness. The school became wrought up to an extraordinary pitch of excitement in which even the masters joined after a period of incredulity.

When the proper stage of frenzy arrived, Hickey took into his confidence a dozen allies.

At exactly two o'clock on a moonless night, Beauty Sawtelle, waiting, watch in hand, gave a horrid shriek and sent a baseball bat crashing through his window, where he afterward swore four masked faces had glared in on him. At the same time the Egghead raised his window and emptied a revolver into the air, shouting, "Thieves, thieves, there they go!"

Immediately every waiting boy sprang out of bed armed with revolvers, shotguns, brickbats, Japanese swords and what not, and rushed downstairs, shouting, "Stop thief!"

Mr. Tapping, startled from his slumbers by the uproar, seized a bird gun and, guided by Hungry Smeed and the Red Dog, rushed out of doors and valorously took the lead of the searching party. By this time the racket had spread about the campus and boys in flimsy garments, ludicrously armed, came pouring out of the other houses and joined the wild hunt for the masked marauders. Suddenly, from the direction of Foundation House, a series of shots exploded amid yells of excitement. At once the mass that had been churning in the middle of the campus set off with a rush. The cry went up that the burglars had been discovered and were fleeing down the road to Trenton. Five minutes later the campus was silent, as boys and masters swept along the highway, their cries growing fainter in the distance.

Meanwhile, Hickey had not lost a second. Hardly had Mr. Tapping's pink pajamas rushed from the Dickinson when Hickey, entering the study, locked the door and set to work. In a jiffy he had the mattress and bedclothes out the window, down into the waiting hands of Macnooder and the Egghead, who piled them on a ready wheelbarrow. In less than five minutes the iron bedstead, separated into its four component parts, followed. The whole, packed on the wheelbarrow, was hastily rushed into the darkness by the rollicking three. According to the plan, Hickey directed them past Memorial and into the baseball cage, where, by the light of the indispensable dark-lantern, they put the bed together, placed on it the bedding, and saw Hickey crawl blissfully under cover.

When Mr. Tapping returned after an hour's fruitless pursuit down the dutsy road, it had begun to dawn upon him, in common with other athletic members of the faculty, that he had been hoaxed. Mr. Tapping was very sensitive to his dignity, and dignity was exceedingly difficult in pajamas, in the chill of a night with a ridiculous bird gun over his shoulder and an assorted lot of semi-bare savages chuckling about him. Tired, covered with dust, and sheepish, he returned to the Dickinson, gave orders for everyone to return to his room and wearily toiled up to seek his comfortable bed.

The vacancy that greeted his eyes left him absolutely incredulous, then beside himself with rage. If in that moment he could have laid his hands on Hickey, he would have done him bodily injury. That Hickey was the perpetrator of this new outrage, as of the previous ones, he never for a moment doubted. His instinct needed no proofs, and in such enmities the instinct is strong. He went directly to Hickey's room, finding it, as he had expected, empty. He sat there half an hour, an hour, fruitlessly. Then he made the rounds of the house and returned to the room, seated himself, folded his arms violently, set his teeth and prepared to wait. He heard four o'clock strike, then five, and he began to nod. He rose, shook himself, returned to his seat and presently fell asleep, and in this condition Hickey, returning, found him.

The bell rang six, and Mr. Tapping, starting up guiltily, glanced hastily at the bed and assured himself thankfully that it was empty. Moreover, conclusive evidence, the counterpane had not been turned down, so Hickey had not gone to bed at all.

By prodigies of will power he remained awake, consoled by the fact that he held at last the evidence needed to debarrass himself of his tormentor. At seven o'clock the gym bell rang the rising hour. Mr. Tapping rose triumphant. Suddenly he stopped and looked down in horror. Something had moved under the bed. The next moment Hickey's face appeared under the skirts of the trailing bedspread—Hickey's face, a mirror of sleepy amazement, as he innocently asked, "Why, Mr. Tapping, what *is* the matter?"

"Hicks!" exclaimed Mr. Tapping, too astounded to gather his thoughts. "Is that you, Hicks?"

"Yes, sir."

"What are you doing under there?"

"Please sir," said Hickey, "I'm troubled with insomnia and sometimes this is the only way I can sleep."

At two o'clock Hickey was a second time summoned to Foundation House. He went in perfect faith. Nothing had miscarried, there was not the slightest evidence against him. If he was questioned he would refuse to answer—that was all. It had been a morning of exquisite triumph for him. Tabby's bed had not been discovered until ten o'clock, and the transferral to the Dickinson, made in full daylight, had been witnessed by the assembled school. He went across the campus, light of feet and proud of heart, aware of the scores of discreetly admiring eyes that followed him, hearing pleasantly the murmurs which buzzed after him:

"Oh, you prodigious Hickey—oh, you daredevil!"

Of course, the Doctor would be in a towering rage. Hickey was not unreasonable, he understood and expected a natural exhibition of vexation. What could the Doctor do, after all? Ask him questions which he would refuse to answer—that was all, but that was not evidence.

He found the Doctor alone, quietly writing at his desk, and received a smile and an invitation to be seated. Somehow the tranquillity of the headmaster's attitude did not reassure Hickey. He would have preferred a little more agitation, but this satisfied calm was disquieting.

He stood with his hands behind his back, twirling his cap, studying the photographs of Grecian architecture on the walls, finding it awfully still and wishing the Doctor would begin.

Presently the Doctor turned, put down his spectacles, shoved back from the desk and glanced at Hickey with a smile, saying, "Well, Hicks, we're going to let you go."

"Beg your pardon, sir," said Hickey, smiling frankly back, "you said—"

"We're going to let you take a vacation."

"Me?"

"You."

Hickey stood a long moment, open-mouthed, staring.

"Do you mean to say," he said, at last, with an effort, "that I am expelled?"

"Not expelled," said the Doctor, suavely, "we don't like that word; we're going to let you go, that's all."

"For what reason?" said Hickey, defiantly.

"For no reason at all," answered the Doctor, smoothly. "There is no reason, there can be no reason, Hicks. We're just naturally going to make up our minds to part with you. You see, Hicks," he continued, tilting back and gazing reminiscently at the ceiling, "we've had a rather agitated session here, rather extraordinary. The trouble seems to have broken out in the Dickinson about the time of the little surprise party at which Mr. Tapping did not assist! Then a few days later our chapel service was disturbed and our janitor put to considerable trouble; next the school routine was thrown into confusion by the removal of the clapper. We passed a very disagreeable period—much confusion, very little study, and the nerves of the faculty were thrown into such a state that even you, Hicks, were suspected. Then there was the political campaign, a subject too painful to analyze. Last night we lost a great deal of sleep—and sleep is most necessary to the growing boy. All these events have followed with great regularity, and while they have not lacked in picturesqueness, we have, we fear, been forgetting the main object of our life here—to study a little."

"Doctor, I—" broke in Hickey.

"No, Hicks, you misunderstand me," said the Doctor, reproachfully. "All this is true, but that is *not* why we are going to let you go. We are going to let you go, Hicks, for a much more conscientious reason; we're parting with you, Hicks, because we feel we no longer have anything to teach you."

"Doctor, I'd like to know," began Hickey, with a great lump in his throat. Then he stopped and looked at the floor. He knew his hour had sounded.

"Hicks, we part in sorrow," said the Doctor, "but we have the greatest faith in your career. We expect in a few years to claim you as one of our foremost alumni. Perhaps some day you will give us a library which we will name after you. No, don't be disheartened. We have the greatest admiration for your talents, admiration and respect. Anyone who can persuade two hundred and fifty keen-eyed Lawrenceville boys to pay one dollar apiece for silver gilt scrap-iron souvenirs worth eleven cents apiece because they may or may not be genuine bits of a stolen clapper—anyone who can do that is needed in the commercial development of our country."

"Doctor, do you—do you call this justice?" said Hickey, with tears in his voice.

"No," said the Doctor, frankly, "I call it a display of force. You see, Hicks, you've beaten us at every point, and so all we can do is to let you go."

"I'll hire a lawyer," said Hicks, brokenly.

"I thought you would," said the Doctor, "only I hope you will be easy on us, Hicks, for we haven't much money for damage suits."

"Then I'm to be fired," said Hickey, forcing back the tears, "fired just for nothing!"

"Just for nothing, Hicks," assented the Doctor, rising to close the painful interview, "and, Hicks, as one last favor, we would like to request that it be by the evening train. We have lost a great deal of sleep lately."

"Just for nothing," repeated Hickey, hoarsely.

"Just for nothing," replied the Doctor, as he closed the door.

At six o'clock, in the midst of indignant hundreds, Hickey climbed to the top of the stage, where his trunks had already been deposited. Nothing could comfort him, neither the roaring cheers that echoed again and again to his name, nor the hundreds of silent handshakes or muttered vows to continue the good fight. His spirit was broken. All was dark before him. Neither right nor justice existed in the world.

Egghead and Macnooder, visibly affected, reached up for the last handshakes.

"Keep a stiff upper lip, old man," said the Egghead.

"Don't you worry, Hickey, old boy," said Macnooder; "we'll attend to Tabby."

Then Hickey, bitterly, from the caverns of his heart, spoke, raising his fist toward Tabby's study window.

"He hadn't any proof," he said, brokenly, "no proof—damn him!"

The Tennessee Shad

ILLUSTRATED BY
F. R. GRUGER

TO MY FRIEND
Arthur B. Maurice

TO WHOSE SUGGESTION
THE BOOK IS DUE

I

THE RISE OF DOC MACNOODER

AT THE TIME when the celebrated Doc Macnooder, that amateur practitioner but most professional financier, first dawned upon the school, he found the Tennessee Shad the admiration and the envy of the multitude. He had not been a week in the school before he, too, was moved to enthusiasm by the Shad's productive imagination—productive in the sense of its consequences to others. Macnooder, at that time unknown, with only the consciousness of greatness within him, conceived at once the mighty ambition to unite this Yankee fertility of ideas to his own practical but imaginative sense of financial returns. This ambition he did not achieve in a day for the firm of Macnooder and the Tennessee Shad was not finally established until Macnooder, by a series of audacious moves, forced himself to that position where he could compel the Shad to choose between a partner and a rival.

When the Tennessee Shad leaned against a wall his empty trousers wrapped themselves like damp sheets around his ankles. When he strode forth like a pair of animated scissors his coat hung from the points of his shoulder blades as though floating from a rake, while his narrow, lengthened head seemed more like a cross-section than a completed structure.

Hickey The Prodigious, after a long period of mental wrestling, had given him the nickname, and the same was agreed to be Hickey's *magnum opus*. It expressed not simply a state of inordinate thinness, but one of incredible, preposterous boniness such as could only have been possessed by that antediluvian monster that did or did not sharpen its sides on the ridges of Tennessee.

The Tennessee Shad frankly confessed his ambition to be a philosopher, his idea of the same being that of a gloriously languid person who resided in a tub and thought out courses of action over which other people should toil.

His first efforts were naturally directed to the greatest saving of personal energy. His window opened, his door shut, his lamp was extinguished by a series of ropes which he operated from his bed. On retiring he drew his undergarments through his trousers, tucked the legs carefully in the socks which in turn were placed in his slippers, and leaned the whole against the chair, on the back of which his undershirt in his shirt, his shirt in his vest, his vest in his coat lay gaping for the morrow. As a result of this precocious grasping of the principles of economics, he was able to spring from his bed fully clothed with but two motions, an upward struggle and a downward kick.

The physical inertia was not, however, accompanied by any surrender of the imagination. On the contrary he liked nothing better than to propose ideas; to lie back, lazily turning a straw in his lips, and to throw out suggestions that would produce commotions and give him the keen intellectual enjoyment of watching others hustle. These little ideas of the Tennessee Shad's, so rapturously hailed at the inception, were not always so admired in the retrospect; especially after the rise of Macnooder to the practical partnership had introduced the element of aggressive financeering.

Now Doc Macnooder came with no surrounding haze of green, but fully equipped with the most circumstantial manner.

It lies in the annals of the Hamill House that within six hours after the opening of his trunks, he had sold a patent bootjack to the Triumphant Egghead, and a folding toothbrush to Turkey Reiter, disinfected and bandaged the foot of Peewee Davis, who had stepped on a tack, and begun the famous Hamill House March which was a blend of the vibrant reiterations of a Chinese orchestra and the beatings of a tom-tom man.

Macnooder's early days, as well as his age, remained closely wrapped in mystery and speculation. Many stories moved about; he had shipped before the mast and fought Chinese pirates off Malay; he had been an enforced pirate himself; he had been an actor, touring the country with barn stormers; he had been a dentist's assistant, a jockey, and a Pinkerton detective. Macnooder never absolutely affirmed any of these reports, and he certainly would never have denied one.

He shortly became secretary and treasurer of his House, of his Form, and of each organization to which he was admitted. He

THE FAMOUS HAMILL HOUSE MARCH

played the organ in chapel, represented twenty firms, and plied so thriving a trade in patent and ingeniously useless goods that he was able to refuse a cash offer from the village tradesmen to abandon the field.

But Macnooder was not content. He wished a reputation not simply for ubiquity, but as a hero of some desperate deed of valor and cunning, and so to enter the company of that Machiavellian spirit, the Tennessee Shad, of Turkey Reiter and of Hickey, the incarnation of mischief.

In the days of which I write smoking had still the charm of Eden's apple. Thundering assaults were directed from the pulpit at the Demon Cigarette, which was further described as a Coffin Nail; and boys whose stomachs rebelled smoked with a thrill at the thought of detection, immediate expulsion, disgrace, and a swift downward career which nothing could check but the gallows.

Macnooder, either in Chinese junks or as a detective to screen his features behind a cloud of smoke, had acquired the deathly practice of inhaling the obnoxious weed, and soon began to cast about for a more safely luxurious method of enjoyment than a mattress beside an air-flue.

Now, the Hamill House, relic of the old school, was a rambling structure which had been patched and altered a dozen times, with the result that each story was composed of several levels.

Macnooder was hastening down the back steps from the third floor one afternoon when the lacrosse stick he carried at shoulder arms came in smart contact with a beam, with the result that he reached the landing without the formality of the remaining steps.

He picked himself up wrathfully, and gazed at the offending beam. It was totally unnecessary, in quite an absurd position, impending over a flight of narrow stairs. The more Macnooder studied it, the more curious he became. If it was only a beam, it was of extraordinary thickness and height. If it was not a beam, it must be a sort of blind passage leading directly from his room. But leading where?

Macnooder went softly up the steps and, stretching on tiptoes, gently sounded the plastered obstruction. It certainly gave forth a most promising hollow sound.

Twenty minutes later, Jay Gould who had waited patiently below, rushed up in a swearing mood.

"Where in blazes is that impudent, cheeky, all-fired, nervy freshman?" he cried, stamping up in pursuit of the greenhorn who had dared to keep him waiting. But at Macnooder's room he stopped in amazement.

"What in the name of peanuts are you doing?"

"Hush!" said Macnooder, pacing the floor. "Twelve feet from the door and six over."

"He's gone dippy," said Jay, not completely surprised at this solution of Macnooder's many-sided personality.

"HE HAD SHIPPED BEFORE THE MAST AND FOUGHT PIRATES."

"Twelve feet minus four leaves eight. Allowing, say, two-and-a-half feet for the width of the passage, it must strike in here somewhere."

Jay Gould, keeping a chair in front of him, carefully advanced, studying first the floor and then the abstracted, concentrated gaze of Macnooder.

"I say, Doc."

"Don't bother me."

"I say, dear boy, is anything wrong?"

"Come here," said Macnooder, suddenly straightening with a look of triumph.

"What do you want?"

"Lift your right hand and solemnly swear."

"Swear what?"

"Never to reveal the secret mysteries I am about to unfold to you."

"Come off. What's the answer?"

"Swear."

"Sure."

"I have discovered that the Hamill House hides a secret chamber, a den of horrors perhaps," said Macnooder darkly.

"How did you find that out?"

"I first suspected it," said Macnooder, rapidly dramatizing the bare facts, "by a strange, pungent, ghoulish odor that has come to me in the dead of the night."

"Poor Doc," said Jay Gould, shaking his head; "he is dippy, after all."

Macnooder, perceiving the time for simple words had arrived, rapidly imparted the accident of his discovery, ending excitedly:

"Jay, that passage starts right above the floor of my closet or you can take your pick of anything I sell, at fifty per cent off."

Gould was convinced at once.

"But where does it lead?"

"Straight over *back* of your room!"

"Back!"

"Exactly. I've worked it all out. There's a blind hole about six feet square directly back of your closet. What do you think of that?"

"Holy cats!" said Jay Gould who immediately bolted for his room with Macnooder at his heels. A short comparison of distances, with a craning survey of the shelving roof, convinced them that, in fact, the greatest discovery of the age was at hand.

"You see, my room is a couple of feet higher than yours," said Macnooder excitedly. "I'll dig for it low down in the wall. You saw a trapdoor through the floor of your closet and we'll have it cinched."

"This must be a profound secret," said Jay Gould slightly pale.

"Your hand!" said Macnooder.

Two minutes later, having locked and barred the door, the wide-eyed discoverers were flat on their bellies in Macnooder's closet,

MACNOODER STANDING ON TIPTOES SOUNDED THE PLASTERED OBSTRUCTION.

Doc stealthily applying a chisel to the plaster which Jay Gould carefully stuffed into a washbag, illegally borrowed from the Pink Rabbit.

"It's hollow, sure enough," said Macnooder, when the plaster had fallen. "Where's the saw?"

"Here you are. Down with the laths."

"Not a sound."

Through the dull rasping of the saw the laths gradually yielded an aperture for the passage of the human body.

"Let's look," said Jay Gould eagerly.

Through the jagged entrance lay a passage mysterious, adventurous, and gloomy, formed by the meeting of the sloping roof and the floor.

"Let's explore it," said Jay Gould, all for action.

"You bet."

"Think of finding it!"

"It's a wonder!"

"Start ahead, Doc."

"Take the honor," said Macnooder magnanimously; "I have had all the fun so far."

"I wouldn't think of it," said Gould resolutely, "you have every right. After you."

"Are you afraid?"

"Are you?"

"Let's toss."

"Beans! I'll go first," said Jay Gould, who feared neither man nor master.

"There may have been a murder," said Macnooder, when Gould was safely in. "If you strike any bones, don't rattle them."

Jay Gould at once lit a match.

"The bite of some rats is peculiarly poisonous," continued Macnooder, wriggling like a snake amid the cobwebs.

The first match was immediately succeeded by a second.

"Great Lalapazoozas!"

"What is it?"

"Look at this."

Macnooder hastily hauling himself upon the passage, found a blind enclosure above five feet square with a chimney at one side.

"Have a coffin nail," said Jay Gould, with perfect calm.

"What shall we call it?" said Macnooder instantly.

"The Holy of Holies."

"Your hand again."

"We'll bring rugs and sofa cushions and crackers and cheese. Eh, what?"

"Sure, Mike."

"Say, who'll we let in on this?"

"It must be a secret locked in the breasts of only a few," said Jay Gould firmly. "Sport McAllister is my roommate, he'll have to go in."

"Of course. But not the Waladoo Bird—no elephants that will stick their feet through the ceiling."

"Well, how about Shingle-Foot Harris?"

"Agreed; and Tinkles Bell—five; no more!"

"We must take a separate oath of secrecy."

"Sure."

"Sealed with blood."

"Quite so."

"And brand the arms with a burning cigarette."

"What!" said Macnooder; "all of us?"

"No—o, the fellows we let in."

"Oh, absolutely!"

The discovery of the Holy of Holies, destined to be passed down for four successive generations (this is not fiction), unsuspected by masters or uninitiated housemates, still left Macnooder short of the national reputation which he felt was his due. Of course, among the midnight brethren his standing was enormous. But this left him as restless as the right hand when the left hand knoweth not its doing.

From the floor of Jay Gould's closet a trapdoor was constructed, fitting cunningly in natural grooves with a bolt to be drawn below. The only moment of dire peril occurred one afternoon when Shingle-Foot, having gone into the Holy of Holies alone, fell asleep and gave forth snores that shook the House. Luckily, no masters were within, and Macnooder hastily diverted suspicion to himself while Jay Gould, scrambling into the den, seized Shingle-Foot by the throat and brutally throttled the disturber.

Still, the veneration of the inner brotherhood sufficed not. Often of evenings, when lights were out, and they were huddled by the warm bricks in whispered ecstasy lit by the winking sparks of their cigarettes, Macnooder would lapse into reverie.

"What's the matter?" one would inquire from time to time.

"I'm working out something—an idea," Macnooder would answer, lapsing into taciturnity.

But the great idea delayed unconscionably. Macnooder's suave good humor turned into a fidgeting irritability. He was only the big man of a House. The nation was beyond these sectional limits with its call to ambition.

Dink Stover had not yet arrived with his Sleep Prolonging Devices but Hickey who had not yet left (by request) had already preempted the lists of history with his nocturnal exploits and above all there was the Tennessee Shad, the fertile originator of busy schemes from recumbent positions. About this time a faculty decree was promulgated against the right of every future American citizen to acquire influenza, bronchitis and the catarrhal substitutes, and it was solemnly announced that henceforth, under odious penalties, every boy should wear a hat.

On the following morning, while the indignation was at its height, a joyful ripple spread over the school, which rushing to the fountain of rumors, beheld the Tennessee Shad lazily slouching across the Circle, equipped with what might legally be termed a hat. The rim of a derby, stripped of every vestige of a crown, reposed upon the indignant upright of his two flanking ears. It had been a hat and it was a hat. It complied with and it defied the tyrannous injunction. A roar of joy and freedom went up and in ten minutes every $3 to $5 derby in the school was decapitated and the brim defiantly riding on the exposed head of each rebellious imitator.

The incident concentrated the already passionate longings of the young Macnooder. He must pass over the limits of the House. He must rise to national scope. He must prove himself worthy of the complexities of the Tennessee Shad. For Macnooder had that critical enthusiasm for the Shad that the man of practical perceptions has for the irresponsibilities of a man of genius. The imagination of the Tennessee Shad must be turned to practical results as Niagara, stupendous in itself, has waited for centuries to be harnessed to the pockets of business. He, Macnooder, would prove his right, capitalize the Tennessee Shad, form the firm of Macnooder and the Tennessee Shad, and putting it on a sound business basis, develop it into a source of revenue.

In this mood he was bumping up the stairs one afternoon, when he came to an alarmed and sudden halt. Directly opposite, from the crack of the Pink Rabbit's door, came a faint, but unmistakable odor of tobacco.

Now the Pink Rabbit was among the cherubim and seraphim of the school. Macnooder could hardly believe his senses. He advanced a few steps, cocked his head on one side and drew in a deep breath. The odor was strange, but distinctly of the Demon Tobacco.

Macnooder, hastily sliding around the door, beheld, in fact, the Pink Rabbit, propped up in bed, reading a novel, devouring a box of taffy, and smoking a cigarette.

"For the love of Mike, Rabbit! What are you doing?" he exclaimed.

"What's the matter?" said the invalid hoarsely from his couch.

But here Macnooder suddenly sniffed the air.

"Cubebs!" he said.

"Sure."

"But that's smoking."

"Not at all. Doctor Charlie prescribed them—cure asthma, and all that sort of thing."

"Cubebs are not tobacco?" said Macnooder, who had missed the preliminary stages.

"No, you chump."

"And they're good for colds, you say."

"Hay fever and asthma."

"Well, I'll be jig-swiggered."

Macnooder continued to his room in a state of scientific speculation, halted by the window and, digging his fists into his pockets, stared out at the Circle, around which a dozen fellows were laboriously plodding in penance.

"Cubebs aren't tobacco," he repeated for the tenth time. "By the great horned spoon, there certainly is something in that idea."

That night, in the Holy of Holies, Macnooder was more silent than usual, though this time it was with a purpose.

"Doc's in love," said Shingle-Foot, suspiciously.

"I believe he is."

"He certainly acts off his feed."

This sally failed to awaken Macnooder.

"She doesn't love him."

"She loves another."

"Poor old Doc."

Macnooder calmed them with a disdainful flutter of his hand.

"I'll tell you," he said impressively, "what's been occupying me."

"Go ahead."

"I'm tired of local reputations."

"Oh, you are," said Sport McAllister critically; for he thought it was time that even Macnooder should be discouraged.

"I am."

"Indeed, and what will satisfy you, you conceited, brassy, top-heavy squirt?"

"Nothing but an international reputation," said Macnooder, disdaining to notice the mere flight of epithets.

"You don't say so!"

"And now I've got it."

"Dear me!"

"I've got the greatest stunt that was ever pulled off in any school, at any time, in any country."

"Well, we're listening."

"I'll put it this way. What would happen if the faculty got on to the Holy of Holies?"

"I'd be guiding a plow in South Idaho," said McAllister frankly.

"The use of tobacco in any form is prohibited."

"And punishable by suspension," said Jay Gould. "So says the catalog. Pass the coffin nails."

"Well, this is what I propose to do," said Macnooder, "I propose to go two times around the Circle, in full sight of every master in the whole place, smoking a cigarette."

"Repeat that," said Jay Gould.

Macnooder firmly complied.

"Oh, at night!" said Tinkles Bell scornfully; "that's an easy one."

"No, in full daylight."

"And remain in the school?"

"And remain in the school."

"Repeat the whole proposition again."

"Are you a betting man?" said Sport McAllister when Macnooder had stated the proposition the third time.

"First, last and always."

"I will bet you," said Sport McAllister, trying to still the eagerness in his voice, "I will bet you my monthly allowance from now until the close of the year. Take it, it's yours."

"I'll attend to that bet."

"What?" said McAllister, hardly believing his good fortune. "You take it?"

"The word was 'Attend.' "

"To smoke a cigarette while walking twice around the Circle in full daylight, and not get suspended."

"Exactly."

"Will you write that down?" said McAllister, who began to plan how he should enjoy the blessings of Providence.

"We have witnesses."

"When will you do it?" said Jay Gould.

"Within one week."

The next day Macnooder caught a cold which thickened considerably by the following morning. Despite this, he announced to the expectant House that the attempt would be made at one-thirty that afternoon.

Promptly at that hour Sport McAllister, Jay Gould, Tinkles and Shingle-Foot, according to agreement, repaired to the Dickinson House, armed with opera glasses, and spreading the great news. The word having circulated, the five Houses that bordered the Circle, as well as the long outline of the Upper, were suddenly and theatrically alive with spectators, carefully masked (also according to request) by hand screens and window curtains.

"Aw, he'll never dare," said Sport McAllister to the Tennessee Shad, who was furnishing the window.

"Perhaps he's been fired already."

"I'll bet there's a catch in it."

"Why, every master in the place is around now."

"Sure; he couldn't go ten yards before Robinson in the Cleve would nab him."

"Aw, he'll never dare," repeated Sport McAllister. In the misfortune of his friend, he found not only a certain pleasure but a promised easing of the money stringency.

"What's that?"

"Where?"

"Just coming behind the trees."

"It's Macnooder!"

"No!"

"It certainly is!"

It was Macnooder, stepping briskly forward. His throat, to emphasize its delicate condition, was wrapped around with several knitted scarfs; while, besides a sweater, he wore in the warm month of October a winter overcoat.

When precisely opposite the Upper, and in full sight of the Houses, Macnooder deliberately halted and bringing forth a box, lighted a cubeb cigarette.

Then, puffing it forth voluminously, he started around the Circle. The nearest House was the Cleve, wherein dwelt not only the Muffin Head but Brotherly Love Baldwin, the young assistant who had new ideas on education.

As luck would have it, at that precise moment Baldwin was on the threshold, preparing to cross the Circle.

At the sight of Macnooder, steaming briskly along his way, he stiffened one moment with horror, and the next, shot violently after the offender. He did not exactly leap forward, but there was in his advance all the growling rush of a bounding dog.

Macnooder, from the tail of his eye, beheld the sweeping approach and blew forth a particularly voluminous cloud.

"Stop!"

Macnooder came to a halt in gentle surprise.

"How dare you?" exclaimed Baldwin, almost incapable of speech.

"What's wrong, sir?" said Macnooder thickly.

Among the spectators in the Houses there was a sudden terrified craning forward.

"Throw that cigarette down this instant—you young reprobate!"

Macnooder was seized with a fit of coughing.

"Please, sir," he said finally, "I'm trying to work off a cold. It's only a cubeb."

"A what?"

"A cubeb, sir."

Mr. Baldwin began to suspect that he had bounded into a trap. So he said with dignity, "Were these prescribed by Dr. Jackson?"

"Oh yes indeed, sir. Of course, a cubeb isn't tobacco."

"But smoking is forbidden."

"Oh, no, sir."

"What!"

"Catalog only forbids use of tobacco. Cubebs are a medicine."

Mr. Baldwin stood rubbing his chin, thoroughly perplexed. Macnooder, with serious face, waited patiently the outcome of his dilemma. Now, of course, Mr. Baldwin could have ordered him to desist from any public display so liable to misconstruction and so upsetting of discipline. But he did not; and the reason was the very human motive that actuates the oppressor and the oppressed. He had been caught, and he wanted someone else to share the ignominy.

When the spying school (who of course saw only a cigarette) actually beheld Mr. Baldwin retire and Macnooder continue on his way, smoking, a spasm of horrified amazement swept the audience, in the midst of which young Peewee Davis fell from the second story, carrying away the vines.

Nothing more happened until the first turn had been completed when Macnooder encountered Mr. Jenkins, popularly known as Fuzzy-Wuzzy. Mr. Jenkins was nearsighted; and though he taught mathematics, his perceptions were not those of a lightning calculator.

When, on the pleasant meandering speculation of his mind, Macnooder suddenly intruded, he stopped dead, raising his hand to his spectacles to assure himself that he actually saw.

Macnooder, rounding the turn, saluted respectfully and continued his nonchalant way.

"Macnooder?"

"Yes, sir," said Macnooder, stopping at once.

"Er—er."

Macnooder inclined his head in an expectant sort of way until Mr. Jenkins was quite able to frame his words.

"Are you smoking a cigarette?" said the master slowly.

"A cubeb, sir, not tobacco," answered Macnooder. "Breaks up colds, sir."

Mr. Jenkins fidgeted with his eyeglasses and stared very hard at him.

"A cubeb, sir, no tobacco," continued Macnooder, allowing the aromatic odor to drift in his direction.

"A cubeb—" repeated Mr. Jenkins slowly, pulling his beard.

"Yes, sir," said Macnooder.

He waited a moment and tipping his hat went on his way, leaving the perplexed master fairly rooted in his tracks.

Mr. Smith, the Muffin Head, the next to be encountered, was

older in experience and cannier. Likewise, he had witnessed the last encounter so, instead of risking his reputation by rushing madly forth, he took up a book and started ostensibly for the library, carefully calculating his time and distance so as to cross Macnooder's path without seeming to have sought the meeting.

That there was a trap somewhere, he was convinced. So, carefully repressing the instinctive desire to spring upon the flaunter of the scholastic red rag, he approached all alert. A slight wind brought him the unmistakable odor of the cubeb. Now, as it happened, he, too, had suffered from bronchial affliction and was no stranger to this remedy. So when Macnooder came to a stop, he said with a superior smile:

"Yes, what is it, Macnooder?"

"Please, sir, did you want to speak to me?" said Macnooder himself surprised.

"About what?"

"I thought—"

"Oh, about smoking a cubeb? Not at all."

"I beg pardon, sir."

"You have a bad cold, I see."

"Yes, sir! Yes, sir!"

"That's very good for it."

The Muffin Head, chuckling with satisfaction, continued on his way. He, too, in the natural course should have sent Macnooder to his room; but again the little human strain prevented. At the entrance to Memorial, he turned and looked back to see who would fall into the trap he had evaded.

This was too much for the now utterly flabbergasted school—the Muffin Head, of all masters; the strictest of disciplinarians; the most relentless of taskmasters! In rapid succession the school then beheld a dozen more masters take the bait, some fairly galloping down with rage, others suspiciously sniffing the air. By the time Macnooder had completed four rounds, there remained only Mr. Baranson, of the Griswold, who had not been tempted out to investigate.

Macnooder made one more round with his eye on the study of the Griswold, hoping against hope. Finally he said, "Well, here goes! Someone has put him on—he's too cute to come out!"

Then, secure and triumphant, he discarded the stump of the

cubeb and lit a real cigarette, completing, without mishap, twice the rounds of the Circle.

Now Mr. Baranson, who rightly bore the title of the craftiest of the crafty, had witnessed the whole performance, chuckling hugely at the successive discomfitures of his associates and finally guessing the explanation.

The Muffin Head, on his return from the library, hoping that he had not been seen, dropped in for an artful call; and at the proper moment paused before the window, exclaiming, "By George, what's that!"

Mr. Baranson doubled up with laughter at the obviousness of the trap. When he had finally wiped the tears from his eyes, he said in a slightly superior manner, "Smith, if you're going to deal with boys, you must use your imagination. You must out-think them. That's the only way, Smith; the only way. Don't walk into their traps, don't do it. Every time a master lets himself be fooled, he loses some of his authority. Imagination, Smith, imagination!"

But an hour later, at dusk, he began to consider, to weigh and to speculate; and the more he analyzed the situation, the more he began to wonder if he had seen the last curtain. He left the House and went slowly toward the road Macnooder had traveled, and his eyes were on the ground where the last cigarette stump had fallen. Suddenly behind him a voice said solicitously, "Have you lost anything, Mr. Baranson?"

It was Macnooder.

The two stood a long moment, master and boy, the craftiest of the crafty and the ambitious Macnooder, glance to glance, one of those silent interrogatories that can not be described.

"Your cold seems to have gone," said Mr. Baranson at length, dealing out his words. Then he added, with a slightly twitching, generous smile, "I *congratulate you!*"

II

INTRODUCING THE TENNESSEE SHAD

MACNOODER'S SUCCESS in performing the impossible feat of circling the Circle smoking a genuine, bona fide non-cubeb cigarette, brought him at once the national reputation he had yearned for, but still left him short of his ambition. The Tennessee Shad had been too long entrenched in his own particular position of public admiration to relinquish a foot of his vantage simply because a new and ingenious claimant had arrived. He considered Macnooder carefully, even solicitously, and listened with deliberation to his crafty schemes of profitable promoting. He was interested but he was not convinced. Once or twice before he admitted Macnooder's equality he would have put him to the test.

Such was the condition of affairs when one Sunday afternoon the House was gathered in Lovely Mead's rooms recuperating from the fatigues of a categorical sermon preached that morning by a visiting missionary.

"Gee, Sunday's a bore!" said the Egghead, on the window seat, sticking a pin in Lovely Mead's leg to make room for his own.

"Ouch!" said Lovely in surprised indignation. "I've a mind to lick you, Egghead."

"Wish you would—anything for excitement!"

"What let's do?" said Macnooder from under the desk lamp, where he was pretending to read.

"Let's do something devilish."

"Ah, December's too cold."

"I have an idea," drawled out the Tennessee Shad from the fire rug, where he lay pillowed on the Gutter Pup's sleepy form. "Let's eat something."

At this there was a mild commotion on the window seat, where four forms lay curled, puppy fashion.

190

"Eat what?"

"I was sort of speculating on a Welsh rabbit," said the Shad in a nasal drawl.

"That's about up to your usual brand of ideas, you thin, elongated, bony Tennessee Shad," said the Gutter Pup contemptuously. "Where are we going to get anything on a Sunday evening?"

"I have a hunch," said the Tennessee Shad languidly. "I have a most particular hunch that Poler Fox was seen Saturday afternoon buying a luscious, fat and juicy piece of cheese at Doc Forman's. Question to the jury: Is or is not that cheese?"

Four figures sat up.

"Poler Fox?"

"What right has he to a piece of cheese?"

"This should be investigated!"

"It should."

"It will be!"

The Tennessee Shad and the Gutter Pup went softly down one flight of the House and along the corridor where Poler Fox burned the midnight oil. They paused and consulted.

"Had we better swipe it or invite him?"

"Let's try to swipe it first—we can always invite him."

"Whoever heard of keeping a cheese overnight, anyway?"

"That's right; it's positively unhealthy."

"We really ought to complain."

"Who'll swipe it?"

"I'll get him out of his room," said the Tennessee Shad, "and you rush in and capture the milkweed."

The Gutter Pup, for good reason, did not trust to the purity of the Tennessee Shad's intentions.

"Why don't you do the lifting?" he said suspiciously.

"You ungrateful Gutter Pup, don't you see?—you won't be seen. He'll know I was only a blind. But have it your own way."

"No," said the Gutter Pup. "You go ahead and get him out of the room."

He waited, ensconcing himself on the shadowy steps, until he saw the Shad and Poler Fox emerge and disappear down the resounding corridor. Then, quickly gliding to the abandoned room, he stepped through the door, elevated his nose, sniffed and considered.

Cheeses are not usually left unexposed or permitted to lend their aroma to articles that are to be worn. He could discard the bureau drawers and the trunk. He peered through the window; it was not on the sill. He opened the closet and drew a long, ineffectual breath. Then getting down on his hands and knees he started under the bed.

At this moment the Tennessee Shad returned with Poler Fox.

"Why, Gutter Pup," said the Shad blandly, "what are you doing under the bed?"

"I came down to borrow a trot," said the Gutter Pup, looking steadily at the Shad; "and I dropped a dime. I think it rolled under the bed."

"You weren't trying to steal Poler's cheese, were you?" said the Tennessee Shad reproachfully.

"Of course I wasn't," said the Gutter Pup indignantly.

" 'Cause Poler wants to give a Welsh rabbit party," said the Shad softly, "and he mightn't feel like inviting you if you were abusing his confidence."

The procession returned, the Tennessee Shad keeping a safe distance from the Gutter Pup, with Poler Fox clutching the cheese as his passport into the feast.

Then a crisis arose.

"What're you going to put in it?" said the Egghead skeptically.

"You can't make a Welsh rabbit without beer," said Turkey Reiter.

"Rats!" said the Tennessee Shad. "That's all you know. You can put a dozen things in."

The assembly divided radically.

"Come off!"

"What else?"

"Who ever heard of a rabbit without beer?"

"I've eaten them with condensed milk."

"We made 'em in the Dickinson with ginger pop."

"Anything'll do, so long as there's alcohol in it."

"Oh, murder!"

"Poison!"

"Not at all—they're not half bad."

"Order!" said the Tennessee Shad, rapping on the chafing dish. "I guess I've eaten and made more Welsh rabbits than any one in this bunch of amateurs. Hungry Smeed is right—you can make them with anything that's got a drop of alcohol in it."

Turkey and the Egghead put up their noses and bayed at the ceiling.

"Contrary-minded can exit."

The protest subsided at once.

"The next best thing to beer is imported ginger ale," said the Tennessee Shad. "Who's got ginger ale?"

A silence.

"Who's got ginger pop?"

Another silence.

"Root beer?"

More silence.

"Sarsaparilla?"

"I have," said the Gutter Pup, jumping up and disappearing under the window seat.

A cheer went up.

Suddenly the Gutter Pup bounded out.

"I put three bottles of sarsaparilla there Friday night," he said wrathfully. "If I knew the low-livered sneak that would steal—"

"Stealing is contemptible," said the Tennessee Shad softly, while everyone looked indignant. "I continue, who's got any cider? Who's got any lemon squash?"

"It's no use," said the gloomy Egghead. "No rabbit for us!"

"We have still our friends," said the persistent Shad. "I move we begin to sleuth. Remember, ginger ale first—but anything after."

The party went off in couples, all except the Tennessee Shad, the Gutter Pup, who didn't trust the Shad, and Poler Fox, who didn't trust the Gutter Pup.

In ten minutes the Triumphant Egghead and Hungry Smeed returned.

"Anything?" said the Tennessee Shad, ceasing to coax the melting mass of cheese.

"Nope."

Lovely Mead came back, and then Macnooder and Turkey Reiter empty-handed. The gloom spread.

"What a beastly shame!"

"And such a sweet cheese!"

"My, what a lovely smell!"

"Well, we're beaten—that's all."

"I have an idea," said the Tennessee Shad. "Let's try witch hazel."

A howl went up.

"You Indian!"

"You assassin!"

"Eat it yourself!"

"Witch hazel hasn't got alcohol in it, you ignoramus!"

"Why not?" said the Tennessee Shad militantly.

Everyone looked at the Egghead.

"Why not?"

The Egghead found the answer too difficult and remained silent.

"Give me the witch hazel," said the Tennessee Shad stirring the rabbit with determined swoops. "Now just let me give you a point or two. It's only the alcohol that counts, you jayhawkers; the rest evaporates—goes up in steam."

"Hold up," said the Egghead, who had recovered.

"What's wrong?"

"I don't stand for that scientific explanation of yours."

"Nor I," said Lovely Mead, whose father was a chemist. "Say, Doc, you ought to know. How about it?"

Now Doc Macnooder had more than a doubt, but he worshiped the fertility of the Tennessee Shad and moreover was seeking an opportunity to make a direct offer of partnership. So he looked wise and said, "The Tennessee Shad is right with this important distinction. The witch hazel will resolve itself into a modicum, ahem, of alcohol if heated separately and kept from contact with the cheese which you understand, in a state of transmutation, has certain lacto-bacillic qualities that arrest vaporization. It's quite simple if you understand it."

The Tennessee Shad gave him a grateful look.

"Say, Sport," said Turkey, only half reassured, "you may be right, but go slow—sort of coddle that witch hazel. Let it taste more of Doc Forman's grocery, if it's the same to you."

"Sure!" said the Tennessee Shad. "I'll put in an extra load of mustard and cayenne. Get those plates ready, you loafers. Dish out the crackers. Here goes!"

Eight plates stood untasted.

"Strange how my appetite's gone," said the Egghead dreamily.

"I don't feel a bit hungry."

"Someone taste it."

"Taste it yourself."

"Here, this won't do," said the Shad, frowning. "Let's all begin together."

Eight spoons made a feint toward the new species of rabbit.

The Tennessee Shad looked thoughtful, then spoke.

"Fellows, I've got an idea! Let's make it sweepstakes."

"Good idea."

"Why, Shad, you're getting intelligent."

"We'll each chip in a nickel and the first one through takes the pot," said the Shad. "Hungry, pass the toothmug."

The nickels fell noisily.

"One, two, three!" said the Tennessee Shad.

Eight spoons brandished in the air and rose again empty.

"Well, let's make it worthwhile," said the Shad. "Let's sweeten it with a quarter apiece. Sweepstakes, two dollars and forty cents. Hungry, lead the mug around again."

Each, as he dropped in a quarter, gazed deep into the mug, drew a breath and set his teeth—two dollars and forty cents was a fortune two weeks before Christmas.

"Everyone in?" said the Tennessee Shad. "No hunchin', Gutter Pup and Hungry, start fair—one, two, three, go!"

Not a boy faltered—Hungry Smeed won from the Gutter Pup by several strings and dove for the pot.

Then they sat and looked at one another.

"Gee, I feel queer!" said Turkey, with an expression of inward searching on his face.

"So do I."

"I believe we're poisoned."

"I know I am!"

"Honest, no joking, I do feel devilish queer."

"What in the deuce did we do it for?"

"Who suggested witch hazel?" said the Gutter Pup, clutching at his indignant digestion. "I'll fix him."

"Yes, who did?" said Turkey, rising with difficult wrath.

"Tennessee Shad!"

Seven writhing forms sprang up furiously.

The Tennessee Shad, with a perfect comprehension of dramatic values, had slipped away, leaving his plate untouched.

III

THE BEGINNING OF THE FIRM

Doc Macnooder bore no grudge. Even the recollected spasms of what might properly be termed his youthful *In*digestion, brought with them no feeling of malice toward the Tennessee Shad. On the contrary though his attempts at a mercantile union were continually repulsed, the determination held fast within him to turn to profit what was now only turned to mischief, and accident finally supplied the welding touch in the following manner.

In those days when the Gymnasium was still an oft-promised land, the winter term, from January to April, was to the embattled faculty what the Indian season was to the early pioneers. Four hundred-odd, combustible boys, deprived of outlet, cooped up for days by slush and sleet, presented in miniature that same state of frothy unrest from which spout forth South American somersaults and Balkan explosions.

It takes usually two weeks for the exhausted boy to recuperate from the Christmas vacation, but from about the twentieth of January the physical body overtakes the imagination and things begin to happen.

Toward the first week of February there gathered in the Triumphant Egghead's room ten disgusted members of the House, utterly wearied with life, especially bored with the present and without the slightest hope for the future.

Outside a steady, sleety downpour brought feeble icicles from the roof and ran rivulets through the muddied snowbanks.

"Now, it's turned to rain again," announced Hungry Smeed, with his nose applied to the windowpane while his waving heels cast shadows on the wall. "Nice, wet, oozy, luscious rain."

"Let's all go bicycling," said Lovely Mead facetiously.

"What time is it?" asked the Gutter Pup from the crowd on the couch.

"Just two o'clock."

A groan went up.

"Is that all?"

"Thought it was after four."

"What is there to do?"

"It's still raining, fellows," said Smeed from the window, and the conversation ceased.

"Do you think Yale'll beat Princeton?" asked Turkey Reiter at last.

"Stop trying to make conversation," said Doc Macnooder resentfully, "and don't move any more; you're the deuce of a soft pillow."

"Who's going to the Prom?" inquired Crazy Opdyke feebly.

"Crazy, you annoy me," said Butcher; "you annoy me and disturb my rest. Don't propound questions."

"Say, fellows!" said Smeed in great excitement.

"What?"

"It's snowing!"

The door opened a crack and the Tennessee Shad slipped in.

"What's doing, fellows?"

"We're exhausted with excitement!" said Old Ironsides Smith sarcastically. "We're trying to rest up for the next debauch, you precocious young skeleton."

"Say, fellows, I've got an idea," said the Tennessee Shad, draping himself over the desk.

"Oh, go away!"

"It's a corker!"

"Huh! Another of those witch hazel rabbits?"

"No, no," said the Tennessee Shad, hurriedly skipping that disastrous episode. "This is a sensation!"

"Of course!"

"Never mind—let him speak his piece."

"Let's form," said the Tennessee Shad slowly, "let's form a Criminal Club."

"A what?"

Macnooder, with an awakening hope, sat up, wondering if the brain factory was again working.

"Criminal Club—convicts and that sort of thing. We'll shave off our heads and go about lockstep."

"And initiate new members?" cried Goat Finney.

"Sure."

"And go into chapel tomorrow morning lockstep?"

"Of course!"

"Gee, what a peach of an idea!"

"Can you see the Doctor's face?"

"Oh, mother!"

"Hurray!"

"Hurrah!"

"Hurroo!"

Into the dry pit of baffled energy an idea had fallen, and in a moment all was flame and fury.

"Shad, this is a good one," said Turkey, rousing himself. "We'll call it quits on that rabbit—only—only, remembering the past, we would like to have assurances from you, assurances and guarantees."

"I second the motion most emphatically," said the Gutter Pup revengefully.

The fate of the Criminal Club hung in the balance.

"Look at this," said the Tennessee Shad. And he removed his sombrero.

From ear to ear, from the nape of his neck to the blade of his nose, he was as smooth as a china egg. The day was won in a rollicking cheer.

"Oh, look at him! Look at him!"

"Isn't he wonderful?"

"Bee-oo-tiful!"

"Me for a convict!"

"Can you see the sensation?"

"Bully for the Shad!"

"Let's do it now."

"Come on!"

Five minutes of scurrying to and fro for scissors and shaving kits, and the Triumphant Egghead's room presented the spectacle of an improvised barber shop.

"How'll we begin?" said the Gutter Pup.

"Who goes first?"

"Supposin' we draw for it."

"Who does the shaving?"

"We can't shave back of our own ears."

"The way to do it," said Macnooder, looking at the Tennessee Shad, "is for one-half of us to shave the other half."

"That's it."

"Let her go at that."

"Who first?"

But here a difficulty arose. No one cared to go first.

"This won't do," said the fiery-headed Gutter Pup, repulsing the offers of Doc Macnooder. "If I'm going to shed my shade trees—I don't trust any man, least of all Doc Macnooder."

"What do you mean?"

"I mean no one scalps any of my hair till I get a guarantee off his."

"Rats!" said the Tennessee Shad. "Gutter Pup's a natural-born kicker. Go ahead, Doc, and give him an object lesson."

But Macnooder, though sympathetic to the Tennessee Shad, was on the defensive as far as it concerned the Gutter Pup.

"In the present state of the Gutter Pup's mind—no!" he said thoughtfully. "No, I've got to see a nice white boulevard on those red lands before I consent to laying out mine."

"Will someone else start her up?"

In the silence that ensued Old Ironsides noisily dropped a pin.

"Shad," said the pessimistic Egghead, "it's a good scheme of yours, a bully good scheme; the only trouble is there doesn't seem to be enough mutual confidence. I guess the verdict'll have to be premature death."

"Shad, old sporting print," said Turkey, "have you any suggestion for harmony?"

"Nothing easier," said the Tennessee Shad, locking the door and pocketing the key. "There's one guarantee and here's another. Stand up, form a circle, everyone face the man to his right, grab the shoulders of the man in front of you, sit down slowly on the knees of the fellow behind you, the fellow in front sits down on yours, slowly, *slowly*. There you are. That's the way the Zouaves do it."

The ten found themselves in a circle, comfortably seated and seating.

"There's the answer," said the ringmaster triumphantly; "you shave and get shaved, no first and no last; the happy family; safety razors only. Now, get up, stick on the towels and start with the scissors first."

The Tennessee Shad enthroned himself on a table as master of ceremonies, while the hilarious circle formed about him in a bedlam of exclamation.

"How the deuce is Hungry Smeed going to reach up to Turkey?"

"Stick him on a chair, you chump!"

"I don't want the Gutter Pup."

"Aw, send him over here."

"Stop bobbing that head, you Butcher."

"Shorten the circle."

"I can't get Crazy's scalp lock."

"When do we begin?"

"Say when, Shad."

"All ready."

"Let her go!" said the Tennessee Shad from his perch.

Pretty soon protests broke out.

"Ouch!"

"Do you think you're biting them off?"

"Be a little less careless back there."

"Say, who's got the Gutter Pup? Murder him!"

"Moses!"

"Kezowy!"

"Help!"

"Better be careful," said the Tennessee Shad warningly; "in a moment you're going to face the other way."

The shears snipped more gently.

"What do we do when we get through the back?" said Goat Finney.

"You lather it and shave."

"What about the rest?"

"The front's easy enough; anyone can do that."

In an hour every head was as bald as a sapling in a hurricane. They stood and gazed at one another, shrieking with laughter. They hugged one another, rolled on the floor in joyful battling groups, and blessed the imagination that had turned a slough of despond into a vaudeville. On the last stroke of the dinner-bell, solemnly, in lockstep, led by Hungry Smeed and grading up to the mighty Turkey Reiter, eleven glistening heads in sequence descended on the dining room. At the same moment, from the north entrance, appeared a chain gang of eight, equally void of hair, led by Mucker Reilly, followed by Snorky Green, Beauty Sawtelle,

Tough McCarty, Charley De Soto, Piggy Moore, Pink Rabbit and the Waladoo Bird!

The duplicity of the Tennessee Shad was forgotten in the masterly climax he had imagined. The rival clubs met and agreed to proselyte and divide the school.

At eight o'clock the next morning, when the Doctor, all unaware, stood in his pulpit, rubbing his glasses and shooting careful glances along the crowded pews, suddenly a shriek went up. Marching proudly with gleeful faces, two gangs of baldheaded boys suddenly appeared abreast, and in rhythmic step came down the aisles amid the gasps, the shrieks and roars of the school.

Now, there are two things a headmaster must control: his temper and, above all, his sense of humor. The situation was serious; a smile would have been fatal. Something had to be done at once or within a day there would not be enough hair left in the excited school to tuft the head of a Japanese doll. He set his teeth and stared his most terrific stare at a point where the double row of bald heads faded from the vision. Luckily the service allowed him to stifle his amusement and fan up his wrath by calling up the horrible vision of the threatening epidemic.

"Never in my experience, in my whole experience as a scholar or a teacher," he began, glaring with painful ferocity at the denuded culprits, "never have I known such willful, malicious and outrageous desecration of the house of the Lord as you young scalawags have shown today. I do not know whether I shall expel you outright or deprive you of your diplomas; I shall wait until I can consider the matter more calmly. But this I can say right now, if any other incipient imbecile in this school dares to imitate this exhibition of monumental asininity, that boy will leave this school within an hour and never return. I will see these deluded boys in my study after lunch."

The members of the newly formed Housebreakers' Union went out quietly, stealing apprehensive glances at one another.

At two o'clock, as they huddled together in the solemn study, each striving to occupy an unexposed position, T. Dean Smith, secretary, appeared, and, after gazing in fascination at them, said, "Well, boys, you certainly have riled the Doctor this time. You'd better go back quietly."

"Oh, Smithy, won't he see us?" said the Pink Rabbit in a panic, while others exclaimed:

"Is he going to fire us?"

"Will he take away our dips?"

"What does he say?"

"Is he mad as a hornet?"

"He says he won't trust himself to see you now," said Smith gravely, without mentioning the reason why the mirth-tortured Doctor wouldn't trust himself to face that sidesplitting spectacle. "I'd lay pretty quiet for a while, if I were you fellows. Let it blow over a little."

"Gee!" said the Tennessee Shad in disgust, as they filed through the gloomy portals. "Can't he have a sense of humor?"

T. Dean Smith glanced at the curtains of the Doctor's sanctum, but did not reply. Instead he stood on the top step gazing down on them with a sardonic smile.

"You'll be a beautiful sight at the Prom, you will!" he said and entered the house. His words fell like a bomb.

"Geewhilikens!"

"Holy cats and mice!"

"I never thought of that!"

"Give me the dunce cap!"

"Of all the fools!"

"Goats!"

"Asses!"

"Idiots!"

"My whole family's coming."

"The family's not what's worrying me."

"Who started us on this fool stunt?"

"The Tennessee Shad."

"Roughhouse him!"

"Hold up! I'm in the same boat," cried the Tennessee Shad. "Don't lose your blooming heads; the Prom's two weeks off!"

"Two weeks?" shouted the Gutter Pup, with a glitter in his eye. "What's two weeks going to do? Do you think we can get respectable in two weeks?"

"Nothing easier," said the Tennessee Shad. "Hair tonic!"

"Fall in line," said Macnooder, seizing instantly the suggestion.

The eleven convicts and the eight Housebreakers assumed a chain gang formation.

"About face!"

"Mark time!"

"Right, left!"

"Forward, march!"

Lockstep, pounding the ground, they went swiftly toward the village and descended on the vendors of hair lotions.

That night the commercial Macnooder appeared at the rooms of the Tennessee Shad and found the door barricaded. He knocked gently in a coaxing friendly way.

"Who's that?" said the Tennessee Shad after their eyes had met through the keyhole.

"Hist! It's Doc Macnooder. Open up."

"I'm studying," said the Tennessee Shad, too tired to choose his lies.

"Shad I come not to take your hard-earned money but to do you good," said Macnooder soothingly, using his well-known formula. "Will you listen?"

"Elucidate," said the Tennessee Shad, drawing up a chair on his side of the door.

Macnooder, camping down, said with the confidence that a great idea alone can inspire:

"Shad, I've approached you many a time and oft with a few little suggestions for adding a few coupons and bonds to our worldly possessions. You have rejected my partnership."

"I have a soul above money," said the Shad, moving his ear, however, a little closer to the keyhole.

"This is my last, positively last offer," said Macnooder firmly. "Accept it and we sign articles of partnership, share and share alike, in a month you will drive your own horse and carriage, wear diamond studs and sport a jewel-studded gold pencil. Refuse and—"

"And what?" said the Tennessee Shad.

"You won't refuse, you can't refuse! Now listen."

Three minutes later the bolts slipped and the Tennessee Shad led Doc Macnooder to the easy chair and propped him up with cushions.

That night the joyful Macnooder transformed his room into a barber shop, with rows of lotions and glassy ointments, announced the Tennessee Shad as partner and hung out this shingle:

THE IMPERIAL TONSORIAL PARLORS
MACNOODER AND THE TENNESSEE SHAD
BOSS BARBERS
CASH, MORE CASH, AND NOTHING BUT CASH!

Massage .... $ *.03*
Friction with any hair encourager .... *.05*
Vaselining .... *.03*
Three-in-One .... *.10*
Two weeks' treatment *1.25*

No towels supplied.

The Macnooder treatment coaxes forth the hair, seizes and stretches it, makes it long and curly. Long and curly hair means social success at the Prom; social success means retaining the affections of the fair!

Don't hesitate, don't calculate, do it now!
Come early, come often and bring the children!

Two weeks to cover their nakedness, two weeks to meet the all-seeing feminine eye. That night, each greased hopeful went to bed with a prayer for the morrow.

At the stroke of the rising bell the Gutter Pup catapulted out of bed and flung himself anxiously before his mirror and remained transfixed with despair at the sight of two elephantine ears flanking a snow-white cranium that had not been covered overnight with hair. At this moment a groan arose from Lovely Mead's room across the study.

"Is that you, Lovely?" said the Gutter Pup, fascinated by the horrible caricature in the mirror.

"It is."

"What luck?"

"Nothing!"

"Nothing here."

The door opened on the Triumphant Egghead and Hungry Smeed in pajamas.

"What luck, you fellows?"

"Don't ask!"

"I've got a couple of shoots on top," said the Egghead; "but that's where Butcher Stevens' razor missed me. Isn't it awful?"

"When do you suppose it'll come out again?"

"There must be something tomorrow morning."

"What will we look like at the Prom?"

"I'm desperate," said the Triumphant Egghead. "I've got an Apollo Belvedere rival who stays at home. Jerusalem, where will I be now when she sees this!"

"We must load up with starchy food and drink lots of phosphates at the Jigger Shop," said Hungry Smeed wisely.

"Do you think anything'll show up by tomorrow?"

"Oh, Lovely, it must!"

"How're the others?"

"Smooth as a rink."

Every spare hour was spent in following a new theory; if persistency and ingenuity could have done it they would have succeeded, or had there been any faith in newspaper advertisements or honor in the labels of patent hair-restorers.

They rubbed and greased and dosed themselves, they caught at the first shoots and shut their jaws and pulled, morning, afternoon and night, and at last, when the inexorable Prom came galloping in, they went in hangdog fashion, balking and blushing, to meet the shrieks that greeted their first bow.

.   .   .   .   .   .

That night the Tennessee Shad sat among the lonely anti-fussers who roosted on the chilly edges of the Esplanade and scoffed at the gaiety within.

It was cold, uncomfortably cold, and one by one the frost-nipped spectators slipped away until only the Tennessee Shad remained, fascinated. As each stubble-covered, flap-eared dupe bumped his embarrassed way into view he half closed his eyes and smiled a contented, faraway smile.

The Tennessee Shad had never danced!

IV

FIRST JOINT OPERATION

THE RETURNS from the two weeks of rushing business of the Imperial Tonsorial Parlors made quite a respectable dividend to celebrate the inception of the firm, especially as the Triumphant Egghead, who was in difficult competition for the affections of a blonde, had plunged desperately in the vaselining and the massage.

The formation of the firm was still a matter of secrecy, unsuspected by the public, a fact which alone made possible the next operation.

When January and February have been endured, the limbo month of March is certainly the most fatiguing of the whole year. It belongs neither to the winter family nor to the aristocracy of the spring. It is peevish, malicious and the spirit of negation. When it shines overhead, with vaulted blues and lazy clouds that invite soaring baseballs to them, it is treacherous and foul underfoot. When it snows it brings no sleighing. When it freezes it is not to spread the pond for skating but to harden the mud ruts and delay the opening of the diamonds. Month of corduroys and leathern boots, of waiting and longing, when sinkers overrun the table and the vegetables taste of the can, when the greatest boon is a case of pinkeye or German measles (real or feigned) which gives you the right to doze and browse and play games with other fortunate inmates of the infirmary on the Hill.

The Triumphant Egghead sat on the ledge of the Esplanade and expressed these sentiments in more direct terms, while his whole conception of existence was centered in making a tennis ball strike the shoulder of an opposite ledge so as to bound back into his hands. From an upper window the Gutter Pup and Lovely Mead looked out in disgust at the sky because it had no sun, at the earth because it was unfit to gambol on, and more particularly at the Triumphant Egghead for having enough energy to sit there and bounce a ball.

Presently the Egghead's fingers slipped and the ball, escaping, rolled away. He watched it streak wetly down the Esplanade, hesitate and then topple down the steps and trickle languidly along the slimy surface, coating itself with rich yellow ooze. Then, falling off the ledge, he stretched himself and shuffled heavily up to join the Gutter Pup in Turkey Reiter's room.

"My, you're energetic!" said Lovely Mead.

The Egghead grunted, selected a soft spot and lay down.

The Gutter Pup continued gazing out the window with malicious joy at Cap Keefer and the candidates returning from their mud bath in the baseball cage.

"Hello!" he said suddenly. "There goes Doctor Charlie into the Dickinson with his little green bag."

"Wonder who's sick," said the Egghead. "Lucky fellow!"

"Wish I were," said Turkey Reiter.

"Same here," said the Gutter Pup.

"It's such a pleasure to be ill with Doctor Charlie," said Lovely Mead ruminatively. "He has such nice little white pills and such round brown pills and such great big black pills that decorate a mantelpiece so nicely!"

"Think of sleeping two luscious weeks at the infirmary."

"Hum!"

"Don't Turkey, don't—it's cruel."

"Why, here comes the Tennessee Shad," said the lookout, "just as fast as he can come. My, just see how he hops along!"

"He'd better keep away from here," said the Egghead, running his head over the still prickly hairs.

"He will, if he knows what's good for him," remarked Turkey Reiter.

"I only wish he would drop in!" said the Gutter Pup, doubling up his fists and annihilating a sofa pillow.

"I think, fellows," said the Egghead, squirming to and fro so as to scratch his back, "I say I think the Tennessee Shad's usefulness in this community is just about over."

"He won't catch me again," said the Gutter Pup. "If he brought me a ten-dollar guaranteed goldpiece on a solid silver platter I wouldn't so much as reach out my hand for it."

"His murder would be quite justifiable," said the Egghead, thinking of the Prom. "It will take me a couple of natural lives to live down the effect of that haircut. I was not beautiful."

"Ugh!"

"Don't—don't recall it!"

"Gee, my girl's stopped corresponding."

At this moment the Tennessee Shad opened the door, inserted a cautious portion of his sharp features and said genially:

"Ah, there!"

Three vicious sofa cushions slam-banged against the door, accompanied by an explosion of wrath.

"Get out!"

"Cut loose!"

"Vanish!"

"Hold up," said the Tennessee Shad, opening the door again. "I've got an idea!"

Two books and a couple of slippers came smashing through the air.

"You'll regret it," said the Shad, bobbing in and out.

The Gutter Pup banged the door and locked it. Outside was heard the scraping of a chair along the hall, then the transom turned and the glittering eyes of the Tennessee Shad appeared over the door.

"Shad, you are a brave man," said Turkey Reiter ominously. "Go away—do go away while we can still control ourselves."

"Fellows, I have come to apologize," said the Tennessee Shad, while the chair squeaked protestingly.

"Keep your apologies," said Lovely Mead. "We loathe the sight of you. Get out!"

"To apologize and atone," added the Tennessee Shad, keeping a watchful eye on the Gutter Pup who was reaching out for a baseball bat.

"Atone!" said the Egghead with a bitter laugh. "Much good that'll do me."

"Yes, atone, Egghead," said the Shad firmly. "I'm sorry; I feel bad—I do feel bad. I'll admit that my ideas sometimes miscarry, but I have had good ones—you know I've had good ones, and this idea is a good one!"

The Gutter Pup raised the baseball bat, but Turkey Reiter restrained him.

"No, Gutter Pup; let's hear it," he said; "let's know the depth of his depravity. Let's have no illusions about him."

"I'll back my idea," said the Tennessee Shad stoutly.

"How'll you back it?"

"I'll tell you how I'll back it. I'll back it against all you fellows—the whole longeared lot of you. You let me in and promise to keep your hands off me till you hear my idea and, if you don't fall down and kiss my hand and say: 'Shad you're a public benefactor; can you ever, ever forgive us?'—if you don't say that, well, I'm willing to be massacred any time or anyhow. Now, can you imagine what sort of an idea it is?"

The four looked mutely at one another. Finally Turkey spoke.

"Tennessee Shad, you always did have a persuasive, silvery voice, and as my fondest hope for the future is to be associated with you in selling anything to anybody I'm going to let you in. Pup, let down that bat. Egghead, open the door."

The Tennessee Shad glided in, locked the door in turn and shut the transom with much mystery.

"First," he said, "give me your word of honor that you'll keep this a dead secret. No blabbing and no one else to be let in on it. Promise."

"Hold up, this wasn't in the agreement," said the Egghead stubbornly.

"No promise, no secret!"

"That's fair," said Turkey.

They raised their right hands and solemnly swore.

"And no mental reservations," said the Tennessee Shad severely, looking at the Gutter Pup, "if you're gentlemen!"

"Of course not. Say, what do you think we are?"

"All right."

The Tennessee Shad climbed on a chair and roosted on the back in his familiar manner, plucked forth a pencil, chewed it meditatively and said, "Are you happy?"

"What the deuce has that got to do with it?" said the Gutter Pup, tightening his grip on the baseball bat, while the Egghead added irately, "Turkey, it's a con game—he's kidding us."

"Oh, let him tell it his own way," said Turkey.

"Are you happy? Are you cheerful?" continued the Tennessee Shad pursuing the Socratic method. "Do you enjoy your meals? Do the words fresh vegetables mean anything to your jaded appetites? Do they?"

"Go on, and don't be idiotic."

"Does the prospect of wallowing two weeks in the mud fill your soul with rapture? Are you still eager to rise at an unearthly hour, to eat the deadly sinker and the scrag bird?"

"What are you driving at?" said Turkey, mystified. "You know the answers as well as we do. What's your scheme?"

"How would the idea of spending these next two weeks like this appeal to you?" said the Tennessee Shad, point-blank: "Sleeping late, eating cream in your coffee—not cream, but *real* cream—thick, lumpy, soggy cream—no chapel, no recitations—nothing! Would two weeks in the infirmary appeal to you as an idea?"

"Would it?" said Lovely Mead, opening his eyes. "Jemima!"

The Gutter Pup put away the baseball bat, leaning it gently in the corner.

"Think of nothing to do all day long," continued the Tennessee Shad, half shutting his eyes, "but to read novels and play cards and games! Think of having special steaks and nice, juicy chops to build up your delicate bodies!"

"Oh, Shad!" cried the converted Gutter Pup. "How are you going to work it?"

The Tennessee Shad came back to earth, gave a vicious last bite on his pencil, pocketed it, slapped his knee and cried:

"German measles!"

"German measles?" repeated the four.

"Shad!"

"You don't mean it!"

"Who's got 'em?"

"Oh, joy!"

Now, German measles are not an affliction but a dispensation of Providence, and the boy who in the month of March is thus blessed and discovers it before the doctor does is in honor bound to share his good fortune with his neighbors.

"I know," said the Gutter Pup suddenly. "It's over in the Dickinson. I saw Doctor Charlie trotting in."

"Naw!" said the Tennessee Shad disdainfully. "I've looked into that—that's nothing but Wee-Wee Logan faking up a case of pinkeye. Mine's the real, genuine article. Are you on?"

"Are we on?"

"Say, just lead us up to him!"

"Quick!"

"It's Doc Macnooder, on the second floor," said the Tennessee Shad. "But, mind, only we four get in on this. We don't want to sleep two in a bed."

"But, Shad, how do you know?"

"How can you be sure?"

"Doc knows the symptoms," said the Shad. "He's had 'em before; besides, he's going to be a doctor."

"For Heaven's sake, fellows, let's get to him."

"We mustn't lose a minute."

"Come on."

"Hold up," said the Tennessee Shad. "There's a condition attached to it."

The four seekers after infection drew up and eyed the glib impresario.

"There generally is a string to your ideas," said the Gutter Pup; "and we're getting very much to dislike those strings."

"That's dead right!"

"I wouldn't get too careless this time, young sporting life!"

"I never saw such a distrustful bunch," said the Tennessee Shad; "and the whole thing is to protect you, too."

"What do you mean?"

"I mean this," said the Tennessee Shad with an injured air. "I drew up a contract with Doc that we get exclusive rights and have to pay him a dollar down. Do you want the whole House started for the infirmary before we can get a look-in? If you don't think it's worth a quarter—oh, well —I guess I can find—"

"Excuse me," said Turkey Reiter, pulling out a coin, "you are a miracle of foresight."

"Pardon me," said the Gutter Pup, making change.

"Will this bright new quarter do?" said Egghead.

"You fellows ought to think twice before you shout," said Lovely Mead, completing the dollar.

"I had German measles second-form year," said the Egghead as they descended the stairs. "They're delightful!"

"How long does it take to catch 'em?" asked the Gutter Pup.

"About a week."

"That's an awful time to wait!"

"Hush, here we are," said the Tennessee Shad, stopping and knocking on door 48.

A slight swishing sound was heard on the other side and a catarrhal voice said, "Who's there?"

"It's me," said the Tennessee Shad. "It's all right, Doc; open up."

The key turned and they filed into a room encased with green,
black and blue bottles arranged on shelves, heaped in corners, scattered everywhere.

Macnooder, swathed in neck cloths, dressed in a green-and-blue
bathgown, red Mephistopheles slippers and violet garters, sank
back into an easy chair and disappeared a moment behind a voluminous handkerchief.

The four proselytes stood by the door.

"Say, old sporting Tootlets," said the cautious Turkey, "German
measles is most pleasant, but real measles isn't what we're looking
for. What's to guarantee us we get what we pay our money for and
not a gold brick?"

"You can't have measles twice, you ignoramus," said Macnooder
with a sneeze. "I had 'em four years ago."

"You'll guarantee us?" said the Gutter Pup.

"Not to have measles? Sure, I will. I'll post a forfeit, five apiece."

"That's good, straight talk," said the Tennessee Shad briskly.
"Don't be an ass, Gutter Pup. Now, Doc, if you'll give us your word
not to let anyone else in on this, here's that dollar we agreed upon."

"So help me!" said Macnooder, jingling the coins in his pocket.

"Hold up there," broke in Lovely Mead; "all very well, but
how're we going to know you'll carry out the bargain?"

"He's going to Trenton this afternoon," said the Tennessee
Shad. "He's got an aunt living there."

"Is that so, Doc?"

"Just as soon as I get through with you fellows and get in Doctor
Charlie."

"Well," said Turkey, "I don't see but what it's a go."

Macnooder rose, drew a carpet over the crack under the door,
stuffed the keyhole with cotton and lit an alcohol lamp.

"What's that for?" said the Egghead, whom the presence of so
many labeled bottles rendered uneasy.

"Cold kills germs, heat develops them," said Doc with a superior
air. "Come on, Shad, you first!"

The Tennessee Shad seated himself opposite, touching knees and
foreheads, while the others looked on in fascinated admiration.

"Grab my hands," said Doc solemnly, "and take long breaths."

One week later the Gutter Pup began to cough, Lovely Mead to sneeze and Turkey Reiter and the Triumphant Egghead to snuff and sniffle; only the Tennessee Shad remained disconsolate. Doctor Charlie, joyfully summoned, found the five waiting in Turkey Reiter's room, applied a thermometer and looked very solemn.

"Catarrhal symptoms and febrile disturbance," he said. "Pack up your things and get right up to the infirmary." Then, considering the Tennessee Shad thoughtfully, he added, "You have a slightly heightened temperature, but that may be only imagination. However, I think I won't risk it; you go up, too."

An hour later the five were shaking hands and slapping one another on the back in the cozy parlor of the infirmary.

"Well, you old growlers," said the Tennessee Shad proudly, "are my ideas always useless?"

"Shad," said Turkey, "you are reinstated in our affections. We love you. You are our pride and joy."

"I hope," said the Egghead, drawing up by the crackling fire, "that it'll rain and slush the whole time we're here."

"Gee, it certainly is good indoors," said Lovely Mead, squatted before the bookshelves.

"What'll come next?" said the Gutter Pup with thick speech. "I certainly have got you all beat on the snuffles."

"Look out for a little pink rash tomorrow morning," said the Egghead wisely.

"Does it itch bad?"

"Naw, it only tickles for a day."

"I suppose we'll have to stay in bed one day at least."

The Tennessee Shad stood, legs akimbo, gazing into the fire.

"Why so silent, old Shad?" said the Triumphant Egghead.

"I don't understand it."

"Understand what?"

"Why I didn't take," said the Shad dejectedly, "I haven't any symptoms at all. I faked up a temperature, but I can't keep that up."

"Old sporting life," said Turkey with a grin, "this is one on you!"

"It certainly is, Shad," said the Egghead with a chuckle.

"Poor old Shad!" said the Gutter Pup, winking at the others. "What an awful sell. But it was coming to you, old hoss; it certainly was coming to you."

"You ungrateful, spiteful little beast," said the Tennessee Shad.

There never was such a dinner as they sat down to that night.

"My, what a steak," said the Gutter Pup languidly, "soft and red and juicy."

"Say, are these mashed potatoes?"

"A little more, please."

"Um—if there's anything I love it's creamed onions."

"Ice cream for dessert."

"No?"

"Fact—coffee ice cream."

"Say, was that a tomato soup, eh?"

"Think of a week of this!"

"Pass my plate."

"Let's begin all over again."

"Hope you stay with us, Shad."

"Shut up," said Shad, "and be a gentleman with those onions!"

They slept late, had breakfast in bed and rose just in time to drop in to lunch.

"Why, where's the Shad?" said Turkey Reiter.

"He's gone."

"Fired!"

"Thrown out!"

"Hurray!"

They took their knives and forks and beat a gleeful tattoo on the table, then burst into peals of laughter.

"This is where we score."

"Oh, mamma, what a story to tell on the Shad!"

"Will we tell it?"

"Oh, no!"

"Are we it?"

They rose and shook hands, then sat down and looked at one another critically.

"Say, where's the little pink rash?"

"Search me."

"I haven't got it."

"Nor me."

"It ought to have come," said the Egghead thoughtfully.

"I feel bum enough to have a dozen, all right."

"Shut up!" said the Egghead, jumping up so as to catch the first view, "here comes lunch!"

"What is it?"

"Veal cutlet."

"With brown sauce?"

"Brown sauce—fresh peas and tomatoes!"

"Say, sports," said Turkey Reiter suddenly, "is this cutlet tough to you?"

"It certainly is."

"It cuts all right."

"Well, it hurts me to chew it."

The Egghead laid down his knife and fork with a clatter.

"Why, Egghead, what's wrong?"

"Do your jaws ache?"

"Sure!"

"They do."

"Have you ever had the mumps?"

"No!" cried in horror Turkey, the Gutter Pup and Lovely Mead.

"Well, you have them!"

.   .   .   .   .   .

They not only had the mumps, but they had them violently, outrageously, swollen to ridiculous proportions. On the third day, while the Gutter Pup from his bed was gazing in the opposite mirror at a face that looked like a chipmunk with a coconut in either cheek, a word of consolation came to him in the shape of the following scrawl:

> *Say, Gutter Pup, it was all Macnooder. I didn't know—honest, I didn't. Square me with Turkey.*
>
> *Yours,*
>
> *SHAD.*

P. S.—I've had the mumps.

V

THE FIRM FINDS A NEW VICTIM

SHORTLY AFTER the firm of Macnooder and the Tennessee Shad had been established on a dividend basis, they discovered to their alarm that the scope of the future operations was exactly limited by the luster of their past successes. Not that there was any stop in the output of fertile ideas or astute practical financiering. The trouble was, to use Wall Street phraseology, with the market and the lambs. If Macnooder sought to launch an idea he was greeted with derisive smiles and the cry, "Fine, tell it to the Tennessee Shad!"

When the Tennessee Shad languidly and artfully proposed, the reply was similar and more insulting:

"Try it on Macnooder, you assassin and bunco steerer!"

Famine set in relentlessly and there is no telling what might have happened had not chance, as shall be related, brought them a victim made to order and a field of exploitation which for a time seemed more inexhaustible than the diamond field of Africa. Had either the avarice of Doc Macnooder or the mischievous imagination of the Tennessee Shad been capable of restraint, the firm might have gone the full course in fattening prosperity; but as both were but mortal, the speculation was profitable but unfortunately short. Here endeth the parenthesis.

When Montague Skinner had completed sixteen gentle and luxurious years in the hansoms and continuous vaudevilles of New York City, it chanced that the select private school which he reluctantly graced, becoming unduly elated with the phenomenally triumphant eleven which represented it, issued a challenge and bore down on The Lawrenceville School, Lawrenceville, New Jersey, with a betting commissioner and faces which they desperately strove to render without malice or guile.

As the hospitality of their hosts saw them to the Trenton depot, they reached New York on their return-trip tickets and arrived at their homes, delaying the cabdriver no longer than the time required to borrow the fares from their sympathetic butlers. The Metropolitan papers obligingly concealed the score in obscure corners while the business manager hurriedly revised the schedule for the ensuing season, excusing himself to the Lawrenceville Football Association on the ground that the two hours required to make the trip was unfortunately found to be a serious infringement on the scholarly routine of the school.

The experience was exceedingly upsetting to young Skinner who, being a very large frog in a very small pond, could not remember without profound unrest the very much larger frogs he had seen disporting themselves on the surface of the considerably larger waters.

Now Skinner had not simply been born with a gold spoon in his mouth, but literally amid a shower of golden spoons, forks and knives. Joshua M. Skinner, proprietor and manager of The Regal Hotel, blissfully regarded himself as but a humble instrument in the advancement of his only child's career, and secretly rejoiced when his son lectured him on the proprieties of masculine attire and the vernacular of select society.

At fifteen, Montague was installed in his private suite and given his particular valet, likewise a coachman and coupé to be at his orders all hours of the day. Accounts were opened at the best of tailors and haberdashers, and Joshua M. Skinner doubled an exceedingly elastic allowance, resolved that money should never be lacking to the proper equipment of Montague's genteel sporting proclivities. Mrs. Skinner was all that a fond and perfect mother should be and the only time that the semblance of a disagreement had arisen between her and her son was on one vulgar occasion when she had beheld Montague and three companions returning from school in a *hired* cab.

Despite this tender paternal solicitude, Montague had passed through so much of the disillusionment of worldly existence that he had quickly come to assume that air of complete boredom which goes with a stockade collar and a limply pendant cigarette. He never burst into roars of laughter. The most excruciatingly mirth-provoking turns of the vaudeville headliners never stirred him to more than a tolerantly amused smile. He never applauded. At the age of sixteen he had never fallen in love. He spoke of the chorus as "homes for old women," and from his superior knowledge, smiled down at his more impulsive comrades who, blinded by the flood of lights and a painted cheek, occasionally borrowed from him the price of a timid bouquet. He had never lost his temper as he was surrounded by those who never quarreled with his choice of The Regal Hotel Special Cigars or the daintily served dinners, and generously left him the choice of the evening's entertainment —and the buying of the seats. He had never been guilty of anything so vulgar as a rough-and-tumble fight. He had never saved up to purchase something that gave him the thrill of unhoped-for possession. His trousers had never bagged at the knees. His glossy hair was never ruffled and Bucks, the devoted valet, saw to it that his cravats were never allowed to fade upon the constantly renewed shirts of specially imported French lawn.

He was just over the five-foot line, very carefully washed, reddish hair well subdued, a slightly raw countenance, perpendicular ears and a short chin which hung on the brink of a three-inch Piccadilly collar. Despite a creaseless coat that ran over the stoop of his shoulders and the distinction of his racing vest, he still had the look of one who had been forced into long trousers by hothouse processes.

On Saturday morning he rose promptly at ten, extended his unmuscular arms to Bucks who solicitously encased them in a wadded wrapper and opened the door to the already prepared bath.

By half-past-eleven he went out on the avenue dragging a bamboo cane, for a visit to his shirtmakers whose obsequious attention gave him a little lukewarm satisfaction. Later he met his cronies at an expensive restaurant where the headwaiter in person placed him in his chair with a deferential, "What can I do for you today, Mr. Skinner?"

Sometimes he ordered from his profound and nice knowledge of how such delectable repasts should be ordered and sometimes he said in a bored way, "Just shake us up something tasty, will you?"

Then he initialed the bill without looking at it, to the sidelong admiration of his guests.

In the evening, if the matinee had been too fatiguing, they ensconced themselves in Montague's private salon and sat into the early hours about a green table laden with different colored chips of the sort that on other tables are used in a sport entitled tiddledy-winks.

And yet, because way down beneath all the sham and superficiality with which doting parents were trying to smother the real impulses, because the spark of the boy is invincible and cannot be completely extinguished, young Skinner began to wonder and to dream. He saw again, beyond the heavy, crowded, towering buildings the glimpse of a strange life that ran joyously over green fields and around ivy-clad houses of brick and tile, a life where the boy and the man were strangely joined, where the world was the world of that youth of which he had known nothing and toward which he began strangely to yearn.

And so it happened to the amazement of his precious cronies, of Bucks the flabbergasted valet, of Skinner's father and mother, and most of all to himself, that at the beginning of his seventeenth year, in the month of September, Montague Skinner of Broadway and Fifth Avenue, renounced the metropolis and took his way toward The Lawrenceville School in Lawrenceville, New Jersey.

Doc Macnooder, perched like a sentinel hawk, sat in the open window of the Triumphant Egghead's room surveying the arrival of the appetizing freshmen. His legs hung out, his heels rapped an occasional tattoo around the clinging ivy, but his glance was distant and circling upward in the speculative heights of financial dreams.

Across the way, from Dick Stover's room in the turret of the Dickinson, the thin shanks of the Tennessee Shad protruded in a similar attitude. From time to time their carnivorous glances sought the front porches below them and fastened intently on the stir of an incoming freshman.

About the long, green reaches of the Circle, the last stages were discharging their vociferous or bashful occupants—a last belated buggy was streaking toward the distant Cleve, *ventre-à-terre*. Below on the stone steps the committee on introduction was catechizing a rumpled candidate who clasped a valise to him with a despairing loneliness.

"Oh you Macnooder man!"

Macnooder, screening his eyes, discovered under the pendant legs of the Tennessee Shad the wolfish eyes and star-pointing nose of Dennis de Brian de Boru Finnegan.

The call was repeated.

"Hello yourself," said Macnooder.

"What luck?"

"What luck over there?" said Macnooder who from theory always reserved the last word.

"Gilt-edged, premium-down, bang-up—strictly fresh and all that sort of thing," said Finnegan, who (as has been related) considered himself the discoverer of the double adjective.

"What have you got?"

"Two brutal sluggerinos who played professional feet-ball in the slums of Chicago."

Macnooder received this with a languid yawn.

"The champion peroxide blond halfback of Des Moines, Iowa."

"How interesting!"

"A millionaire baby from Philadelphia wrapped up in greenbacks, and Cyclops Berbecker, the one-eyed wonder of the wandering eye."

"Fact?" said Macnooder, the impresario at once keenly alert and addressing the Tennessee Shad, the senior partner of the firm of Macnooder and Self.

"Fact," said the Shad solemnly, "glass eye, detachable and most sociable."

Macnooder's glance was a glance of envy. Seeing which Finnegan chirped up, "Well, old pawnbroker, what have you got to boast of?"

"Nothing," said Macnooder sadly. "Supplies very poor this year, boys."

At this moment back of him burst forth a chorus of exclamations.

"Keeroogalum!"

"Holy Cats!"

"What is it?"

"Hold me up!"

"Have I lived to see it!"

Below, two suburbanally distinguished horses, drawing Trenton's proudest hackney coach, had stopped and from the front seat a being, obsequious and mechanical, had sprung to his heels, touched his hat and waited at attention.

"Hush!" said the Triumphant Egghead, "don't frighten it, it'll fly away."

"It's a beadle," said Turkey Reiter.

"It's a dentist."

"It's a butler."

"A butler your grandmother—it's a valet."

"My word!"

"So it is."

"A real live young valet."

"What's he going to do now?"

"Hush!"

Bucks, in obedience to a command, came toward the steps, perceived Macnooder suspended from the sill, like a wooden monkey on a stick, and bringing his heels to attention, touched his finger to his hat and said, "Beg pardon, sir, but is this the Dickinson House?"

Macnooder put his hand to his throat, gulped and nodded, incapable of speech. The silence everywhere had fallen like the crash of thunder. Even Dennis de Brian de Boru Finnegan was clinging to the window frame awed and speechless.

Bucks returning, imparted the reassuring information, the door opened, and Montague Skinner emerged, supporting his languid body on a light bamboo cane, slapping the annoying dust from his beautiful trousers, and, leaving the vulgarities of the baggage to Bucks, sauntered, not too eagerly and in no wise embarrassed, up the stone flags to the house.

Upstairs, the pent-up indignation burst forth with a roar.

"Murder!"

"Desecration!"

"Outrage!"

"Lynch him!"

"Pie him!"

"Strip the hide off him!"

"Mangle him!"

The door resounded with the impact of furious bodies.

"Stop!"

The voice was the voice of Macnooder, the mastermind. The mob paused in suspense.

"Come back—sit down!"

"Sit down?" thundered the Triumphant Egghead. "Sit down! When we're disgraced—laughing stock of the campus—sit down?"

"Exactly. Would you kill the goose that lays the golden egg, you nincompoop!"

A light began to dawn. The Triumphant Egghead scratched one

ear, loosened his collar and collapsed in a chair.

"What this house needs is style," said Macnooder firmly, "style and proper banking facilities."

"Aha!"

"When a young Van Astorbilt arrives, you'd make a noise, would you, and frighten him away."

At this moment Hungry Smeed at the window announced shrilly, "The valet, the valet, he's driving away!"

"Let him go," said Macnooder with great calm.

"I say," said Butcher Stevens wrathfully, "are you going to let a fashion plate, a candy dude, insult us in this way and do nothing about it?"

"Butcher, you're so crude," said Macnooder crushingly, sitting down and gazing out of the window with the eye of a cat who knows what is waiting on the sill. "Just think—this belongs to us—all of us!"

The Great Big Man came scooting through the door, his little knickerbockered legs shaking with excitement.

"His name is Skinner and his father owns The Regal Hotel, New York City."

"Wire at once to reserve the bridal suite," said Macnooder triumphantly. "Where's Klondike?"

A moment later Klondike, the houseman who was advertised to shake up the beds of the Dickinson, was found and brought in grinning, while the mystified veterans gazed at Macnooder expectantly.

"No, he doesn't look like a valet," said Macnooder sadly. "Not at all like a valet."

"But we can dress him up," exclaimed Turkey Reiter, the first to seize the idea.

Ten minutes later, Klondike encased in a battered stovepipe, supplied with white mittens and a selected pigeon's blood cravat received on a salver a dozen calling cards which he was instructed to present one at a time, and departed in search of Montague Skinner after the stovepipe had been decorated with a chicken feather in lieu of a cockade.

"Remember," said Macnooder imperiously before the gathering dispersed, "nothing brutal, nothing coarse, we must do nothing to discourage capital, we must be kind to Van Astorbilt, we must educate him—gently, for he belongs to us—all of us!"

Skinner's first days were replete with disturbing surprises. He, the big frog, had sunk with a splash, dwindled into a very small tadpole among a myriad of other little tadpoles.

Of course he had expected a certain amount of ragging. When Klondike, in his circus paraphernalia had appeared with the calling cards, he had recognized the patness of the caricature. Still, this had surprised him. He had never thought of the incongruity of arriving with a valet, nor that it would be an isolated phenomenon. It was rather upsetting to find himself in a world where valets failed to impress.

Another thing that rather puzzled him was the studied attitude of deference assumed toward him by the Dickinson House. He was not always quite sure of this attitude. At times it seemed to him that a lip twitched or that a roguish gleam lurked in eyes that were set for gravity.

Now, of course, this was all rather ridiculous, for they were nothing but children, whereas he—he had lived. He had known things beyond their ken, had lived the life of a man of fashion, a cosmopolite, and of course if they found his costumes rather individual, equally of course he could not be expected to descend to jerseys and corduroy "pants."

He had had quite an interesting experience with that minor detail of scholastic life—the curriculum. He had hesitated a long while in deliberation over the requirements for admission into the Fifth Form and then modestly decided to lengthen his sojourn amid pleasant places. The day following his arrival he spent an annoying morning and afternoon being examined for the Fourth. The following morning he was assigned to the Third, where his recitations commanded such solicitous interest from the Natural Enemy that he agreed to descend another rung on the ladder. There he remained long enough to become pleasantly acquainted and wearily acquiesced in his final drop into the First Form, where all travel ceases.

Luckily, he did not regard the curriculum seriously. One thing, though, annoyed him. He had passed through the fire of baptism and had been renamed the Uncooked Beefsteak. Whether this was a tribute to himself as a product of The Regal Hotel or whether it was an attempt to express felicitously the red hair and singularly raw hue of his complexion, the fact remained that he, Montague Skinner, cosmopolite, was publicly known as the Uncooked Beefsteak. The worst of it was that he could not see the humor of it. It hurt his pride that he of all men, before whom headwaiters and haberdashers bowed down, should be so misunderstood.

Now there are only two ways to treat a nickname; either to grin and hope for some future coincidence that will substitute a more acceptable name, or to place a chip on your shoulder and announce publicly in the fashion of Sow Emmons and Vulture Watkins that any use of the abhorred name will have to be accomplished by an exhibition of the manly art.

The first alternative was beyond the knowledge of Montague Skinner and the second was brutal and mussing.

He fell back on his knowledge of the weaknesses of human nature. He would do what he had always done—open the pocketbook and win by Roman display.

Doc Macnooder roomed across the hall in that secret place into which few were allowed to penetrate. Montague liked the ubiquitous Macnooder. He was so natural and friendly and he showed him the deference that proved that Macnooder at least realized the difference between a tumbling cub and a man of experience. About this time the distinction of Macnooder's cravats became a matter of public comment; likewise a variegated vest that materially added to the charm of his personal appearance.

One afternoon as the Uncooked Beefsteak was sitting forlornly on his window seat, there came a knock and the round, guileless face of Doc Macnooder beamed through the doorway.

"Ah there, old sporting life," said Macnooder in a sympathetic way, "feeling pretty chipper?"

"Fine," said the Uncooked Beefsteak with a painful smile.

"Food's better in Little Old New York, isn't it?" said Macnooder, his eye roving among the gay cravats that hung from the bureau corner. Skinner sighed; a famished gluttonous sigh.

"I'd like to take you out for a little snap or two at some places I know of," he said regaining his worldly air.

"Caviar and asparagus?"

"*A vol-au-vent* with a cold salmon trout first."

"And a real *beefsteak*," said Macnooder, opening a bureau drawer hungrily.

Montague shrank back, glancing at Macnooder suspiciously.

"I say, Doc."

"Hello!"

"I wish you fellows wouldn't call me the Uncooked Beefsteak."

"Why, that's a stunning nickname."

"Well, I wish you wouldn't."

"Does it worry you?"

"It does."

"All right, Beefsteak, I'll try not to."

Montague bit his lip but Macnooder's face showed only the zest of the explorer.

"I don't see any," said Macnooder after a minute.

"Any what?"

"Any filthy weeds."

Montague, slipping to the door, shot the key and proceeding to his trunk brought forth a long, low box decorated with custom stamps and foreign gilt.

"This is what I smoke," he said carelessly, extending the box.

Macnooder's glance trembled in spite of himself.

"Black as ink and half-a-mile long. Fifty Centers?"

"They're private stock," said Montague in a bored way. "Take one if you like."

"Not now," said Macnooder, with visions of bigger game as he sat and watched with wolfish eyes Skinner return the box under lock and key.

"Gee, Beefsteak, pardon me, Montague old chap, you certainly are a dead game one."

"Oh, I've knocked about a bit," said Skinner, stretching his arms languidly.

"I say you really are a devil of a fellow," said Br'er Rabbit with his imagination centering on the miraculous cigars. "There are a couple of champion smokers around these modest little diggin's but my aunt's cat's pants, I believe you could smoke them to a finish!"

"Champion smokers!" said Skinner pricking up his ears.

"Oh, we pull off a couple of smoking championships a year," said Macnooder, stooping to tighten his shoelaces, "secret Ku Klux Klan, dead-of-midnight affairs."

"That interests me," said Skinner, approaching.

"They're great old powwows," said Macnooder, skillfully dropping the subject. "Got any grub?"

"We might wander over to the village," said Skinner, now intensely alert.

"Why not?"

"I say Doc," said Skinner as they shuffled over to Laloo's Hot Dog Palace, "when do they hold these championships?"

"Championships?" said Macnooder, pretending ignorance.

"Smoking championships."

"One's due now."

"I'd like to get into that, you know."

"Hm, rather difficult. They're quite select—the Tennessee Shad —old fellows—inner gang—crême de la crême and all that."

"Oh," said Skinner in great disappointment, "couldn't you work me in?"

"Hardly."

"I'd like a go at it."

"Let me think," said Macnooder whose fertile brain had already achieved daylight.

With the object of stimulating a favorable mental process, Skinner not only ordered up a pack of steaming frankfurters but forced down two indigestibles himself.

"Well, have you thought up anything?" he said anxiously, after they had consumed a jelly roll and steered for Appleby's, the second station on the road from the Aching Void.

"I'm thinking hard," said Macnooder, who gave the high signal to Appleby and soon was floundering among the pastries.

Skinner, to be democratic, after considerable epicurean hesitation, chose a Turkish Paste as the least of many evils and nibbled a little on the edge.

"Beefsteak," said Macnooder, in a friendly way as Skinner paid up, "you're really quite the bounding boy. Really now—we'll just cool off at the Jigger Shop—really now, you ought to get into the swim here."

"That's just what I want to do," said Skinner a little too eagerly. "I'd like to know the real crowd you know."

"I see, sort of break into high society," said Macnooder, who bit his tongue to keep from choking.

"Well," said the Uncooked Beefsteak, blushing a little.

"Oh, that's all right—perfectly proper—just a little expression of mine. Besides you belong—you're it—you're the real thing—you're a sport, you know."

"I say, have you been thinking up a scheme?" said Skinner, not only anxious but a little suspicious of Macnooder's admiration.

"I have a glimmer," said Macnooder, nodding to Al, the guardian of the Jigger, and elevating three fingers as a signal for the maximum, "yes, I may say a twinkle. I wish the Tennessee Shad were around. Try half-a-dozen éclairs, you old gormandizer. Shut your eyes and imagine you're denting the menu at dear old Del's. No? Well, thinking it over, I think I will. Al, transport the éclairs."

"You said a twinkle," said Skinner patiently figuring out Macnooder's greatest possible cubic capacity.

"Exactly that," said Macnooder, who continued to assist his stomach to stimulate his mind.

"Well, what have you hit upon?" said Skinner, expectantly.

"A good one," said Macnooder, leaving with one hand upon the belt and a lingering backward glance.

"Let's go back to the room and talk it over."

"Never!" said Doc in alarm. "We might be overheard—we'll just roll up to Conover's and get a quiet corner, and eat a few pancakes while we're discussing the details."

"I'm not hungry," said Skinner defensively.

"That's all right," said Macnooder cheerfully. "I am."

"You think you can work me in, then," said Skinner, after waiting for Doc to open the subject.

"Not in the championships," said Doc. "You have to be elected to the Sporting Club and all that—most select. I have another way, though, but it's expensive. You get the word—expensive."

Skinner handed Mrs. Conover a ten-dollar gold certificate.

"You reassure me," said Doc with a summery smile.

Skinner had a sudden feeling of uneasiness.

"We were speaking of breaking into society," said Macnooder. "That's the idea."

"How so?" said the Uncooked Beefsteak, looking decidedly raw.

"You give a banquet—an introductory banquet—a sort of débutante affair, you know."

"How could it be pulled off?" said the Beefsteak, caressing the idea.

"Terrific secrecy, dead of midnight, banks of the canal, and all that."

"But the smoking championship?"

"Aha!" said Macnooder, looking very subtle. "That's where the real idea comes in. For the entertainment of your guests you give an invitation smoking meet."

"I see," said Skinner joyfully.

"And put up as first prize a nice, long, fat, juicy box of *expensive* cigars."

"But suppose I win?"

"You won't."

"Oh, I don't know."

"Well, are you fond of my idea?" said Macnooder proudly.

"I am," said Skinner, resting his hand on Doc's shoulder as a mark of special favor. "But I say, how do you work a smoking championship?"

"Leave that to me."

"Who'll I invite?"

"Likewise to me. I'm the little social secretary."

"What'll I get?"

"Caviar," said Doc firmly.

"Something in the line of pâtés?"

"Truffled pheasants and all that sort of thing."

"A lot of sweets."

"But no *beefsteaks*," said Macnooder who departed hastily to roll off his laughter on the soft lawn behind the Kennedy, where he and the Tennessee Shad sat long in gleeful consultation.

Skinner was complacently elated at the new prospect. After all, big schools were very much like small ones and the way into high society lay clear, whatever the geography. The more he thought over Macnooder's scheme, the more it appealed to him. He had no vulgar envy in his nature. He did not aspire to be a hero—all he asked was to be the patron of heroes.

Full of confident expectations, he wrote a letter to Bucks, the marooned valet, outlining a program of Lucullan prodigality. After Doc Macnooder had dropped in for a few words of suggestion, two large boxes stuffed with The Regal Hotel's transported best duly arrived and were placed in safe keeping.

Finally, the great social night arriving, Skinner received the first real thrill of his misdirected little existence—the thrill of forbidden fruit. At ten o'clock the shivering Beefsteak, completely dressed, beheld a thin, roving bar of light trickling under the crack of his door. The next moment, Doc Macnooder preceded by a bull's-eye lantern stole noiselessly into the darkness.

"Who's that?" said the Uncooked Beefsteak in a chilly whisper.

"Hush," said Macnooder hoarsely, "not a breath!"

"What's that for?" said the Beefsteak, alarmed at the sight of a black cloth that shrouded the mysterious face, burglar-fashion.

"We must never be recognized!"

"Is there any danger?"

"Heaps. Old Greek-roots sleeps on a trigger. Put on this hand-kerchief. Get off those shoes. All ready now?"

"I say, what'll we do if he nabs us?"

"Soak him on the point of the chin," said Macnooder very sol-emnly. "If you miss him, I'll get him and then scud for your room. Come on now, on your tiptoes."

Guided by Macnooder, the now thoroughly alarmed Beefsteak slipped along the horribly proclaiming halls and through Hungry Smeed's window out into the steaming night.

"Gee!" said Montague, using that vulgar exclamation for the first time. "Gee, that was great!"

"First time?"

"You bet."

"Danger's not over yet. What's that? Down on your pantry!"

"Someone's moving towards us."

"Grab my hand. Come on now. Run for your life."

Guided by Macnooder, stumbling and swaying, Skinner felt the soft turf rush under him. They dodged between the chapel and the accursed abode of Compulsory Bath, skirted the baseball diamonds, and stopped to draw breath behind the safe confines of the laundry.

"Narrow squeak."

"Great," said the palpitating Beefsteak.

They passed through Negro settlements, dimly emerging in the suffused light of the approaching moon, rattling their sticks along picket fences to the indignation of furious dogs that came bound-ing after them, while from ahead came faint echoes of other parties similarly engaged. Gradually their group was augmented until as they reached the banks of the canal they mustered a dozen in free marching order. Another dozen under the leadership of the Ten-nessee Shad were splashing in the none-too-fragrant waters or dry-ing their ghostly limbs ashore. Answering shouts went up.

"Here we are."

"Where's the grub?"

"Oh, Turkey Reiter!"

"Hello there, Butcher Stevens!"

"Have you got Van Astorbilt?"

"You bet we have."

"Open the boxes."

"Give us the grub."

"Am I hungry?"

"Oh, no!"

The strange zest of adventure disappeared in Skinner. He was again in his element, he the purveyor of banquets and the patron of heroes. The swimmers came in dripping, hastily scrambling for places in the festive ring.

At this moment there was a disturbance near the provender, and Finnegan came rushing up to Macnooder.

"I say, Doc! Here is the Coffee-colored Angel who's sneaked up on us and wants a share of the swag."

"Throw him out!"

"He says he is on to the game and will give the whole shooting match away. What's to be done?"

"Welcome him with open arms," said Macnooder, who had the instincts of the politician, "and kick the slats out of him tomorrow."

"Start her up!" cried a score of voices.

"Give us the truffles!"

"Trot out your venison!"

"Little girls and little boys," said Macnooder, who loved to speak, but was seldom allowed to finish, "when the evening star, swimming across the sun-kissed horizon—"

"Cut it out!"

"No elocution!"

"Come down to earth!"

"My friends," said Macnooder, complacently yielding, "before opening this evening's entertainment, I would draw your attention to a few articles of daily necessity which I am prepared to furnish at prices—"

"No business!"

"You can't flimflam us tonight."

"Come to the point."

"Gentlemen," said Macnooder, looking about him doubtfully, "you forget. Where are your manners? Remember this is a débutante affair. Gentlemen, I have the honor to socially introduce to you Mr. Montague Skinner, the Fifth Avenue Narcissus, one of the leaders of the crême de la crême of Metropolitan fashion. Mr. Skinner's perfect pants are the feature of the famous annual poultry exhibition. Mr. Skinner's socks are the limit—of gentility. Mr. Skinner's neckties are destined to revolutionize local styles."

"You ought to know, Doc!" said a voice.

"I do know," said Macnooder, with an evil look into the crowd, "and I know likewise the skulking author of that aspersion. I resume. Mr. Montague Skinner in making his début into the crême de la crême of Lawrenceville society comes before you, not simply as the spoiled favorite of the lobster palaces, but as an athlete!"

"A what?" cried a dozen mystified voices.

"I said athlete," said Macnooder. "Mr. Montague Skinner is the holder of all Metropolitan junior smoking records, from the one-minute cigarette dash to the one-hour record on cigars. As a preliminary to the opening of the evening's banquet, Mr. Skinner will meet in friendly competition the leather-lunged champions of the school. In order to add a little sportiness to the evening, as well as to soften the edge of his munificence, Mr. Skinner will supply each guest with three cigars. You start on a crouching start, and the first to finish, the first at the grub. Two prizes will be offered—one open to all present for the first to finish these same diamond-backed goldplated cigars; the second for the contest of champions."

"What's that?"

"It will be a finish fight—no quarter asked or given! Each contestant has nominated his particular brand of leather. There are five Would-Bes. There will be five distinctly different poisonous rounds. In deference to our host, the first round will be at cigars known as the Pride of The Regal Hotel; second round at corncob pipes specially loaded; third round at stogies; fourth round at political cigars, and fifth round at a final death-defying test proposed by Butcher Stevens—the terrible Hubble-Bubble—the Hookah or Persian Water Pipe!"

"Supposin' they live through it!" said a voice.

"They won't," said Macnooder. "But if they do, a new series will begin at once until a decisive knockout shall be scored."

"A regular ten-second knockout?"

"Each contestant, as he drops by the wayside, will be allowed one hour and twenty minutes to recover and then a doctor will be summoned."

"What doctor?"

"Doctor Macnooder."

"I resign," cried a dozen voices.

Macnooder, whose soul was above mosquito bites, continued, "The Hon. Rinky Dink Stover, Tough McCarty, the champion gum chewer of the Woodhull; Mr. Dennis de Brian de Boru Finnegan, our little silent boy, and the Tennessee Shad, the Apollo Belvedere of the Blue Ridges, have unselfishly agreed to serve as judges, spongers, and ambulance corps."

"Cheese it!" said the voice of the rebel.

"Why don't they smoke up?" cried another.

"Mr. Stover and Mr. McCarty," said Macnooder suavely, "as far as can be discovered, are bound by a secret oath never again to touch tobacco. Mr. Finnegan is desisting in the hope of ultimately reaching five feet, and the Tennessee Shad refrains from fear of scorching his bones."

"Gee, Doc, but you are a peach!" said the voice of one who was still cramped by the facts.

"Any more questions?"

There were none.

"I will now introduce to you Mr. Montague Skinner, the pet of the lobster palaces and the Prince of Wales of New Jersey fashions."

As Skinner rose to bow his blushing acknowledgments, Macnooder, with a wave of his hand, transferred the box of cigars to the Tennessee Shad who emerged from the shadows and proceeded to distribute. Just what took place in that shadow is locked in the secret archives of the firm of Macnooder and the Tennessee Shad, but the answer might explain much that proceeded to happen.

Quite deceived by the vociferousness of the false applause that greeted him, Skinner felt again the pleasant tickling sensations that recalled the prodigal days of the metropolis. He withdrew with all the old gorgeousness to join the group of champions. The risen moon flung leafy shadows over the half-naked circle of contestants, where each novice was resolved to die a martyr's death rather than miss the opportunity of smoking a genuine one-dollar cigar. At a command from Macnooder, the matches crackled into flames like the points of distant picket fires, accompanied at once by a gradually increasing chorus of coughs and choking. Still not a descendant of Eve, lover of the forbidden, flinched at his awful task.

"I will now present the champion of champions," said Macnooder in cadence. "Mr. Montague Skinner, the conqueror of the Rockfellerite, the cigar that the Czar of Russia calls for with his morning coffee, you have just had presented to you. The second contestant is Mr. Butcher Stevens, who smokes the terrible Hubble-Bubble as a baby swallows a hatpin. Mr. Stevens is absolutely confident of success."

Butcher Stevens arose amidst applause and performed a bow by means of a scraping motion of his left foot.

"The third contestant is Mr. Slush Randolph, known as the White Terror or King of the Cigarette Fiends. Mr. Randolph takes great pride in his yellow-tipped fingers, which he waggishly calls his Meerschaums. Mr. Randolph is absolutely confident of success."

Slush Randolph smiled a sickly smile and tumbled backward to a place beside Butcher Stevens.

"Our fourth contestant," continued Macnooder, "is Mr. Stubbs, the White Mountain Canary. Mr. Stubbs' speeches for the Democratic ticket not only defeated Mr. Bryan but wrecked his party. Mr. Stubbs bases his hopes for victory on the training he received in smoking political cigars, five of which, the gift of a Prohibitionist candidate for dogcatcher, he is confident no man can smoke and live to tell the tale. The White Mountain Canary is absolutely confident of success."

Stubbs, who had listened to this biography in awestruck amazement, gasped and sat down, still keeping a fascinated glance on the orator of the evening.

"The fifth and last contestant," continued Macnooder, "is Gomez, the Black Beauty, the Dark Horse from Cuba. Beauty, although a freshman just arrived, has a reputation second to none. In Cuba it is said he smoked his first cigar at the age of three years and two months. He is absolutely confident of success."

As the fifth contestant awkwardly slouched forward and bobbed his head, a suppressed murmur ran the rounds of the burning circle while Tough McCarty and Dink Stover were seen to bend warningly over the form of the Coffee-colored Angel, who had been making remarks.

"First Round, on Mr. Montague Skinner's suggestion, at the Rockfellerite coupon-bearing cigar. Ready! Go! All other contestants are reminded that three cigars must be finished before denting the grub, the sooner the finish, the more the grub! Smoke up, you gormandizers!"

Skinner drew in his first puff with complacency, assuming a position of ease and dignity against a tree. He studied his rivals, discounting at once Slush Randolph and the White Mountain Canary, who already were smoking lip-deep, but considering uneasily the professional precision of Butcher Stevens and the Black Beauty.

He finished his favorite cigar with a slight but noticeable feeling of heaviness, due, no doubt, to the distance from the last feeding hour. Butcher and Black Beauty were already waiting, having ended together. The White Mountain Canary was permitted to continue, after a slight altercation with the judges as to the amount consumed, while the White Terror, coughing through the last heated puffs, unbuckled his belt and removed his upper garments with gladiatorial resolution.

"Round Two, contribution of Mr. Slush Randolph, corncob pipes with Mr. Randolph's special mixture, known as The Blacksmith's Delight."

Skinner received his pipe with less elation. The first puff made him glance up sharply, half suspecting a practical joke. To his surprise the White Mountain Canary, albeit with an expression of pain, was resolutely at work, while the White Terror's face showed an expression of malignant ecstasy.

At the conclusion of Round Two the honors were plainly with the Black Beauty who had drawn slightly ahead of Butcher Stevens, while a considerable interval separated Skinner and Slush Randolph from the White Mountain Canary.

"Round Three," said the cold, unfeeling voice of Doc Macnooder; "political cigars, name unknown, at suggestion of the White Mountain Canary."

The cigar was worse than the pipe. A slight haze began to rock slowly down from the overhanging boughs. In desperation Skinner tried quick, short puffs, expelled as soon as taken, but at that he began to cough uneasily. The outer circle of contestants had disappeared from his consciousness, he saw only his little area, the tense faces of Slush and Stubbs, the determined jaws of Stevens, and the indolent figure of the Black Beauty, who, as regular as a teakettle, was enjoying every puff.

At Round Four, Slush Randolph had crawled away and the White Mountain Canary lay on his back with one leg elevated in token of the surrender he was unable to utter.

"Round Four," said the joyful voice, "resignations of the White Mountain Canary and Slush, the King of the Cigarette Fiends, received and accepted. Still resolved on asphyxiation, Butcher Stevens, Montague Skinner, and the Black Beauty. Round Four, suggested by the Dark Horse from Cuba, will be at the famous Seaman's Stogy, a charming little thing used either as a pastime or to lash the tiller. Are you ready? Go!"

Butcher Stevens took two short, jerky puffs, glanced very hard at Macnooder, and immediately threw up the sponge. The sight brought no feeling of joy to Skinner—he had tried the Stogy, with a pain like an electric needle shooting through his lungs. Still he would not give in. He would show them that courage was a relative thing, that they could fail where he could rise superior. His head rocked and weird forms danced before his eyes, but still he kept on. Suddenly he looked about him. Of the dozen who had started in the common race, not one was left upright. He had the feeling of a conqueror on the battlefield of his own defeat. Muttered curses and objurgations seemed to buzz about him in indistinct gasps. He heard them not at all. His flickering energies were concentrated on keeping alive the red spark at the end of the thing that burned like a wet rope coated with tar.

Halfway through, the haze cleared, and he suddenly perceived the Black Beauty deliciously on his back, legs crossed, expelling huge volumes of smoke, INHALING every breath! At this sight all resolution oozed from him. He tried one last discouraged pull, then allowed the reeking weed to slip from his limp fist, and digging his fingers in the warm turf, desperately strove to steady the careening world.

Once only he opened his dizzy eyes—at the sound of a clattering plate. In the middle of the circle, laughing ghoulishly, Macnooder the traitor, Stover, McCarty, Finnegan, and the Tennessee Shad were literally stuffing themselves with the banquet that was to have fed the score, that now lay in groaning groups vowing vengeance on him, Skinner, who had sought only popularity.

In this one horrid glance he had a vision of the Black Beauty, who, disdaining food, still gloriously on his back, was burning up the delicious cigars with the rapidity of a prairie fire.

"I hear you had a party," said Al, watchdog of the Jigger, when the next morning Skinner had stolen over during forbidden hours.

"They tell me I did," said Skinner, weakly ordering a bromo-seltzer.

"I hear quite a few young bruisers are laying for you."

"I am not very popular," said the Uncooked Beefsteak slowly, reflecting with a new enlightenment how ungrateful republics may be.

"I suppose you know how Macnooder and the Tennessee Shad flimflammed you," said Al, who harbored a little professional jealousy.

"No."

"Worked in a lot of doped cigars and cornered the grub."

"I don't care," said Skinner, to whom even French cooking would never mean anything again.

"They tell me, though, you are pretty good at the weed," said Al to console him.

"I thought I was till I struck that fellow Black Beauty."

"Who?"

"The fellow from Cuba—Gomez," said the Uncooked Beefsteak with reluctant admiration.

"Huh—there goes your Gomez now," said Al with a short, barking laugh.

"Why, that's Blinky!" said Skinner, perceiving the one-eyed purveyor of illicit Sunday papers slouching across the street.

"Sure," said Al, looking pityingly at the young innocent. "Macnooder worked him in to take no chances. Blinky could set fire to a rubber hose and smoke it with ease and pleasure."

VI

A SLIGHT DISPUTE IN THE FIRM

IF THE smoking championship had blighted Montague Skinner's young and tender illusions, it had also its sting for its promoters. The immediate consequence was an abrupt and violent rupture in the firm of youthful promoters on the following abstruse point of moral and financial etiquette.

When the final division had been made of cigars, slightly damaged sandwiches, mixed meat pastes, half-filled bottles of root beer and ginger ale, uneaten éclairs and French pastry turning slightly to the sour, and the same had either been forced into the Aching Void or sold to rank outsiders for cash considerations, the Tennessee Shad discovered by accident that Macnooder had actually collected from Blinky and each of the challenging smokers the sum of twenty-five cents for the privilege of smoking the miraculous cigars. The Tennessee Shad demanded an equitable accounting of all sums gained from whatever source. Macnooder refused, claiming certain perquisites as financier and underwriter and on this point an instant estrangement took place.

The Tennessee Shad, nursing the bitterness a creative genius feels for the pettinesses of a commercial partner, was curled up on the window seat of his high station at the Kennedy when a sudden outburst of shrieks sounded opposite.

"Beefsteak, this way!"

"Come on, you son of The Regal Hotel!"

"Beefsteak, clean my shoes!"

"Beefsteak, shake up this coat!"

"Beefsteak, tidy up my room!"

"Shake a leg!"

"On the jump!"

"Oh, you Beefsteak!"

The Tennessee Shad uncoiled as a snake uncoils, and lifting his head listened curiously to the insistent chorus that was borne to him from the open windows of the Dickinson opposite. From time to time the frantic figure of Montague Skinner could be seen rushing through the rooms in a confused attempt to serve many masters.

"That's quite a speedy valet service they've organized over there," said the Gutter Pup enviously.

"It's a mistake," said the Tennessee Shad in lazy disapproval.

"How so?"

"The Beefsteak won't stand it. He'll run away—ship before the mast and all that sort of thing. They're overdoing it."

"Well, can you blame the crowd?" said the Gutter Pup, thinking of the smoking fiasco. "Why, I can taste those cigars yet."

As this was a delicate subject and the Shad was quite aware that his own motives were under the gravest suspicion, he turned the conversation with a yawn.

"All the same I'd like to swipe that young gold mine for one little week," he remarked.

The expression was casual and without malice, but no sooner uttered than it became a moving idea. Unseen by the Gutter Pup, the Tennessee Shad experienced almost a physical shock. His head rose eagerly and his eyes focusing on the noisy Dickinson fixed themselves in a dreamy stare.

"Supposin' I did swipe him?" he said softly to himself.

Now, of course such an act was in direct defiance of all law and precedent which forbids poaching beyond territorial limits. The Tennessee Shad, however, was one who bequeathed precedents rather than followed them.

With this predatory scheme in mind the Tennessee Shad became keenly alive to the turbulent course of the Uncooked Beefsteak's education in the Dickinson.

Shortly afterward Skinner, voyaging toward the Jigger Shop, was agreeably surprised to perceive the thin, elongated body of the Tennessee Shad bearing across his path with the most friendly intentions.

"Why, it's the Pet of the Lobster Palaces!" said the Shad, seemingly surprised by the encounter.

Skinner who had had nicknames showered upon him like flowers about a prima donna, accepted the title without demur.

"Going over to the village?" said the Shad cheerily.

"A SPEEDY VALET SERVICE THEY HAVE ORGANIZED OVER THERE."

"Yes."

"Come on. How are things going?"

"Oh, all right," said the Beefsteak wearily adopting the answer *de rigueur.*

"Not very chipper, though?"

"Oh, well—"

"The merry little sunshine smile not exactly working, eh?"

"No—o."

They had now come to that short and narrow dash that leads to the Jigger Shop, and the Uncooked Beefsteak, not only seeking sympathy, but willing to buy it, said, "How about a few jiggers?"

The Tennessee Shad, who was always subtle, brushing aside an immediate advantage in order to launch more securely his future maneuvers, replied, "Thanks, old Hippopotamus, but I'm out for exercise."

Now, had Skinner been anything but a newcomer the monstrosity of this statement would have put him at once on the *qui vive*. As it was, he was overwhelmed by a stranger sentiment. For the first time since his advent to the school he had offered and received a refusal. With this unexpected shock all defiance and suspicion died away.

"Who's putting you through the paces?" said the Tennessee Shad, observing the result with satisfaction.

"Why, it's no particular one," said Skinner sadly.

"But Macnooder is the worst!" said the Shad, striving for an advantage.

"Perhaps."

"Pretty strenuous, eh? what?"

Skinner passed his hand over his moist forehead and admitted without qualification the justice of the observation.

"That's the trouble with Macnooder—he's so coarse!"

Skinner, thus artfully encouraged, blurted out, "I don't mind the rest, but it's the scrubbing-up the shoes, the blacking, that gets my nerves."

"You've got good nerve though," said the Shad, examining critically the stained fingers.

"Oh, I'll stick it out."

"Good boy. Too bad you're not with us."

"I say, how long—" said Skinner, who then balked and stopped.

"How long will you have to be the Merry Little Bootblack?"

"Yes—that's about it."

"Um—m. That depends. Now I'll tell you what to do," said the Tennessee Shad, carefully choosing the best means to prolong the period of servitude that now seemed to promise him such fair returns. "Jolly right up with them!"

"What?" said Skinner amazed.

"Sure. Show you're one of them. Walk right up and swat 'em on the back!"

"No!"

"Jump in and tickle 'em right under the ribs—be playful."

"Playful?"

"That's the game. Start a few jokes at 'em yourself."

"What kind?"

"Crease the trousers the wrong way—a little mucilage in their shoes, camphor balls down the lamp chimney, and all that sort of thing."

"But what'll they do?"

"Do? Why, they'll discharge you for a bum valet!" said the Tennessee Shad with tears in his eyes.

"By George, I'll try it."

"Do, and say—"

"What?"

"Start on Macnooder."

"Why Macnooder?"

"You see, Doc's got more sense of humor than the rest."

Skinner, longing for company, suggested Conover's and pancakes. The Tennessee Shad refused. On the return Skinner pleaded again the attractions of the Jigger Shop. The Tennessee Shad refused again but it was an awful wrench. They parted, Skinner made gorgeously happy by an invitation to visit the treasure rooms of the Tennessee Shad who dove around a corner to give liberty to his true feelings.

When the Dickinson scouts reported for the fifth successive time that the Uncooked Beefsteak, property and perquisite of the House, had met the Tennessee Shad and led him from one gormandizing result to another, paying all bills—great was the indignation thereof.

"Look here, boy," said Turkey Reiter to Doc Macnooder at the hastily summoned council of war, "what are we going to do about it? Supposin' we let up a bit? The Beefsteak isn't so worse, after all."

"There's no use in letting the Tennessee Shad get away with the goods," said the Triumphant Egghead, who also felt defrauded by Skinner's constant excursions with a member of a foreign state.

Now Macnooder had been the chief victim of the Tennessee Shad's artful advice to Skinner, but he had no intention of publishing the fact. Equally he was resolved not to allow the Tennessee Shad to force him to a change of policy.

"The trouble with you cheap sports is your accounts are busted, and you want to be fed," he remarked witheringly.

"Well what of it?" said the Egghead brazenly.

"Don't you see it's all the Tennessee Shad's doings? He's put it into the Beefsteak's head that he can starve us out."

"Of course he has got to be kept in subjection," said Turkey Reiter, "but couldn't we relent a little?"

"Never!" said Vulture Watkins. "The trouble with that New York dude is the moment you treat him decent, he gets unbearable."

"He certainly has been fresh enough lately!"

"Still," said Turkey Reiter, "I don't see why we couldn't relent a little."

"Why should our import trade be deflected," added the Triumphant Egghead. "Skinner belongs to us, doesn't he? Well, then, what right has he to fatten up the Tennessee Shad?"

"In the first place," said Macnooder, raising his voice to quell the mutiny, "the Tennessee Shad won't fatten. In the second place, just sit back and wait. When the Beefsteak really gets to know the Tennessee Shad he'll come limping straight back to us. In the third place, I will have a few fat little words with the Tennessee Shad and tell him what we think of him."

In pursuance of which, choosing his time, Macnooder crossed the path of the Tennessee Shad at the moment when his late partner, having left Skinner, was returning languidly home, well fed and rejoicing.

"Hello," said Macnooder, assuming a critical position.

"Why, it's Macnooder isn't it?" said the Shad blandly. "Have you come to divvy up on that little graft of yours?"

"I've come," said Macnooder wrathfully, "to tell you just what we think of you, you low-down, body snatching nursery maid!"

"What strong words!"

"See here! What right have you got to interfere with the business of the Dickinson?"

"I, interfere? Gracious goodness! Do you mean little Montague?"

"I do. What right have you got to come poaching over on our grounds?"

"Are you vexed because Beefsteak buys me hot dogs and jiggers and Turkish paste and éclairs and root beer and pancakes?" said the Shad smiling, "and lots and lots of other juicy things?"

"Look here, the Beefsteak is fresh as paint. It's up to us to edu-cate him and it's up to you to keep off!"

"Why, hasn't he improved?" said the Shad looking at Macnoo-der with a malicious eye. "Doesn't he attend to your boots as a real valet should?"

"Will you let him alone?"

"Why don't you be kind and gentle with him? If you're hungry ask him po-litely!"

"Shad, if you weighed a hundred pounds I'd whang the life out of you!"

"Thank you, I weigh just ninety-eight and a half."

"If you weighed a hundred, I'd kick the slats out of you!"

"Don't boast," said the Shad softly. "If I weighed a hundred, you'd settle up with me."

"Then you won't keep off?"

"Alas!"

"Look out!"

"Threats?"

"We'll get you yet!"

"Try."

"Anyhow, you bunco steerer, I'll bet you can't keep him a week!"

"Why, Doc," said the Shad brightening, "that is the first real word of sense you've spoken. But do remember that I'm doing it all because I am so very fond of Montague, and not because I'm trying to even up matters with you. Oh, dear no! Ta! Ta!"

"Just the same," said the Tennessee Shad to himself as he left the infuriated Macnooder. "There's a good deal in what Doc says. I wonder how long I can keep my hands out—really out of that stuffed bank from New York."

Three days later, Dennis de Brian de Boru Finnegan, gamboling in, found the Tennessee Shad on the window seat in the reflective attitude of Sherlock Holmes, the character he most admired, mum-bling to himself. Finnegan, listening, heard strange muffled words.

"Why not end it all—sooner or later? What's the dif?"

"End what?" said Finnegan, mystified. "What's wrong?"

"It's the Beefsteak," said the Tennessee Shad perceiving him. "Irishman, did you ever try to resist temptation?"

Finnegan sat down and tried to remember.

"I'm resisting—but oh, it hurts!" said the Shad.

"The Beefsteak is some fresh vegetables, isn't he?" said Finnegan understanding.

"It isn't that," said the Shad, "though that is bad enough. It's the thought of all the green goods he is just itching to buy."

"Why don't you?"

"But then he'll go back to the Dickinson."

"Well, why do you?"

"But if I don't, then Macnooder will."

Finnegan ceased to offer suggestions.

"It's wrong," he said.

"Of course."

"You're interfering in his kindergarten education."

"I know."

"And the Beefsteak has just got to be educated out of those sporting ideas of his."

"Don't I have to listen to them?"

"My advice," said Dennis who was all for discipline, having signally evaded it, "is to wrap up one beautiful gold brick, an eighteen-karat smasher, coupon buster, soak it to him and quit the game."

"I am such a creature of habit," said the Tennessee Shad, thinking of the pleasant, refreshing trips to the village.

At this moment from below came a timid hallo.

"Oh, Tennessee Shad!"

Finnegan, hanging over the window sill, perceived below the irresolute figure of the Uncooked Beefsteak and summoned him up. Now Skinner had never yet gathered his courage to the point of a visit to the distinguished room. As it was, he shifted a long moment from foot to foot before daring to enter.

"Look at the Dickinson," said the Tennessee Shad gleefully. "Why, the whole house is boiling up."

Opposite, every window seemed tenanted with indignant spectators.

"Now is your time," said Finnegan hurriedly. "Sell him the whole blooming shooting match."

"No."

"Yes!"

"I mustn't."

"You must."

The door opened gently and Skinner, visibly overcome, stole in on his tiptoes and bumped down into the nearest chair. As Finnegan had calculated, no sooner had this first temperamental weakness passed than Skinner's gaze clearing, fastened in wonder upon the strange collection of real and bogus trophies which literally choked the walls from floor to ceiling. Each article recalled a chapter in the mercantile progress of the Tennessee Shad and Dink Stover, and some were reminders of youthful gullibility. Notably was this the case in a souvenir toilet set of seven colors which Stover in his salad days had bought from Macnooder with the joy of a Pittsburgh millionaire stumbling on an original Rembrandt. With his rise to fame, Stover, turning philosopher, had refused to part with this reminder of past enthusiasm, keeping it prominently displayed as a sort of anchor to common sense when too great a satisfaction with self should tend to raise his feet from the ground.

No sooner did the Beefsteak perceive this variegated assortment of odd china than he sat erect and asked.

"Gee, what's that?"

Dennis, with a triumphant glance at the Tennessee Shad, assumed an auctioneering attitude and rapturously detailed the many imaginary points of interest that could lend value to such a collection.

Propped up on the window seat, the Tennessee Shad watched through half-closed eyes the responsive eager flush on Skinner's face.

"He would buy it, he would, he certainly would," he said to himself, mastering his emotions with difficulty. "Think of selling it back, right under the nose of Old Macnooder!"

At this moment, as though to add to his trials, Skinner having listened enraptured to Finnegan's recital, exclaimed, "You don't say so! By jingo, wouldn't I like to have that, though!"

Finnegan yawned, as is customary when a strong emotion is to be concealed, and said in a sort of haphazard way, "Why, you can always fling out a nice juicy young bid. You never can tell. Perhaps Stover's hard up."

"Really?" said the Uncooked Beefsteak, turning to the joint proprietor.

The Tennessee Shad swallowed hard, glanced out the window to resist temptation, and said almost angrily,

"Not for sale."

"Perhaps Skinner here would like a chance at the football shoes," said Finnegan who at first believed the Shad was simply working up the scene for a slaughter *en masse*.

"What's that?" said the Beefsteak at once.

"The identical, historic, specially preserved shoes that Flash Condit wore when he scored on the Princeton Varsity," said Finnegan, who disappeared in quest.

Of course Skinner listened, admired and wanted to buy. The Tennessee Shad again refused, but with difficulty and in a weaker voice. Finnegan scratched his head, sorely vexed, and led the Beefsteak up to the consideration of several articles of fabulous history, including a watch charm supposed (but not guaranteed) to be made of that clapper whose theft had once thrown the school into such a turmoil. The Uncooked Beefsteak admired everything without reserve, coveted everything, and showed extreme willingness to pay spot cash.

The Tennessee Shad, had he been tied to a stake to the accompaniment of twenty howling savages, could have suffered no more. Finally almost overcome, he rose and hastened from the room. Finnegan, quite amazed, followed and last of all, Skinner with the reluctant step of the disappointed collector. Halfway down the second flight of stairs the Tennessee Shad could go no further. He turned, leaning against the banister, facing the Uncooked Beefsteak.

"Say, you don't really want to buy?" he said faintly, hoping against hope that Skinner would return a contrary answer.

"You bet I do!"

"Cash?" continued the Tennessee Shad still hoping. "It's got to be cash down."

Skinner, back in a familiar way, flashed a bundle of bills and said, "Why boy, just look these over."

"Go back!" said the Tennessee Shad.

He watched Skinner spring up the stair, the roll of bills carried insolently in his hand.

"Well, it's sending him back to Macnooder," he thought wistfully, "making him a present, but I can't resist my nature!"

Dennis de Brian de Boru Finnegan, who, of course, could sus-

THE IDENTICAL SHOES THAT FLASH CONDIT WORE

pect only a little of the inner conflict, pressed his hand covertly in admiration of what he at once considered the highest mercantile strategy.

When, half an hour later, the Tennessee Shad and the ebullient Skinner again descended the stairs to seal the compact in the usual way (Finnegan being detained by the annoyance of a recitation) the Tennessee Shad felt not the slightest elation. He glanced gloomily at Skinner's immaculate creases going before him on the narrow walk and a feeling of remorse came over him, the flat, heavy, tasteless feeling that succeeds the plunge into temptation.

"It's the last time," he thought, glancing back at the Dickinson where several wolfish eyes still watched his progress. "It's the last time that walking safe deposit will ever open for me. Well, there's only one thing to be done. If it is the last, I'll eat till I bust!"

With this colossal heroism in mind he said to prepare the Beefsteak for the hecatombs that were to come.

"Skinner, Old Sporting Tootlets, I feel rather hungry."

"My boy," said the exultant purchaser, "go as far as you like."

The tone was the tone that answered obsequious headwaiters in expensive metropolitan restaurants. The patronage decided the Tennessee Shad. The Beefsteak was really impossible when you treated him like a human being. He would show him no mercy.

"Well, Old Gazello," said the Uncooked Beefsteak, in imitation of Turkey Reiter, "pick out anything you want. You can't scare me, I've got the wad!"

He clapped him on the shoulder as a patron of gladiators might. The Tennessee Shad winced as from a blow and the last grumbling of his thin conscience died away.

"Shad, old boy!" said Skinner, throwing back his coat and allowing the tips of his pink fingers to slide along the blazing vest into the pockets. "You don't know what a real gorge is. I can't stand with you on this food here. It really is dyspeptic, you know. But say, wait till Thanksgiving, come up to the hotel with me and I'll show you what a real blowout is. I'll put you up against some real sports, I will."

The Tennessee Shad swallowed his wrath, glancing about to make sure no one was within hearing distance.

"My boy," continued Skinner, forgetting himself, "you young ones here don't know me!"

"We don't, eh?"

"Not a bit. Why, when I come in, every headwaiter in New York comes up on the jump. They have named a couple of dishes after me."

"You don't say so!"

"Fact."

"You're a little tin wonder, aren't you!" said the Tennessee Shad, beginning to be angry.

The constant opening of the pocketbook had stripped Skinner of the last semblance of awe toward the Tennessee Shad. He laughed a short, disagreeable laugh.

"A wonder? I'm a real sport—no ten-cent article like you put up with around here—the real dead game variety!"

This last indiscretion was too much for the Tennessee Shad. He left abruptly and dashing across the street, plunged through the doors of the Jigger Shop, straight into the arms of Mr. Lucius Cassius Hopkins, the Old Roman himself. For a second, face to face with that supreme flunker of boys, all thought deserted him. Then, assuming a look of combined grief and terror, he cried, "A roll of court plaster and a bandage Al, quick's you can! Fellow at house cut his foot!"

But at this moment the Uncooked Beefsteak all unprepared, flopped in, crying hilariously, "Lord, Al, open up a whole can!"

Then he saw the Roman.

"A can of—court plaster? Yes?" said the Roman with a little joyful burbling sound. "Well, speak up."

"No, sir."

"Not court plaster?"

"No, sir."

"Just the ordinary destructive, daily poison—well?"

"Yes, sir," said the Tennessee Shad slowly.

"So."

The Roman paused and, shooting up an eyebrow, fixed them with his long glance as though to petrify them first and punish them after. Montague Skinner was chilled to the bone, a sensation further enhanced by perceiving from his angle of observation, a more fortunate pair of legs, *en cachette,* behind the counter.

Now the Roman ruled not simply by the weight of an iron hand, but by the terrors of an imagination endowed with humor and satire. And so, remembering that it was the Tennessee Shad who waited before him, he decided to fit the punishment to the criminal.

"No excuse—no further excuse—none at all? Imagination numbed—not working today? Too bad. Ten times around the Circle. Do it now."

The Tennessee Shad was thunderstruck. He went out in high indignation. Of course the Roman had done it on purpose. There were a dozen punishments he might have selected—sent him to Penal for an afternoon—but to choose this, knowing his aversion to muscular strains! It was an outrage.

"Why, ten times around the Circle is over two miles," he said furiously as they tramped away. "I've never walked that in my life. The old rhinoceros, he did it on purpose! It's unfair. It's discrimination—persecution—tyranny. I've a mind to go right up to the Doctor."

"The Old Roman's down on you," said Skinner, who had learned a number of the routine formulas.

"Course he is, always has been. Nice mess you've got me in."

"How was I to know?" said Skinner.

The Tennessee Shad relapsed into gloomy meditation. What he did not voice aloud was that the real humiliation threatened was the spectacle of himself, yoked to the Beefsteak, parading before the hilarious audience of the school. Of course, Macnooder, of all persons, and the Dickinson cohorts, with the memory of defrauded threats, would come piling out to hoot him—caught in his own trap, publicly exposed as the boon companion, the bosom friend of the stolen Beefsteak.

The moment was critical, one of those public trials that changes in a twinkling a reputation and fastens a label of ridicule to a career of honor. What is more, the Tennessee Shad knew the peril.

In this state of immense mental perturbation and excited brain effort, the Tennessee Shad, heeled by the contrite Skinner, arrived at the edge of that vast area known as the Circle and gazed in horror, as the adventurous sailors of Columbus gazed at the limitless waters.

But fortune favored him. Directly in front stood a wheelbarrow waiting the reappearance of the gardener. His gaze left the stretches of the Circle and paused at the thing on wheels at his side. A moment later he said breathlessly, "Beefsteak!"

"What?"

"Do you remember what the Roman told us?"

"Sure, ten times around the Circle."

"But the exact words?"

"That's it, ten times around the Circle."

"He didn't say *walk* ten times?"

"Why, no."

"Ah!" The Tennessee Shad drew a long, comforted breath. He was saved. Then, carefully considering the inexperienced Skinner, he said carelessly putting one foot on the wheelbarrow, "Gee, if I could turn the laugh on the Old Roman! If I could get the best of him some way! They could fire me, I wouldn't care."

Skinner's glance in turn fell on the wheelbarrow.

"Eureka!"

"What is it?" said the Shad, wondering if he had taken the bait.

"I say! I have a wonderful idea. The wheelbarrow!"

"What about it?"

"We take turns, one gets in the wheelbarrow and the other wheels him around."

"Skinner, you're a genius," said the Tennessee Shad with great effusion. "It's the greatest joke ever heard. It'll kill the Roman. He'll explode. You're a hero, my boy. The whole school will cheer you on. How *did* you think of it?"

"Who'll start?"

"I will," said the Shad, hastily slipping into the wheelbarrow. "I weigh hardly anything, let her go."

Now the legs secreted behind the counter at the Jigger Shop belonged to Hungry Smeed, who as soon as the Roman departed, had gone scampering gleefully back to the Dickinson with the joyful tale of the Tennessee Shad's having been caught with the Uncooked Beefsteak. In one minute the entire house came rushing out to behold the humiliation of the crafty usurper of their own property. What they beheld instead was the lank limbs of the Tennessee Shad stuffed into the wheelbarrow that Skinner was trundling with an air of strained but supreme content.

"Well, I'll be jig-swiggered," said Macnooder ruefully.

"Can you beat him?"

"The Shad certainly is a wonder."

"How the deuce do you suppose he got him to do it?"

"Why, he's got the Beefsteak so hypnotized that he's grinning all over."

"He certainly is!"

"Boys, we can't help it, we'll have to give the Shad a cheer," said Macnooder. Overcome with admiration and soaring for once above the earthly line of dollars and cents in his enthusiasm for the artist, he said to himself, "I certainly must compromise, the firm has got to go on!"

"We certainly will."

The cheer that went rollicking over the campus, waking up the inmates of the Houses, encouraged Skinner wonderfully. He took it as a personal tribute. Startled by the unexpected clamor, the school came rushing to the windows, beheld the extraordinary voyage of the Tennessee Shad and sure of a sensation, came swarming out.

"Take it easy, Montague, old chap," said the Tennessee Shad. "Rest every half time around. Besides, we want the whole bunch to get on to us."

"Say, it's about your turn," said Skinner, happy but very hot.

"Never," said the Tennessee Shad firmly. "You're safe; you run no risks. But it's ten to one they fire me."

"I'll take the risk," said Skinner.

"No, you won't," said the Shad tragically. "Besides, it's a wonderful sell on the Roman, if I never touch foot on the ground. Oh, wonderful!"

"Still," said the Beefsteak doubtfully.

"My boy, the glory is all yours. You had the idea, you get all the credit," said the Shad, manfully resisting the temptation. "Hear that cheer? Look at the mob running over from the Upper—with cameras, too. It's the finest thing ever happened. Twice around now, that's a fifth the distance already. Keep a-going."

By this time the Circle was lined with rollicking, roaring boys, vying with one another who should cheer the loudest for the Tennessee Shad.

"Don't cheer me fellows, cheer the Beefsteak," cried the Shad, giving the high sign. "It's his idea, he thought it up. Cheer for the Uncooked Beefsteak."

And the school, gazing on the perfectly satisfied countenance of Skinner, understood the part it had to play. Immense cheers for the unsuspecting dupe rolled forth, jumping from group to group that before respective houses crowded down to the edge of the roadway.

The Uncooked Beefsteak, with every muscle strained, saw only the triumph in front, knowing nothing of the hilarious groups behind his back that locked arms and danced with joy.

"Isn't he wonderful?"

THE TENNESSEE SHAD STUFFED
INTO A WHEELBARROW THAT SKINNER WAS TRUNDLING.

"Look at the Shad's face!"
"How does he look so solemn!"
"And the Beefsteak thinks he is it!"
"Oh, joy!"
"Oh, rapture!"
"Cheese it. Here he comes again."

"Three cheers, fellows, for Beefsteak!"

The rolling accompaniment of cheers spurred Skinner on to supreme efforts. He was absolutely, airily happy. He beamed on the procession of excited faces that shouted forth their encouragement and at times was so convulsed with his own humor that he was forced to stop to let the gale of merriment spend itself.

He waited no longer than was necessary to rest the ache in his armpits, and then was off on the glorious journey. At the completion of the sixth round, the Tennessee Shad insisted that he should be massaged and a dozen hands fought for the honor; another crowd, with flapping handkerchiefs fanned air on his boiled complexion, while from all sides he heard the plaudits.

"Beefsteak, you're it!"

"The grandest scheme—"

"How did you think of it?"

"Keep it up."

"It's a record breaker."

"You're strong as an ox."

"All ready?' said the Tennessee Shad with maternal solicitude. "Here, wrap those handles with handkerchiefs, some of you loafers. Clear the way there, for Beefsteak!"

Intoxicated with the strong intoxication of the multitude, the seventh round was completed before he knew it. Then the roadway seemed suddenly to harden and strike his feet with the impact of every step. The Tennessee Shad began to grow to the proportions of P. Lentz and the circle to widen like the journeying ripples from a dropped stone. Four times he set down the awful burden and gasped for breath before the welcoming shouts went up.

"Eight rounds!"

"Only two more."

"Bully for the Beefsteak!"

"Strong as a blacksmith."

"More massage."

"Rub down the Beefsteak."

He began the ninth round; the chorus of shrieks and cheers was one steady howl in his ears, handkerchiefs and caps fluttered over his head, while dimly he heard new shouts.

"Go it there, you Beefsteak!"

"Show your speed."

"Hit up that pace."

"Make a record!"

Then he saw nothing but the interminable white space over the peaked head of the Tennessee Shad. Every fifty feet he set the wheelbarrow down to rest, doggedly resolved not to fail. Then the tenth round, the final triumph began. Ready to drop, paying for every yard gained by a hundred shooting pains, stopping, jerking along blindly, unheeding, he came at last to the supreme quarter and wheeled the Tennessee Shad straight to the entrance of the Kennedy House, set down the wheelbarrow and turned gloriously to view the triumph.

Suddenly he heard a shout wilder than all the rest and looking at the terrace of the Kennedy, beheld a sight that swept away the clouds of his illusion like a clap of wind. On the top step stood the Old Roman, a handkerchief at his eyes, doubling over with laughter, shaking hands, actually shaking hands, with the *Tennessee Shad.*

VII

FACTS LEADING TO A RECONCILIATION

AFTER THE Beefsteak's brief but disillusioning visit with the Tennessee Shad, Macnooder observed with satisfaction that while he had suffered—he had not improved.

Just what was the matter with the Uncooked Beefsteak was still a puzzle to the Dickinson House. It was quite evident that so long as he was oppressed and forced to the menial exercises of bootblacking and clothespressing, he was moderately inoffensive. It was equally evident that the moment the ban was lifted in the slightest and he was restored to human intercourse, he became absolutely unbearable. But the reason thereof was not to be found.

"What the dickens is the matter with him anyhow," said Turkey Reiter. "We have certainly given him enough exercise."

"Ah, he'll never learn," said the Egghead, who always took a gloomy view.

"He's all right when he is cleaning out the room," said Hungry Smeed, who had never enjoyed the luxury of a valet.

"We certainly treat him like a dog."

"We certainly do!"

"It's a crime!"

"Well, what are you going to do about it?"

"You'd think he would learn a thing or two."

"Well, at any rate," said Macnooder, "he's stayed on the reservation lately. No wandering from the fireside, and all that sort of thing. I'll bet the Tennessee Shad's tongue is hanging out every time the Beefsteak goes over to the village."

Macnooder spoke vindictively, harboring vindictive impulses toward the Tennessee Shad ever since the return of the souvenir toilet set to the Dickinson. Likewise the Uncooked Beefsteak, innocently acting on the artful suggestion of the Tennessee Shad, had returned to Macnooder, in the joyful belief of restoring a sacrificed heirloom, the football shoes which Flash Condit did *not* wear when he crossed the Princeton goal line. As the restoration was made in private, Doc Macnooder accepted it with admirable gravity and saved thereby a public advertisement. But the blow told.

It would not do, however, any longer to risk open warfare with the Tennessee Shad, backed by the busy imaginations of Dink Stover and Dennis de Brian de Boru Finnegan. Another would have sought revenge. Not so Macnooder. His instinct was always financial. If he could not destroy, he would combine. With this idea in mind he began, introspectively and outwardly, to seek for some scheme worthy to offer to the Tennessee Shad as basis for a new treaty. After a season of wandering dreamily, straw in mouth, cap set ruminatively on the incline of his head, a fortunate conjunction developed an idea which almost resulted in a football riot and did produce a situation that should be brought to the attention of the omniscient body of rules-makers if only to avert a lurking danger which might turn a scholarly clash of gladiatorial universities into a shambles.

Macnooder, after a week of fruitless searching, was gazing hopelessly out of the window at the departing candidates for the House elevens, when a knock was heard and the voice of the Uncooked Beefsteak meekly sought admission.

Now for two days the ban had been lifted on the dispenser of Skinner's wealth, and Montague had been treated like a citizen; which, translated, means that the features of Turkey Reiter, the Triumphant Egghead, Macnooder et cetera, had once more returned to the hostile interiors of the Jigger Shop and Conover's.

"Come in," said Macnooder.

The Uncooked Beefsteak found his way through the litter of bottles and boxes and joined Macnooder on the window seat.

"Well, what's up?" said Macnooder critically, perceiving at once an air of importance and pride about his visitor.

"I say, Doc," said Skinner, heedless of the cold and antagonistic glance, "what do you say to injecting a little sporting life into this dead hole?"

"Oh, you think it is a dead hole," said Macnooder softly.

Skinner stifled a yawn and ran two fingers down the creases of his trouser leg.

"Come off, now. You know it's dead."

"Say, you must have an idea."

"I have."

"Touch her off."

"What do you say to getting up a book on the house games?"

"Gambling, Rollo?" said Macnooder, turning over the thought rapidly.

"Oh, rot!" said Skinner. "Don't josh me now."

"I'm thinking hard."

"It's quite sporty and heaps of fun."

"You've done this before?"

"Sure."

"But don't you think that was very wrong of you, Montague?" said Macnooder, who had not yet determined on a course of action.

"If you are talking like that—" said Beefsteak blushing a little, and rising.

"Sit down, sport," said Macnooder dreamily. "Elucidate a little on this here proposition of yours. Where would you begin?"

"I'd begin," said Beefsteak eagerly, "with the Kennedy–Woodhull Game next week."

"The Kennedy?" said Macnooder with a little start of interest.

"Why not?"

"But that's a cinch. No one would bet on that. Varsity men can't play this year and the Woodhull ought to win thirty to nothing."

"Bet on the score, then."

Macnooder took a long time before replying. His gaze traveled across and up to the eyrie of the Tennessee Shad, and rested there fondly.

Finally, smothering his enthusiasm, he said slowly, "Yes, I suppose that could be done."

"Same thing as betting to win and betting for place," said the Beefsteak in a sort of worldly way.

"But is this a square game?" said Macnooder.

"Oh, rather," said the Beefsteak. "Why, a bookmaker is the squarest thing a-going. I know a dozen of them."

"Now, he's off again on that eternal dead game sporting idea of his," said Macnooder to himself, mentally debating whether or not to consign him at once to the blacking brush. However, he temporized.

"Where do I come in?"

"You are an expert adviser," said the Beefsteak with just a touch of patronage. "You know the crowd better than I do. You'd better work up the bets."

"Oh, really!"

"And you get a third of the profits," said the Uncooked Beefsteak hastily.

"You supply the capital?" said Macnooder warily.

"Any amount!"

"It's most debauching!"

"Pooh! every gentleman places a little bet now and then," said the Beefsteak in his grandest manner.

At this moment a call resounded along the hall.

"Oh, you, Beefsteak, come here and press my pants!"

The gentleman of fashion disappeared in a twinkling. Skinner looked at Macnooder in a mute appeal.

"Better go," said Macnooder, thus relieved of all responsibility, "and tomorrow I'll give you an answer."

That night by recognized routes, Doc Macnooder journeyed in safety over to the Kennedy and the lair of Tennessee Shad. The conference was secret, complete, and satisfactory to all parties interested, and the first result was that the next morning the Uncooked Beefsteak was made happy by Macnooder's agreeing to act as a sporting partner in what was agreed should be a deliberate attempt to trim the Tennessee Shad.

Since the national game of football has been shorn of horns and hoofs, a little of the truth may be told of the joyful hecatombs of those earlier games in the nineties. Baseball on a professional field smooth as a billiard cloth, under the protecting vision of clubbed discouragers of assault and battery, is one thing; the same pastime on a back lot amid boulders and broken bottles, with opposing gangs waiting and willing on the lines, is quite a different risk—rated according to insurance tables.

Such was the relative position of the house games in the realm of football. They were strenuous affairs—rare opportunities when the best of friends could physically experiment on each other without an afterthought. Of course all this is changed, but it was a good school, though a rude one, for the masculine animal, who, refine him as you may, must somehow fight his way through this world.

Now, the Kennedy having four members of the Varsity, was accordingly weakened in its House eleven. The Tennessee Shad, who, as may be remembered, was thinner than his own shadow, was not exactly the most corpulent member of the eleven but a fair representative of the average. He was at quarterback, and Fatty Harris at center, a combination which looked very much like a cannon ball and a musket. Hungry Smeed, who even after he had consumed forty-nine pancakes, never weighed over one hundred and twenty, was at one end and Dennis de Brian de Boru Finnegan at the other. The guards weighed one hundred and forty and the tackles, the Gutter Pup and Lovely Mead, ten pounds less, and the situation is best understood when it is baldly stated that the team was so mortified that it had refused to stand up and be photographed.

The Woodhull team, on the contrary, was strong with second-team men, averaged over one hundred fifty pounds to a player, and was already conceded the house championship.

All of which made the conference of Kennedy enthusiasts on the evening before the game a most oppressively silent gathering.

"It's a joke," said the Tennessee Shad, reclining on P. Lentz's cushioned frame, to save himself for the morrow's fray.

"The faculty sprung this dodge about debarring Varsity members just to beat us out of a championship."

"Sure!"

"They're down on us."

"I'll bet Old Baranson at the Woodhull worked it through himself."

"I'll bet he did!"

"Well," said Lovely Mead cheerily, "they'll beat us about thirty-six to nothing."

"Fifty-six!"

"A hundred and six!"

"Never mind, I'll get a crack at Cheyenne Baxter," said the Gutter Pup, who came from the same town and loved his friend.

"I've got a few love pats for Butsey White myself."

"They outweigh us twenty pounds to a man."

"Why, if a wind should start up blowing we wouldn't stay on the field!"

"If you fellows would only spring some of my trick plays," said Dennis de Brian de Boru Finnegan, "they'd never get hold of the ball."

"What's your pet idea?" said Stover, yanking the Irishman to him by an ankle and a wrist.

"It's called the fan-wedge," said Dennis, who never resigned hope. "It's just like this, see! The quarter gives the signal, everyone on the team runs back and out in the lines of the spokes of a fan, and the center snaps the ball when they are on the run. The fan divides and sweeps toward each end and the quarter makes a long pass to whichever side looks best. See?"

"Dennis," said Stover severely, "go stand in the corner."

"It'll work, Dink, you see if it won't!"

"What idea is the Shad browsing on?" said Stover, squelching Finnegan by covering his head with a sweater.

"Oh, I'm kind of thinking of something," said the Tennessee Shad in a noncommittal way.

"Something that is good for thirty-six points?"

"My idea is a secret," said the Tennessee Shad loftily, "but if it works it will most certainly reduce the score."

At this came an interruption.

"Here comes Macnooder!"

"And the Beefsteak!"

"What's his game?"

"He's coming over to give us the laugh."

"Keep quiet," said the Shad quickly. "Don't get in a huff. Just let me draw him out."

There now appeared, followed by the Uncooked Beefsteak at a valet's distance, Doc Macnooder with a pair of uncased opera glasses strapped to his back, trailing a bamboo cane, a pencil over one ear and a note book in one hand. His approach was received in various ways; by the younger members with expectant grins, by the veterans with wary defensive looks, while the Gutter Pup openly and insultingly took the twenty-two cents that burdened his change pocket, counted them, and slipped them down his sock.

"Ah there!" said Macnooder, affably saluting with his bamboo cane. "Very pleasant evening, gentlemen. Nice day for ducks— white ducks, of course! Let me present to you Mr. Montague Skinner, my betting commissioner."

"Your what?" said two or three voices.

"I think I said betting commissioner," said Macnooder in his most inviting way. "Monte, did I say betting commissioner? I did. This, gentlemen, is a little betting account, called a book, that I finger thus between my thumb and my first finger. I am told there are a number of gents, called dead game sports, in this House, and I just dropped over to accommodate them. A little flier on the game, eh?"

At this there was a low, rumbling, portentous sound and Dink Stover, as President of the House, was about to order the proper measures when he suddenly beheld the left eyelid of the Tennessee Shad fluttering on his bony cheek.

"Now, little bounding boys," said Macnooder, genially poising a pencil, "we will do this in professional fashion; winner first, place afterward. Any Sporting Life eager to place a bet on the Kennedy to win tomorrow's game, step up. Step up, but don't crowd. We give you two to one, Woodhull to win. Did I hear a noise?"

"You are a dead game sport, you are," said P. Lentz sarcastically. "Why don't you ask us to give you the money?"

"Three to one," said Macnooder instantly.

"How generous!"

"Five to one."

"We're still listening."

"Six and seven to one. Eight to one. Dollars to doughnuts, in jiggers, in bank notes, in thousands. Come one, come all. Our capital is unlimited. Ten to one, then. Ten to one the Woodhull wins the game!"

"Ten to one the grass comes up in the spring," said the Gutter Pup sarcastically.

"Ten to one the earth goes around the sun."

"Ten to one *you* don't lose whichever way it comes out!"

At this, Doc Macnooder hastily changed the subject.

"Anyone want to bet on the score? Any dead game Kennedy sport got any feeling of confidence at all?"

"What do you want to bet?" said P. Lentz at last, stung into action.

"Even the Woodhull wins by fifteen points."

P. Lentz looked at Macnooder as Al at the Jigger Shop was wont to look when the charge account had been overstretched.

"Well, now, what's your idea?" said Macnooder professionally. "Speak up my man, speak up!"

"I'll bet you even," said King Lentz very slowly, "that they don't score over twenty-four points."

At this juncture a little lukewarm enthusiasm began to appear, and when Macnooder, after a whispered conference with Skinner, expressed his willingness, quite a number of wagers were recorded. The Tennessee Shad however, remained obdurate until thirty points had been conceded, when he at length responded, entraining in his fall Finnegan and the Gutter Pup.

"Say, it's a cinch," said Macnooder knowingly to the Uncooked Beefsteak, when they had returned to their rooms.

"Why, thirty points is nothing at all," said Skinner joyfully.

"Nothing!"

"Gee, I certainly wanted to get back at that Tennessee Shad."

"Sure you did. Well, you got him. He swallowed the whole fishing pole."

"But can we collect?" said Skinner, struck by a sudden horrid thought.

"Now, that's an idea," said Macnooder. "We must fix that. I tell you what. Give me your money, and we'll make Turkey Reiter stakeholder and I'll round up those paper collar sports in the Kennedy and make them plunk up tonight."

The Uncooked Beefsteak became so superhumanly unbearable under the stimulus of his new venture that the House in self defense was forced to set him to darning socks. So sure was he of his approaching victory over the Tennesseee Shad that not even this additional humiliation could disturb his equanimity. In the afternoon, after scrubbing off the degrading stains of blacking from his fingers, he slanted his pearl gray fedora at the proper rakish angle on his head, and, rejoicing inwardly, sauntered down to the third field to watch the preliminaries of the game.

The shivering line of the Kennedy was running through the signals in a weak discouraged way, while the well-nurtured, brawny team of the Woodhull, as though disdaining superfluous exertion, was languidly tossing the pigskin to and fro.

The Uncooked Beefsteak spread his feet, clasped his hands behind his back and, looking over the antagonists, smiled a thoroughly satisfied smile. About him reassuring comments went up.

"Say, it's a shame!"

"They'll never be able to count the points."

"The Woodhull ought to lend them a couple of men."

"They'll tire themselves out running down the field."

"Why, there won't even be a first class scrap in it!"

Macnooder came up, looking very canny.

"Say, Beefsteak, I've worked the Shad into doubling all his bets. How about it?"

The Uncooked Beefsteak wrung his hands furtively but with great feeling.

Jack Rabbit Lawson, referee, a fifth former with a flower in his buttonhole and a choker tie of several antagonistic shades, now passed languidly on to the field, and called the teams together, announcing in routine, half-hearted fashion, as he had done in a dozen games before, "Of course fellows, no roughing it."

"Oh, no!"

"Nothing brutal, nothing coarse!"

"Oh, dear no!"

"Remember, this is a gentleman's game."

"You bet we will!"

"I shall be very strict."

"Yes, Mr. Referee."

"The Woodhull wins the toss. The Kennedy kicks off. Are you ready?"

By common consent, the first line-up was devoted to a friendly exchange of amenities, with honors about even between Cheyenne Baxter and the Gutter Pup, who came from the same town, and Butsy White and Fatty Harris, who were too closely related.

With the second line-up the game began in earnest. There were many scores to wipe out between the two houses, and Ginger Pop Rooker at quarter for the Woodhull had no intention of losing the verbal opportunity of the present advantage.

"Oh, I say, fellows," he said in a careless, bored way. "What's the use of using the signals? Let's tell 'em where we're going. Ram the ball right through Lovely Mead and that little squirt of an Irishman! On your toes! Let her come!"

The humiliated Kennedy swarmed frantically to the point attacked, only to be borne back for a five-yard loss. The Woodhull came gleefully to its feet, laughing hilariously.

"Good eye, Ginger!"

"Tell them every time!"

"Poor old Kennedy!"

"All ready," said Rooker to the shrieks of the spectators. "Put it right through the Gutter Pup this time. Hard now!"

For thirty yards the outraged Kennedy was swept back before a fumble stopped the insolent advance. Cheyenne Baxter, at left half, for the Woodhull, owing to a retiring left eye, either saw imperfectly or with his battling right eye fixed on his chum, the Gutter Pup, momentarily forgot the technical presence of the superfluous football.

At any rate the Kennedy lined up, plunged at the opposing line and were carried back five yards to the accompaniment of derisive shrieks from the squabs of the Woodhull on the side lines.

There was a hurried consultation in which the Tennessee Shad was seen with his lips to Fatty Harris's ear, and then the team massed for a plunge on center. The ball was passed, there was a forward lunge, a churning movement; half the players went down in a heap and suddenly a report like a dynamite explosion was heard. Among the spectators a clamor arose.

"What the deuce has happened?"

"They've squashed Fatty Harris!"

"Fatty Harris is blown up!"

"Punctured!"

"Squashed flat!"

"Exploded!"

"No, it's the ball!"

"He's bust the ball!"

"He certainly has."

"Flat as a pancake."

"Fatty has smashed the ball!"

"Well, where *is* the ball?"

This last cry quickly communicated itself to the frantic Woodhull team, who, throwing themselves on Fatty Harris, rolled him over and discovered that the pigskin had vanished.

At this moment a wild, gleeful shriek arose from behind the Woodhull goal posts, and the Tennessee Shad was seen extracting from under his sweater the flattened pigskin. Instantly the field overflowed with the shock of waters, triumphant or frantic.

"Touchdown!"

"Robbers!"

"Touchdown for the Kennedy."

"Call him back!"

"Dead ball."

"Hurrah for the Tennessee Shad!"

"Muckers!"

"No mucker tricks!"

"The ball was down."

"Call it back!"

"Judgment!"

"Judgment, Mr. Referee!"

Jack Rabbit Lawson, hauled to and fro between the contending parties, found himself in the most serious predicament into which a referee can fall, when a decision must be given and either decision requires an escort of police. Moreover, each contending party, to clinch the judgment, had precipitated itself upon him and the struggle for his possession raged like the contention of Greek and Trojan over the body of Patroclus.

"Don't let those thugs bluff you, Jack!" shouted the Kennedy cohorts, in possession of an arm and a leg.

"Square deal, no cheating!" retorted the Woodhull with a commanding grip on the other extremities.

Fresh arrivals surged in, seeking to fasten on him.

"Touchdown!"

"No touchdown!"

"Square deal!"

"Justice!"

"No intimidation!"

"No mucker tricks!"

"Hands off," shouted Jack Rabbit Lawson. "Let go of me!"

"Mr. Referee," said the Tennessee Shad, artfully cool, "I demand that the game go on."

"The game must go on," said the referee, immensely relieved.

"Never," shouted the furious Woodhull.

"Mr. Referee," said the Tennessee Shad with magnificent impudence, "they know we've got 'em licked! I demand that the game go on. Settle the point afterward!"

At this, just as he intended, the Woodhull quite forgot that it was only a question of walking through the unresisting line in their fury at the trick sprung on them. With one accord they responded.

"We won't go on!"

"Don't give the robbers a point!"

"Don't you stand for it!"

"Judgment, Mr. Referee!"

"Let go of me, there, will you?" said Jack Rabbit Lawson for the tenth time. "I'll look it up in the rules."

Churning at his heels, the whole mass swept him on to the Upper, except where in spots little detached groups of enthusiasts sought their own solutions. At the Esplanade the crowd waited vociferously while Lawson went to his room, accompanied by the Tennessee Shad for the Kennedy and Ginger Pop Rooker for the Woodhull.

Lawson, having closed his collar and coaxed his necktie back into a normal position, looked sternly at Rooker and said, "Now, what's your argument?"

"My argument," said Ginger Pop turbulently, "is that a ball is dead when it is a dead ball! And furthermore, we are playing a game called football, and not 'Button, button, who's got the button,' or 'Going to Jerusalem,' or 'Post office,' or—"

"Hold up there," said Jack Rabbit magisterially, "that's enough. Your argument is a good one. Now, Shad, what's yours?"

"I have three arguments," said the Tennessee Shad, rising, with his thumb over the second button of his waistcoat. "First, the play had never stopped; second, you won't find anything against it; and third, this bunch of soreheads would have done the same thing if they had had a cute little boy like me."

"Your position is very strong," said Jack Rabbit Lawson, nodding to the Tennessee Shad. "I will now look it up in the rules."

He read through the fine print laboriously and solemnly and closed the book.

"Well?" said the rival counsels in a breath.

"There are things here," said Lawson judiciously, "that I want to think over. I will announce my decision in an hour."

At that time the mob gathered once more. Jack Rabbit Lawson appeared at his window and announced that he had read the rules again and was still deliberating, but that his decision would infallibly be given at five o'clock.

Suddenly, their fury having had a certain time to cool, the Woodhull all at once woke up and grasped the amazing fact of their own blunder in not continuing a contest that could have but one outcome.

Consequently as the Tennessee Shad, camped on the Esplanade in the midst of the embattled Kennedy, was receiving congratulations, a suave delegation from the Woodhull headed by Ginger Pop Rooker with his blandest smile, approached, and the following conversation took place.

"Hello there, you foxy old Shad!"

"Hello, yourself."

"Say, you certainly worked a slick one over us."

"Is it possible?"

"Look here, it did make us rather hot at first, but we certainly have to take off our hats to you. That was a corking idea, a wonder, a peacherino, and perfectly square."

"Oh, don't make me blush."

"I say, old boy, we give in!"

"You do, eh?"

"Yes, we admit your claim. We'll agree to a touchdown. So now let's go back and finish the game."

The Tennessee Shad looked long and sadly at Rooker, then he laid his head on P. Lentz's shoulder and began to laugh. The laugh irritated Rooker and likewise alarmed him.

"I say, Shad, shall we play it over now or tomorrow?"

Then the Tennessee Shad spoke languidly, "No, dear boy, no. You had your chance on the field, and you refused, think of it, you *refused* to go on! Of course we'd have licked you to a scramble anyway, but, oh, well, we'll let it go at six to nothing."

"What, you won't play it over?" cried a dozen angry voices.

"Don't ask me."

"Why, you robber!" said Rooker, immediately changing his tone, "you low-down robber!"

"Thank you!"

"You little sneak thief!"

"A baby trick!"

"Mucker gag!"

"We'll appeal to Walter Camp."

"Do," said the Tenessee Shad, "keep on appealing. But you're licked, and remember this, that I rushed the ball right through you, right through the whole Woodhull line!"

This being a little super-insulting, the Kennedy took up a little stronger defensive position as the Woodhull advanced. The tension, however, was fortunately averted by the sudden appearance at his window of Jack Rabbit Lawson, who, having locked and fortified his door, now addressed the crowd.

"Fellows, I have read over the rules a third time, and I have come to a decision."

"Hurray!"

"Touchdown!"

"No score!"

"Woodhull!"

"Kennedy!"

"Shut up!"

"Let him talk!"

"Fellows, I have decided," said Jack Rabbit Lawson firmly, in the midst of a hollow silence, "I have decided TO RESIGN!"

And closing the window abruptly, he withdrew, nor could threats or cajolery ever draw from him an opinion on the case.

To avert a civil conflict, the Doctor at once appointed a faculty committee to render a decision within the half-hour. This committee, rejecting as immaterial the Woodhull's contention that the Tennessee Shad had used a sharpened nail, was guided by an almost analogous incident in the Harvard-Carlisle game, where, it may be remembered, a touchdown was scored by an Indian concealing the pigskin under the back of his jersey, and running the length of the field through the bewildered scholars. The tremendous classic prestige of Cambridge being decisive, judgment was rendered for the Kennedy, with this proviso: that the game should not be played over, and all adherents were ordered quarantined in their respective Houses for twenty-four hours.

The Uncooked Beefsteak, shocked and bewildered, went limply toward the Dickinson. Halfway, Turkey Reiter, stake-holder, accosted him.

"Hello there, Sporting Tootlets!"

The Uncooked Beefsteak stopped and feebly responded, "Oh, hello!"

"Rather bad day for bookmakers, eh?"

"I don't understand it at all."

"Well, I paid over the stakes," said Turkey Reiter mercilessly. "Say—rather expensive educating us, isn't it?"

Skinner shook his head.

"I don't understand. Where's Macnooder?"

"Doc? Over with the Tennessee Shad."

"With the Tennessee Shad!" said the Beefsteak, shocked. "Why, we got this up to trim him!"

"Look here, son," said Turkey Reiter, relenting a little, "you put this down from me—the only way to trim either of those weasels is to trim them together!"

Skinner took off his hat and slowly spun it on one finger, gazing stolidly at the windows of the Tennessee Shad.

"And now, Old Gazello," said Turkey, who enjoyed an occasional lapse into moralizing, "really you are not up to teaching these con men anything as yet, let alone sinful, wicked practices. *Savez?* Better sit down at our feet and pick up a few pearls."

The Beefsteak, incapable of reply, moved slowly away.

"Don't try to be a bad man," continued the moralist. "Don't listen too much to the chink of the coin in your pockets. Don't try to buy your way here, because it won't go—it won't go, my boy! But—if nothing will stop you, if you've got to get rid of the dough, for the love of Mike, give me a chance!"

VIII

THE BEEFSTEAK APPLIES FOR ADMISSION

FORTUNATELY FOR the firm, despite his previous trying experiences, it must be confessed that the Uncooked Beefsteak still clung to those sporting proclivities which, in more worldly communities, are regarded as the natural distinctions of a gentleman. Reduced by his disrespectful housemates to menial degradations as humiliating as endured by other kings in exile, the spirit of ambition was yet strong in him—the spirit to excel in some field, to rise from the mass at whatever cost, to be known as an individual and not a type.

Unfortunately, the field was limited. He was not an athlete and he lazily had no desire to be one. He neither sang nor was the cause of melody in instruments. He did not act nor was he given to journalism. All this was in the undeveloped area into which he had never ventured, satisfied with his own beau ideal of a man of fashion.

However, it did seem to the Beefsteak, despite certain disillusionment which he had encountered since his advent to Lawrenceville, that the school was sadly in lack of what is vulgarly known as a true gentleman-sport—the two names, in his mind, being complementary, if not synonymous. Of course, a number of the fellows rejoiced in the very common nickname of "Sport," but the title had certainly been conveyed without the slightest notion of its distinction.

To Skinner's critical mind a gentleman-sport was not only a disciple of that magnificent Englishman, Beau Brummel, but of that other distinguished Britisher, the Marquis of Queensberry, who, while laying down the full etiquette of the law, was always found at the side of the prize ring and never within it. Likewise this ideal was one who never counted his change, never quarreled over a bill, who played with existence and wagered on the simple turns of fate with anybody for anything. To be a gentleman-s then, was to be magnificent, elegant and racy; and to be the first gentleman-sport in the school was, in a word, the ambition to which the Uncooked Beefsteak still clung, despite all reverses and the combined educational efforts of his housemates.

However, his skirmishes with the Tennessee Shad and Doc Macnooder had instilled in him a spirit of canniness. He no longer exposed his roll of bank notes, trailing it so to speak, on a string behind him. Instead, his first instinct when approached, was a convulsive movement toward the more secure buttoning of his coat. This educational result of their efforts was not, it must be confessed, so pleasing to Doc Macnooder and the Tennessee Shad, who, having become reconciled, sought separately but fruitlessly to enlist the Beefsteak in several schemes to humiliate the other.

Turkey Reiter alone was not suspected, for Turkey as President of the House had undertaken a series of lectures on moral conduct. These excursions into morality were delivered, strangely enough, in only four places: at Laloo's, to the bubbling noise of the steaming hot dogs; at Appleby's before the Turkish paste; at the Jigger Shop, and at Conover's. Why the spirit should refuse to move elsewhere went unnoticed by the Uncooked Beefsteak, who was immensely flattered by the solicitude of the great Turkey Reiter, listened a little and always begged the privilege of standing treat. The Beefsteak, still persistent, recurred to the Tennessee Shad and Doc Macnooder.

"Gee, I'd like to get back at those bunco steerers," he said, digging his teeth viciously into an unresisting frankfurter.

"Be humble, son," said Turkey Reiter, with paternal impressiveness.

"I'll get them yet."

"Others have tried," said Turkey Reiter, with a reminiscent twinge. "Your game, young rooster, is to be humble."

"Well, now," said the Beefsteak, with a sudden access of frankness, as they were alone, "say just what is the matter with me anyhow?"

"It's not just one thing, Old Gazello," said Turkey, comfortably. "Though, of course, there is one thing that is dead against ʌgly."

"What's that?"

"ɔu're a billionaire."

The Uncooked Beefsteak stared very seriously at the can where the hot dogs were bubbling, and said, "I wonder if that is it?"

"Sure, you're fair game. You're the fresh meat for every hungry coot who is strapped and waiting for the first of the month to come around. Say, bub, do you know what I'd do if I were you?"

"What?"

"Burn the bank and strip to a dollar a week," said Turkey, rushing on enthusiastically, either because moralizing was apt to run away with his discretion or because the near approach of a recitation rendered impossible any further favors from the munificence criticized.

"Oh, I say—"

"Sure," said Turkey, become like many another, the victim of his own argument," these are wise words, sonny. Cut out the treating, get down in our midst, and let us educate you on proper lines. *Savez?*"

"What! Never treat?"

"Never."

"No one at all?"

"Well, only—" said Turkey, pausing a bit and clapping the Beefsteak on the shoulder in an extra amicable way, "only a fellow who's doing you good."

The Beefsteak watched Turkey Reiter go, chuckling, helter-skelter back to recitation and remained a moment in thoughtful meditation over the dubious interpretation of his last words. Then he paid the bill and went slowly up the village street.

Directly in front of him, in full possession of the walk, was a bulldog, of no more reassuring aspect than bulldogs usually are. As Appleby was at the window and several fellows lounging in the doorway, Skinner marched resolutely forward expecting the passage to be yielded. Ten feet away, as the maneuver only resulted in a certain disconcerting fixity of the brute's gaze, he made a wide detour and deferred to another day the issue whether or not the irreproachable aroma of trousers made at New York's most expensive tailor, would appeal to that sense of aristocracy which is said to be instinctive in the canine.

The dog, who was felicitously named Tough, was the property of Blimmy Garret of the Woodhull, who besides rejoicing in the distinction of having risen to six feet six, was, on account of his possession of a mustache and a real discouraging bulldog, generally regarded as filling the position to which Skinner longingly aspired —the premier dead game sport of the school.

The companionship of Tough had been rather expensive to Blimmy. Due to several cases of carelessness on the dog's part, he had been forced to buy the silence of Klondike, who shook up the beds in the Dickinson, and pay Blinky, the one-eyed purveyor of cigarettes, ten dollars and replace the shredded trousers.

Tough was supposed to inhabit a suite in the village, but being by nature inclined to good society he had learned at the sound of a professorial tread to retire under the window seat and remain until the danger had passed. Despite which, the All-Seeing Eye was decidedly fixed in the direction of Tough and waiting a logical excuse.

The Uncooked Beefsteak had no sooner completed the outer trail than a patter of feet and a slight asthmatic snort behind revealed the fact that the brute was deliberating at his heels. Now if the Beefsteak's courage had never been tested by a frontal attack, it was doubly uncertain when momentarily expecting a crisis behind. There was still twenty yards to the Jigger Shop and an acceleration of pace might have fatal results.

At this moment, the Uncooked Beefsteak, looking ahead, thankfully perceived the true cause of the commotion at his heels.

In front of Bill Orum's, the cobbler, another dog, with certain marks that would permit him for purposes of classification to be described as a setter, was rounding the corner with tail set and carefully poised step. The last animal was Henry Clay, the property of Bill Orum, who stoutly declared that his dog could annihilate anything that attacked him on the *left* side; the right eye having gloriously gone in a victorious career.

Just which side the bulldog selected in his forward movement would be hard to determine, but in another second the joined bodies were revolving in the dust much after the fashion of a giant pinwheel that has jumped its fastenings. At the uproar that fell upon the street, a crowd came rushing out while the rival owners, hastening up, finally secured possession of the hindquarters of their respective champions. Then it was found that the bulldog had a secure grip on the pride of the cobbler shop at the throat directly beneath the closed right eye.

In this *impasse* Al, from his wisdom, produced an ammonia

bottle and Tough yielded to science what he would not have yielded to nature. Blimmy Garret hastily smuggled the victorious Tough to a place of concealment while the crowd, drifting away, left a few to listen to Bill Orum's haranguing on the result and his repeated assertion that Tough would have been a dead dog by now if he had attacked on the *left* side.

"That dog of Blimmy's certainly needs a licking," said Al, whose eyes and throat had received their measure of the ammonia.

"He certainly does," said Skinner, in full agreement.

"A lot of reputation he's got," said Al contemptuously, "licking a lot of curs and a walleyed setter whose teeth have to be tied in!"

"I'd like to bring a real bruiser down here," said Skinner, with a knowing look.

"Go ahead."

"By jingo, I will," said Skinner determinedly as he walked home. "Or, at any rate, I'll find a pup who'll make mincemeat of that sassy coyote."

Now, the Beefsteak's mind did not as yet work with that instinctive flight toward a novel idea that was the characteristic of the veteran. As a consequence, it was only after having repeatedly expressed a desire to get even with the brute who had given him such a chilly few moments that the complete idea finally took shape.

He stopped as though he had stubbed his toe, overcome with the beauty of his inspiration. His first impulse was to rush with it to Macnooder and the Tennessee Shad with a request to be admitted into the firm. But though he had learned little, he had learned something. Bridling his enthusiasm he forced himself to go twice around the Circle, working out the details of his scheme.

"Gee, the greatest ever. I'll be a chief promoter myself, and get up a dogfight," he confidently proclaimed.

When the Uncooked Beefsteak approached the firm of Macnooder and the Tennessee Shad he did so with so much business discretion that the veterans were clearly amazed.

"I want a few words with you two," said The Beefsteak, with a certain manner. "No bluff—but an out-and-out understanding!"

"Why, Montague, how you have aged!" said Macnooder in soft surprise.

"It's no joke this time," said Skinner, waving the persiflage aside. "I've got a scheme and I want an understanding. Now I'll be frank."

"Hello," said Macnooder, who from constant use of this last assurance became suspicious of the words on another's tongue.

"You fellows are about the cutest thing out. You've flimflammed me, and you've done it well. I'm not kicking, only I've got my eyes open now. And you'll never get me again."

At this tempting challenge, Macnooder looked over the roofs of the houses, afraid to meet the eye of the Tennessee Shad.

"See here," continued Skinner, with more gravity, as he mistook their silence, "I'm for you fellows and I want to get into your game on the ground floor."

"What game?"

"Promoting."

"Bring us an idea," said Macnooder.

"I have."

"You've got me."

"The best."

"What is it?"

"Get up a professional dogfight, Blimmy's bull-pup and some other dog we'll get. Sell tickets and run it off in the woods at midnight."

Macnooder looked at the proud Beefsteak and then solemnly at his partner.

"Shad," he said, "extend to Monte the right hand of fellowship."

"We must get a dog, though, that will dine off Tough," said Skinner.

"I know one," said the Tennessee Shad dreamily.

"Where?" said the Beefsteak eagerly.

"Trenton," said the Tennessee Shad, "a long-haired dog, that's the game. Bulldogs are pie before long-haired dogs—can't get at the throat."

"The Tennessee Shad'll look after the challenge, then," glibly said Macnooder, who from old experience read aright the note of dreaminess in his partner's voice and knew something was brewing. "Who'll referee?"

"I will," said the Uncooked Beefsteak.

Macnooder glanced at the Shad and saw a little smile of satisfaction on those thin lips.

"I suppose I've got to be secretary and treasurer then," he said, with false weariness.

"That's the stuff," said the Beefsteak autocratically. "Besides,

I've seen a real fight and know the game."

"It's a good idea," said Macnooder after the vow of secrecy had been passed and the Beefsteak had gone, walking a little lightly on his toes.

"Yes."

"But, couldn't we put it over on the Beefsteak just once more—just one little final touch?" said Macnooder, to learn what the Shad was planning.

The Tennessee Shad remained a long time in cloudy speculation. Then he scratched his head, replaced his cap, and said carefully, "Tomorrow, Doc, I'll tell you all about it—tomorrow."

The Uncooked Beeksteak's eagerness to claim the limelight was quite in accordance with the plans of Macnooder and the Tennessee Shad. The more Skinner took upon himself, the more complacently they viewed the outlook. For some time it had become increasingly difficult for the firm of Macnooder to arouse any general enthusiasm for its speculative offerings. Particularly was this true of any attempt to collect before the fact.

Consequently, with great magnanimity, they assured the unsuspecting Skinner that the honor being his, they were determined he should have all the glory and suggested that whatever publicity was needed should come from him.

Skinner was allowed to announce the great event, to challenge Blimmy Garret in behalf of his champion and most important of all, to sell as many tickets as he could at the rate of fifty cents a head. Macnooder, modestly keeping in the background, received the receipts and safeguarded them, urging that no mention should be made of this trifling service.

By thus prominently displaying the Uncooked Beefsteak, they succeeded in working up a tremendous amount of enthusiasm in quarters which would have been decidedly lukewarm had the great sporting event borne the names of Macnooder and the Tennessee Shad.

When Skinner had collected and turned over to Macnooder the proceeds of thirty tickets, and had arranged the date and selected an ideal location in the groves that border the distant canal, he suddenly became rather panicky as to the mysterious champion whom the Tennessee Shad was to provide, and rushed all in a flutter to the Kennedy for reassurance.

"Be calm," said the Tennessee Shad, "I have the dog."

"Have you seen him?"

"I have."

"When?"

"This afternoon."

"Then he's near here?" said Skinner, surprised.

"I have him in training quarters," said the Tennessee Shad, with a mysterious wave of his hand. "Within a mile of where I stand."

"Training?" said Skinner, mystified.

"Feeding him on raw veal and mustard. You can spread the report that he's bitten two men in the last three days. That shows what he'll do to that china bull-pup of Blimmy's."

"You said he was a collie?"

"German Collie, a bruising ugly-tempered, rampaging collie."

"Supposing Tough licks him?" said the Beefsteak anxiously, contemplating a wager.

"A long-haired collie?" sad the Shad loftily. "Greatest fighter in the world. Why, Tough will never get his tooth in him. Put up all your money on it!"

"I wish I could see him," said the Beefsteak doubtfully.

"Course you do," said the Shad sympathetically. "But if you do, then Blimmy has a right to see. And say, if Blimmy sees this living death—it's all off. No bets, and no fight."

"Really?"

"Keep it quiet."

"By the way, what's the dog's name?"

"Dynamite."

The next afternoon the Shad arrived with a worried look.

"Say, Beefsteak, can't you put ahead the date?"

"What's the matter?"

"Why that brute of mine is chewing up everything in sight."

"No!"

"Fact. He tore the feathers off a duck and mangled a milk pail they left by mistake. We've got him boxed now."

"Supposing we pull it off tomorrow night."

"I don't think we can hold him any longer."

When Blimmy Garret heard the tales of butchery emanating from the opposite camp he was equal to the occasion.

"You go back, young stripling," he said imperiously to Skinner, "go back to whoever backs that ki-yi, and tell that old four-flusher

"YOU GO BACK, YOUNG STRIPLING."

that if his mongrel isn't any fiercer than that there won't be enough of him to line a pair of mittens!"

"They keep him shut up in a box," said the Beefsteak doubtfully.

"They do, do they? Well, you tell 'em we're holding Tough in a trunk with a couple of shot-laden trays over him too."

"They say he's even attacked a milk pail!"

"Oh, he has?" said Blimmy, growing indignant. "Well, tell them Tough is so wild, we've had to wedge his jaws."

"What for?"

"To keep him from wearing down his teeth when he thinks of that pup Dynamite," said Blimmy very seriously. "And say, go back and tell your friend that we don't want even another day. Pull the affair off tonight, or I won't answer for the spectators."

"All right," said Skinner, running off.

"Oh, I say!"

"What?"

"Tell him Tough will be there in a box, all right!"

"All right."

"And hold up, are you putting up a bet?"

"No—o," said Skinner, "I'm the referee. I can't."

When in the watches of the night, a shivering band of would-be sports bent on feverish dissipation gathered expectantly by the light of half-a-dozen lanterns in a distant and gloomy spot, the ferocious rumors from the rival camps had become common property and in certain quarters there was a marked impulse to seek places of security rather than the natural points of vantage.

"Have you ever been at one of these things?" said Shrimp Davis, who was the youngest allowed to qualify as a sport.

"No," said Peewee Bacon in the same woodland whisper. "It's pretty risky, isn't it?"

"There ought to be a ring with a high wall around it," said the Triumphant Egghead, who was always critical. "Something to protect the spectators."

"That's right."

"There's no telling what a dog will bite."

"And if his jaws set on you, they never let go."

"Say, this is a rotten place for a fight."

"Well, I wore leather boots and shin-guards."

Meanwhile, Skinner, dressed to kill in the flashiest of all his flashy vests and ties, checked suit and feathered fedora, was anxiously superintending the marking-off of the ring, and carefully selected a level glade among a clump of melancholy pines. Four stakes were driven in and several lengths of ropes stretched around.

"Say, the Beefsteak's quite the fellow, isn't he," said Peewee much impressed.

"He certainly has seen a lot of life."

The preparations for the safety of the public did not impress.

"What are they stringing up ropes for?"

"Huh, to keep us out of the ring."

"Is that all the guarantee we get?"

"And they say both pups haven't had a square meal in thirty-six hours."

"Oh, mother!"

"A dog's bite is poisonous, isn't it?"

"Sure, they burn you out with a red-hot poker."

"Oh, joy!"

"What's that?"

"Have they come?"

A series of yelps were now heard approaching from opposite directions and presently two wheelbarrows bearing sinister noisy boxes appeared out of the gloom. There was a rush in the direction of the Tennessee Shad and Macnooder, but all lingering incredulity was dissipated when the light of a lantern revealed behind the slats of an improvised cage, the dim head of a large collie —German or otherwise.

Macnooder, who had a strong dramatic instinct, was in sweater and high boots, a rag over his forehead and several crosses of black court plaster on his cheeks, which were at once taken to be proofs of the fighting qualities of the challenging Dynamite.

Both dogs, as a result of the exceedingly lumpy journey they had come, combined with the prodding received from two zealous owners, were in a humor more human than canine. As a consequence, no sooner had the full effect of their anger reached the crowd, than there began a curious shifting movement among the spectators; those in front slipping to the back while those who were promoted surrendered instantly their vantage.

The two boxes were placed at opposite sides of the ring, and the seconds summoned by Skinner met in the middle for conclave.

"So *you're* back of this!" said Blimmy comprehending Macnooder's connection for the first time.

"I'm slightly interested, Blimmy," said Macnooder with a smile.

"And you think you've got a dog can lick Tough, do you?"

"My dear old boy, we don't *think*."

"Are you backing your opinion?" said Garret furiously.

"It's all over. We don't want to *steal* your money!"

"Will you bet?"

"Wait," said Macnooder, who made a gesture to the Tennessee Shad, who immediately produced a spade.

"What's that for?" said Skinner, mystified.

"To bury Tough," said Doc, with a bland gesture.

"Begin," said Blimmy, in a rage.

At this there was suddenly heard a noise among the trees, like an army of squirrels. A third of the audience, their courage departing, were now seen making their way along overhanging branches.

Skinner, more thoroughly frightened than ever before in his life, remained alone in the middle of the ring, suddenly realizing the responsibilities as well as the glory of high office. Blimmy and Macnooder pushing the front of their boxes up to the ropes stood with their hands on the bolts.

"Stop!" cried the Tennessee Shad in a purposely tense voice. "Stop a moment."

"What's the matter?" cried a dozen alarmed voices.

"The Beefsteak must get out of the ring or I won't answer for the consequences."

At this another third of the audience took to shinnying up the most available trees, while the rest, including P. Lentz who couldn't, to have saved himself, lifted his two-hundred pounds from the ground, began to cast calculating glances to the rear. The Beefsteak, without a pause, retired outside the ropes while the tree dwellers with returning interest began to shout:

"Even on Dynamite!"

"I'll back Macnooder's dog."

"Goodbye to Tough."

"Stuffed dog tomorrow!"

"Ten to one someone gets chewed."

"What show has a Beefsteak got?"

"Jemima, they're fierce!"

"Give us the carnage."

"Blood!"

"Are you ready?" cried the Beefsteak, in a high falsetto. "Let 'em out."

There was a volley of cheers from the trees and a unanimous rushing movement to the rear on the part of the remaining spectators, a flight conspicuously led by Macnooder and the Tennessee Shad with well-acted fright.

The shutters dropped simultaneously, but only Tough bounded forth in furious solitary possession of the ring. From the released cage of Dynamite nothing stirred.

Conflicting shouts now sounded from the trees.

"What's the matter?"

"Where's Dynamite?"

"Why doesn't he come out?"

"Just wait till he does."

"When he makes up his mind, look out."

"Rats, he's afraid!"

"Go on, give him time!"

A full minute passed and still the only occupant of the ring was Tough with four legs stiffly planted, growling his defiance. From behind the tree trunks some of the most daring began to steal back to where the Beefsteak, puzzled, waited in suspense for the living destruction to burst forth.

Reassured, the crowd began to throng the ringside, shouting:

"Come on, Dynamite!"

"Sic 'em!"

"Poke him up!"

"Shake him up!"

"Kick the box!"

Acting on the hint, the Beefsteak shook the box with a thundering boot. A furious snarling, which momentarily restored confidence, answered him, but no Dynamite appeared.

"He's there all right!"

"What's the matter with him?"

"Hear him growl!"

"He's coming."

"The deuce he is!"

"He's gone to sleep."

"Where's the Tennessee Shad?" cried the Beefsteak.

The Tennessee Shad had disappeared.

"Where's Macnooder?"

The cry was taken up in vain. Suddenly the same suspicion seized the group of would-be sports who, rushing to the box, over-turned it. At the same moment, Tough, springing forward, came to a disgusted stop, more in sympathy than in anger, before an aged, moth-eaten, toothless dog, who, emerging in snarling protest, sank immediately to a reclining position. At once it was a riot.

"Why, he's a billion years old!"

"No teeth!"

"No eyes!"

"Hair dropping out!"

"Even Tough wouldn't bite it!"

"Jemima, if it isn't Old Sally!"

"Sure, it is!"

"Belongs to Laloo!"

"Why, she is thirty years old!"

"A grandmother!"

"It's a put-up job!"

"Fraud!"

"Fake!"

"Skin game!"

"All bets off!"

"Murder!"

"Stop, thief!"

"Oh, what a bunco game!"

"Money back!"

"Give us our money back."

"Catch the Beefsteak."

"Hold him, boys!"

But that great sporting promoter, too amazed to think of flight, was gazing in dumbfounded horror at the blinking, ragged anemic specimen which the Tennessee Shad had advertised as Dynamite.

"Hold up, I say, it's the Tennessee Shad," he cried vainly, "catch Macnooder and the Tennessee Shad—they've got the money!"

Then the mob reached him.

IX

THE LAMB RETREATS

HAVING FOUND by successive disillusioning experiments with the firm of Macnooder and the Tennessee Shad that the school was neither impressed by his own worldly personality or ready for the launching of genteel sporting practices, Montague fell into a period of abysmal depression that was the more overwhelming in that he could see no guiding streak of light in the completeness of his darkness.

He had failed to impress. There was no doubt on that score. And as his moral education, by sharp processes, began to be accomplished, he himself began, curiously enough, to lose the zest for the ways and distinction of complete manhood and to long wistfully, unbeknownst of his comrades, for the simple frolics of a mere boy.

The trouble was that he was always an outsider. He perceived it despairingly as he perceived the vital truth, that a night feast on indigestible tinned food and dyspeptic root beer was still a banquet and a banquet that needed no more fortunate patron.

When Turkey Reiter had indiscreetly informed him that his fatal drawback was the reputation for billions, he spoke the truth, and he might have added that every billionaire in such an assemblage is held to be impossible, dudified and deserving of hard labor until he has removed the burden of suspicion.

Now the Uncooked Beefsteak could not comprehend this truth —he debated it, he meditated long thereupon in solitary tramps, he tried to comprehend it; but the traditions of his first sixteen years were too strong. It could not be so. It could not be that a generous open purse, a purse waiting to be called upon for the multifarious enjoyments of those he chose to signal out as his friends, could be a handicap. His theory could not be wrong, the blunder must have lain in indiscreet application. Some way there must be to win popularity and stop the humiliating and menial

services to which he was daily condemned by his paternally solicitous housemates. For, unable to perceive the larger good, the Beefsteak could see no useful purpose to be served in this course in
primitive tailoring, complete housework, and general bootblacking.

At times the House relented, hoping that the lesson had been
learned. Unfortunately, Skinner could not seize the subtle class
distinctions which forbade him, a mere bag of money, a noncom-
batant, what was permitted to the nobility of muscle and brain.

Of a consequence, no sooner was the ban lifted than he became
familiar instead of humble, boastful instead of inquiring, pushing
instead of thankfully receptive, and given to using nicknames,
which were reserved for those who had progressed to the second
degree. Upon which, the House would convene and agree that the
Beefsteak was still unfit for human intercourse and assign him back
to the boots and the clothes brush.

Now, in about the tenth period of this recurrent discipline, the
Beefsteak had suddenly a brilliant idea. The Easter recess was
approaching—he would invite Macnooder to spend the week with
him at his father's hotel and by dazzling him with its splendor and
magnificence, awaken him to a proper sense of the Skinner importance.

The result steadied him in his wavering belief in the theory of
the supremacy of capital. Not only was there an instant somersault
on Macnooder's part, a change accomplished between the blacking
of one boot and the withdrawal of the other, but the effect in the
House was electrical.

Half-an-hour after Macnooder had received the invitation, the
Triumphant Egghead smilingly appeared in the Beefsteak's room
with a genial manner. "Hello, Monte, old boy, not studying, are
you?"

"Come in," said the Beefsteak, chuckling inwardly.

"What a perfectly corking room, a peacherino!" said the Egghead, surveying for the first time the walls decorated with photographs of certain theatrical ladies who adorned but did not elevate
the stage, and chromos of national bruisers in boxing tights.

"You like it?" said Skinner carelessly.

"And gee! Look at the Dottie-Dimple-Toes! Say, you don't know
all these damsels, do you?"

"I'll put you next to any of them," said Skinner, relapsing into
the past.

"Gee, I'd like to meet a real live actress," said the Triumphant Egghead, slyly approaching his opportunity.

At this moment the door opened and the Waladoo Bird came hastily in. The Triumphant Egghead shot him a furious glance which was returned by one of suspicion and envy.

Then the Waladoo Bird, giant of the football eleven, sat down and, smiling on Skinner, said with directness, "Say, Monte, I've got to get a couple of suits bitten out for me in New York. You know the whole dressing game from A to Z. Give me a couple of pointers on what's the real thing. Look over my style of beauty and put me on. And say, what's the best hotel to stop at?"

The Waladoo Bird understood but one method of attack and that was a mass through the center of the line. But at this moment the door swung the third time and the Tennessee Shad entered, slightly out of breath, with a glance at the two visitors that sought to seize on the instant if he had been forestalled. Close on his heels came Dennis de Brian de Boru Finnegan, who beat to the threshold the Gutter Pup and Lovely Mead.

That night the Uncooked Beefsteak, who had been watched since luncheon by those who were most concerned in watching one another, went off to sleep more thoroughly happy than he had been in months. He had played the trump card and the stakes were his. No more would he lighten the burdens of Klondike, the houseman, no more would he bend in servile postures over the oozing muddy boots of striplings in knickerbockers, no more would he listen in enforced isolation to the whispered merriment of distant feasts; he would select with a ruthless and distinguishing finger his guests among the elite of his comrades; there should be a week of princely entertainment and then he would return, one of the chosen, a member of the crème de la crème.

At the same time Macnooder was saying excitedly to the Tennessee Shad. "See here, I've got the inside track—the Beefsteak will invite anyone I say."

"Little social secretary, eh?"

"Shut up. Do you know what I'm going to do? I'm going to sell excursion tickets, good for one week at the Regal Hotel, all expenses paid, and I'm going to soak each gazebo ten fat young plunks."

"Doc, it's glorious," said the Tennessee Shad, "you certainly will own Fifth Avenue. But say, how much longer do you think we can go on excavating in this here Beefsteak mine?"

"Very, very little. That's why we'll play this for a lalapazooza!"

"The trouble is we have assumed a moral attitude towards Monte," said the Tennessee Shad regretfully. "We are loosening his gold rocks but we are educating him."

"Yes, and when we get him educated and a proper self-respecting citizen—he'll be ungrateful."

"I fear so—I fear me much."

"On to the Regal Hotel!"

"On, Doc, on!"

About three o'clock in the afternoon of the opening of the Easter vacation there debarked at the Cortlandt Street terminal of the Pennsylvania Railroad a party of five in close marching order, consisting of Macnooder and Dennis de Brian de Boru Finnegan in advance, the Waladoo Bird and the Tennessee Shad supporting the center and the Triumphant Egghead guarding the rear.

"Halt," said Macnooder.

"What for?"

"We must consult. How shall we approach the Regal Hotel? On foot, in a swiftly moving trolley, or drawn by prancing horses?"

"Hire a hack, of course," said the Triumphant Egghead, who represented society. "You can't enter a hotel on foot."

"Why not?" said Finnegan.

"It isn't done."

"Rats! I'm for hoofing it. Show me the sights of Broadway and all that sort of thing."

"You're a hayseed and a jayhawker," said the Triumphant Egghead.

"Don't let's quarrel yet," said the Tennessee Shad soothingly, "I've only got sixty cents and I vote for the elevated."

"I think a barouche is an unnecessary expense," said Macnooder, who calculated on the Triumphant Egghead's buying the carriage.

At this moment the Waladoo Bird was discovered filling his pockets with peanuts.

"Merciful heavens," exclaimed the Egghead in horror. "You ignoramus, what are you doing?"

"Eating peanuts," said the Waladoo Bird, suiting the action to the word.

"Are you going through New York scattering shells like a hayseed?"

"I am," said the Waladoo Bird who had the Western contempt for the abode of the unconvicted rich.

"I won't be seen with you."

"Don't."

"If he is determined," said Macnooder meditatively, "he had better work it off. Let's walk."

The Triumphant Egghead immediately engaged a coach and hid himself in the company of the Tennessee Shad whose exertions were always mental.

The Waladoo Bird, flinging out peanut shells with the regularity of a thrashing machine, strode defiantly, flanked by Dennis, who stepped from corner to corner to buy an extra, and Macnooder who showed a lively interest in the new attractions in the shop windows.

A matter of a block behind, at a patient walk, came the hired coach from the recesses of which the Triumphant Egghead gazed upon the offenders with wrath and disgust.

"I wonder what he thinks this Regal Hotel is?" he said furiously. "An actor's boarding house?"

"I know for a fact," said the Tennessee Shad to soothe and comfort him, "that the Waladoo Bird had only two dollars and thirty cents."

"Awful funny, ha! ha!" said the Egghead, who was in no mood for humor.

"He must get filled up sometime."

"If he don't, it's all off. Do you think I'm going to march into the foyer of the classiest thing in New York with an elephant ten feet high cracking peanuts?"

"How far is it uptown?"

"Five or six miles."

"He ought to get away with an awful lot of nuts by then," said the Shad, who began to share his anxiety. "So this hotel is rather flossy?"

"The flossiest."

"Lots of gilt and red plush and all that sort of thing."

"Sure."

"What's the fodder like?"

"The cuisine," said the Egghead elegantly, "is the most fashionable in the city."

"But the Beefsteak sets up for the grub?"

"Yes, you chump."

"Everything we get away with?"

"Sure."

"Perhaps if the Waladoo Bird knew that he would ease up."

The announcement, in fact, produced a decided sensation. The Waladoo Bird finished the last handful outside the carriage at the peremptory challenge of the Egghead and then jarred the carriage springs while Finnegan made the common demand for a show of speed.

When Montague Skinner, moving restlessly in the ante-room of the Regal Hotel, beheld the arrival of the overloaded coach, he was quite touched by the cordiality of the greeting he received.

"Leave it to me," he said, intervening between the reluctant purse of the Triumphant Egghead and the grinning coachman. Then with an ease that made the Waladoo Bird stiffen up and take notice, he summoned a footman and said, "Charles, see what the fare is and have the office attend to it."

"Here, I say!" began the Egghead, with not too much resistance.

"Oh now, Monte, this is ours!" said Macnooder more emphatically as he perceived an absence of danger.

"No," said the Beefsteak finally, but with the lightness that such a triviality merited. "From now on you are my guests."

The Tennessee Shad, who had sixty cents, exchanged a glance of delirious joy with the Waladoo Bird who had a two-dollar bill, and, being thrown together in their voyage toward the elevator, whispered, "It looks good to me."

"It certainly does."

"No expenses."

"None at all."

At this moment the Waladoo Bird was overwhelmed by a fearful thought.

"I say, he's got the bags."

"Who's got them?"

"The Buttons."

"Well, what of it?"

"We'll have to tip him."

"Well, tip him!"

"I've only got a two-dollar bill and a nickel," said the Waladoo Bird in a worried whisper.

The Tennessee Shad nervously shifted his sixty cents to an inner recess, maliciously enjoying the confusion of the giant who was wondering uneasily whether the elevator man would expect to be recompensed.

Macnooder, Finnegan and the Triumphant Egghead were escorted to their quarters by Skinner, after leaving the Waladoo Bird and the Tennessee Shad in the adjoining room assigned them.

The Buttons, having deposited the bags, was languidly busy straightening the window curtains and shifting the chairs with that perfect, expectant manner that is instinctive wih those whose fortunate mission in life is to be tipped.

"What'll I give him?" said the Waladoo Bird in a muffled roar.

"How do I know?"

"I can't give him a nickel."

"Never!"

"I say lend me a half a dollar."

"Can't. Macnooder's got my purse."

The Waladoo Bird, who had faced the Princeton Varsity without a tremor, quailed before the spruce representative of bellboys. For a moment his fingers hesitated over the plebian nickel and then, blushing with combined rage and embarrassment, he blurted out, "Here—take this."

And he thrust upon him the two-dollar bill.

The Tennessee Shad, who had the profoundest respect for capital, was furious.

"You jackass, what did you do that for?"

"I had to give him something, didn't I?"

"Yes, but, Holy Cats, you can *buy* a bellboy for two dollars!"

"Well, what was I to do?" said the Waladoo Bird, who, clutching his last nickel, began to feel the despairing loneliness of one who is stranded in the great city.

"Do, you blockhead? Ask him to get you some change."

"Ask him—" said the Waladoo Bird in stupid amazement. "Well, why in thunder didn't you tell me?"

"Humph! Thought you'd been weaned from the bottle," said the Tennessee Shad, who now felt a sense of personal loss.

"Well, by gravy, I'll do it now," said the Waladoo Bird, bolting into his coat.

"Hold up! What are you going to do?"

"I'm going to track that young highwayman down and shake it out of him!"

"Hold up! You can't do that."

"Can't I? Just watch me!"

"Hold up! You'll make a social blunder!"

"Beans!"

When the Triumphant Egghead with Macnooder and Finnegan entered the room they found the Tennessee Shad in an attitude of deep dejection with one ear trained for the outburst of an expected cyclone.

"What in blazes is the matter?" said Macnooder. "And where is the Waladoo Bird?"

The Tennessee Shad explained.

"My aunt's cat's pants, that is awful!" said the Triumphant Egghead with a shiver.

"Wriggling snakes, what do you suppose he's doing?"

"He'll smash the crockery!"

"Had we better tell the Beefsteak?"

"Never!"

"Why the deuce didn't you look after him?"

"What do you expect?" said the Tennessee Shad aggrieved, "Do I look like a tug-of-war team?"

"This is awful," said the Triumphant Egghead, wiping his forehead.

The door opened and the Waladoo Bird plumped in.

"Did you get him?" said the five in chorus.

"Get him?" said the Waladoo Bird in a rage. "Why, there are one hundred-and-fifty bellhops below, all hopping around, and every mother's son of them looks alike! Say, what color hair did that pirate of ours have?"

The Tennessee Shad promptly forgot.

"Look here, boy!" said the Triumphant Egghead. "This will never do. You'll queer the whole bunch."

"I gave him two dollars," said the Waladoo Bird, sitting down with a crash that brought a groan from the light furniture.

"And don't go making a woodpile of everything you sit on!"

"HOLD UP! WHAT ARE YOU GOING TO DO?"

"What's wrong?"

"You. You're wrong. You're not fit to come into the parlor. A nice time we'll have with you. Didn't you ever see a hotel before?"

"Are you speaking to me?" said the Waladoo Bird, rising.

When the altercation had subsided, another serious question arose.

"Where'll we dine?" said Finnegan who had been coached. "Supposin' we grub with the Beefsteak—private dining room, special dishes and all that sort of thing."

"I vote for downstairs," said the Waladoo Bird, who had been put in a contrary humor.

"Why?"

"I want to get a chance at a real bang-up menu."

"And I vote to put this guy in seclusion!"

The Waladoo Bird gave the Egghead an evil look and was about to reply when Macnooder suavely arose.

"The Waladoo Bird is quite right. We will dine in public."

"Everyone will be dressed to kill."

"Then we shall be taken for Western millionaires. But—I say *but*—we are going to pull off this thing in classy style."

"No social blunders," said the Tennessee Shad.

"And no trying to split the menu," said the Triumphant Egghead.

"We will pick out the daintiest dishes," said Macnooder, trying the power of suggestion on the Waladoo Bird, "the *recherché*, expensive dishes, and we will take little careless dabs at them."

"Fine!" said the others, with the unique exception of the Waladoo Bird.

"Tomorrow we'll rip the stuffing out of the bill of fare, we'll mangle it, we'll blow holes in it, tear it up the back and drive it to its corner!"

"Tomorrow!"

"Tomorrow! But tonight we'll go down in a bored sort of way. We'll put up an awful bluff, tired of caviar and nightingales' tongues and all that sort of thing. We've got to keep the Beefsteak in his place—remember that! Show him we're old birds."

"Righto," said everyone; that is, everyone except the Waladoo Bird.

"Just take a nibble here and there and then push the plate away," said Finnegan, wishing to be helpful.

"Righto!"

"And stretch your arms and yawn in a high-bred, classy sort of way."

"You chump!" said the Triumphant Egghead. "Where have you been brought up?"

"The last suggestion is now withdrawn," said Finnegan modestly.

"Now, we're all agreed," said Macnooder, with an expanding smile. "Our object is to take the wind right out of the Beefsteak's sails—to show him what! Nothing but short sprints tonight, all long-distance records postponed until tomorrow."

"All right!" said the majority, minus one.

The dinner passed without any exhibition of Gargantuan powers on the part of the Waladoo Bird, but this was due to no surrender to social prejudices but to the fact that, placed as he was to command a view of the foyer, his whole attention was concentrated on the perplexing passage of flitting bellboys.

The Uncooked Beefsteak was slightly disappointed by the reticence of his guests, but this sentiment was soon lost in the blissful enjoyment of his new social footing. Nothing, in fact, could have been more delightfully intimate than their bearing toward him. He was not simply a patron—he was one of them.

He took them to the theater, in a box, to a vaudeville performance over which a year ago he would have yawned himself weary. To his amazement, he found himself caught up in the general hilarity, wildly applauding slapstick comedians who caused Dennis de Brian de Boru to weep for joy. He applauded! He had never done such a thing before. He actually stamped his feet and rattled his cane, demanding renewed encores. And when the show was over and the Tennessee Shad proposed that, instead of dividing into two cabs, henceforth whenever they went they should all crowd into one and send an empty cab before them as a sort of guard of honor, he gleefully embraced the idea and balanced on the bony ridges of the Tennessee Shad, waving his hat to the crowds of Broadway with the zest of restored youth.

When, late at night, after the Waladoo Bird had consumed a terrifying number of oysters, Finnegan had eaten three Welsh rabbits, and Skinner had seen his guests to their rooms, he returned gorgeously to his private suite.

Bucks, the confidential valet, was in wait.

"How do Bucks? How are you?" he said languidly.

"Thank you, sir. It's good to see you back, sir."

"The old boarding house is still doing a fat young business?" asked Skinner, surrendering his coat and falling into the vernacular of the admired Turkey Reiter.

"I beg pardon, sir! Oh! Yes, sir," said Bucks, momentarily mystified. "I hope you enjoy the school, sir?"

"It is wonderful, Bucks, wonderful. Glorious times! Glorious fellows!"

"That Mr. Walader, sir, certainly is something of a man," said Bucks, with great respect.

"He could wipe the ground up with any cop in New York," said Skinner stoutly. "And at that you ought to see P. Lentz. He weighs two hundred and sixty."

Here the telephone began to buzz angrily.

"Hello," said Skinner, going to it.

"Hello. Is that you, Monte, old boy?" said the excited voice of the Tennessee Shad.

"Yes, here I am."

"Say, look here, the Waladoo Bird has gone clean through his bed!"

"What?"

"Punctured a hole clean through it! Say, fix him up, will you? He's in mine now!"

"All right," said Skinner, who, turning from the telephone announced with pride, "What do you think of that? He's smashed the bed, Bucks—couldn't hold him! See to it, will you?"

"Yes, sir."

"Get something very solid."

"Yes, sir."

"One of those things they rig up for cattle kings."

"Certainly, sir."

When the noiseless valet had slipped away, Skinner stood a moment in contemplation of the glorious feat.

"By George!" he exclaimed, "Won't old Fatty Harris be wild when he hears of it—he's only smashed a football. The Waladoo Bird is a wonder. By George, I never had a better time in my life! Gee, what a difference though it makes when you once get in!"

Then he sat down very seriously on the edge of his fragrant bed, staring at the toes that peeped forth from the gorgeous lavender silk pajamas.

"By George!" he said suddenly, with a great moral resolve. "I know what I'll do. I'll hire a tutor I will! I'll slave all summer. But I'll get to college with that bunch or I'll injure my health!"

When the stage had lumbered away after depositing the last returned convict, the inmates of the Dickinson House, exhausted and sleepless after that Easter period which the curriculum still persists in ascribing to rest and recuperation, foregathered once more on the steps and the young green banks in lively discussion.

The Uncooked Beefsteak from his room directly above, looked down with satisfaction, pausing in the process of arranging three new resplendent vests. It had been a never-to-be-forgotten week. His hospitality had gone beyond the limits where even a prince might hesitate. If there was a dish on The Regal Hotel public menu that Finnegan, Macnooder and the Waladoo Bird had not contended with, it was solely because the season outlawed it. They had neglected not a single theater, riding to and fro always with an empty cab ahead as an outrider. The totalled record of meals consumed and carriages provided had made Skinner pater blink with amazement and there had been a few words on the subject, including a cash offer if the visit could possibly be abbreviated.

But this was pure inconsequential persiflage and had been silenced at once by the announcement of Montague's highly virtuous intention to secure a college education.

The Beefsteak, fondly secure of the affections of his late guests, brazenly deployed an array of theatrical neckwear where it would most dazzle and astound.

Of course he had that admiration for the Waladoo Bird that d'Artagnan entertained for Porthos, Dennis de Brian de Boru fascinated him and the Tennessee Shad moved him to envy with the dark and devious strategy of his mind. But, after all, it was Macnooder, the financier, and the Triumphant Egghead, the representative of society, who really stirred his heartstrings, and they should be his special cronies, singled out from the multitude.

He finished the task of sorting his marvelous wardrobe and yielding to an impulse, boldly arrayed himself in his latest tailored creation, a noticeable concoction in large brown and green squares. He surveyed with genteel pride the thin, perfect line of the red silk necktie, passing his hand over the speckled vest with large white buttons. He liked to dress well, in perfect taste yet with distinction, and now at last he dared gratify this taste.

Secure as a Braddock in his complacent confidence, he went down the steps and burst in full vision upon the group.

"Well, old gazebos," said the Beefsteak, throwing back the sides of his coat, peacock fashion, "How do you like the spring styles?"

Turkey Reiter looked at Doc Macnooder and sadly shook his head, while in the group an ominous silence began to spread.

The Uncooked Beefsteak, all unaware, sauntered down to a position beside the Triumphant Egghead and clapped him on the shoulder.

"Egghead, old sporting life, tell the multitude about the classy food I corralled for you."

Then spoke Turkey Reiter, the czar, solemnly, "Beefsteak, there is a pair of old muddy boots, standing right in front of my wash-stand. The mud is rather hard and doesn't improve the boots a bit. Better go up now—quietly—and see what you can do with them."

"What!" said the Beefsteak, every hair of his head starting up with horror.

"Take great care of them," said Turkey Reiter softly. "They are my favorite boots."

"You don't mean it!" said the Beefsteak, turning desperately to Macnooder, "Oh, I say, not again!"

"It's for your own good, you blasted millionaire," said Mac-nooder sadly. "It hurts us more than it does you."

A great lump rose in the Beefsteak's throat. He turned wildly to the Triumphant Egghead.

"Yes, Macnooder is right," said this last hope. "We're really doing you good. So, Beefsteak when you finish the boots up nicely, come down on your tiptoes and brush up a few of my things. My clothes have been kept in such rattling good order lately that I should hate—"

But the Beefsteak zigzagging in his walk, had wabbled up the steps. He went to his room and sat down, steadying his head in his hands. And there at last the full light broke over him.

That evening as the House was gathered for supper, Butcher Stevens suddenly exclaimed, "For the love of Mike, look at the Uncooked Beefsteak!"

Around the corner came Skinner, clad in an ill-fitting pair of ink-stained corduroy trousers, a jersey in place of the loud vest and a slouch hat over his eye.

"Merciful heavens!" said the Triumphant Egghead, with a shock. "Beefsteak, where did you get that rig?"

"I traded it," said the Uncooked Beefsteak firmly. "Got it for my last $85 tailor suit."

"Dear boy, what does this mean!" said Macnooder, with a horrible misgiving.

"Read that!" said the Beefsteak, thrusting a paper on Turkey Reiter.

"What is it?"

"It's a telegram I've just sent home. Go on, read it!"

And Turkey Reiter read:

Joshua M. Skinner,
The Regal Hotel,
New York City.
Cut my allowance to a dollar a week.

Montague.

"Explain!" said the Tennessee Shad heartbroken.

"I will," said the Beefsteak militantly. "It means I am on, I'm wise. It means you've educated me and I know my lesson. From now on the bank is suspended. I'll start even. And remember this," he added, looking steadily at Macnooder, "I may still be a Beefsteak, but there's nothing uncooked about me—I'm done to a crisp!"

X

LAST HISTORIC EXPLOIT OF THE FIRM

Say did you pass? Then set 'em up!
Good work, my brilliant brother.
Say, did you flunk? Then pass the cup!
Hard luck! Let's have another!
It heightens all the joys of Greek,
Soothes Mathematics' rigor,
In each event of life we seek
The ever-flowing jigger.

Refrain

The jig, jig, jigger,
The jig, jig, jigger,
The jig, jig, jigger, the jigger,
But we, when waves of trouble roll,
We hie us to the jigger.

"FOR HEAVEN's sake, shut up, Goat! You're 'way off the tune," said the Tennessee Shad irritably.

Now, the Goat knew he was not off the tune and, likewise, perfectly understood the cause of the irritation. Wallowing gorgeously on heaped-up sofa cushions, breathing in the perfumed breeze at the open window, his chin in his hands, he looked down maliciously to where the Tennessee Shad, indolently on his back, retired under the brim of his sombrero, was nibbling at the pink-and-white petals that rocked languidly down. Then, with malice aforethought, the Goat's floating tenor resumed:

It cools in heat, it warms in cold,
If sick it can restore us,
And when our health becomes too good,
'Twill fix the matter for us;

So eat aplenty while you're small,
Eat more when you are bigger,
And lest we do not grow at all,
Let's take another jigger.

"Chorus now, Shad!"

The jig, jig, jigger,
The jig, jig, jigger,
The jig, jig, jigger, the jigger.
But we, when waves of trouble roll,
We hie us to the jigger.

Whereupon the Goat, seized with the idea, disappeared from the dormer window and presently shuffled out on the Esplanade.

"They're fresh strawberry jiggers, Shad," he exclaimed tantalizingly; "for the first time too."

The Tennessee Shad snored loudly.

"Would you like me to set you up?" said the Goat, frisking as near as he dared. "Would you like to forget the past and have a jigger on me—would you, Shad? My hair's long and curly now."

The Tennessee Shad was too wary to be caught by any such hypothetical invitation to which he knew very well the answer to his answer; so he snored again, but keeping an eyelid batting on the chance that the Goat would venture too near.

"Strawberry jiggers, nice, fresh, creamy strawberry jiggers!" said his tormentor. "My, I'm going to eat a dozen! Sorry you don't care about 'em. Ta-ta!"

The Tennessee Shad opened one eye and watched the Goat go gamboling toward the village, as goats should go who are glad to be alive in the best of all months, who have ravenous appetites and something jingling in their pockets to lay down on the counter.

The Tennessee Shad had all the requisites for perfect happiness except the last—there was nothing in his pockets to sound musically, not even one miserable nickel to strike against another. Not only was he devoid of credit, but, as the result of the education of Beefsteak, of the Criminal Club, and the search for German measles, he was not quite restored to that social standing which would warrant his approaching a past victim with the demand direct.

Despite these incontestable facts which should have allowed him to withdraw under the spell of his philosophy, one disturbing, buzzing little sound persistently and mockingly persecuted him, "Fresh strawberry jiggers!"

Now, there are three great epochs in the annual of the school: the first appearance of the strawberry, the arrival of the raspberry, and that happy moment when the spoon plunges into the creamy jigger and strikes upon the juicy shreds of the peach. And, the greatest of these is the inauguration of the strawberry season.

The Tennessee Shad drew in his cheeks and ran his tongue over his lips until he could bear it no longer. He sat up, blowing the sprinkled apple blossoms from his coat, and began to consider seriously.

"I must see Doc Macnooder," he said at length, after a vain examination of his own artifices. He stood himself up by a process of jerks and, acquiring sufficient momentum by his first movements, entered the House, bumped around the corners and rubbed his way to Macnooder's room, where he gave the agreed signal. No answer returning, he applied his eye to the keyhole, and then, chinning himself, surveyed by way of the transom the deserted bottles, the stuffed owl and the dangling dried bats.

"Doc must be in the village," he said. "If he is in funds I certainly ought to be good for a touch there."

For those who knew the Tennessee Shad his gait told all. When under the magic of a possibly productive idea he went rapidly in a beeline, his thin legs seeming to shut and close with the agility of a tailor's shears. On the present occasion, being in a deeply meditative mood, he went in little stumbling steps, often stopping to change his stride, scratching his head and, being lonely, altering his stride to kick along some stone larger than the rest.

In this mode he suddenly perceived the plump, Capuchin figure and round head of Doc Macnooder sauntering toward him, hands sunk in his pockets, his glance wandering in the clouds. At the same moment Macnooder perceived him and the following colloquy ensued:

"Hello, there."

"Hello, yourself."

"I was looking for you, Doc."

"I was trailing for you."

" 'Em—you were?"

"I was."

"That means you are strapped."

"You don't mean to say you are?"

"Why, Doc, you're an old millionaire. I thought you—"

"My money's all tied up," said Macnooder. "Invested in stocks and that sort of thing."

"You were my last hope," said the Tennessee Shad, "If the firm's bust what are we going to do about it? We've got to find something."

"Let's see what's doin' first," said Macnooder. "Let's reconnoiter."

"We might try Laloo," said the Tennessee Shad thoughtfully. "I gave him the idea of hot dogs. He's made thousands on it."

But as they approached, Laloo, basking lazily at the entrance of the frankfurter palace, shifted his toothpick and ominously drew out a little memorandum.

The two stopped.

"There's gratitude for you," said the Tennessee Shad bitterly.

"You should have struck a bargain with him," said Macnooder, the banker: "ten per cent and your personal account."

"Shall we try Appleby?" asked the Shad.

"What's the use?" replied Macnooder.

They proceeded up the leafy street to where, before the Jigger Shop, a score of ravenous boys were clinking their spoons against their glasses. In front a huge placard announced:

FRESH STRAWBERRY JIGGERS

"Let's work the Hickey Flimflam on the bunch," said the Tennessee Shad, perceiving Turkey Reiter, the Goat, Butcher Stevens and the Gutter Pup.

"All right—I'm desperate," said Macnooder under his breath; "but wait till Turkey Reiter clears out. He's on."

"Turkey's a square sport," said the Shad; "he wouldn't give it away."

They reached the crowd on the steps and saluted.

"Pretty good, eh?"

"You bet your sweet life!"

"Nothing like the strawberry, is there?"

"Um-um!"

"How's the supply hold out?"

303

"Say, Doc," said the Tennessee Shad, closing one eye and cocking his head toward the counter where Al's steely glance was turned upon them, "do you think, could you be persuaded—eh, what?"

"What, *again?*" cried Doc in simulated astonishment.

Al's eye opened and his finger stole softly across his politician's mustache as he bent forward the better to listen.

"Oh, come on! There's always room for another," said the Tennessee Shad. "Just to be sociable."

"Why, you old gormandizer!" said Macnooder. "You'll swell up and bust!"

"Then you won't?"

"You bet I won't!" said Macnooder, loosening his belt. "And you're a bigger fool than I took you for if you do. However, go ahead and commit suicide if you want!"

"Well, I guess I won't," said the Shad softly, slipping his belt to an easier hole and sitting down. "I just wanted to be sociable, that's all."

They ensconced themselves in the group, chatting aimlessly for a quarter of an hour, with surfeited unconsciousness of the melting jiggers that circulated beneath their noses.

Finally, it being his turn to treat, the Beefsteak, in fancied security, maliciously addressed Doc Macnooder.

"How about it, Doc?"

Macnooder emitted a long whistle and said indifferently, "I oughtn't to, but if the Shad will take one, too, I'll be sociable."

"Only a single, Doc," said the Tennessee Shad; "I couldn't eat any more—I couldn't."

The Beefsteak, who not for the world would have offered to treat had he believed them ravenous and destitute, once persuaded that further jiggers might be accompanied by physical pain and exertion, insisted maliciously.

"How about it, Shad?" said Doc. "Come along, be sociable."

The Tennessee Shad in turn drew a long breath.

"Oh, very well," he said, "but only a single."

Al, in the act of filling the glasses, stopped and looked long at the Tennessee Shad.

"Now, what's the game?" he said to himself.

The Tennessee Shad looked indifferently into the coveted glass, stirred the solitary jigger a little with the spoon, nibbled without appetite and relapsed into conversation.

"Say, Shad, I'd like to bet you couldn't eat six doubles," said Doc facetiously, winking at the Beefsteak.

The Tennessee Shad snorted.

"You don't want a cinch, do you?" he said crushingly.

Turkey Reiter stopped, caught Macnooder's eye, smiled reminiscently and nudged the Beefsteak.

"I thought you'd bet on anything," said the Beefsteak.

"So I will."

"Well, I'll bet you can't do it right now!"

"Eat six double jiggers?"

"That's what I say."

The Tennessee Shad jingled his keys in his trousers.

"Why don't you pick my pockets?"

"You're a quitter," said the Beefsteak, warming at the thought of the many old scores he had to wipe off. "I'll bet you half-a-dollar even you can't do it, and the loser pays for the jiggers right now. And if you don't take it up you're a paper-collared sport and a bluff."

"That's pretty strong talk, Shad!" said Macnooder.

"It's all very well for you to talk," said the Shad angrily. "This is one of your put-up games!"

The Beefsteak, egged on by Turkey, insultingly flashed the half-dollar under the Tennessee Shad's nose, exclaiming:

"Oh, you bluff, you cheap sport! Will you take me? Will you?"

"You be hanged!" said the Tennessee Shad wrathfully. "If there ever was a cheap sport, it's you. You never would bet unless you had a cinch. Well, I'll take you—on one condition."

"What?"

Doc and Turkey looked surprised while Al at the counter, with his hand on the spigot, cocked his head slightly.

"That you make the same bet with Doc Macnooder."

Macnooder was on his feet protesting.

"Oh, I say, hold up. I'm not in this."

The crowd found against him.

"Hold up, there," said the Beefsteak, scratching his head. "That's a pretty big bet."

The Tennessee Shad saw the dawn of suspicion in the Beefsteak's eyes, and shifted his attack forthwith.

"Well, I'll make that bet myself," he exclaimed. "Who's the quitter now?"

The Beefsteak, reassured, stated the terms cautiously.

"Half-a-dollar even you can't eat six double jiggers—"

"Strawberry jiggers."

"Strawberry jiggers—in an hour."

"Let it go at an hour."

"Shake?"

"Shake!"

Then the Tennessee Shad turned aggressively on Doc Mac-nooder.

"Same thing goes with you?"

"Confound you!"

"Half-a-dollar even?"

"Well, yes."

"Shake?"

"Shake!"

"Al, serve 'em up!"

Then Doc and the Tennessee Shad, not too fast, but as with great physical effort, each ate six double jiggers.

The Beefsteak, whose hopes had been alternately raised and lowered with this comedy, paid sixty cents for the jiggers the Shad had consumed and sullenly tossed him the shining half-dollar. The Tennessee Shad, having lost to Macnooder, gravely transferred the coin, and Macnooder, rising, tendered it to Al, saying, "I'm a dime short, Al—but that's the price of admission."

"Keep it, my boy," said Al enthusiastically, putting the half-dollar away from him. "Keep it; it's yours. I'd be ashamed to touch a penny of it."

Turkey Reiter solemnly offered his hand to the Tennessee Shad, saying, "Old sporting print, I never saw it better done, not even by Hickey, God bless him!"

"Thank you!" said the Tennessee Shad. "Why, where is the Beefsteak?"

They crowded to the window and saw the Beefsteak, collar up, brim down, hands sunk in his pockets, deliberately tracking for home.

Half-an-hour later, the audience having shifted, they caught the Gutter Pup and repeated with equal success.

Arm-in-arm, fed to satiety, each with five nickels jingling in his pocket, Doc and the Tennessee Shad rolled hilariously back to the House.

"It was brilliant," said the Shad, thinking of future strawberry jiggers. "But it is limited, Doc. We were lucky to get the Gutter Pup."

"It leaves us about where we were."

"We've got to do something—something big—on a swipe scale!"

"We certainly have."

"You haven't anything up your sleeve?"

"Lots of 'em, Shad—but they're all on the flimflam order. This time we've got to produce some goods."

They proceeded, each searching inwardly until almost to the House. Suddenly from the north door Alcibiades, the waiter, with a splash of white linen over his arm, emerged and disappeared around the back. The Tennessee Shad stopped.

"Did you see him?"

"Who?"

"Doc, I've got an idea!"

"Fire away!"

"No—no," said the Tennessee Shad ruminatively, "not now, Doc; not just now. It needs thinking over. What time does it get dark?"

"Eight o'clock," said Macnooder mystified.

"Meet me at half-past eight, thirty feet behind the baseball cage —alone!"

The Tennessee Shad, on taking his seat at the table that night, fixed his gaze on Alcibiades, the waiter, in such a concentrated glare that that menial, in his nervousness, violently did offense to Slush Randolph's ear with the platter of incoming sinkers.

"Confound you, Shad," said Slush, "quit rattling Alcibiades. What's wrong with him, anyhow?"

The Tennessee Shad stared haughtily at Slush and addressed Hungry Smeed.

"What do you know about him?"

"Who? Alcibiades?"

"Yes, what's his real name?"

"Finnigan—Patsy Finnigan," said Smeed, who didn't know.

"Correct. Now does anything strike you as peculiar about him?"

"Naw," said Hungry Smeed, annoyed at being delayed in his eating and watching Slush from the corner of his eye to make sure he didn't beat him to a second helping.

"Look again."

"He looks like a prizefighter."

"Oh, you do see that, do you? Well, he was a prizefighter."

At this startling announcement Slush, Butcher Stevens, the Triumphant Egghead and Hungry Smeed raised their heads with a simultaneous jerk and gazed at the circling Alcibiades.

"Come off; he's too thin," said Butcher Stevens with a critical glance.

"Look at his jaw. Look at his bullet head. Look at those bloodshot eyes."

"Why, he's a feather!"

"Featherweight, that's it."

"Say, you old Tennessee Shad," said Butcher Stevens directly, "you know something. You've got something up your sleeve. Do you know he's a prizefighter?"

"Well, supposin' I do?" said the Tennessee Shad.

"A prizefighter!"

"It can't be true!"

"He does have the jaw."

"Shut up!" said the Tennessee Shad. "Do you want everyone to hear?"

"Say, Bub, what's doing?"

"I've got an idea," said the Shad with dignity, "a real imported, patent-applied-for idea, and I want you fellows to clear out and give me a chance. Mind, now, whatever you do, don't tell a soul what I told you!"

A moment later the astonished Alcibiades received from the hands of the Tennessee Shad, accompanied by a terrific look of mystery, a covert scrawl with a whispered: "Read at once."

At half-past eight, while Doc Macnooder, lurking in the gloom behind the baseball cage, was straining eyes and ears for the approach of the Tennessee Shad, suddenly, from the ground in front of him, a thin, black silhouette sprang up.

"What's that?" cried Macnooder, bounding back.

"Shh, Doc, it's me!" said the familiar nasal voice of the Tennessee Shad.

"Confound you! What do you mean by sneaking in on me like that?"

"Hush—I had to be sure you weren't a spy," said the Tennessee Shad, grasping his arm. "No one must know our errand here!"

"Well, what the deuce is our errand?"

"We are waiting for someone," said the Tennessee Shad mysteriously. "Sit quietly now and keep your fingers crossed, for if we pull this off, Doc Macnooder, we're going to buy a safe to stuff our spondulix in."

"Pull off what?"

"Silence!"

After ten minutes' tense breathing suddenly the Tennessee Shad spoke: "Doc?"

"Yes."

"Do you hear anything?"

"Not a sound."

"Well, I do—pebbles crunching over there. Now! Look!"

"Where?"

"To your right, squint down along the fence, just past where the moonlight hits the second tree. See?"

"There's someone coming."

"Hush!"

Presently the Tennessee Shad sent forth a cautious whistle. The approaching figure loomed larger, stopped, advanced, stopped and looked about defensively.

"He's carrying a stick," said Macnooder.

"It's all right," said the Tenneessee Shad, rising. "We'll go to meet him."

Advancing rapidly he exclaimed, "Mr. Finnigan, shake hands with Mr. Macnooder. Doc, shake hands with Mr. Finnigan."

"Why, it's Alcibiades!" exclaimed Macnooder.

"Of course it is," said Tennessee Shad. "Come, Finnigan, we're not safe here. Come quickly. Follow me."

"Where you takin' me?" said Alcibiades, planting the stick in front of him.

"Down by the pond in the woods where no one'll hear us."

"Thanks, but I'll stay here."

"Shucks, Alcibiades," said the Tennessee Shad soothingly. "All we want is to put a little sporting proposition to you."

"Well, you can put it here."

"Don't you trust us?"

"No, you young devils; you bet I don't. If you've got anything to say, say it or I'm going back."

The Tennessee Shad consulted with Macnooder and, taking a step toward Alcibiades, said firmly, "Finnigan, you're a prize-fighter!"

"Huh?"

"You're an ex-prizefighter!"

"What's that got to do with it?"

"Are you?"

Alcibiades scratched his head and considered.

"And what then?" he said cautiously. "What's the answer?"

"I knew it!" said the Tennessee Shad joyfully. "Finnigan, give me your hand. I'm proud to shake it!"

The startled Alcibiades then suffered his right hand to be enthusiastically pumped by Macnooder, but kept with his left a convulsive grasp on the stick.

"Now, Finnigan," said the Tennessee Shad professionally, "here's the point. What would you say to putting on the mitts just once more?"

"No you don't!" exclaimed the little Irishman, springing back.

Macnooder and the Tennessee Shad gazed in astonishment.

"What the deuce is the matter with him Doc?"

"Guess he thinks we want to kidnap him and make him fight Turkey or Butcher."

"Don't be a fool, Alcibiades," said the Tennessee Shad sharply. "None of us wants to fight you."

"Well, what do you want, then?" said Alcibiades, still on the defensive.

"Do you know any of the profession down in Trenton?"

"In Trenton?"

"Yes. Could you get anyone from there to come up and go a mill with you?"

"Could I? You want *me* to find someone?"

"That's it. Do you know anyone there?"

"Oh, yes! Sure, I know a lot of men there. But what do I want to be puttin' on the gloves for, anyway?"

"Why, we put up a purse, of course."

"Well, now, why in the devil didn't you begin with that?" said Finnigan, dropping the stick. "That's talkin'. Sure I mistrusted you were tryin' to play a trick on me."

"So you think you could make a match, Finnigan?"

310

"Maybe so, maybe. I'm running into Trenton tomorrow morning. I might look around a bit. It all depends on the purse, you know. Now what might be your idea on that?"

Macnooder and the Tennessee Shad withdrew and whispered. Macnooder, as the man of affairs, continued the operations.

"Well, now, Finnigan, what would you say was a fair proposition? Come, now, speak right up!"

"For how long a fight?"

"Oh, fifteen good slashing rounds. Come, now, what would you say?"

"Well, I don't know what I'd say."

"How about fifteen dollars—dollar a round?"

"Sure you young bloods can do better than that."

"Well, twenty-five dollars—lump."

"There's the expenses from Trenton?"

"Five dollars more for the rig. Is it a go?"

"Well, I'll have to see a bit."

"Fix it up for tomorrow night if you can, and have your man here on the stroke of midnight."

"Well, I'll see what I can do."

"Twenty-five-dollar purse, five for the rig and fifteen good slashing rounds. That's the terms. All right? Put it here!"

The Tennessee Shad and Macnooder, having watched Alcibiades flit back into the far shadow of the Upper, withdrew to the secret banks of the pond where the lugubrious moon fell in a shining splash amid the mossy reflections of the wood.

"Shad," said Macnooder, breaking the silence, "this is a wonder. It is beautiful. I really am touched. As a bonanza investment it takes me back to the late lamented Hickey and his no-guarantee silver-gilt clappers."

"Let's reckon up," said the Tennessee Shad professionally. "First, expense account. Purse and rig from Trenton, thirty dollars. Hiring of baseball cage, nothing. Advertising, nothing. Bribing of police, nothing. Subsidizing press, nothing. Can you think of anything else?"

"I can't."

"Total expenses—thirty dollars. Now for the rub. What'll we make the admission—one plunk?"

"Two."

"That's pretty stiff."

"We'll make that for reserved seats, front row. Just before the fight we can issue ordinary admissions at one bone."

"Cash?"

"Absolutely."

"Now, Doc," said the Tenneessee Shad seriously, "we must look at all sides of this, and there's one snag and it's a big one."

"Which one?"

"Our past reputations."

"Um!"

"The Egghead's sore on me because that haircut before the Prom queered him with his girl, and the Gutter Pup for several reasons, but principally for my leading him into mumps instead of German measles. He had 'em bad, Doc, very bad."

"Well, I suppose we'd better cut 'em out, then?"

"On the contrary, don't you see, they're the only ones can help us to general confidence."

"I know it's a good one," said Macnooder somewhat puzzled, "but it hasn't quite got to me yet. How the deuce are you going to get those two yaps who are gunning for you to help you inspire general confidence?"

"I'm going to make them my officials—Gutter Pup shall be referee, and the Triumphant Egghead timekeeper."

"I see," said Macnooder enthusiastically; "salve them over with a few plunks apiece."

"Doc," said the Tennessee Shad from the heights of a loftier genius, "you are really only fit to be a money changer and a pawnbroker. When will you rise to the truths of high finance?"

"I am humbly listening," said Doc. "What is it?"

"I am not going to do anything so low-down, easy and commonplace as to pay them to do what I've got to have done."

"No?"

"No! I'm going to make the Gutter Pup and the Triumphant Egghead give me the sanction of their re-spec-ta-ble names and I'm going to make 'em *pay me for doing it!*"

Doc Macnooder humbly knelt and struck the ground with his forehead.

"Oh wonderful Tennessee Shad! When you get into business let me be your office boy?"

"That's already promised," said the Tennessee Shad, pleased. "Turkey Reiter has the call. And now to biz. I let off a bit at the dinner table about Alcibiades being a prizefighter and told the boys not to breathe a word; so, by this time, it ought to be all over the Upper. The Gutter Pup'll be primed. Let's swoop down on him."

"If we pull this off," said Macnooder sadly "it'll be just about the last, Shad."

"Alas!"

"They'll never stand for another deal from us!"

"They've stood for a good many."

"Shad, here ends the firm of Macnooder and the Tennessee Shad."

"Perhaps, but Doc this is the great and only Lalapazooza. We may go down, but it'll be with the band playing and the dear girls strewing flowers!"

"Say, what are we going to call Alcibiades?"

The Tennessee Shad paused and reflected.

"Patsy the Brute."

"Then he ought to pad," said Doc doubtfully. "He looks more like chills and fever."

"Good idea. I'll see to that. The other fellow is the Trenton Terror."

The Tennessee Shad, accompanied by Doc, rapped softly and stole in as innocently as Br'er Rabbit. The Gutter Pup, alone, entrenched behind a desk, lifted the green shade from his eyes and looked at the intruder deliberately, with an appetizing, fox-eyed glance.

"Hello, you old Gutter Pup!" said the Tennessee Shad in a friendly way, while Doc slid to a seat. "Am I welcome?"

"You are not! Get out of here!"

"Does that little jigger episode rankle?" said the Shad, sidling forward. "Because I've come to pay you back."

"What!" said Gutter Pup, startled from his attitude.

"I've come to pay you back," said the Shad, jingling the three remaining nickels to sound like a pocketful; "that is, if—if you think it wasn't a square catch."

"Humph—that's the string to it."

"No, no, I'm serious. I want to be fair and aboveboard. If you think—well, what do you think?"

"Oh, you caught me all right."

"I'll tell you what I'll do," said the Tennessee Shad suddenly; "I'll help you to work it on Lovely Mead or the Egghead. I'll square it that way. What do you say? It certainly would be a corking sell on Lovely!"

At this astute appeal to frail human nature, the Gutter Pup's scowl of vanity gave place to a smile at the soothing thought of leading his dearest chum into the same trap into which he had fallen.

"Let her go at that."

"Good," said the Tennessee Shad, extending his hand. "No hard feelings. Gutter Pup, you're the sport of the bunch. Shake."

The Gutter Pup shook hands gravely.

"Now, Gutter Pup, we want your advice," said the Shad cheerily. "I've got an idea."

"No," said the Gutter Pup firmly.

"It's a beautiful idea."

"Never again!"

"Just hear it!"

"No and no!"

"What! Haven't you any curiosity?"

"I haven't!"

"But, Gutter Pup—"

"Not a word."

"It's just this—"

The Gutter Pup sealed his ears with his fingers and looked stonily at the Shad. The Shad looked at Macnooder, shrugged his shoulders and made a sign of capitulation. The Gutter Pup disdainfully maintained his attitude. The Tennessee Shad sat down, picked up a paper cutter and gazed at it with such set melancholy that, from sheer curiosity, the Gutter Pup released his ears.

"Gutter Pup," said the Shad pathetically, "do you realize that your conduct hurts me?"

"Glad of it."

"Do you realize that in a short month all we old friends are going away from here to part forever? Can't you understand that your conduct and Egghead's and all the rest hurts me and makes me feel bad? Don't you realize that I want to do something to wipe out the past and win back the friends, the good old friends again?"

"Yes, you do!"

"Yes, Gutter Pup, I do—I feel lonely. I want to be restored to the old feeling of confidence."

"Mumps!" said the Gutter Pup, blushing a little.

"That's just it," said the Shad instantly. "I wanted you to say that! That's just what makes me feel bad. I want to make amends; to give you fellows something that'll wipe off the slate. Now, my little idea."

Up went the Gutter Pup's fingers again. The Tennessee Shad looked very sad, sighed, rose and offered his hand in farewell.

The Gutter Pup, smiling scornfully, extended his.

"It was only a prizefight," said the Tennessee Shad hurriedly, clutching the hand in both of his. "Never mind. Goodbye! Come on, Doc."

He went toward the door; Doc did not rise.

"Hold up!" said the Gutter Pup.

"Well?"

"You said prizefight?"

"I did."

"What do you mean by that?"

"I meant a crocheting sociable, of course," said the Tennessee Shad. "That's what is always meant by prizefight! Well, goodbye."

"Wait a moment now; don't be so thundering touchy."

"I am touchy."

"Rats! Can't you take a joke?"

"Not some jokes. Come on, Doc."

"Look here, Shad," said the Gutter Pup, slipping past him and locking the door. "Say, I take it back. Go on, now, let me in on this. Who's the scrap between?"

The Tennessee Shad stared at Doc and then at the Gutter Pup.

"I said nothing about an amateur boxing exhibition."

"What do you mean?"

"I'm talking about a really professional prizefight."

"A prizefight between professionals—real professionals?"

"Exactly that."

"Then it's straight about Alcibiades?"

"Who told you?" cried Macnooder and the Tennessee Shad in simulated anger.

"No matter," said the Gutter Pup hastily. "I promised not to tell."

"Well, it is true," said the Tennessee Shad. "His real name is

Patsy the Brute and Doc and I have matched him to go fifteen rounds against a bruiser we're smuggling up here called the Trenton Terror. Now ask me to sit down, and put a soft cushion behind my back!"

The Gutter Pup, rendered weak by emotion, grabbed the Tennessee Shad's arm and clung to him. In his underform years (as has been related) the Gutter Pup had fought battles galore for the pure love of battling, and was now the President of the Sporting Club (*vice* Hickey once removed), an organization devoted to the scientific healing of animosities without recourse to debasing exhibitions of billingsgate. Likewise the Gutter Pup possessed on his wall, as the proudest ornament of the school, a signed photograph of John L. Sullivan. For all which reasons his clutch tightened, as though he were afraid the Tennessee Shad would slip away through the transom.

"Oh, Shad, do you mean it?" he said at last.

"I'm telling you."

"But how are you going to get them?"

"Of course we've got to raise a stiff purse," said the Tennessee Shad as an opening wedge, and then, observing the Gutter Pup thoughtfully replacing the key in the lock, he added: "but that's not what we came about."

"What then?" said the Gutter Pup, looking at him long and critically.

"We want your advice as the leading sporting authority in the school," said the Shad solemnly. "It's all a question of the referee. Doc's for Butcher Stevens and I'm for Turkey Reiter. What do you think?"

"Why not me?" said the Gutter Pup instantly.

Macnooder looked profoundly at the battling photograph of John L. reposing on the American flag—profoundly, with a concentrated glare. The Tennessee Shad climbed to his familiar roost on the back of the chair and replied with embarrassed reluctance, "Gutter Pup, I wish we could offer it to you. You really know more about such things than any of us. You're really it. I wouldn't hurt your feelings for the world; that's why I want you to understand our reasons before we ask anyone else."

"I don't see," began the Gutter Pup, cut to the heart.

"Now, let me put the case before you. We've got to pony up a stiff purse. You know professionals and you understand. If we could let the whole school in, why we'd have no trouble. We can't. This thing's got to be pulled off with terrific secrecy at midnight, down in the baseball cage. At most, we can't let in more than thirty or forty fellows. So the only way is to give the prime jobs to the fellows who'll put up for them. There you have it. Turkey and Butcher will uncork like a flash at the chance. Gee, who wouldn't? Do you see, Gutter Pup? You'll understand, won't you? You won't take it hard. We'll leave it all to you. Which one— Turkey or the Butcher?"

"I suppose you'd want a stiff contribution," said the Gutter Pup, his appetite in his eye.

"Pretty stiff," said the Shad with charming frankness.

"I could put up a fiver."

"I'm afraid that wouldn't do," said the Tennessee Shad sadly. "Don't think about it any more. Besides, we've got to have some bruiser like Turkey to keep things in order."

"Shad," said the Gutter Pup, now almost tearfully, "haven't I always kept things in order at the Sporting Club? Now, look here: Turkey's a mutt, and the Butcher—well, you simply can't invite a couple of real professionals unless you give 'em a referee who knows the rules; you simply can't."

"But what are we going to do?"

"See here," said the Gutter Pup desperately. "Make it eight! I'll borrow another three somewhere and somehow."

We rather counted on more," said the Tennessee Shad doubtfully. "What do you say, Doc?"

"Pretty cheap, Shad. Think of the glory of it!"

"I tell you how it might be done," said the Tennessee Shad thoughtfully. "If we could get someone to put up ten for timekeeper—"

"Leave that to me," exclaimed the Gutter Pup, grasping at the straw. "I've got just your man—Goat Finney. His father's a billionaire."

"I wonder if the Triumphant Egghead would put up five to be one of the seconds?" said the Tennessee Shad.

"Let me see him!" said the Gutter Pup enthusiastically. "Give me the chance."

"Well, on these conditions I am willing," said the Tennessee

Shad after sufficient deliberation. "If you can raise more, why, do it. How about it, Doc?"

"We always did want Gutter Pup to referee, you know."

"Get at it quick," said the Tennessee Shad, rising.

"You bet I will!"

"Cash," said Macnooder warningly. "Paid in five hours before the fight."

The Gutter Pup departed running.

At half-past ten that night, at the Tennessee Shad's dictation, Doc Macnooder entered in the joint account book the following items:

Goat Finney, for holding the stopwatch	$10.00
The Triumphant Egghead, for being permitted to rub down the Trenton Terror	5.65
Turkey Reiter, for being permitted to rub down the Trenton Terror	5.00
The Beefsteak, for the privilege of sponging off Patsy the Brute	3.75
Tough McCarty, for the privilege of sponging off Patsy the Brute	3.00
Slush Randolph, for the right to supply the sponges	2.50
Gutter Pup, for refereeing and procuring the above officials	8.00

Under cover of these confidence-inspiring names, Macnooder and the Tennessee Shad sold their tickets rapidly without a hitch, no questions asked.

At twelve o'clock the next day Alcibiades slipped the Tennessee Shad a note confirming the arrangements and guaranteeing the arrival of a local bruiser that night.

At seven o'clock each official eagerly presented himself in the Tennessee Shad's room and made cash payments. Meanwhile the subscribers for reserved seats were receiving from Doc Macnooder, in exchange for two dollars, a green ticket inscribed:

RESERVED SEAT

Doc Macnooder and the Tennessee Shad Offer

THE TRENTON TERROR

vs.

PATSY THE BRUTE

THE TENNESSEE SHAD

*For the Professional Featherweight Champion-
ship of Mercer County, in Fifteen
Slashing, Terrific Rounds
Under the Auspices of the Sporting Club
Present Ticket at 11:45 at
Baseball Cage
$2.00*

At ten o'clock a supplementary issue of one-dollar general admission tickets, open to all comers and presentable at 12:10, was
eagerly snatched up.

At half-past eleven the Tennessee Shad and Doc Macnooder,
armed with Legs Brownell's bull's-eye lantern, stole down by the
pond to meet Patsy the Brute and the Trenton Terror. They
found them side by side, amicably reclining under a tree, puffing
vigorously on ill-smelling cigars. Doc Macnooder turned the lantern on the new arrival; the scrutiny was not favorable.

"Are you a prizefighter?" he said, discouraged.

"Why not?"

"You don't look it."

"I'm a better man than this fellow."

"Remember, they're featherweights, Doc," said the Shad.

"Well, give us the goods," said Macnooder. "Fight like demons.
We want fifteen slashing rounds!"

"All right, boss."

"You're the Trenton Terror."

"That suits me."

"And, Alcibiades, you're Patsy the Brute."

"That's fierce enough. Where's the coin?"

"You'll get that in the cage."

"No you don't—we get it now."

"Don't you trust us?"

"I'd rather feel the coin."

The Tennessee Shad consulted with Macnooder and Doc paid
over thirty dollars and stationed himself so as to command the
retreat of the Trenton Terror. On the stroke of twelve they stole
up to the cage and entered by the back by means of three large
boards prudently loosened for the occasion to secure a retreat.

319

The ring was already roped off. Four dim lanterns at the corners lighted up the white sweaters and rat-like eyes of the silent, breathless crowd. Above, a swallow or two, disturbed by the unusual spectacle, were frantically scurrying among the rafters. At moments the door opened and a whispered recognition was heard.

Macnooder presented the combatants to the Gutter Pup and sent them to their corners to strip for action.

Murmurs of surprise began to rise from the amateurs as the ribs and collarbones of Patsy the Brute appeared from under the red flannels.

"Gee, he's thinner than the Shad!"

"He's wasted away."

"He must be awfully scientific."

"His blows wouldn't annoy a fly."

"Me for the Trenton Terror."

But at this moment the upper anatomy of the visitor was disclosed.

"Lord, he's thinner still!"

"I can look right through him."

"He looks more like a professor of chemistry."

"How many ribs can you count?"

"Featherweight? Paperweight you mean!"

The Tennessee Shad, prepared for such criticism, advanced swiftly to the middle of the ring and held up his hand.

"Ladies and gentlemen, before opening the festivities tonight I desire to say a few words in explanation. We are placing before you tonight, at much expense and great personal danger, one of the most unique, I may say *the* most unique, bona fide, high-class professional exhibition in the history of the school. I will say, for the benefit of a few experts on baby carriages and tiddledywinks who seem to be unusually vociferous tonight, that these gentlemen are not bloated middleweights. They are featherweights; each man is trained to the second; there is not an ounce of superfluous flesh on their bones. Each man is a streak of lightning, with muscles like whipcords, skilled in every trick and artifice of the game. We have tried to put before you not a lumbering exhibition of fatty degeneration, but a sizzling, rearing, tearing spectacle of fast, furious and sanguinary fighting. Are there any criticisms of the management?"

There were none.

Macnooder arose and made a sign to the seconds, and the contestants lumbered forward, Alcibiades girt with the school colors, his antagonist decorated about the waist with a blue-and-white pennant loaned by the Duke of Bilgewater.

"The contestants tonight," continued Macnooder in singsong, "are, on my right, Patsy the Brute, who will uphold the red and black; on my left, the Trenton Terror. Both men have ferocious reputations. In explanation I would say in confidence that Patsy's retirement from the professional ring was simply due to his having accidentally killed a man by a terrific wallop on the solar plexus, an accident which he profoundly regrets. The contestants are old enemies, they have already met three times in three bruising contests, and they do not want to conceal that this is a fight for blood! At their personal request the rules will be stretched so as to permit of the most deadly slaughter. The presence of our well-known sporting authority, the Gutter Pup, as referee, will, however, be a guaranty that this fight, though slashing, will be absolutely square and aboveboard! Rounds, three minutes each—one minute interim. Everyone be seated!"

The Gutter Pup whispered a moment to the contestants and then sprang back, crying, "Time."

The Trenton Terror and Patsy the Brute stood confronting each other, visibly embarrassed.

"Make 'em shake hands, Gutter Pup," said the Tennessee Shad quickly.

"Did you see that?" said Doc Macnooder, on the other side. "They didn't want to shake hands. Gee, but they've got it in for each other."

The first round was not exactly thrilling.

"The light and the ground bother 'em," said Macnooder. "Just wait till they get their bearings."

"Funniest style I ever saw."

"Why, they hold their fists down by their knees."

"Featherweights always have styles of their own."

"Don't see how they can strike from there."

"They're quicker than others. You'll see all right."

Round number two passed like the first.

"When are they going to begin?" said a voice.

"Push 'em together."

"Tie 'em together."

"They're sizing each other up," said Macnooder loudly. "Planning out the campaign."

In round three their gloves met twice.

"Each is afraid of the other's wallop," said Macnooder more loudly. "One blow'll decide it. Great footwork, wasn't it?"

Suddenly in round four, just as a few polite blows had been struck, a hoarse voice at the back whispered "Cheese it!"

Instantly the cage was plunged in darkness, while a confused murmur rose.

"It's the Doctor."

"We're trapped."

"We'll all be fired!"

"Let's get out."

"Silence!"

"Shut up, everyone. The Shad's gone to reconnoiter."

Presently the Shad's voice was heard, "Light up, there isn't a mouse stirring."

The lanterns flickered up again.

"Who yelled 'Cheese it'?" said Turkey angrily.

Everyone stood up and looked about.

"If anyone's afraid he can get out now quick," said the Gutter Pup. "We don't want to cheat the cradle."

Strangely enough no one availed himself of the opportunity.

Round four, being resumed, ended with the professionals clinched desperately. Then another delay arose. The contestants refused to fight unless the hat was passed for additional contributions. Macnooder calmed the angry crowd by explaining that the ground was so rough and the light so bad that the Trenton Terror was really running the risk of twisting his ankle. The hat showing only five dollars and twenty cents, the management was forced to add five dollars more before the fighters consented to go on. Macnooder having taken the precaution to hold up the bonus until one good round had been fought, the hopes of the whole company were raised by a few resounding thumps, accompanied by a great amount of prancing about the ring.

Toward the end of round seven, again the sepulchral voice was heard.

"Hi! Cheese it!"

Again every light was doused while everyone waited with calculated breath. Again the Tennessee Shad slipped out by the back, reconnoitered and angrily returned. This time everyone, slightly unnerved, made a determined search for the alarmist, accompanied by such inviting requests to show himself that it was no wonder the search was unproductive. They returned to the ring.

"This is getting on my nerves," said Goat Finney, blowing on his fingers.

"Wish the deuce it was over."

"The Doctor'll be sure to hear of it."

"Course he will."

"He always does."

"Why don't they hurry up?"

The next round, as the result of another strike, the hat was passed again. In round nine another alarm arose, with another fruitless search for the disturber. By this time the feeling of panic was becoming epidemic.

At the end of round ten an angry consultation took place in the middle of the ring. The Trenton Terror positively refused to continue unless the stakes were increased. Macnooder addressed the turbulent meeting, "Say, fellows, a word, one word, please. This is the situation. This fight is illegal. You don't realize that. If the police get the tip we might be jugged for a year. These continued fake scares are getting on the nerves of these gentlemen, naturally. They're the ones who're taking the risk and they feel they ought to be paid more for it. Now I'll leave it to you. Shall we pass the hat again or call it off now?"

At once a discussion broke out.

"No, no!"

"We want our money's worth."

"Do you call this a fight?"

"Gee, I've had enough."

"Call it off."

"Nothing of the sort."

"Go on."

"No baby act."

"Pass the hat."

The mysterious possibility of prison gave a thrill to the imagination that lifted the tame contest into the realm of the heroic. The Gutter Pup passed the hat.

Meanwhile, the Tennessee Shad and Macnooder were solemnly consulting.

"Gee, Doc, if this goes on another five minutes, where'll our profits be?"

"I know it."

"Each time it hits us harder."

"Well, what are you going to do about it?"

"Lord, if the Doctor would only come, Macnooder," said the Tennessee Shad in a solemn whisper. "He *must* come!"

The pair exchanged a deep, silent glance of comprehension. The Tennessee Shad smiled and disappeared carefully in the direction of the safety exit.

The collection was announced at three dollars and sixty cents. Public opinion forced from the ruthful Macnooder the disbursement of a sufficient sum to make up the stipulated ten dollars. Round eleven began with threats from all quarters directed against the management and the fighters.

Suddenly outside the gravel crunched under a firm tread and three startling knocks fell on the door. Everywhere the whisper went up:

"The Doctor!"

"Police!"

"Douse the lights!"

"Through the back, you chumps."

"Hurry!"

In less than a minute, amid a scurrying of frantic figures racing for the woods, the last vestige of the furious and terrific professional prizefight had vanished.

.   .   .   .

The next afternoon, ensconced in the Jigger Shop, Turkey Reiter, the Gutter Pup and the Triumphant Egghead considered the reckoning of the night before.

"I'm out ten plunks," said the Egghead. "I got reckless when they passed the hat. How did you make out?"

"I'd hate to tell," said the Gutter Pup.

"Funny the Doctor didn't refer to it in chapel."

"Say, that was queer."

"What was the fight like?" said Al, who had listened.

"Frightful," said Turkey Reiter. "There was bad blood between them!"

"How long did it go?"

"Ten slashing rounds."

At this moment the Triumphant Egghead, looking out the window, exclaimed, "Hello!"

"What's the matter?"

"There they are!"

On the opposite sidewalk Alcibiades and the Trenton Terror were sauntering affably together.

"Is that what you call Patsy the Brute and the Trenton Terror?" said Al dreamily.

"Sure."

"Was this one of the Tennessee Shad's little parties?"

"Why, yes."

"Doc Macnooder, too?"

"Yes, he was in it."

"Hem," said Al thoughtfully, "I see where two back accounts get paid up."

"Al," cried the Gutter Pup, "what do you know? Do you know those fellows?"

"The Finnigan brothers? Rather—used to steal watermelons together."

"Brothers!" said the Gutter Pup with a gasp.

"Brothers!" said the Triumphant Egghead.

"Brothers!" said Turkey Reiter.

"But, Al, they *are* prizefighters, now, aren't they?" said the Gutter Pup desperately.

"Well, they have done a good deal of boxing," said Al, polishing the faucets.

"Ah, they have done that?"

"Oh, yes, down at Katzenbach's grocery. They used to box lemons."

.   .   .   .

The Gutter Pup, Turkey Reiter, Goat Finney, the Beefsteak and the Triumphant Egghead sat on the steps of the Esplanade, nursing their feelings and their pocketbooks. Boys with tongues in their cheeks looked at them as they passed, and snickered at a good safe distance. Others shouted to them, joyful, insulting gibes.

Presently the Tennessee Shad and Doc Macnooder loped up in a friendly manner and stood looking down at them.

"Hello, Turkey!" said the Shad hopefully.

Turkey's gaze remained set.

"Hello, Lovely!"

Lovely drew a breath and looked down.

"Aren't you going to say howdy?" pleaded the Tennessee Shad. "Egghead—Gutter Pup—oh, Gutter Pup?"

The Gutter Pup's lips moved and set again, while Macnooder was observed departing on tiptoes.

"I suppose you're sore on me," said the Tennessee Shad sadly. "Well, I don't blame you. I'll never forgive myself—never!"

He sat down opposite, took a handful of stones, juggled them in the air, sighed, and fell into their silence.

All at once he brightened, looked up and said, "Say, fellows, I've got an idea!"

Then they surged up and fell upon him.

"Macnooder! Doc, help there; stand by me! Ouch!"

But Macnooder, purely the spirit of commerce, scudding for the west, called back, "Sorry, Shad—can't do it; the firm's dissolved!"